Desert Heat

By Request

Desert Heat

THE DESERT BRIDE
by
Lynne Graham

WHIRLPOOL OF PASSION
by
Emma Darcy

HOSTAGE OF THE HAWK
by
Sandra Marton

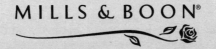

MILLS & BOON®

*MILLS & BOON and MILLS & BOON with the Rose Device
are registered trademarks of the publisher.
Harlequin Mills & Boon Limited,
Eton House, 18-24 Paradise Road, Richmond, Surrey, TW9 1SR*

DESERT HEAT
© by Harlequin Enterprises II B.V., 1999

The Desert Bride, Whirlpool of Passion and *Hostage of the Hawk* were
first published in Great Britain by Mills & Boon Limited
in separate, single volumes.

The Desert Bride © Lynne Graham 1996
Whirlpool of Passion © Emma Darcy 1987
Hostage of the Hawk © Sandra Myles 1994

ISBN 0 263 81539 0

05-9907

*Printed and bound in Great Britain
by Caledonian International Book Manufacturing Ltd, Glasgow*

Lynne Graham was born in Northern Ireland and has been a keen Mills & Boon® reader since her teens. She is very happily married with an understanding husband, who has learned to cook since she started to write! Her three children keep her on her toes. She has a very large old English sheepdog, which knocks everything over, and two cats. When time allows, she is a keen gardener. Lynne has been writing for Mills & Boon since 1987 and has now written over 25 books, which are loved by readers worldwide—she has had more than 10 million copies of her books in print in many different languages.

THE DESERT BRIDE
by
LYNNE GRAHAM

CHAPTER ONE

THE sheer opulence of Al Kabibi airport stunned Bethany. The acres of glossy marble floors, the huge crystal chandeliers and the preponderance of gold fittings made her blink and stare.

'Pretty impressive, eh?' Ed Lancaster remarked in the slow-moving queue to Visa Clearance. 'And yet five years ago there was nothing here but a set of concrete sheds and an unrelieved view of the sand dunes! King Azmir pumped the oil but he stockpiled the profits. His tight-fisted attitude caused a lot of resentment, not only with the locals but with the foreign workers as well. Conditions used to be really primitive here.'

The American businessman had joined their flight at a stopover in Dubai. He hadn't stopped talking for thirty seconds since then, but Bethany had been grateful to be distracted from the grim awareness that, had her departmental head not decreed that she centre her research on this particular part of the Middle East, nothing short of thumbscrews and brute force would have persuaded her to set one foot in the country of Datar!

'When King Azmir fell ill the crown prince, Razul, took over,' Ed rattled on, cheerfully impervious to the fact that Bethany had stiffened and turned pale. 'Now he's a different kettle of fish altogether. He's packed fifty years of modernisation into five. He's an astonishing man. He's transformed Datari society...'

Beneath her mane of vibrantly colourful curls Bethany's beautiful face had frozen, her stunningly green eyes hardening to polar ice. All of a sudden she wanted Ed to shut up. She did not want to hear about

Prince Razul al Rashidai Harun. Nor did she have the smallest urge to admit that their paths had crossed quite unforgettably during Razul's brief spell at university.

'And the people absolutely adore him. Razul's like their national hero. They call him the Sword of Truth. You mention democracy and they get *real* mad,' Ed complained feelingly. 'They start talking about how he saved them from civil war during the rebellion, how he took command of the army, et cetera, et cetera. They've actually made a film about it, they're so proud of him—'

'I expect they must be,' Bethany said flatly, an agonisingly sharp tremor of bitterness quivering through her.

'Yes, sirree,' Ed sighed with unhidden admiration. 'Although this divine cult they've built up around him can be painful, he *is* one hell of a guy! By the way,' Ed added, pausing for breath, 'who's coming to collect you?'

'Nobody,' Bethany muttered, praying that the monologue on Razul was over.

Ed frowned. 'But you're travelling alone.'

Bethany suppressed a groan. Actually, she hadn't been alone at Gatwick. A research assistant had been making the trip with her. But, with only minutes to go before they boarded, Simon had tripped over a carelessly sited briefcase and had come down hard enough to break his ankle. She had felt dreadful simply abandoning him to the paramedics but, aside from the fact that she barely knew the young man, work naturally had had to take precedence.

'Why shouldn't I be travelling alone?'

'How on earth did you get a visa?' Ed prompted, suddenly looking very serious.

'The usual way… What's wrong?'

'Maybe nothing.' Ed shrugged with an odd air of discomfiture, not meeting her enquiring gaze. 'You want me to stay with you in case there should be a problem?'

'Of course not, and I see no reason why there should be a problem,' Bethany informed him rather drily.

But there *was*. Ed had just moved off with an uneasy wave when the Datari official scrutinised her visa and asked, 'Mr Simon Tarrant?'

Bethany frowned.

'According to your visa, you are travelling with a male companion. Where is he?'

'He wasn't able to make the flight,' she explained with some exasperation.

'So you are travelling unaccompanied, *Dr* Morgan?' he stressed, with a dubious twist of his mouth, as if he could not quite credit the validity of her academic doctorate. That didn't surprise her. Female children had only recently acquired the legal right to education in Datar. The concept of a highly educated woman struck the average Datari male as about as normal as a little green man from the moon.

'Any reason why I shouldn't be?' Bethany demanded irritably, her cheeks reddening as she was drawn to one side, the embarrassing cynosure of attention for everyone else in the queue.

'Your visa is invalid,' the official informed her, signalling to two uniformed guards already looking in their direction. 'You cannot enter Datar. You will be returned to the UK on the next available flight. If you do not possess a return ticket, we will generously defray the expense.'

'Invalid?' Bethany gasped in disbelief.

'Obtained by deception.' The official treated her to a frown of extreme severity before he turned to address the other two men in a voluble spate of Arabic.

'*Deception*?' Bethany echoed rawly, unable to credit that the man could possibly be serious.

'The airport police will hold you in custody until you depart,' she was informed.

The airport police were already gawping at her with

blatant sexual speculation. Even in the midst of her incredulous turmoil at being threatened with immediate
deportation, those insolent appraisals made Bethany's
teeth grit with outrage. Sometimes she thought her physical endowments were nature's black joke on the male
species. With *her* outlook on the male sex she should
have been born plain and homely, not with a face, hair
and body which put out entirely the wrong message!

'You are making a serious mistake,' Bethany spelt
out, drawing herself up to her full height of five feet
three inches. 'I demand to speak to your superior! My
visa was legitimately issued by the Datari embassy in
London—' She broke off as she realised that absolutely
nobody was listening to her and the policemen were already closing in on her with an alarming air of purpose.

A sensation new to Bethany's experience filled her. It
was fear—sheer, cold fear. Panic swept over her. She
sucked in oxygen in a stricken gasp and employed the
single defensive tactic she had in her possession. 'I
would like you to know that I am a close personal friend
of Crown Prince Razul's!'

The official, who was already turning away, swung
back and froze.

'We met while he was studying in England.' Her
cheeks burning with furious embarrassment at the fact
that she should have been forced to resort to name-
dropping even to earn a hearing, Bethany tilted her chin,
and as she did so the overhead lights glittered fierily over
her long torrent of curling hair, playing across vibrant
strands that ran from burning copper to gold to Titian in
a glorious sunburst of colour.

The official literally gaped, his jaw dropping as he
took in the full effect of that hair. Backing off a step,
his swarthy face suddenly pale, he spoke in a surge of
guttural Arabic to the two policemen. A look of shock
swiftly followed by horror crossed their faces. They

backed off several feet too, as if she had put a hex on them.

'You are *the one*,' the official positively whispered, investing the words with an air of quite peculiar significance.

'The one what?' Bethany mumbled, distinctly taken aback by the staggering effect of her little announcement.

He gasped something urgent into his radio, drawing out a hanky to mop at his perspiring brow. 'There has been a dreadful, unforgivable misunderstanding, Dr Morgan.'

'My visa?'

'No problem with visa. Please come this way,' he urged, and began to offer fervent apologies.

Within minutes a middle-aged executive type arrived and introduced himself as Hussein bin Omar, the airport manager. His strain palpable, he started frantically apologising as well, sliding from uncertain English into Arabic, which made him totally incomprehensible. He insisted on showing her into a comfortable office off the concourse, where he asked her to wait until her baggage was found. He was so servile that it was embarrassing.

Ironically, the very last thing Bethany had wanted was to draw any unwelcome attention to her arrival in Datar. Suddenly she fervently wished that she had kept her stupid mouth shut. Her reference to Razul had been prompted by a shameful attack of panic. Why on earth hadn't she stayed calm and used logical argument to settle the mistaken impression that there was something wrong with her visa? And why all that silly fuss about the fact that she was travelling alone?

Fifteen nail-biting minutes later the airport manager reappeared and ushered her out…out onto a *red* carpet which had not been in place earlier. Bethany began to get all hot and bothered, her nervous tension rocketing to quite incredible heights. The VIP treatment staggered her. Everybody was looking at her. Indeed it was as though the whole airport had ground to a dead halt and there was this strange atmosphere of what could only be described as...electric excitement.

It *had* to be a case of mistaken identity, Bethany decided, struggling to hold onto her usually bomb-proof composure. Who on earth did Hussein bin Omar think she was? Or did an acquaintance with Razul automatically entitle one to such extraordinary attention at the airport?

What an idiot she had been to claim friendship with him...especially as it was a lie...a really quite blatant lie, she conceded inwardly, grimly recalling her last volatile meeting with the Crown Prince of Datar, slamming down hard on the piercing pain that that memory brought with it. She had had a narrow escape—a damned lucky narrow escape, she reminded herself fiercely. She had very nearly made an outsize fool of herself, but at least *he* had never known that. She hadn't given him that much satisfaction.

A whole column of spick and span policemen were standing to attention on the sun-baked pavement outside. Bethany turned pale. The heat folded in, dampening her skin beneath the loose beige cotton shirt and serviceable trousers she wore. Her discreet little trip to Datar had gone wildly off the rails.

'Your escort, Dr Morgan.' Hussein bin Omar snapped his fingers and a policeman darted forward to open the door of the waiting police car.

'My escort?' Bethany echoed shakily just as a young woman hurried forward and planted an enormous bunch of flowers in her startled hands. As if that were not enough, her fingers were grasped and kissed. Then for a split second everybody hovered as though uncertain of what to do next.

'*Allah akbar*...God is great!' the airport manager suddenly cried. Several other excited male voices eagerly joined him in the assurance.

At that point Bethany simply folded backwards into the police car. The whole bunch of them were crazy! Instantaneously she scolded herself for the reflection. As an anthropologist trained to understand cultural differences, such a reflection ill became her. As the car lurched into sudden motion and the driver set off a shrieking siren to accompany their progress she told herself to be calm, but that was difficult when she noticed the two other police cars falling in behind them.

Common sense offered the most obvious explanation. Hussein bin Omar had been appalled by the mistake over her visa because she had claimed that she knew Razul. In short, this outrageous fuss was his attempt to save lost face and simultaneously demonstrate his immense respect for the Datari royal family. That was why she had been supplied with a police escort to take her to her hotel outside the city. All very much over the top, but then this was *not* England, this was Datar—a feudal kingdom with a culture which had only recently begun to climb up out of the dark ages of medievalism.

She closed her eyes in horror as her driver charged a red light, forcing every other vehicle to a halt. Fearfully lifting her lashes again, she gazed out at the city of Al Kabibi as it sped by far too fast. Ultra-modern skyscrapers and shopping malls mingled with ancient, turquoise-domed mosques, the old and the new coexisting side by side.

As it left the lush white villas of the suburbs behind, the broad, dusty highway forged a path through a landscape of desolate desert plains. Bethany sat forward to get a better view of the fortress-like huge stone walls rising out of the emptiness ahead. Her driver jabbered excitedly into his radio while endeavouring to overtake a Mercedes with only two fingers on the steering wheel.

Bethany was on the edge of her seat, praying. And

then, without any warning at all, the car swerved off the road outside the fortress and powered through a set of enormous turreted gates. A clutch of robed tribesmen suddenly appeared directly in their path. They were brandishing machine-guns. The driver jumped so hard on the brakes that Bethany was flung along the back seat, and then she heard the splintering crack-crack of gunfire and threw herself down onto the floor, curling up into as tight a defensive ball as possible.

The car rolled to a halt. She stayed down, trembling with fear, wondering if the driver had been shot but not prepared to raise her head until the bullets stopped flying. The door clicked open.

'Dr Morgan?' a plummy Oxbridge voice enquired expressionlessly.

Bethany peered up and met the politely questioning gaze of a dapper little Arab gentleman with a goatee beard.

'I am Mustapha—'

'The g-guns…?' she stammered.

'Merely the palace guards letting off a little steam. Were you frightened? Please accept my apologies on their behalf.'

'Oh…' Feeling quite absurd, Bethany flushed and scrambled out of the car; only then did alarm bells start ringing. 'The *palace* guards?' Wide-eyed, she stared at the older man. 'This isn't my hotel?'

'No, indeed, Dr Morgan. This is the royal palace.' He permitted himself a small smile of amusement. 'Prince Razul requested that you be brought here without delay.'

'*Prince Razul*?' Bethany repeated in a strangled voice, but Mustapha had already swept off towards the arched and gilded entrance of the vast sprawling building ahead, clearly expecting her to follow him.

The airport manager must have contacted Razul about her arrival, Bethany registered in horror. But why on earth would Razul demand that she be brought to the palace? After the manner in which they had parted two years earlier he could not possibly wish to see her again! Lifelong conditioning to the effect that he was every woman's fantasy did not prepare an Arab prince for the shattering experience of having his advances rebuffed. By the end of their last, distressing encounter Bethany had been left in no doubt that Razul had been very deeply offended by her flat refusal to have anything to do with him.

Yet she had planned what she would say to him in advance, employing every ounce of tact at her disposal. She had known the strength of his pride. She had gone to great lengths in her efforts to defuse a volatile situation gently. Her face shadowed now, the cruel talons of memory digging deep. Razul had unleashed his temper and goaded her into losing her head. She wasn't proud of the derision with which she had fought back but he had been tearing her in two. She had been fighting for her own self-respect…why not admit it?

As she followed the older man into a huge, echoing hall lined with slender marble columns she was in a daze. Her exotic surroundings merely increased the sensation. Tiny mosaics were set into wildly intricate geometric patterns in shades of duck-egg green and ochre and palest blue on every inch of the walls and ceiling. The effect was dazzlingly beautiful and centuries old. A tiny sound jerked her head.

A giggle…a whisper? She looked up and saw the carved *mishrabiyyah* screens fronting the gallery suspended far above her. Behind the delicate yet wholly effective filigree barrier she caught flutters of movement, fleeting impressions of shimmering colour and then a burst of girlish laughter, excited whispers emerging from far more than one female voice and then swiftly stifled. A drift of musky perfume made her nostrils flare.

A tiny window onto the outside world for the harem? Bethany froze and turned white, a terrible pain uncoiling inside her. The thesis which had earned her both her doctorate and her current junior lectureship at a northern university had been on the suppression of women's rights in the Third World. *This* was not the Third World but, even so, the dreadful irony of her almost uncontrollable attraction to Razul had boiled her principles alive two years ago. Her colleagues had laughed their socks off when he'd come after her...an Arab prince with two hundred concubines stashed in his harem back home!

'*Dr Morgan*!' Mustapha called pleadingly.

Numbed by the onslaught of that recollection, Bethany moved on again. At the far end of the hall two fierce tribesmen stood outside a fantastically carved set of double doors. They wore ceremonial swords but carried guns. At a signal from Mustapha they threw back the doors on a magnificent audience room. The older man stepped back, making it plain that he was not to accompany her further.

At the far end of the room sunlight was flooding in from doors spread back on an inner courtyard. It made the interior seem dim yet accentuated the richness of its splendour. Her sturdy leather sandals squeaked on the highly polished floor. She hesitated, her heartbeat hammering madly against her ribcage as she stared at the shallow dais, heaped with silk cushions and empty. But a terrible excitement licked at her every sense and she felt it even before she saw him—that frightening mix of craving and anticipation which for the space of several weeks two years earlier had made her calm, well-ordered life a hell of unfamiliar chaos.

'Dr Livingstone, I presume?'

She jerked around, that honey-soft accented drawl sending a quiver down her taut backbone. Her breath shortened in her throat. Thirty feet away on the threshold of the courtyard stood the living, breathing embodiment of a twentieth-century medieval male—Razul al

Rashidai Harun, the Crown Prince of Datar, as uncivilised a specimen of primitive manhood as any prehistoric
cave would have been proud to produce.

'All that outfit lacks is a bush hat. Did you think you
were coming to darkest Africa?' Razul derided lazily,
and her serviceable clothing suddenly felt like foolish
fancy dress.

She couldn't take her eyes off him as he walked with
cat-like fluidity towards her. Breathtakingly good-
looking…terrifyingly exotic. With those hard-boned,
hawkish features, savagely high cheek-bones and that
tawny skin he might have sprung live from some ancient
Berber tapestry. He was very tall for one of his race.
Sheathed in fine cream linen robes, his headdress bound
by a double royal golden *iqual*, Razul gazed down at
her with night-dark eyes that were as hard as jet.

It took enormous will-power to stand her ground. Her
mouth went dry. Razul strolled calmly around her, for
all the world like a predator circling his kill. It was not
an image which did anything to release her tension.

'So very quiet,' Razul purred as he stilled two feet
away. 'You are in shock…the barbarian has at last learnt
to speak proper English…'

Bethany lost every drop of her hectic colour and
flinched as though he had plunged a stiletto between her
ribs. 'Please—'

'And even how to use your dainty Western cutlery,'
Razul imparted with merciless bite.

Bethany dropped her head, anguish flooding her. Did
he really think that such trivia had mattered? Her heart
had gone out to him as he'd struggled, with all that savage pride of his, to fit into a world which his suspicious
old father had denied him all knowledge of until he'd
reached an age when the adaptation was naturally all the
more difficult to make.

'But the barbarian did not learn one lesson you sought
to teach,' Razul murmured very quietly. 'I had no need

of it for I know women. I have always known women. I did not pursue you because I was prompted by my primitive, chauvinistic arrogance to believe myself irresistible. I pursued you because in your eyes I read blatant invitation—'

'No!' Bethany gasped, galvanised into ungluing her tongue from the roof of her dry mouth.

'Longing...hunger...*need*,' Razul spelt out so softly that the hairs prickled at the nape of her neck. 'Those ripe pink lips said no but those emerald eyes begged that I persist. Did I flatter your ego, Dr Morgan? Did playing the tease excite you?'

Appalled that he appeared to recall every word that she had flung at him, Bethany was paralysed. He had *known*. He had known that on some dark, secret level she'd wanted him, in spite of all her protestations to the contrary! She was shattered by the revelation, had been convinced that her defensive shell had protected her from such insight. Now she felt stripped naked. Even worse, Razul had naturally interpreted her ambivalent behaviour in the most offensive way of all. A *tease*...? Sexless, cold and frigid were epithets far more familiar to her ears.

'If you believe that I misled you, it was not intentional, I assure you,' Bethany responded tightly, studying her feet, not looking at him, absolutely forbidding herself to look at him again, not even caring how he might translate such craven behaviour. Maybe she owed Razul this hearing. He was finally having his say. Two years ago his fierce anger had not assisted his efforts to express himself in her language.

The silence smouldered. She sensed his frustration. He wanted her to fight back. Funny how she knew that, somehow understood exactly what was going through that innately devious and clever brain of his. But fighting back would prolong the agony...and she *was* in agony, with the evocative scent of sandalwood filling her nostrils and the soft hiss of his breathing interfering with her concentration. It took her back—back to a terrifying time when her safe, secure world had very nearly tumbled about her ears.

'May I go now?' She practically whispered the words, so great was her rigid tension.

'Look at me—'

'No—'

'Look at me!' Razul raked at her fiercely.

Bethany's gaze collided with vibrant tiger-gold eyes and she stopped breathing. The extraordinary strength of will there mesmerised her. Her heartbeat thudded heavily in her eardrums. All of a sudden she was dizzy and disorientated. With a sense of complete helplessness and intense shame, she felt her breasts stir and swell and push wantonly against the cotton cups of her bra as her nipples pinched into tight little buds. Hot pink invaded her pallor but there was nothing she could do to control her own body. The electrifying sexual charge in the atmosphere overwhelmed her every defence.

Razul dealt her an irredeemably wolfish smile, his slumbrous golden eyes wandering over her, lingering on every tiny hint of the generous curves concealed by her loose clothing. Then, without warning, he stepped back and clapped his hands. The sound was like a pistol shot in the thrumming silence.

'Now we will have tea and we will talk,' Razul announced with an exquisite simplicity of utter command that made Bethany recall exactly *who* he was, *what* that status meant and *where* she was. This rogue male was one step off divinity in Datar.

Bethany tensed and jerkily folded her arms. 'I don't think—'

Three servants surged out of nowhere, one with a tray bearing cups, one with a teapot, one with a low, ebonised, brass-topped table.

'Early Grey…especially for you,' Razul informed her,

stepping up on the dais and dropping down onto the cushions with innate animal grace.

'Early Grey'? She didn't correct him. The oddest little dart of tenderness pierced her, making her swallow hard. She remembered him surreptitiously shuffling that 'dainty Western cutlery' he had referred to at a college dinner. Then she locked the recollection out, furious with herself. Miserably she sank down onto the beautiful carpet, settling her behind onto another heap of cushions, but her disturbing thoughts marched on.

She had been infatuated with him—hopelessly infatuated. Every tiny thing about Razul had fascinated her. She had been twenty-five years old but more naïve in many ways than the average teenager. He had been her first love, a crush, whatever you wanted to call it, but it had hit her all the harder because she hadn't been sweet sixteen with a fast recovery rate. And she had been arrogant in her belief that superior brainpower was sufficient to ensure that she didn't succumb to unwelcome hormonal promptings and immature emotional responses. But *he* had smashed her every assumption about herself to smithereens.

'There was a bit of a mix-up over my visa at the airport...I wouldn't have mentioned your name otherwise,' she heard herself say impulsively, and even that disconcerted her. She was not impulsive, but around Razul she was not herself. The china cup trembled betrayingly on the saucer as she snatched it up to occupy her hands and sipped at the hot, fragrant tea.

'Your visa was invalid.'

'I beg your pardon?' Bethany glanced up in astonishment, not having expected to hear that nonsensical claim again.

'Young women are only granted visas under strict guidelines—if they are coming here to stay with a Datari family, can produce a legitimate employment contract or are travelling with a relative or male colleague,' Razul enumerated levelly. 'Your visa stated that you would be accompanied. You arrived alone. It was that fact which invalidated your documentation.'

Bethany lifted her chin, her emerald-green eyes flashing. 'So you discriminate against foreign women by making lists of ridiculous rules—'

'Discrimination may sometimes be a positive act—'

'Never!' Bethany asserted with raw conviction.

'You force me to be candid.' Brilliant dark eyes rested on her with impatience, his wide mouth hardening. 'An influx of hookers can scarcely be considered beneficial to our society.'

'Hookers?' Bethany repeated in a flat tone, taken aback.

'Our women must be virgin when they marry. If not, the woman is unmarriageable, her family dishonoured. In such a society the oldest profession may thrive, but we did not have a problem in that field until we granted visas with too great a freedom.'

'Are you trying to tell me that I was mistaken for some sort of tart at the airport?' Bethany gritted in a shaking voice.

'The other category of female we seek to exclude I shall call ''the working adventuress'' for want of a more acceptable label.'

'I'm afraid I don't follow,' Bethany said thinly.

'Young women come here ostensibly to work. They flock to the nightclubs that have sprung up in the city. There they dress, drink and conduct themselves in a manner which may be perfectly acceptable in their own countries but which is seen in quite another light by Datari men,' Razul explained with a sardonic edge to his rich vowel sounds. 'A sizeable percentage of these women do not return home again. They stay on illegally and become mistresses in return for a lifestyle of luxury.'

'Really, I hardly look the type!' Bethany retorted witheringly, but her fair skin was burning hotly. 'And, fascinating as all this is, it's time that I headed for my hotel.'

'Lone women in your age group are not currently accepted into our hotels as guests.'

Bethany thrust a not quite steady hand through her tumbling hair. 'I beg your pardon?'

'No hotel will offer you accommodation when you arrive alone.' His strong dark face utterly impassive, Razul surveyed her intently. 'Had I not brought you to the palace you would now be on a flight back to the UK.'

'But that's ridiculous!' Bethany suddenly snapped, her nervous tension splintering up through the cracks in her composure. 'It's hardly my fault that my assistant broke an ankle before we boarded!'

'Most unfortunate.' But he said it with a faint smile on his beautifully moulded mouth, and his tone more than suggested that he was not remotely interested in the obvious fact that her planned stay in Datar had now run into petty bureaucratic difficulties, which she was quite sure he could brush aside...should he want to.

Bethany pushed her cup away with a very forced smile, behind which her teeth were gritted. 'Look...this is an important research trip for me—'

'But then you take all your work so seriously,' Razul pointed out smoothly.

Her facial muscles clenched taut. 'I am here in Datar to research the nomadic culture,' she informed him impressively.

'How tame...'

'Tame?' Bethany echoed in shrill disconcertion, having assumed that his own cultural background would necessarily prompt him to treat the subject with appropriate respect.

'I have read your paper on the suppression of women's rights,' Razul murmured very softly.

'You've read my paper?' Bethany found herself gawping at him.

'And, having done so, intend to generously offer you research in a field which could make you famous in the academic world when you return to the West.' Burnished golden eyes suddenly struck hers with ferocious force.

'What field?' Bethany queried, a frown-line dividing her brows as she shifted uneasily on the cushions, instinctively reacting to the humming tension in the air.

Razul unleashed a predatory smile upon her. 'A way of life never before freely opened to the scrutiny of a Western anthropologist. I feel remarkably like Santa Claus.'

'Excuse me?' The atmosphere was suffocatingly tense. Bethany scrambled upright and involuntarily backed away from the controlled menace that emanated from Razul in vibrating waves.

'A prolonged stay in my harem will not only provide you with liberal scope for academic research, it will provide me with a long-awaited opportunity to teach you what being a woman is all about,' Razul told her with silken self-satisfaction.

CHAPTER TWO

'YOUR harem?' For the count of thirty seconds Bethany simply stared at Razul, her bright green eyes open to their fullest extent. Then she visibly bristled, her naturally sultry mouth compressing into a thin, unamused line. 'Very funny,' she said flatly, but there was an unevenness to her response as she fought against the giant tide of bitterness threatening to envelop her.

'You walk in my world now.' Razul issued the reminder with indolent cool. Veiled dark eyes slid over her in an all-encompassing look that was as physical as a caress. 'When you walk from it again you will be a different woman.'

Her aggressive stance—feet apart and arms taut—quivered as a tide of fury surged through her, leaving her light-headed. 'If you look at me like that once more, so help me I will knock your teeth down your throat!' Bethany blistered back at him.

A scorching smile slashed his hard mouth, perfect white teeth flashing against his golden skin. He surveyed her with intense pleasure. 'My father said… "Is this woman worth a diplomatic incident?" If he saw you now, truly he would not have asked such a question.'

'What do you mean, "worth a diplomatic incident"?' Bethany demanded, her voice half an octave higher.

'Sooner or later you will be missed,' Razul pointed out gently. 'Questions will be asked, answers must be given. Our ambassador in London will be called to the Foreign Office. But I suspect it will be many weeks before we reach that stage—'

'The Foreign Office?' Bethany shook her head as

though to clear it, a daze of utter disbelief beginning to enfold her.

'You see, you have so few people in your life to notice that you are missing. You write to your mother only once a month. You communicate with your father not at all. Your sole close friend is currently enjoying an extended honeymoon in South America—her fall from grace in allowing a man into her life very probably loosened the ties of that friendship. As for your academic colleagues…?' Razul enumerated these facts in the same calm, measured tone, as though he was well aware of her growing incredulity. 'This is the long summer vacation. I doubt if they will be expecting to hear from you. I find your life of isolation a sad testimony to your wonderful Western civilisation.'

The pink tip of Bethany's tongue crept out to moisten her dry lower lip. Shock was reverberating through her in debilitating waves. 'How…how do you know all these things about me?' she whispered jerkily.

'An investigation agency.'

'You put a private investigator on me? But when? You didn't even know I was *coming* to Datar!'

'Did I not? A liberal endowment to your university ensured your eventual arrival—'

'I b-beg your pardon?' Bethany stammered, a painful throb of tension beginning to pulse behind her browbone.

'Why do you think your superiors insisted that you base your research on Datar?'

'The nomadic tribes here have not suffered the same level of exposure to the modern world as in other countries,' she informed him harshly, her hands clenching in on themselves.

'True…but who suggested the subject of your research?'

Bethany went rigid. The idea had come down from on high. It had not emerged from the anthropology department itself. Indeed there had been resentful mutters to the effect that she must have admirers in high places because such research opportunities abroad were, due to a shortage of finance, currently at an all-time low.

'I'm building your university a brand-new library,' Razul shared with her gently. 'And my carefully chosen British representative, who stressed his special interest in Datar and also mentioned how very impressed he was by a series of lectures you gave last year, insisted on absolute and complete anonymity in return for the endowment.'

Bethany was starting to tremble. Without a flicker of remorse he was telling her that she had been lured out to Datar on false pretences. 'No...I don't believe you...I *refuse* to believe you!'

'I have known the date of your arrival since you applied for your visa. I was not, however, prepared for you to arrive alone at the airport,' Razul conceded wryly. 'Or for the subsequent furore over your visa, but your solitary state has worked to my advantage. You now have no companion to raise the alarm...and I have you in my possession that much sooner.'

'You have not got me in your possession, you maniac!' Bethany snatched up her duffel bag and stalked to the exit doors. 'I've listened to this nonsense long enough as well!'

'You are prepared to endure bodily restraint?'

'Meaning?'

'Without my permission you are not allowed to leave the palace.'

'Nobody *allows* me to do anything...I do what *I* want to do!' Bethany spat back at him, and jerked at the ornate handles with furious fingers. 'And I am returning to the airport!'

'If you force my men to put their hands upon you they will be severely embarrassed that you should invite such an indignity…but they will not flinch from their duty,' Razul warned.

The doors sprang open. Instantly the two guards outside spun round and faced her, yet they did not look directly at her and she remembered how at the airport, after she had mentioned Razul, the male eyes had swiftly averted from her as she'd passed. It was an insult for an Arab man to stare openly at an Arab woman who was not of his family…but she was *not* one of their women. Such pronounced respect ironically sent a shudder down her backbone, and the mere concept of instigating a pointless struggle with those fierce-looking men made her cringe. In one violent movement of frustration Bethany thrust the doors shut again.

'If you don't let me out of here I'll scream!' she hurled down the length of the room at Razul.

'It will only make your migraine worse.'

How did he know that she got migraine headaches? How did he know that she could already feel the first dismaying signs of an attack?

'You think I won't scream, don't you? You think I'm so damned impressed by your utterly ridiculous threats and your blasted throne room, I haven't got the bottle!' Bethany fired off at him, shaking all over with rage.

'"The bottle"?' A frown-line divided his winged ebony brows as he rose fluidly upright and began to move towards her.

'Stay away from me…I'm *warning* you!' On the edge of hysteria for the very first time in her life, Bethany threw back her shoulders and screamed. It hurt her ears, it hurt her throat, it hurt her head. But what shook her even more was the reality that nobody came running to see what was amiss.

'Ask yourself what happiness your life in the West has brought you,' Razul urged her softly as he moved towards her. 'You work relentless hours. You drive yourself like a mouse on a treadmill and deny yourself every feminine pleasure.'

'I am extremely happy!' Bethany launched back rawly, her back pinned to the doors. 'I'm totally fulfilled by my work.'

'Being totally fulfilled by me will be infinitely more satisfying. It will release all that pent-up tension—'

'The only way I am likely to release my pent-up tension at this moment is by physically attacking you...if you don't keep your distance!' Bethany swore, fighting against the increasing pounding of the building migraine, feeling her skin dampen, her stomach lurch. 'Now maybe you think this little power game of yours is amusing but it has gone far enough...do you hear me? I want transport back to the airport *right now*!'

'If I gave you what you say you want you would regret it for the rest of your life,' Razul asserted wryly. 'I will not permit you to make so foolish a decision.'

'Back off, Razul!' As he got too close Bethany took a defensive leap along the wall and saw swimming spots in front of her aching eyes, but she fought her own weakness to the last ditch. 'The joke has gone stale. You cannot possibly intend to keep me here against my will. I couldn't possibly be your type—'

'I have catholic taste—'

'Intellectually I find you—'

'A challenge? When you have rested for a while you will feel more adjusted to the wonderful change in your circumstances. No longer are you alone—'

'I *like* being alone!' Bethany screeched.

'You are afraid to share yourself—'

'I am not sharing anything with you!' It was a cry of despair. Suddenly, without warning, she snapped, the rigidity going out of her, hot tears burning her eyes, making her cover her rapidly working face with shaking hands.

A pair of strong hands inexorably peeled her off the

wall which was supporting her. 'No!' she gasped in horror.

An even stronger set of arms relentlessly swept her off her feet. Her head was spinning in a cartwheel of fire. Her gaze clashed with glittering gold eyes set between lush ebony lashes longer than her own, and a stifled moan of mingled pain and defeat was dredged from her.

'Stop fighting me.'

'Put me down,' she sobbed weakly.

'Shush…' he whispered softly, soothingly. 'Surrender can be the sweetest pleasure of all for a woman. You were born to yield, not to fight.'

She closed her water-clogged eyes, feeling too ill to try and struggle against overwhelming odds. *Overwhelming odds*…Razul in a nutshell, she reflected wretchedly. Two years ago she had blown every penny she'd possessed on a trip to Canada to stay with her aunt to escape him. Like a drug addict she had suffered withdrawal symptoms of sleepless nights, lost appetite, mood-swings and, worse, the frightening conviction that she had a streak of masochism more than equal to anything that her martyred mother had ever displayed in her dealings with her wandering husband.

Razul was carrying her and without any apparent effort. The scent of him so close washed over her…clean, warm, intensely male. They had never been *this* close before. But she had wondered—oh, yes, she had wondered what it would feel like to be in his arms. Now it had been thrust on her when she was defenceless and, worst of all, she *liked* it, she registered in horror—*liked* the fact that he had taken charge, liked the soft, rich feel of his robes against her cheek, the raw male strength of him, the steady thump of his heartbeat. A sob that had nothing at all to do with her migraine escaped her.

A clamour of anxious female voices chattered in Arabic as she was laid down on a bed. A cool hand

rested on her forehead. Razul. A part of her wanted to
retain that contact and that made her feel worse than
ever. He lifted her up. 'Drink this…'

Her medication was in her bag but she drank the
herbal concoction, lay back, weak as a kitten, and momentarily lifted her heavy eyelids. Two young women
were kneeling on the carpet several feet from the bed
and they both wore fixed and matching expressions of
frantic concern and unholy fascination. Melodrama was
born in Arabia, she thought helplessly.

'The doctor is coming.' Razul smoothed the fiery
tangle of curls off her damp brow. His hand wasn't quite
steady. 'Close your eyes; relax,' he instructed in that
dark, deep voice of his. 'Tension must increase the pain.'

Relax? A spasm of anguish snaked through her. He
had brought her to the harem. Those had to be *his*
women watching her. Wives, concubines— Oh, dear
heaven, what did it matter what they were? she asked
herself bitterly. He was still one man with two hundred
young and beautiful women at his disposal—*gifts* from
his father's adoring subjects.

Datar had made an official complaint to the British
government when a certain notorious tabloid had spilt
what the Dataris considered to be very private beans to
an agog British public. Diplomatic relations had been
cut off for six months. Contracts which should have gone
to British firms had suddenly been awarded elsewhere.
Since then the media had been tactfully silent about the
Crown Prince of Datar's exotic sex life. Not a murmur
had appeared in print since those revelations two years
earlier.

Razul had been shattered when she'd dared to fling
those same facts in his teeth—so outraged, so furious,
so nakedly incredulous that any woman should dare even
to mention such an unmentionable subject, never mind
berate him with a personal opinion of his morals, that
he had forgotten every word of English that he *did* have,

slamming back at her in his own language before he'd stormed out, leaving her sobbing and empty and bitter as gall.

In a haze of surprising drowsiness and broken shards of memory Bethany drifted at first, like a boat on a storm-tossed sea, but the boat slowly came into the calm of harbour, drawn there by the cool, strong fingers reassuringly linked with hers. Feeling inexpressibly relaxed, she slid into a deep, dreamless sleep.

Bethany wakened to the sound of chattering birds and stretched languorously. Her dark lashes lifted and she saw not a ceiling but a dome of incredibly beautiful stained glass far above her. She sat up with a stifled gasp. There was another shock awaiting her. She was not alone. Three brightly smiling young girls were kneeling in total silence on the carpet.

'You are awake, *sitt*.' One of them rose gracefully and shyly lifted gorgeous almond-shaped eyes to hers. Her slender body was garbed in a colourful, tight bodice and swirling skirt, her feet shod in embroidered slippers, gold jewellery tinkling with her every movement. 'I am Zulema. We have been chosen to serve you. Many wished for this honour but only I speak English. Prince Razul say I speak English very good…is good enough?' she checked in sudden dismay, the query undoubtedly prompted by the fact that Bethany was gaping at her.

Bethany snatched in a gulping breath, striving to get a grip on herself as she took in the fabulous room and its alarming unfamiliarity, then glanced down and fingered the equally unfamiliar filmy white silk gown she was mysteriously clad in. 'You speak wonderful English, Zulema,' she mumbled weakly.

'I will run a bath for you, *sitt*. You must long to be fresh. You had a very long journey, but it is so thrilling, I think, to fly on a plane. Once I travelled to London with Princess Fatima—' Zulema's animated little face abruptly clouded and she dropped her shining dark head as if she had dropped a clanger.

Fatima…who was Princess Fatima? Razul's sister, mother, aunt…wife? Bethany knew nothing about his family.

As Zulema hurriedly pressed the other girls into activity Bethany absorbed their unhidden high spirits and the rather discomfiting way they kept on stealing fascinated glances at her. Were they maids or was their connection with Razul of a more intimate nature? After all, every one of them was wearing enough gold jewellery to sink the *Titanic*. Dear God, Razul had put her in his harem just as he had promised. And he had *drugged* her to keep her here last night!

What had been in that seemingly innocuous drink that she had trustingly taken from his hand? She had never managed to sleep through a migraine before. Whatever he had given her had knocked her out cold. She had slept through what remained of yesterday late into a new day. And right now she was in shock—so much shock that her brain was traumatised. The sound of running water came noisily through a door now flung wide. In a sudden motion Bethany slid from the bed. Zulema gasped and surged to proffer slippers as if the wonderful, silk-soft rug were insufficient to protect her feet.

'Please…' Please leave me alone, she wanted to plead, but when Zulema looked up at her with a horribly embarrassing look of near-worship, as if she were some sort of goddess instead of a perfectly ordinary woman the same as herself, Bethany was struck dumb.

'We will bathe you, *sitt*.'

Bethany, who found even communal changing rooms a mortification, was appalled by the suggestion. Fighting to hide the fact, she murmured tightly, 'You don't need to serve me, Zulema.'

'But you are the one…you must be served,' Zulema protested anxiously.

The one *what*? Bethany almost screamed, recalling that same phrase from the airport but restraining herself. 'Where I come from,' she said stiltedly, 'we do not share bathrooms.'

Zulema giggled and delightedly shared this barbaric desire for privacy with her companions. Bethany took advantage of the huddle to slide past them into the bathroom and close the door. The ultra-modern appointments were reassuring. The bedroom, furnished with antique cedarwood inlaid with silver, had given her the disorientating impression that she had been snatched back to the time of Sheherazade. Peeling off the gown, she climbed into the bath which had been run for her, but she sat rigid in the richly scented water like a puritan invited to an orgy, furiously washed herself and clambered back out again as fast as she possibly could.

By the time she had finished with Razul he wouldn't be able to get her back to the airport quickly enough! Was he crazy? Did he really imagine that he could make a prisoner of her? *Of course*, he could not seriously mean to try and keep her here by force. But everything he had told her the previous night flooded back to her—the endowment to the university...the strict anonymity demanded...her own surprise, as a junior member of the department, when she had been offered the research trip.

She emerged from the bathroom wrapped in towels. 'Where are my clothes?'

With pride Zulema indicated the fabulous heap of jewel-coloured silks now strewn over the bed.

'*My* clothes...my suitcase,' Bethany extended tautly.

Neither was forthcoming. Ignoring her audience, Bethany flicked open chests and closet doors. *Nothing*, not a stitch of her own clothing in sight! She wanted to stamp her feet and scream with temper, and it must have showed because Zulema and her helpers looked worried sick, as if any sign of dissatisfaction on her part was likely to bring punishment down on their unprotected heads.

'OK...I'll wear this stuff. Choose something for me,' Bethany invited grudgingly.

Smiles broke out again like magic. Zulema extended an emerald-green silk caftan edged with gold, and a filmy pair of lace briefs and matching bra, the likes of which Bethany had never harboured in her plain white cotton underwear drawer. A flush of increasing rage mantling her cheeks, she dressed and stood at the mirror with a silver-backed brush, yanking it brutally through her long, wild mane of tangled curls.

'I have displeased you, *sitt*?' Zulema pressed in a small, tearful voice. 'Why you not like my help?'

Bethany felt all mean and small-minded and contemptible and handed over the brush, taking a seat on a divan. How the heck could you force the principle of equality on someone when equality was neither acknowledged nor desired?

'Such glorious hair. I have never seen such wonderful hair,' Zulema sighed, delicately teasing out each snarl with reverent fingers. 'It *is* the colour of the setting sun, just as was said.'

'Said by whom?'

Zulema giggled shyly. 'Prince Razul's guards, they talk... It is forbidden that they talk, but men, they gossip too. A long time ago we hear about the English lady with the hair of glorious colours...soon all our people know and talk and the King, he got very angry indeed to hear the whispers about his beloved son. Ah...the English breakfast is here!' Zulema carolled excitedly as the door opened.

What kind of whispers? Bethany wanted to know as she stood up, but Zulema threw wide yet another door, revealing a dining table and chairs. 'Just like home,' she told Bethany as a procession of servants bearing trays followed in her wake.

Open-mouthed, Bethany stared as the trays were un-loaded and the lids on the metal dishes were lifted one by one. Fruit juices, cereals, toast, croissants, breakfast rolls, wheaten bread and every possible kind of preserve. Fried eggs, boiled eggs, scrambled eggs, *even* coddled eggs. Kippers, devilled kidneys, beef sausages, fried bread, tomatoes and French toast. It was lunchtime but she was receiving breakfast.

Zulema pulled out a chair and Bethany collapsed down onto it, surveying the banquet before her. She was hungry but never in her life had she seen such a spread for one individual. The entire table was covered.

'You like?'

'I'm very impressed.' Her voice wobbled in the pres-ence of such shamelessly conspicuous consumption.

'Prince Razul bring in chef from Dubai. If you not like his cooking, he go back,' Zulema informed her cheerfully.

Razul had hired a chef specifically to cook Western food for *her*? Heavens, did he actually think that she would be staying long enough for it to matter? Bethany took a deep breath, feeling more and more as though she was existing in some outrageous fantasy world, aeons removed from her own life of quiet, sensible practicality.

She was finishing her tea when Zulema approached her again.

'The Prince…he say he meet with you now,' Zulema whispered, as if she were setting up an incredibly excit-ing romantic assignation.

Bethany stood up and straightened her narrow shoul-ders with Amazonian spirit. 'And don't spare the horses.'

'The horses?'

'Never mind.'

The palace was an astonishingly large building. It ram-bled all over the place in a hotchpotch of corridors, screened galleries and sunlit courtyards.

At the head of a superb marble staircase Zulema abruptly halted and drew back several steps. 'We must wait, *sitt*.'

Bethany looked over the wall down into the magnificent courtyard below, but her attention had not been attracted by the lush selection of tropical plants and the beautiful playing fountains. It was Razul she saw, his luxuriantly black, slightly curly hair gleaming like raw silk in the strong sunlight…and then the woman, sobbing and clutching frantically at his ankles.

'We go for walk, *sitt*,' Zulema urged uncomfortably.

'No, thanks.' In all her life Bethany had never seen a woman humiliate herself to such an extent. She was appalled. She needed no grasp of Arabic to interpret that distraught voice, that subservient posture and the passionate intensity with which the poor woman was hanging onto him.

Razul hissed something in his own language and literally stepped over her. As she attempted to follow him he snapped his fingers furiously at a cluster of servants cowering in a corner. Within seconds they were rushing to lift the woman from the ground and hurry her away through one of the archways off the courtyard.

'Who is that woman?' Bethany whispered.

'The Princess Fatima,' Zulema muttered thinly. 'Prince Razul take only one wife. Always he say that…only the one.'

Bethany's stomach lurched sickly. Perspiration broke out on her brow. So Razul was married. Dear heaven, that tormented woman was his wife, and it did not take great imagination to comprehend the source of her hysteria, did it? Razul had brought another woman into the palace and the poor creature was quite naturally distraught. The sheer cruelty of his behaviour devastated Bethany. He was every inch the savage, despotic Arab prince, who believed his own desires to be innately superior to any mere female's wants and needs.

In a tempest of pain she refused to acknowledge Bethany descended the marble stairs. Razul swung round, his starkly handsome features flushed and still set with cold anger and hauteur. And then, as his stunning golden eyes settled on Bethany, the tension went out of him. A dazzling smile completely transformed his strong dark face.

That smile hit her like a shock wave, made her steps falter and her heart give a gigantic lurch behind her breastbone. For a split second she was hurled back two years to the evening they had first met. She had been coming out of the library. He had been leaning against the bonnet of his Ferrari, surrounded by gushing female students, every one of whom had been blonde and not known for her inhibitions with men. And then he had looked up and focused on Bethany and perceptibly stilled, treating her to a narrowed, intent stare before suddenly flashing that spectacularly glorious smile. Riveted to the spot, she had dropped her books.

But *not* this time, she swore to herself, despising her own shameful susceptibility and the disturbing emotions and responses which could block out every rational thought.

'I've always been told that the Arab male cherishes and protects the women in his family,' she shot at him in stark challenge, 'but report really doesn't match reality, does it? The Princess Fatima does not appear to qualify for even an ounce of your respect.'

His smile vanished as though she had struck him. A dark rise of blood delineated his hard cheek-bones. 'You saw...?'

'I saw,' Bethany confirmed shakily.

'I am disturbed that you should have witnessed so distressing a scene but, in honour, I may not discuss it with you,' Razul delivered in a grim undertone.

Bethany turned away. She could not bear to look at him. So he had that much decency—a tiny kernel of loyalty to his wife. And he was profoundly embarrassed that she had seen that distasteful encounter…amazing. It was almost as though he expected her to pretend that these other women did not exist in his life. Concubines *and* a wife.

Yet she had never been able to hate him properly for his lifestyle. Just as she was a product of her world, he was a product of his. Nor was she foolish enough to imagine that Datar was the only country in the world where concubines were kept. It was not a subject referred to; it was a subject politely ignored lest people in high places be offended. And she had often wondered how many Western males could truthfully say that, given the same opportunity and society's silent blessing, they too would not indulge in the freedom of such sexual variety.

'Did you sleep well?'

A laugh that was no laugh at all bubbled in her throat. 'You should know…you drugged me—'

'You were in great pain. I could not bear to see you suffer,' Razul imparted tautly, on the defensive. 'A sleeping potion allowed you to rest.'

A sudden unbearable sadness swept over her. She found herself sinking down on the stone edge of a fountain, and she let her fingers trail restively in the water. 'And how do you answer the kidnapping and imprisoning charge?'

'You gave me no other option.'

Bethany breathed in deeply and looked at him where he stood, brushing aside the disturbing realisation that in the superbly tailored dove-grey suit which outlined his broad shoulders, narrow hips and long, lean legs he looked achingly familiar to her. On the outside touched by Western sophistication, she thought painfully, on the inside not touched at all, and not about to apologise for it either.

'You know I won't let you get away with a cop-out like that,' she whispered.

'Cop-out?' Razul queried flatly, standing very tall and taut.

'An evasion.' She guessed that the women in his life let him off the hook every time he smiled, and then doubted if he even had a passing acquaintance with being pinned between a rock and a hard place by her sex. Fatima had been crawling round his feet like a whipped dog, not standing up to him like an equal.

Pain trammelled through her afresh. Was that what had attracted Razul to a woman outside his own culture...to her? Her spirit, her independence? In Datar even the male sex walked in awe of Razul al Rashidai Harun. One day he would be their king.

'You cannot seriously intend to imprison me here—'

'It does not have to be a prison. Give me your word that you will not attempt to escape and you may roam free.'

'Something of a contradiction in terms.' Unwarily she connected with smouldering golden eyes intently pinned to her and her throat closed over. Why am I talking to him so calmly instead of screaming at him? she wondered. Her own pain had risen uppermost, swallowing up the anger. Worse still, there was a treacherous part of her that greedily cherished every stolen moment in his company. The knowledge filled her with a deep, abiding shame.

'*Je te veux...*' he had said two years ago. 'I want you.'

'*Tu es à moi,*' he had purred like a sleek jungle cat. 'You are mine.'

Temptation—sinful, sweet, soul-destroying...

'You are an educated man,' Bethany muttered not quite steadily.

'On the surface. Don't flatter me,' Razul said with

sudden harshness. 'I know your opinion of me. My father allowed thousands of Datari men to attend British and American universities over the last two decades. He did this only because it became clear to him that our country would become totally dependent on foreign workers if he did not encourage our young men to seek education and technological training in the West. But he would not permit me to enjoy a similar experience.

'I am well aware that reading many books and spending a short spell at university does not make me an educated man…especially not in the eyes of a woman who has a string of letters after her name and many academic accomplishments.'

In the hot, still air the tension pulsed and throbbed, beating down on her from the electric force of his challenging gaze. He possessed one very powerful personality, one very volatile temperament which was also unashamedly emotional, but you were never in any doubt of the ferociously strong will that lay behind it all. But only now did she register the innate humility with which he viewed himself on an intellectual level, and that discovery pained her and made her want to put her hands round the throat of his obstinate old father, who had denied his own son what he freely gave to his subjects.

Her throat thickened. 'Razul, nobody who has seen what you have managed to achieve here in Datar over the past five years could possibly think you anything other than an educated man.'

'I make use of many advisors from all levels of our society. I will not tolerate nepotism, for placing the unfit in authority is the curse of the Arab world. I seek to liberalise our culture for the benefit of our people…but I know what you think, *aziz*, as I say this.' He sent her a dark, level appraisal. 'You think how can I talk of liberalisation and then steal a woman.'

'I'm well aware that stealing women is an element of

the tribal culture,' Bethany informed him in a frozen voice. 'But—'

A brilliant smile crossed his beautifully shaped mouth. 'It is not a crime as long as the woman is treated with respect and honour,' he smoothly inserted.

Bethany bent her fiery head, staggered to find herself on the brink of laughter. When it suited Razul, he was wondrously, deviously simplistic, and her mere admission that woman-stealing was a tradition practised for centuries in his culture delighted him in so far as he saw that as ample justification for his conduct.

'But naturally the marriage must take place within a short space of time,' Razul remarked softly. 'It is expected.'

Her head flew back, shimmering green eyes fixing on him in unconcealed shock.

The silence stretched, taut as a rubber band, between them.

With a muffled expletive in Arabic Razul took a long stride forward and then stilled, sheer incredulity sufficient to match her own flashing across his staggeringly handsome features. 'In the name of Allah, *aziz*…surely you could not think I would insult you with anything less than an offer of marriage? Last night…was this why you panicked?' he demanded starkly, and reached for her hands to tug her relentlessly upright. 'I brought you here to become my wife!'

His *second* wife. In a storm of outrage Bethany looked at him in absolute disbelief, and then she tore her hands violently free and fled.

CHAPTER THREE

PASSING beneath the nearest archway, Bethany found herself in an elaborate reception room. Fighting for self-control, she closed her eyes. 'Prince Razul take only one wife. Always he say that...only the one.' Zulema's explanation for Fatima's distress returned to her now. Seemingly Razul was now prepared to break that promise to his wife, and in a society where he was all-powerful what could the wretched woman possibly do? Presumably she could live with her husband's other female diversions but felt both betrayed and threatened by the prospect of another woman acquiring the same status as herself.

Marriage...woman-stealing was all above board as long as you offered holy matrimony to satisfy the conventions. A strangled laugh, empty of amusement, escaped her. Little wonder she had been treated like royalty at the airport, little wonder she was being waited on hand and foot. Everybody *but* her had expected marriage to follow her arrival!

A polygamous marriage. The teachings of the Koran taught that a Muslim was entitled to up to four wives at any one time. In a lifetime he could get through many more than that number, if he so desired, by the judicious use of divorce. The ex-wives, of course, had to be liberally provided for. One of the reasons why polygamy was becoming less prevalent in the Arab world was the sheer expense of maintaining multiple families. But Razul was fabulously rich.

Oddly enough it had never occurred to her two years ago that Razul might already be a married man. The tabloid hadn't picked up on that…but then maybe he had not been married then. She raised trembling hands to her stiff, cold face.

'Why are you distressed?' It was a ferocious demand, raw with a frustrated lack of comprehension. 'Perhaps you are ashamed to have misjudged me so badly,' Razul suggested with savage bite. 'This is not Bluebeard's castle. I am not some filthy rapist who would force his unwanted attentions upon an unprotected woman! Do you seriously believe that my father would have agreed to me bringing an Englishwoman here had I not intended to marry her? Do you think us savages?'

Bethany wanted to howl with hysterical laughter and slap him hard to express her emotions at one and the same time. 'The Princess Fatima?' she whispered chokily.

'Fatima must learn to adjust. This is not my problem,' Razul dismissed, slashing the air with an angry and imperious hand. 'I do nothing to be ashamed of. I have waited two long years for you and she is well aware of this…'

Bethany gazed at him in horror. 'Your compassion is overwhelming,' she muttered sickly.

'Compassion is not infinite…no more is tolerance. Why do you treat me to this response?' Razul launched at her. 'It makes no sense!'

'Last night…' Bethany was struggling to think straight while dimly wondering what he could possibly find incomprehensible about her response. Dear heaven, did he fondly imagine that a *marriage* proposal two years ago would have been sufficient to change her attitude towards him? Did he think that she would have fallen gratefully at his feet in welcome? And when he now offered what he no doubt saw as the ultimate of honours, did he think that that would magically overcome her resistance?

'*What* last night?' Razul appealed with driven emotion.

'You kept on saying that when I went *back* to my world... You weren't thinking of marriage then!' she reminded him.

Razul set his incredibly eloquent mouth into a grim line. 'I was making it clear that were you to be unhappy I would set you free. I would give you a divorce, but *only* after you had given our marriage a fair and reasonable trial.'

Inside herself, beyond her angry disbelief, she hurt. She turned her head away. She would never have married Razul in any circumstances. Even if he hadn't had Fatima and those other women, she reflected painfully, she still would have said no. Marriage was not for her and would never be for her. She had seen far too much of the misery of marriage while she had been growing up, and, beyond that again, the even greater misery of a cross-cultural union.

Even so, she was shattered by the idea that Razul would *want* to marry her. Two years ago he had wanted an affair...and she wouldn't have been his first affair on campus—no, far from it! She might not have met Razul until his second term but she had *heard* about him...oh, boy, had she heard! His fame had gone before him.

Razul had flung himself with immense enthusiasm into a world where women were willing to share his bed without the smallest commitment on his part. Blessed by gorgeous good looks, charming broken English intermingled with fluent French, enormous wealth and the certainty that he would one day become a king, Razul had hit the female student body much like a winning lottery ticket blowing in the wind, hopefully to be captured by the most determined of his many admirers. A kind of communal hysteria had reigned in his radius, she recalled painfully.

'I could never marry you,' Bethany informed him tightly.

'Do not say never to me…I will not accept it.'

'I insist that you call a car to take me to the airport!'

'I refuse.' Razul sent her a raw, shimmering glance of gold.

'You are thinking of the loss of face…' Bethany assumed, suddenly wishing that she did not understand his culture to the degree that she did. If he had informed his family that he intended to marry her and she refused, it would be a humiliation for him. A public humiliation. There was undoubtedly not a woman in Datar who would deny herself the great honour of becoming one of his wives.

'Again you go out of your way to insult me.' Razul slung her a look of wrathful reproach, his hands clenching into fists by his sides. 'What lies between us runs too deep to rest on something so superficial as what you term a "loss of face"!'

Bethany was paper-pale, but rigid with a strength of will every bit as unyielding as his own. 'There is nothing between us and there never will be. You *must* accept that. In my opinion my sole attraction in your eyes is the fact that I said no two years ago! Your ego can't live with the startling concept that there exists one woman in the world who wants nothing to do with you!'

'When you speak such barefaced lies I lose all patience with you!' Razul blazed at her with such explosive suddenness that she flinched. He closed the distance between them in one long, panther-like stride and reached for her. 'These lies are naked provocation!'

As he hauled her into his arms Bethany stiffened in shock. Glittering golden eyes roamed over her startled face with a scorching heat that made her skin tauten over her bones. 'You burn for me as I burn for you—'

'*No!*'

'I saw your hunger last night.' Razul lifted a shapely

hand and knotted long fingers very slowly into the fiery tumble of her long hair. 'I hold you and your heart beats as madly as that of a gazelle hunted down in the desert. It beats for me and for no other man. Yet I have never touched you,' he breathed, in a throaty undertone of frustration which sent taut quivers rippling down her rigid spine. '*Never*... How many men in your world could say that of the woman they longed to possess? How many men would treat you with such unquestioning respect?'

His thumb was rubbing against the lobe of her ear. A tiny little shiver ran through her, fracturing her breathing. Eyes as keen as those of a hawk in flight scoured her hectically flushed face, beating down on her with merciless insight. She trembled, a whirling tide of dizziness assailing her, the hiss of her indrawn breath shatteringly loud in the stillness. 'Razul, I—'

'You trust me to observe the boundaries...why?' Razul demanded roughly, yet the long forefinger he lifted to trace the tremulous fullness of her lower lip was tormentingly gentle, brushing across the tender skin with innate eroticism. 'In the mood I am in your trust is a step too far. Perhaps I have been too honourable...I made it too easy for you to drive me away in England, but I will not make it easy *this* time.'

'Let go of me,' Bethany mumbled thickly, her slender length slipping from rigidity into sudden, shivering weakness as that expert finger slid against her trembling mouth. A tide of sexual awareness strong enough to wipe out her every defence was infiltrating her now.

'Have other men not held you...touched you?' Unhidden anger harshened his rich dark voice. 'Why do you expect me to be different?'

Her breasts rose and fell, heavy, swelling, her nipples peaking inside the gossamer-fine covering of her bra. A languorous heat was uncoiling between her thighs, making her shift like a cat arching its back in the sunshine, but in the depths of her unthinking mind lurked an equally animal fear of her own responses. *'Don't!'*

'But your eyes say *do*…and if I had behaved as a man of your world you would not have shunned me two years ago. I allowed you to stay free,' Razul intoned with mesmeric intensity. 'Do you know why an unmarried woman is not left alone with a man in Arabia? A man is expected to sin and a woman is deemed too weak to resist temptation, for was she not fashioned to be the greatest pleasure of a man's existence? As you will be mine, heart, soul and body…for that I promised myself in England and I will fulfil that promise more sweetly than you can believe…'

'Airport!' Bethany said jerkily, as if he had yanked a string and that was the best her blitzed reasoning powers could come up with by way of a contradiction.

Razul laughed softly. A lean hand sank to the shallow indentation of her spine and pressed her closer as he slowly lowered his arrogant dark head. 'The image of a jet taking off…the heavens opening as the gates to your secret garden…most fitting, but then you are an extraordinarily sensual woman,' he murmured thickly. 'Did I not sense that from the first?'

A violent shudder snaked through her as his warm breath fanned her cheek. He took her mouth in a hot, hungry surge of possession and dragged her down so deep and so fast into a world she didn't know, she was lost. He prised her lips apart with the tip of his tongue and probed the moist, tender interior that she instinctively opened to him. With a strangled moan Bethany caught fire in a surging blaze of passion.

Excitement, raw, wild and overpowering, took her by storm. With every fevered kiss she hung on the edge of desperation for the next, crushing her thrumming body into the hard, lean heat of him for the closeness that every fibre of her femininity greedily craved. Her hands swept up and found his broad shoulders, dug in there briefly to trace the hard stretch of his taut muscles beneath the rich fabric of his jacket before convulsively linking round his strong brown throat, her seeking fingers flirting deliciously with the luxuriant black hair at the nape of his neck.

With a stifled groan he suddenly tightened his arms around her as he lifted her up against him, kissing her breathless with an intense urgency that stoked the flames of her arousal to unbearable heights. She clutched at him, knotting her fingers into his thick, silky hair, for he was the only stable influence in a whirling vortex of violent passion. He muttered something rough against her swollen mouth, momentarily stiffening as if to withdraw, but she held him there, kissed him again with the same raw, answering hunger that he had chosen to awaken in her.

He drew her down, down onto softness and support, crushing her quivering length just as swiftly beneath his superior weight. As he sealed his long, muscular body to hers the heat of desire washed over her with such strength that she burned, her hips arching up, her legs torturously confined in the clinging cloth of her caftan. His hand closed round her breast and she gasped, shocked by sensation, instinctively straining her swollen, seeking flesh upwards to meet that possessive hold.

Razul dragged his lips free of hers, staring down at her with blazing golden eyes, his cheek-bones harshly delineated beneath his smooth, sun-bronzed skin as he snatched in a ragged breath. He loosened his grip, ran a torturous fingertip over the shamelessly distended nipple poking against the fine silk barrier, sending fire shooting to the very centre of the throbbing ache between her thighs. She closed her eyes in an agony of excitement and shuddered as if she were in a force-ten gale.

'I cannot do this,' Razul breathed with subdued ferocity, abruptly pulling back from her and yet carrying her with him, his strong hands grasping her arms as he tugged her upright again. 'To do this is to shame you, and I will not have regrets between us. You will come to me as my bride or you will not come at all!'

He settled her down like a doll onto a low divan. Bethany didn't know what had happened to her. Her entire body felt as though it had acquired a life of its own, and right now it was screaming with a clamouring dissatisfaction which was cruelly unwelcome. In short, she ached—ached for a physical completion which she had never desired in her life before—and she sat there, struck dumb by sheer horror as her mind fumbled up out of the darkness of complete shut-down to reason again. And yet she did not want to think...

'I always knew that your desire would match mine,' Razul confessed with rough satisfaction. 'Now you must acknowledge that too and be grateful that my control is greater...though in truth it was not that which restrained my ardour...the doors are ajar.'

Be grateful? Bethany sat there in the burnt ashes of self-discovery, her fire ignobly doused by a bucket of cold reality. She had never endured such a tumult of agonised emotion. She was seized by shame and loathing for both herself and for him. 'Fatima...' she whispered strickenly, and hung her head, wondering how any man could possibly reduce her to such a level of selfish, mindless insanity.

'What has she to do with us?' Razul demanded with savage impatience. 'Do not speak her name to me again!'

How *could* he talk like that? Nausea stirred in her cramping stomach. She was so unbearably ashamed of her own behaviour. How could she have forgotten Fatima for one moment? How could she have? Feverish tears scorched her lowered eyelids as she scrambled upright. 'You must let me go!'

'You are the most stubborn woman I have ever met,' Razul condemned harshly, frustratedly. 'Why can you

not talk to me? Why do I *still* meet the same silence?
Are you so prejudiced against my race that you cannot
listen to your own heart?'

The charge of racial prejudice hit her like a final intolerable blow. Bethany shot him a look of bitter reproach and took off as if all the bats in hell were on her
trail.

Strangled sobs were clogging her throat when she
found Zulema waiting for her on the gallery above. She
rammed them back with every atom of fierce discipline
that she possessed and lifted her head high, concealing
the agonising strain threatening to tear her wide open.

How dared he bring her here...how dared he subject
her to such an intolerable situation? He was stirring up
feelings from the past—angry, disturbing emotions
which she had thought had been laid to rest. It was her
pride which was hurting, she told herself. Her stupid,
childishly irrational crush on him two years ago was a
memory which now made her cringe. That she should
be forced back into contact with him again was naturally
a nightmare of mortification. It was like returning to the
scene of the crime.

Back in her palatial suite of rooms, she paced the
floor, too frantically strung up to sit down. She knew
what was *really* wrong with her. She was still reeling
with shock from the physical response that he had ex-
tracted from her, was barely able to credit that that wanton woman in his arms had been her. After all, that kind
of physical stuff had always left Bethany cold. Even in
the grip of infatuation she had assumed that the reality
of any closer contact with Razul would pretty much
match her distasteful grappling experiences with other
men. But *now* she had learned the shattering extent of
her own vulnerability and she was disgusted with herself.

How could she have allowed him to touch her like
that...how could she have? Maybe it was her own fault,

she thought grimly. She was a twenty-seven-year-old virgin...but that had never bothered her, never caused her the least discomfiture or regret until *he'd* landed in her radius! She had never felt the slightest bit repressed until *he'd* awakened those grossly uncomfortable feelings of curiosity and awareness two years ago. Only now did she face the fact that she must have denied the physical side of her nature for far too long when a *married* man could put his hands on her and make her behave like a sex-starved wanton!

In two long years Razul had not forgotten her...why? Good old-fashioned lust and the challenge that she had foolishly made of herself. In England Razul had laid siege to her as though he had been conducting a military manoeuvre. She had been deluged with flowers and gifts of expensive jewellery. A couple of months on campus had taught Razul exactly what most Western women expected from an Arab prince. She had returned the jewellery. But when she had failed to be impressed, had he given up and returned to more appreciative admirers? *No way.*

Whatever Razul had to fight for was one thousand times more desirable to him than what came easily. His shrewd intelligence and resourcefulness had come into play as he'd focused more on the kind of woman she was. An exquisite Persian kitten had landed mysteriously on her doorstep. When she had worked late at the library an anonymously prepaid taxi would be waiting outside to take her home again. He had invited her to the opera and to external lectures instead of discos and nightclubs.

And she had kept on saying 'no', 'sorry', 'no' and 'no' over and over again, pleading pressure of work and other social engagements, never once saying, until the very last, 'I'm not interested...I'm not attracted to you...I don't like you,' because those had been lies—the most outright lies she had ever told. And the terrible thing had been that Razul had known that she was lying and had been bitterly angered by her refusal to recognise the fierce attraction between them. That was why he had not forgotten her.

She covered her face with unsteady hands, feeling as though her whole being was in wild turmoil, and it terrified her. How the heck could he do this to her? What was it about him that he could *still* get to her to such an extent? She was appalled by her own inability to think straight. And when she looked back on the conversation that she had had with him in that courtyard she was even more unnerved by the peculiarities of her own conduct. She had sat there trailing her fingers in that fountain and actually *talking* to him! Was that rational behaviour? Why hadn't she demanded her freedom in terms which could not be ignored? Why hadn't she threatened him…got him by the throat…and told him that he was a kidnapper?

Her head was spinning over these inconsistencies. Somehow she had to make Razul let her go. She focused on that dark, driven frustration of his last words to her. Surely his own instincts would do the persuading for him? Whatever response Razul had expected to his proposal, he had not received it. Indeed, she had the extraordinary suspicion that Razul had actually believed that she might be flattered that he should have gone to such incredible lengths to bring her to Datar, especially when his manoeuvres were accompanied by the assurance of wholly honourable intentions.

Honourable? The human male didn't come much more basic than Prince Razul al Rashidai Harun. She had severely dented his ego when she'd rejected him outright in England. So in that immeasurably arrogant, obstinate way of his he had put together what he saw as a winning package which no woman in her right mind could conceivably refuse…marriage! He was insane. Apart from the obvious fact that she absolutely loathed him, could he not see the vast gulf of understanding and cultural indoctrination which separated them…why did he refuse to see it? She wanted to scream and tear her hair out at the same time.

Without warning the bedroom door burst open. Startled, Bethany focused on the ravishingly beautiful brunette standing on the threshold. She was wearing a fabulous lemon brocade suit which shrieked designer sophistication. Huge, lustrous brown eyes set above exotically tilted cheek-bones zeroed in on Bethany, and the pouting red mouth twisted into a vicious line of rage.

'I am Fatima…'

Bethany was paralysed by a clutch of emotions, but horror rose uppermost. Razul's wife. She couldn't have opened her shocked mouth had her life depended on it. She wanted a large dark hole to sink into.

Fatima surveyed her with raw loathing. 'Hair the colour of carrots!' she spat. 'You ugly English bitch!'

This was no poor, weeping, tormented woman, Bethany noted dumbly. In fact, there wasn't a sign that there had *ever* been tears on that remarkably beautiful face. There was a look of such simmering violence and uncontrollable fury that Bethany actually feared a physical assault.

'You think you can take my place…but let me tell you what Razul will give you!' Fatima ranted, stalking forward. 'He'll give you a fake marriage, not the real thing! *Mut'a*…you're so clever, you should know what *mut'a* means. It is a marriage contract for a day, a week, at most a month or two. It doesn't even require a divorce! Men use it to take the woman they want and then toss her aside again!'

Bethany had only a very vague idea of what *mut'a* entailed, and even though it was totally irrelevant she found herself thinking that she had not known that Dataris recognised temporary marriage contracts. Such agreements could satisfy the strict conventions of a society which condemned sexual relations outside the bonds of matrimony. Sin and shame were thus avoided. Even a one-night stand could be deemed respectable if it observed the rules.

'Fatima—' Bethany began painfully.

'You are shocked!' Fatima rejoiced in shrill interruption. 'You are also stupid! King Azmir would never permit his son to marry a Western woman under any other circumstances!'

'Fatima...please forgive me for the pain I have caused you just by being here,' Bethany pleaded tautly, no longer able to meet the brunette's eyes, so deeply ashamed did she feel, even though she had not asked for the ghastly situation she now found herself in. 'And please believe that I have no desire to marry your husband—'

'*My*—?' Fatima screeched.

'Razul refuses to allow me to leave the palace!' Bethany didn't want any more distasteful screeching and rushed in to interrupt.

'Refuses to allow...?' Fatima sounded dazed, which Bethany could well understand since the woman obviously believed that she was here by free choice. 'You do not want to be here? You do not want to marry Razul? I cannot believe this—'

'Nevertheless it is the truth!' Bethany broke in fiercely. 'I want absolutely nothing to do with him. I had no idea that Razul intended to bring me here or even that he was a married man—'

'Ah...' Fatima's pouting little mouth slowly set into a coldly malicious smile of comprehension. '*This* is why you wish to leave him.'

Bethany flushed hotly. 'Only *one* of the many reasons,' she stressed curtly.

'If you truly wish to leave, *I* can easily get you out of the palace,' Fatima informed her, with a glinting little smile. 'The old women in our family still hide themselves behind the veil when they go out. Who could tell what lies beneath the *chador*?'

'I would be very grateful for your help—'

'I will make the arrangements.'

The brunette yanked open the door and loosed a terse volley of Arabic on Zulema, who was waiting outside. The girl cowered and then fell down on her knees, trembling as if she was terrified. With a most unlikeable air of malicious satisfaction Fatima walked out, leaving Bethany alone. What a bitch, Bethany couldn't help thinking, and then she bent her head, asking herself what right she had to stand in judgement. This was not her world—oh, no, indeed, this was not her world, and the sooner she was out of it again, the happier she would be, she told herself fiercely.

Bethany was lying on a divan, glancing abstractedly through a glossy magazine, when she caught a disturbing glimmer of movement in the reflection of a tall mirror to one side of her and turned her head. Shock shrilled through her, her breath escaping her in a sudden hiss as she shot to her feet.

'Try not to scream...' Razul sent her a smile of raw amusement that acknowledged her astonishment. 'These are the women's quarters, and in honour of your reputation I should not be here—'

'Damn right...you shouldn't be!' Bethany spluttered breathlessly. 'How the hell did you get in here?'

'SAS training. I crossed the roof and dropped down onto the balcony.'

She hadn't heard a sound but then he had always moved with the silent prowl of a natural predator. 'You could have broken your stupid neck!' she snapped. 'What do you want?'

'Obviously I should have come at night and brought the chocolates,' Razul sighed with lazy mockery. 'You do not have a romantic bone in your body, Dr Morgan.'

Bethany flinched, her facial muscles tightening.

'But we can work on that problem together. You ask why I am here…and I am tempted to ask, Are you joking?' Razul drawled. 'You retreated at speed from a serious discussion.'

'I made my feelings quite clear,' Bethany said shakily.

Razul shoved his hands into the pockets of his well-cut trousers and elbowed back his jacket, displaying the solid breadth of his chest and the taut flatness of his stomach, not to mention the now sleekly defined lines of his lean, muscular thighs. Colour ran up into her cheeks, her tongue sliding out to moisten her dry lips in a darting motion.

Eyes of vibrant gold flicked to her, catching her in the act of appraisal, and his innately sensual mouth curved with instantaneous recognition. Dense ebony lashes screened his eyes down to a smouldering sliver, returning her gaze with earthy masculine amusement. 'When you have not got the restraint to prevent yourself from visually ravishing me, how am I to accept these extraordinarily confused feelings you insist that you have made clear?'

Another tide of hot pink surged up beneath her fair skin. 'I was not—'

'You were,' Razul slotted in silkily. 'You watch me as I watch you. Green light…but then red stop-light. It infuriates me…and right at this moment it makes me want to throw you down on that bed and release that promise of passion again, until you sob against the exquisite torture of my lovemaking and beg me for that ultimate fulfilment. After that experience I seriously doubt that you will again offend my hearing with the lie of your lack of interest.'

Standing there, wordlessly entrapped by the dark, intensely passionate lure of him, Bethany was pretty doubtful too. Her colour fluctuating wildly, she backed away from him, her skin hot and tight as it stretched over her quivering nerve-endings in involuntary response to the electrifying sizzle of raw sexual awareness now churning up the atmosphere.

'I don't deny that...that there's a certain attraction between us,' she heard herself confess between gritted teeth, feeling herself under threat and ready to make that one concession if it held him at bay.

'This is very sudden,' Razul derided.

'I b-beg your pardon?'

'You finally admit the truth, but it is no longer enough.'

Rampant frustration filled her. 'What point is there, then, in admitting such a truth?'

'A crumb from the table when I want the whole loaf?' His sensual mouth hardened as he sent her a swingeing look of scorn. 'I want everything you have to give...and then more. I do not stand at your door like a humble suitor. I will take what you seek to deny me. I will possess you as you have never been possessed, and when it is over you will never forget me...*this* I promise you!' he swore in a biting undertone that sent tiny chills of fear rippling down her rigid spine.

She had thought that finally acknowledging that attraction would satisfy him. Instead, for some reason, that admission had inflamed him. 'What could we possibly have in common?' she demanded starkly.

'You are innocent indeed if you do not know that there are more exciting things between a man and a woman than similarity.'

'No! I know all about *that* kind of excitement!' Bethany slung the assurance at him in disgust as she spun away, her entire body thrumming with the strength of her emotional turmoil. 'And it's not for me.'

She was painfully well acquainted with the sort of violent sexual attraction which could spring up between radically different people. It had happened between her parents. Her irresponsible, utterly self-centered and vain father had waltzed in and out of her childhood as and when it had suited him: when another relationship had broken down, when he'd been short of money, out of work or simply wanting home comforts for a while. He had been far too clever to get a divorce. And her loving mother had kept on opening the door, forgiving, trusting, always ready to hope again that *this* time he would be different and he would stay.

Time and time again Bethany had been urged to make her father feel at home, keep him happy, act as if he were a permanent fixture rather than someone just passing through. Even remembering that period of her life made Bethany's stomach churn sickly. She had promised herself then that, unlike her mother, she would find her fulfilment in a career. She would be independent and self-sufficient. She would never, ever make herself vulnerable by building her life round some man.

'Who taught you such a lesson?' Razul probed.

Dragged back in a shaken state from her own painful memories, Bethany focused on him, feeling that wild, crazed lurch of her every sense and hating him for having the power to do that to her. It was terrifying to feel that she was no longer in control of her own responses.

'Twenty-seven years old and you behave like a mixed-up teenager... Why do you fight me like this?'

'Because this is an impossible attraction...why the hell can't you see that and accept it?' she practically screamed at him from her turmoil of ragged nerves, on the edge of a breakdown. 'Why couldn't you just leave me alone? Don't you ever think about anybody but yourself? Luring me out here and subjecting me to this nightmare is positively sadistic! *You...are...hurting...me!*' And then her voice broke off in horror that she should have revealed that reality.

His veiled dark eyes were impenetrable. 'You hurt yourself, *aziz*. When you gain the courage to see that, perhaps you will also have the grace to be grateful that I chose to give you a second chance.'

Her mouth wobbled below her outraged emerald-green eyes. 'A second chance?' she parroted in a strangled voice, scarcely believing her ears.

'Which you have yet to prove yourself deserving of. Did I not desire you so greatly, I would have set aside all thought of you a long time ago,' Razul delivered harshly.

'I hate your guts…can't you see that?' she blistered back at him rawly.

'What I see is…fear.'

'Fear?'

'There's nowhere to run this time. And when you retreat I advance. You are losing ground fast.'

'Are we playing war games now?' she derided shrilly.

'This is no game.' Razul glanced with irritation at his watch. 'I have a meeting—'

'You *have* to let me go!' Bethany asserted, incredulous at the lack of effect she was having on him.

He took a step closer. Bethany leapt back. He laughed with genuine amusement, tremendous charm in that sudden, spontaneous smile. Approaching her, he lifted a hand and curved long, caressing fingers to the taut line of her jaw. 'I anticipate a long, hot summer in which you will change from the woman you are into the woman you could be… You will not want me to let you go,' he forecast with immense confidence.

'Don't touch me!' Bethany jerked her head back out of reach of that disturbingly intimate caress, trembling all over, feeling cornered and menaced and infuriated by the unfamiliar sense of inadequacy that he was evoking within her.

In answer Razul knotted his fingers into a hank of curling hair and brought his mouth down on a collision course with hers. Almost incoherent with rage, she tried to evade him but he held her fast, forced her to be still and kissed her, and she went down into the heat of hell-fire and damnation without a murmur, electrified by the force of her own hunger. He pressed her back against the wall, both of his hands linking fiercely with hers, and kissed her breathless, crushing her ripe mouth under his until her senses swam in hot, drowning pleasure.

'I will count the hours until I have you in my bed…' Razul confessed raggedly, and withdrew from her.

Wildly dizzy and dazed, she stayed upright on the power of shock alone. She opened her heavy eyes. He was gone. She slid down the wall like a boneless rag doll and shivered and shook, devastated by what he could make her feel, emotionally and physically drained by her own turmoil. What the hell was she going to do if Fatima didn't help her? How long would it take the brunette to make what she had called 'arrangements'?

But Fatima reappeared within half an hour of Razul's exit. Again the door opened without any prefatory knock. A veiled shape stood on the threshold. Fatima was cloaked in the voluminous folds of the *chador* which screened the female form from head to toe, and it was indeed an effective disguise. Bethany only recognised her visitor by her acid-yellow court shoes. A bundle of cloth was tossed at her feet.

'Hurry…the car is waiting for us!' Fatima hissed impatiently.

'Now?'

'Have you changed your mind?'

'Of course not!' Bethany gasped.

Her heart beating like a drum, she pulled on the tent-like *chador*.

'Conceal your hands in the pockets,' Fatima instructed. 'And keep your head down and do not speak.'

There was no sign of Zulema in the corridor outside. Bethany found it incredibly difficult to walk with all that fabric flapping around her. When I get home I'll laugh about this, she promised herself, but she knew that she wouldn't... Indeed, all she could think about was the fact that she would never, ever see Razul again, which made her furiously, bitterly angry with herself.

CHAPTER FOUR

FATIMA led Bethany out to a dusty, cobbled yard bounded by a long line of garages. A Range Rover was sitting there with the engine already running. Bethany clambered into the back like a drunken sailor in her companion's graceful wake. The car roared off and, mindful of the driver, Bethany continued to keep her head bent. Half an hour would take them to the airport—maybe a little more, she conceded, fingering the weight of her shoulder bag beneath the *chador*. She had her passport but no flight ticket… Hell, a seat on a flight anywhere would do as long as it got her out of Datar!

The car lurched and jolted, the engine thundering. They were moving at considerable speed. Bethany finally emerged from her reverie to notice that the drive was taking a lot longer than she had expected. Twisting, she peered out of a side-window and was astounded to realise that the four-wheel drive was crossing a flat salt plain and there was no sign of a road or, indeed, of any other traffic. Her lips parted. 'Where—?'

A startled gasp of pain escaped her as a set of pincer-like nails bit into the back of her exposed hand. Her head spun round. Her eyes collided with seething brown ones and she gulped. She dug her hand shakily into the pocket again but she could feel the slow seep of blood from the stinging slash of Fatima's assault.

Tense minutes passed. Bethany didn't know what to do. Ahead of them the plain vanished into a rolling landscape of dunes. Where on earth was Fatima taking her? There was a sudden rustle of movement from the front of the car. Bethany gasped as a veiled female shape un-

60

coiled from her hiding place on the floor and settled herself into the front seat.

'Two women left the palace and two women will return,' Fatima informed her smugly. 'Nobody will suspect that you left in my company.'

'Where the heck are we?'

The Range Rover lurched to a halt in the shadow of a great rolling dune. Springing out, the driver opened the door beside Bethany.

'Get out!' Fatima planted both hands on her and gave her a violent push.

Bethany got such a shock that she was easily unbalanced and went flying out headlong onto the ground. It knocked the breath out of her lungs but didn't deprive her of hearing Fatima's shrieked abuse and the prophecy that the sun would wreck that pasty white skin of hers and make her hair fall out so that no man would ever want her again.

Bethany picked herself up and wrenched herself out of the suffocating folds of the *chador*. 'You *can't* leave me out here alone!'

As the Range Rover raked into reverse she very narrowly missed being knocked flat by the swinging door that Fatima had yet to pull shut. She leapt out of harm's way and then stood there in the burning heat of the sun, gripped by a brand of quite paralysing incredulity that anyone could do such a thing. Then she was furious with herself for trusting a woman who she had known was blazing with jealousy and rage. She checked her watch and paled. How many miles could that car have covered in well over an hour? Worse, it would be dark soon.

Seeking a lookout point, she started climbing the sliding wall of sand with raw determination. It took her far longer and required far more effort than she had expected. Near the top she bent double, struggling to breathe in the hot air and overwhelmed by dizziness. Finally achieving her objective, she strained her eyes against the fiery blaze of the sun and thought that she was hallucinating when she saw the lines of black tents beginning less than thirty yards below her.

She blinked dazedly and looked again. Her terror of being found as a set of bleached bones after a long and painful decline brought on by thirst and third-degree sunburn died there and then. Indeed her attack of panic now made her feel distinctly foolish. It *was* a Bedouin encampment and a very large one. She did not believe in so miraculous a coincidence. It would seem that Fatima's driver might appear to do her bidding but he was *not* a maniac and he had chosen the drop site, aware that Bethany could come to little harm here. She started down the slope.

A clutch of colourfully clad children saw her first. They ran ahead of her, shouting at the top of their voices. Women peered out of dim tent interiors. Bethany followed the children until a whole horde of men piled out of an enormous tent and blocked her path, their dark, weather-beaten faces arranged in expressions that went from initial shock to outright rigid disapproval. They stood around her exchanging volleys of excitable Arabic and waving their hands about with gusto. Their reaction, so entirely foreign to the indelible rule of Arab hospitality, completely disconcerted Bethany.

A tubby little man with a grey beard, clad in gold-edged blue robes, paced forward and fixed stern black eyes on her. 'You are Prince Razul's bride?'

Red hair in Datar was like having two heads, Bethany decided. When some idiotic Englishwoman with a flaming head of hair came huffing and puffing out of the desert wastes wearing a silly, strained smile, evidently the locals could name her on sight. Zulema had not been exaggerating when she'd said that *everybody* knew about her. Now…should she say that she was *not* Razul's intended or should she play dumb?

'I am Razul's great-uncle, Sheikh Abdul al Rashidai Harun.'

Dumb wasn't likely to carry her through, she registered. Her smile slid away. She sensed the principles of family solidarity looming large, and she had the nasty suspicion that Sheikh Abdul found the sight of Razul's bride apparently loose and on the run in the wrong direction an offence of no mean order.

'I got lost,' she muttered stupidly, but she was so hot and so exhausted that the world around her was beginning to spin.

'You will not become lost again,' Sheikh Abdul announced, producing a mobile phone from his sleeve with a flourish. 'My nephew has a temper like a sandstorm, most dangerous when roused. It is a joy to behold.'

As Bethany swayed a woman tugged at her sleeve and she was carted off to the welcome shelter of a large tent. In daunting silence she was brought water to wash with, then was served with tea and a delicious selection of food. As darkness folded in the elaborate brass lamps attached to the tent-poles were lit. Left alone, she sank down on a kelim-covered ottoman and curved her cheek into a silk cushion, the vibrant colours of the gorgeous Shiraz rugs hung on the cloth walls of the tent swimming before her as her weighted eyelids sank down.

When Bethany finally awakened after a very restless night she was lying under a blanket which she immediately thrust off her, the stickiness of her skin telling her that a new day had begun. She shifted and sat up, her tumbled hair falling round her like a vibrant curtain of flame as she glanced at her watch. It was only eight. She lifted her fingers to thrust the tangle of curls off her damp brow and then she froze.

Sheathed in desert robes, Razul was standing mere feet away with the stillness of a graven image. Sizzling gold eyes as brilliant as sunlight in that hard-boned, hawkish face splintered into her with powerful effect. His complete silence was intimidating. But the most menacing thing of all for Bethany was the instant flood of pleasure and relief she experienced. That instinctive response was her worst nightmare come true.

She turned her head away. 'OK, so I made a break for freedom and ended up a long way from the airport,' she conceded in a tone of nervous irony. 'So what now? You bury me up to the throat in sand at the hottest part of the day, paint me with honey and set scorpions on me? Or do you just send me in disgrace? What *is* the traditional approach?'

'According to tradition, I beat you.'

Bethany lost every scrap of colour, plunged into sudden, unavoidable recall of her aunt's disastrous marriage to an Arab. Violence had played its part in the final breakup of that union. 'That's something of a conversation-killer, Razul,' she murmured not quite steadily.

'*You left me.*' The intense condemnation with which he spoke mirrored the powerful anger that he was visibly struggling to contain.

'That's the problem with stealing women,' Bethany retorted with helpless defiance as her chin came up. 'The stupid creatures may well cherish a peculiar desire to regain their freedom.'

'Do you want me to lose my temper?' Fierce strain was etched on his startlingly handsome features.

And Bethany discovered that *yes*, she did. She *needed* a cure for the madness afflicting her, and the proof that he was the kind of male likely to employ his infinitely greater strength to the task of subjecting a woman would surely provide quite unparalleled therapy. She bent her head, her emotions in so much conflict that she felt torn apart. The madness of her own reasoning hit her hard. Had she enjoyed a single truly rational thought since she'd entered Datar? Angry bitterness consumed her in a sudden, scorching tide.

She slid upright, her jewel-bright eyes slicing back at him. 'Why not? Isn't this whole crazy mess your fault? It's certainly not mine! How dare you bring me to this country? And how dare you stand there now and try to intimidate me?'

'Do not raise your voice to me here where we may be overheard.' The pallor of his increasing anger had spread savagely across his high cheek-bones.

'I'll do whatever the hell I like. I don't belong to you like some sort of rug you can walk on when you feel like it, and you have no rights over me!' she blazed back.

'Have I not?' Razul bit out very softly.

'None whatsoever, so you can keep the macho-man act for your harem!' Bethany spat at him in a mood of pure vitriol, wanting every scornful word to find its target. 'Your chances of reducing me to the level of crawling round your feet are zero...I'd sooner slit my throat! How dare you talk about your *honour* when you've already got a wife? When I called you primitive, barbaric and uncivilised in England I was understating the case!'

His strong face a mask of fury, Razul moved forward with such terrifying abruptness that Bethany threw herself backwards over the ottoman and screamed. A powerful hand closed over her shoulder and began hauling her bodily back up onto the seat which she was endeavouring to employ as a defensive barrier. The sheer strength he exhibited sent her into even deeper panic, and another few strangled yells escaped her before Razul laid the palm of his hand firmly across her trembling mouth, enforcing her silence.

Huge green eyes, dark with fear, looked up at him as he pinned her flat.

'Keep quiet,' Razul intoned.

That controlled command wasn't at all what she had expected. As she braced herself for a blow, her shocked eyes grew even bigger. Her heart was pounding fit to burst behind her breastbone. The hard heat and weight of his body imprisoned her as securely as chains.

'My people will think I cannot control my woman but I know very well how to control my woman,' Razul asserted with savage quietness. 'In bed and out of bed. But I have never yet sunk to shameful violence, nor would I. Do you understand that, or is that beyond your understanding?'

In a daze of quivering uncertainty she stared back up at him and drowned helplessly in the entrapment of compelling golden eyes raw with anger and derision.

'So, *aziz*…one more scream and all you get is a bucket of water over you to douse your hysterics. Am I speaking English clearly enough for comprehension?'

Bethany gave a mesmerised nod under his hand.

With a final searing glance he released her.

She was still in a condition of such bemusement that she couldn't function. She had gone from rage to terror within seconds and lost control. A kind of appalled embarrassment was beginning to steal over her.

Razul stared down at her. 'You said…you said that I already had a wife. Was that some childishly inept attempt to further defame my character?'

She closed her eyes in sudden agony, assuming that he intended to lie to her. 'I *know* that Fatima is your wife.'

'I have never had a wife. I was betrothed at the age of twenty-two to Hiriz, my second cousin. Five years ago she died in a car accident shortly before we were to be married. Hiriz had a younger sister called Fatima,' Razul proffered in the same harsh, unemotional tone, although his biting tension was palpable. 'She is not my wife. Perhaps you would like me to call witnesses to this truth?'

Bethany slowly began to sit up. She was trying to remember what Zulema had said, and recalled that Fatima had at no stage claimed Razul as her husband but had certainly looked pretty smug when Bethany had made reference to what she had believed to be fact.

A quiver of darkly suppressed emotion rippled through Razul's lean length as he studied her with icy dark eyes. 'Had you sought to know me at all, you would already be aware that I do not believe in the practice of polygamy. Nor indeed does my father. One wife at a time is quite sufficient for any man. But *no*!' Razul uttered a harsh laugh. 'You do not see this. Your blind prejudice is shameful, your assumptions for an academic mind inexcusable!'

White as snow and deeply shaken, Bethany made a tiny, uncertain movement with one hand and then her fingers dropped again. 'Razul, I—'

'In the name of Allah, an apology would be an even grosser offence. No doubt you are still suffering from the fantastic notion that my family harbour concubines as well! We may be primitive, backward and painfully unwesternised in our ways, but our standards of sexual behaviour are far higher than those of your own society!'

Sinking ever deeper into a pool of stricken self-examination while being engulfed by the greatest mortification she had ever been forced to endure, Bethany could no longer meet that coldly condemning appraisal.

'After the death of Hiriz, young women were sent to my father in the hope that I would choose a bride from their ranks. While they were within our household they were strictly chaperoned. They were also educated, clothed and dowered at my family's expense...one very practical reason why those daughters were offered by their fathers. Until the spoils of oil wealth were shared, many of them found it impossible to arrange suitable marriages for their daughters. My relatives made matches for them.'

'How could I have known that?' she whispered unsteadily.

'You did not want to know it,' Razul condemned.

'You preferred to believe the outrageous slander which appeared in newsprint. That article was a deeply offensive vilification which caused great distress to my family and to the families of the young women concerned. It was beneath our dignity to issue a denial of such salacious rubbish.'

Her head was spinning. He accused her of not having wanted to know the truth—a charge which pierced right to the heart of her turmoil, forcing her to see herself in a light which painfully exposed her every flaw. Her throat ached. It was as if he had held up a mirror and she wanted to shrink from her own reflection. Like most of her colleagues she had been willing to believe that newspaper article…why? It had provided them with a wonderful opportunity to pontificate on the outright hypocrisy of a society which demanded that young women live as cloistered ideals of perfect purity before marriage, while at the same time permitting the highest in the land to maintain concubines.

But Bethany had had the deepest motivation of all in choosing to accept that story as if it had been written in stone. Anything which she could use to reinforce the barriers she'd seen between herself and Razul had been welcome. It had been more grist to her mill of determined resistance, positive proof that he was every bit as alien in his way of life as it suited her to believe.

Suddenly Bethany, who had always prided herself on her seeking, *open* mind, was appalled by the unreasoning prejudice that she had unquestioningly chosen to harbour…simply because it suited her to do so. How much of that instinctive bias had she acquired in her teens when her mother's kid sister, Susan, had been going through the tortures of the damned in her ill-fated marriage to an Arab?

'I don't know what to say to you,' Bethany muttered unevenly.

He *wasn't* married. He had *never* been married. He

had no other women in his life. Her brain was working in short, electrifying bursts, bringing down the barriers that she had hidden behind for years. Without that protection she felt frighteningly weak and vulnerable. Already she could sense a terrifying surge of relief longing for release inside her. Razul was free…and her last realistic line of defence was being smashed and put out of her reach. That scared the hell out of her!

'How did you injure yourself?'

Her lashes fluttered in bemusement as, without warning, Razul dropped down to her level and reached for her hand. The angry scratches which Fatima had inflicted stood out in stark contrast against her pale skin.

Her fingers quivered in his warm grasp. She looked down at him, watching the ebony crescents of his silky lashes drop near his cheek-bones, scanning the narrow blade of his nose, and her sensitive throat closed over altogether. When he wanted to be, he could be achingly gentle.

Gulping, she threw her head back, anguished guilt sliding like a knife into her heart. Did you really think that he was going to beat you up? she thought. Well, he knows now that you thought that too, and he can take it in his stride beautifully because you have taught him to expect nothing but misjudgement from your corner. She trembled, struggling to rein back the powerful emotions shuddering through her.

'Fatima did this,' he breathed.

'It doesn't matter,' she said chokily, not even caring how he knew that the brunette had been responsible for getting her out of the palace, or how he'd instantly divined who had inflicted those abrasions. Obviously he did know as he hadn't asked any questions.

'She threatened Zulema's family. Zulema had the presence of mind to approach me, but by the time she was able to see me the hour was late. I was with my father. These scratches need to be attended to in case infection should set in. They should have been dealt with last night,' Razul murmured, with a frown, releasing her fingers and straightening again.

She couldn't bear him to move away but she could feel the distance in him like a cold wall holding her at bay. And she didn't blame him—she really didn't blame him for his hostility. Green light…red stop-light. A hectic flush replaced her pallor. She remembered him saying that if he let her go she would regret it for the rest of her life. She remembered how outraged she had been when he'd told her that he was giving her a second chance.

Some truths were very tough on your pride, she acknowledged painfully. What a coward she had been two years ago, huddling blindly behind her prejudices, refusing to listen to her own intelligence except when it told her what she wanted to hear. The reality was that it had been easier for her to refuse him. She hadn't had the guts to cross over the barrier of her own insecurities. She had been afraid of the strength of that attraction, afraid of being hurt, and neither had been an unreasonable fear.

After all, there *was* no prospect of a future with Razul. To talk of marriage was insane. Of course, he hadn't been talking about a *real* marriage, she recalled—at least, not what she understood as a real marriage, though she had no doubt that he viewed this temporary contract business in quite a different light. Naturally his father, whose distrust and dislike of foreigners was well-known, didn't want one in the family on any other basis.

What she didn't understand was how to handle her own emotions. Why the hell hadn't she had an affair with him in England? She would have got this insanity out of her system then and been cured, she reflected resentfully. Within a very short space of time she would have realised that they didn't have a single thought in common, and her infatuation would have died a natural death. There would have been no complications, no agonies, no past to come back and haunt her now with regret and bitterness.

'I think we need to talk…' Bethany muttered uncertainly.

'I am always prepared to talk.' Disconcertingly, Razul's set mouth came very close to a smile.

Bethany swallowed hard, still so bewildered by her own emotional conflict that she was not at all sure that she ought to be saying anything to him. 'I have a…a suggestion to make.'

'Does it relate to your departure?' he breathed tautly.

'Yes…well, obviously it would be sensible for me to go home. But that…well, that doesn't mean that I…well, that I wouldn't be…' her skin burning, she stumbled helplessly over the words to verbalise her own thoughts '…open to the possibility of—well…er…not *here* in Datar, of course, but you can't be here all the time!'

Razul scanned her with unhidden fascination. 'I am lost.'

He wasn't the only one. Bethany had got cold feet. How could she possibly suggest to him that they had an affair? That sounded so cold-blooded, not to mention brazen, but on the other hand it was a considerably more realistic proposal than the idea of marriage in any form, she reminded herself staunchly.

'I am attracted to you,' she began again in a flat tone which concealed her embarrassment, 'and I am prepared to admit that I have not reacted in a very reasonable manner as regards that…er…situation. Had we explored that situation in a relationship two years ago…and again I admit that it was my fault that we didn't…but, had we done so, that would have been by far the most sensible solution—'

'To the problem of this attraction…excuse me…this situation,' Razul slotted in smoothly.

Relieved that he had so easily followed her reasoning,

Bethany's gaze collided involuntarily with shimmering golden eyes and she snatched in a deep breath. 'Therefore it naturally follows that employing marriage as a resolution of the situation would be ridiculously excessive. This is not the nineteenth century, after all, and—'

'This is how I imagine you might speak in the lecture theatre,' Razul remarked.

A pin-dropping silence stretched.

Flames of angry pink burnished her fair skin. She decided to ignore that ungenerous comment. 'And we are both adults—'

'That is indeed a matter of opinion.'

'Look…will you stop interrupting me?' Bethany hissed at him in frustration. 'I am only trying to point out that, while I am not prepared to marry you, I am willing…well, open to the possibility of—'

'Exploring the situation in my bed?' Razul incised in a raw undertone.

Bethany turned scarlet. 'If you *must* put it that way…but I was thinking in terms of—'

'A cerebral affair?' he gritted.

'Well…' Bethany dropped her head, tied up in knots of horrible, mealy-mouthed discomfiture. He seemed to be going out of his way to make this more difficult for her. 'Whatever might conceivably develop…I haven't got a crystal ball—'

'Had you been blessed with one, you would have closed your mouth five minutes ago and kept it shut, but I thank you for your honesty!' There was a whitened edge to Razul's compressed lips now. 'I hope you are equally grateful for mine. My terms are marriage…marriage *or* you will be as one dead to me! I will never voluntarily rest my eyes on you again in this lifetime!'

Her jaw dropped. 'You can't be serious…'

'I have never been more serious,' Razul swore with savage bite.

Bethany was incredulous and furious into the bargain. She had laid her pride and her self-respect on the line. She had offered him a relationship which until today she had never once considered offering to *any* man. That had taken a great deal of courage, and even as she had voiced her proposition she had been frantically worried that she was impulsively overreacting to her own hopelessly confused emotions. 'Right now I could live with never seeing you again just fine!' she told him wrathfully.

Savage golden eyes raked over her. He spread his shapely hands wide and dropped them again with an air of cold finality. '*Inshallah*. Then I give you the freedom that you say you want. You may go. There is a helicopter out there. It will take you to the airport. There is a flight to London in two hours.'

Devastated by the assurance, Bethany gaped at him, her every expectation violently overthrown.

'You have half an hour to make your choice.'

'I don't need half an hour!' Bethany shot back at him, her eyes pure emerald in her hotly flushed face as she squared up to him. 'Five minutes would be too long!'

Razul slung her a slashing glance from molten gold eyes, every line of his lean, muscular length whip-taut. 'That is your decision, but be assured *aziz*…if you stay, you will be my wife by evening.'

'That is as likely as me taking flight without jet engines!' Bethany snapped in ringing disbelief. 'You have to be out of your mind!'

'We will see how out of my mind I am…*this* we will see.' He made it sound like a threat written in blood. His strong, hard features rigid, he swung soundlessly on his heel and swept out.

CHAPTER FIVE

NOTHING like choosing the magic words to speed the parting guest...'wife by evening'? Hah! thought Bethany. Razul was certifiably insane. She knew she would be into that helicopter so fast that she'd leave a trail of little flames dancing in her wake! Release...escape...freedom, here I come! Razul had decided to force the issue, which wasn't surprising, not when you took that mile-wide streak of mean, moody, macho conditioning and added it to all that ferocious pride. Well, she thought with murderous satisfaction, he had made a gross miscalculation. Her little Middle Eastern adventure had come to an end and very grateful she was too!

Her attention fell on the suitcase that she hadn't seen since her departure from the airport. She blinked, reading the message that went with its reappearance. Razul had clearly brought it with him. So, in other words, he had come prepared to face her with that choice. But *first* he had allowed her to make an outsize idiot of herself!

Her teeth gritting, Bethany was fired into sudden activity. She dug out her keys and unlocked the case. She had no plans to check in at Al Kabibi airport dressed in a caftan and silk slippers! Why the heck hadn't she noticed that suitcase sooner? For a few minutes there a tide of remorse had gripped her with temporary insanity. She had actually sunk low enough to offer herself on a plate. If only she had kept her stupid mouth shut she could have boarded that helicopter with every ounce of her dignity still intact!

She took her time getting dressed in a pair of light cotton trousers and a voluminous white T-shirt. Then she combed her hair and finally checked her watch. Fifteen minutes had gone. She walked the length of the tent, pushed aside the ornate hangings and looked outside. The blazing rays of the sun were glinting off the silver body of the helicopter parked in the centre of the camp. Perspiration broke out on her skin. She lifted her case.

You will never see him again.

She could handle that…of course she could; hadn't she got by for twenty-seven years without ever depending on a man?

Never is a long time.

Her teeth clenched. She thrust a furious hand through her tumbling hair. Damn him…damn him to hell and back! She was stronger than this. She was going to do the sensible thing no matter how blasted hard it was to do it!

All her life she had been prudent, practical and realistic. No nonsense, no silly romantic fantasies…well, only one, she conceded with boiling resentment. *Him.* Picking up her books on the library steps, smiling that soul-destroyingly charismatic smile, he had somehow stolen a part of her that she had never got back. Since then…always this nagging sense of loss, separateness, aloneness. She had hated him for having that power over her, and now she hated him ten times more as she wrestled with a hunger as frighteningly irrational as the unfamiliar sense of complete impotence now freezing her in her tracks.

Never is a long time…

What is the difference between an affair and a temporary marriage? an insidious little voice whispered. Stricken by the treacherous thought that had come at her out of nowhere, Bethany pressed unsteady hands to her hot face. She quelled that sly voice. Every fibre of her being revolted against being forced into a position that she had not freely and rationally chosen.

But where was her free choice when her only other option was *never* to see him again? And Razul would keep to that promise. Razul had the kind of dark, driven temperament which could make a sacred shrine out of self-denial. Overwhelmed by the emotional storm battling inside her, Bethany sank dizzily down on the edge of her suitcase. If thoughts had had the power to kill, Razul would have been dead. She was in mental torment. 'Never' stood like a giant wall between her and the freedom she cherished...

The rotor blades of the helicopter started up with a noisy, clattering whirl, and the tent walls rippled. Bethany, who made a virtue out of never crying, shocked herself by bursting into floods of furious tears. She despised herself; she hated him. In the space of forty-eight hours he had torn her inside out. He had cornered her and sprung a trap that she hadn't recognised until it was too late. Dear heaven, she would never forgive him for pushing her to the wall like this and forcing surrender on her!

'What is wrong, *sitt*?'

'*Everything!*' Bethany sobbed passionately before she focused on the speaker.

'Prince Razul was very angry. He was most disturbed for your safety. But on such a day his anger will melt away.'

Bethany's distraught gaze rested on Zulema's sympathetic face as the girl reached shyly for her left hand and clucked anxiously over the scratches. A sob still rattled in her throat as Zulema gently pressed her hand into a bowl of warm water from which the sharp odour of some form of antiseptic wafted. It stung like mad.

'I understand that your family was threatened by Fatima,' Bethany managed tautly.

'But I need no longer fear this threat.' Zulema smiled.

'Now my family live in Prince Razul's protection. He will give my father new employment.'

'I'm glad.' Bethany drew in a shaky breath, drained by her crying jag.

'I am glad our Prince does not marry the Princess Fatima,' Zulema revealed in a rush of covert confidence. 'It is what the King wished but those who know her well did not wish it.'

So Fatima had had the official stamp of royal approval. Razul had not mentioned that fact. No wonder the brunette had been so bitterly hostile to Bethany's arrival.

'What you saw in the courtyard...do not pity her.' The younger woman looked surprisingly cynical. 'She made a big scene to try and shame the Prince into sending you away. It is wrong for a woman to embarrass a man like that. If her father hears of it *she* will be sent away! He would be disgraced.'

Zulema affixed a plaster to the scratches and then stood up and clapped her tiny hands. Instantly her usual two helpers appeared, laden with various articles. There was a burst of voluble chatter from outside the tent. Wrought-iron holders were set up and incense sticks lit, their heavy perfume filling the hot, still air. An aluminium bathtub was marched past her and settled behind the screen at the other end of the tent. Buckets of lightly steaming water arrived one by one.

Bethany hovered in a daze of bewilderment until Zulema drew her behind the screen. Very seriously the little maid covered her eyes. 'I not look, *sitt*...only help.'

Bethany heard herself laugh, her fierce tension suddenly evaporating, and why not? Common sense insisted that Razul could not *possibly* be intending to really go through with his threat to make her marry him. It would be just too ridiculous. He had spoken in anger. Later she would gently call his bluff and reason with him, hopefully without offending that unquenchable pride which was so much a part of him. It had been a very melodramatic threat…but very Arabic and very Razul, she reflected helplessly.

She would accept his hospitality for another few days and see how she felt then. Really there was absolutely no reason for her to go rushing off home like a Victorian virgin threatened with ravishment! That would be a repeat of the same cowardice that she had exhibited in England. There was no good reason why, having come this far, she should not allow herself the luxury of getting to know Razul a little better. What would that cost her? And, in the meantime, she could even begin her research…

She slid into the warm, scented water, wryly accepting Zulema's assistance and bending her head obediently as her hair was carefully wetted and then shampooed. Cocooned in towels, she emerged again and sat down to have her hair combed out and her nails painted. Why all the fuss? she wondered.

'You look tired, *sitt*. Lie down and rest for a while,' Zulema urged. 'The party will last for hours.'

Party? So somebody was throwing a party. Her curiosity satisfied, Bethany smiled and lay down. She could hear a helicopter.

When she opened her eyes again, she could still hear a helicopter, or was it helicopters? She was surprised to realise that she had slept for several hours but then she hadn't had much sleep the night before.

Zulema extended a shimmering, heavily embroidered golden caftan. It was really quite exquisite. The silk flowed across her body with a wonderfully sensuous feel. A vast square of gold chiffon was produced and draped around her head. 'You look very beautiful, *sitt*,' Zulema sighed admiringly. 'You come now?'

Bethany followed her out into the hot, still air. She only had to walk a few yards before she was in another tent the size of a marquee. It was crammed to capacity with richly dressed but mainly middle-aged and elderly women. One by one they came up to greet her and kiss her on each cheek. They were terribly friendly but nobody spoke English and Bethany was quite frustrated, for she would have loved to chat and ask questions. An enormous banquet was spread out on a white cloth in the centre.

Bethany wasn't very hungry but she picked at a few dishes out of politeness. The meal went on for ages but she wasn't bored. There was so much going on around her that she was fascinated, and when the food was cleared away the dancing started to the strains of Arabic music issuing from a huge set of speakers. It got very noisy, but everyone was having a good time and there was a lot of laughter, particularly when a very large woman took the floor to undulate and shake like a belly dancer.

'Please follow me, *sitt.*' Zulema appeared beside her out of the crush. 'It is time.'

As Bethany stood up the music went off. Time for what? she almost asked, but presumably Zulema meant that the party was now over, and she *still* didn't know what the celebrations had been about. There were loud cries of *'Lullah...lullah!'* She assumed these to be some form of goodbye angled at her, and she waved and smiled, which seemed to go down very well, before accompanying Zulema through the hangings at the far end which divided off a section of the tent.

Razul was standing there surrounded by older men. He looked so heartbreakingly handsome in a white linen robe with a dark blue, gold-edged overlay that her mouth went dry and her heart leapt like a dizzy teenager's inside her chest as she crossed the floor to him. A bearded old man was speaking and receiving the utmost solemn attention from his assembled audience.

When that same old man abruptly moved forward,

reached for her hand and looped a scarf round her wrist,
Bethany was astonished. He looped the other end of it
round Razul's wrist and began speaking. Bethany froze.
What the heck was going on? As her wrist was released
again comprehension splintered through her in a violent
wave and plunged her deep into shock. The old man had
to be an imam or priest. Unless she was very much mistaken…but she *had* to be mistaken…

Her stricken gaze flew to Razul. A faint frown-line
divided his ebony brows as he noted her pallor. Her eyes
took a dazed flight over the grave-looking men on either
side of them. Her teeth sank into the soft underside of
her lower lip and the tang of her own blood tinged her
tongue. A tide of dizziness ran over her, leaving her
light-headed. Dear heaven, unless her intelligence was
playing tricks on her, she had just taken part in a marriage ceremony in the role of…?

Bride? She, Bethany Morgan, who was as antimarri-
age as a woman could possibly be, had just played an
unwitting part in a ceremony to which she had offered
no consent? Fathoms-deep in shock, she trembled. It
couldn't be legal—it couldn't possibly be legal when she
hadn't understood a word of it or even what was happening to her! The other men were filing out.

'What is the matter with you?' Razul murmured in a
driven undertone.

Her hands clenched into fists. 'You ought to be locked
up…' she told him in a quavering voice that sounded
alien to her ears. 'I did not consent to marrying you.'

A dark rise of blood accentuated his hard cheek-
bones. Stunned golden eyes flared at her. 'But I told you
we would be married if you remained—'

'And did I say I *agreed*?' Bethany gasped, still seriously weakened by shock.

'You stayed…I took agreement to be given!' Razul
returned in an equally incredulous undertone. '*Finally*, I
believed, you had come to your senses!'

'There's a big difference between staying and getting married.' Bethany pressed damp palms to her cold face. 'Any sort of married,' she mumbled in faint addition, and then her anger stirred and she shot him an accusing look of pure outrage. 'You did it deliberately, didn't you? You knew I didn't believe that you were serious and you took advantage of my ignorance to—'

Without warning Razul closed hard fingers over her shoulder and forced her closer. 'Stop it,' he bit out. 'This is not the place for such a dispute…indeed, where could be the place for such a dispute? You are now my wife.'

His wife. Her stomach lurched. His wife…?

'Do not shame me before my family,' Razul warned, fiercely scanning her shocked eyes. 'For that I will never forgive and nor will they. These are serious proceedings…where is your respect?'

Every last scrap of colour drained from her cheeks. 'But I didn't know…I didn't realise—'

'Did I not tell you?'

'Well…yes, but I didn't *believe*,' she began shakily.

'Believe now,' Razul gritted.

'I don't want to,' she muttered in a very small voice, her lower limbs wobbling because the shock didn't recede, it only struck deeper as the minutes passed.

'Then why did you stay? Why did you not leave for the airport?' Razul demanded with a scorching undercurrent of embittered anger.

'I didn't think you were serious about *marrying* me…not today, here, now,' she whispered dazedly. 'And not in a ceremony like that.'

Had Razul really believed that by staying she was agreeing to marry him? Or had he relied on her lack of Arabic to carry her through to a point where only throwing the most appalling scene would have stopped the ceremony dead? By the time she had realised what was happening it had been too late. And why had she been so blind? When he had talked about marrying her she had not expected an actual *wedding*. A party and witnesses and the solemnity of an imam had not figured in her dim grasp of what such a temporary contract might entail.

'What was wrong with it?'

'Nothing…but I thought…you see, I thought,' she framed unevenly, 'that you were intending some sort of contract—'

'Contract?' he cut in with a frown.

'Fatima said—'

'What did Fatima say?' Razul prompted with sudden menace.

'Well, that you weren't planning on a *real* marriage, that it would be only a temporary arrangement.' Her voice began to join her lower limbs in the wobble effect as a flash of distinct incredulity darkened Razul's eloquent gaze. 'And, you see, I did once come across a written reference to this…er…this practice called *mut'a*.'

'*Mut'a*…' Razul whispered, and then he said it again, his flagrant distaste making Bethany wince. 'In Datar we do not recognise such arrangements for they are open to great abuse. Our rules of marriage are fixed by law and as legally binding as they are in your own country.'

'Oh,' Bethany mumbled.

'Had she told you I was a serial killer, would you have swallowed that as well?' When she failed to meet his fulminating gaze, Razul vented a derisive laugh. 'I am sorry to disappoint you, but we are really and truly married, and you have yet to give me a satisfactory response to the question of *why* you allowed that helicopter to go without you.'

Bethany worried tautly at her lower lip in the electric silence. Her mind was a complete blank.

'Why?' Razul repeated with awesomely unwelcome persistence.

'I plead a fit of temporary insanity!'

His strong features shuttered. Then as the murmur of voices sounded outside the tent his mouth twisted. 'You will feel even more married by the end of this day,' he forecast shortly as he drew back from her.

'And what's that supposed to mean?' Bethany asked shakily. 'I—' And her angry voice was choked off as an older man in a clerical collar came hurrying in, spluttering apologies for his tardiness and closely followed by an elegantly dressed woman and man.

'May I introduce you to the Reverend Mr Wilks, who is chaplain at the Royal City Hospital?' Razul drawled without any expression at all. 'My sister Laila and her husband, Ahmed, who have kindly agreed to act as our witnesses.'

Rooted to the spot, Bethany found herself shaking the minister's hand, receiving a warm embrace from the anxiously smiling older woman and another handshake from her husband.

'Blame Ahmed and me for the late arrival,' Laila told Bethany ruefully. 'We should have been here this morning but, as often happens in the medical world, the best laid plans can be wrecked by an emergency—'

'Your presence was required in the operating theatre and naturally we understand that the call to save human life takes precedence,' Razul interposed.

'But it has messed up things.' The attractive brunette sighed unhappily. 'I know you wanted the ceremonies the other way round and I was supposed to be here to make Bethany feel at home and introduce her to all the relatives, and instead she was left marooned at her own wedding reception... I'm afraid Zulema would *not* have been an acceptable interpreter in the eyes of the older generation. They are all roaring snobs—'

Ahmed moved forward, pressing a soothing hand to his wife's back. 'Do you not think that we should allow Mr Wilks the floor?' he murmured, with a twinkle in his brown eyes. 'You will learn, Bethany, that my wife rarely pauses for breath when she starts talking.'

Bethany summoned up a strained smile. She absolutely could not bring herself to look at Razul. He had intended the English ceremony to take place first, and if it had happened that way she would have known what was going on in time to stop it...but would she have? Would she have had the courage to call a halt in the presence of his family, to shatter the expectations of so many important people by refusing to marry Razul?

Dear heaven, it would have caused a riot, not to mention plunging him into a humiliation of immense proportions... No, she didn't believe that she would have had the nerve to do that to him when her conscience grudgingly suggested that she had played some part in the misunderstanding which had led to this ghastly conclusion.

'Shall we proceed?' the Reverend urged cheerfully.

When Razul had said that she would feel really and truly married by the end of the day, Bethany reflected in furious frustration, he had not been exaggerating. The service was the traditional one. She made her responses unsteadily, and when Razul grasped her hand to slide a wedding ring onto her finger she was as stiff as a clockwork doll. When she had to sign the register, her signature wavered. *Misunderstanding*...? Hell roast him, she thought in sudden, gathering rage; I'll kill him when I get him on his own!

'I am going to adore having another liberated woman in the family!' Laila laughed as the minister fell into conversation with Razul. 'I had to get married to gain my freedom, and our father is still recovering from the shock of seeing what he saw as my eccentric hobby become a career.'

'You're a surgeon?' Bethany questioned, struggling for some form of normal behaviour and finding it very hard.

'An obstetrician. Not much choice really.' Laila pulled a comical face. 'The Datari male is a macho creature but he would run a mile if he was faced with a female medic! But when he discovers there is a female doctor for his wife's most intimate needs he is delighted I exist and the women are too. I am very happy that you have become a part of our family, Bethany,' she said, with an embarrassingly sincere smile. 'And I am sorry that you have had to wait so long to—'

'It is time for us to leave,' Razul interrupted abruptly.

'Why are you in crown prince mode?' Laila asked, with a sudden frown.

'Laila—' Ahmed was flushed, clearly already well aware of the lack of bridal joy in the atmosphere.

Razul's sister subjected Bethany to an uncertain, questioning glance, her bewilderment and concern unconcealed. Bethany went scarlet with discomfiture.

'We will see you very soon. I hope you will be our first visitors,' Razul drawled very quietly.

They got one foot beyond the tent before Bethany heard a muffled surge of Arabic break from Razul's older sister. 'What is she saying?' she whispered helplessly.

'Forgive me if I choose not to translate.' His hard-boned features a mask of grim restraint, Razul headed for the waiting helicopter, leaving Bethany to follow in his imperious wake. Behind them the music broke out as the wedding celebrations started up again.

'Razul—?'

Screaming tension in every line of his lean length, he paused until she drew breathlessly level with him. 'You want to know what happens now? That is very simple,' he stated in a tone from which every drop of emotion had been ruthlessly erased. 'At the end of the summer I divorce you. You go home. I take another wife. I will put this stupid, witless mistake behind me.'

'Take another wife'…? Bethany stared fixedly at the

space where Razul had been. He was already swinging up into the seat beside the pilot. At a much slower pace she clambered into a rear seat where Zulema soon joined her. The rotor blades started up with a deafening whine, mercifully forbidding any further conversation.

CHAPTER SIX

BETHANY was in severe shock. One minute Razul told her that they were really and truly married, the next he dismissed their marriage as easily as if it meant nothing. In other words, it did mean nothing to him. It might just as well have been a temporary contract! Marriage had merely been the convenient device by which he'd intended to get her into his bed on *his* terms. Evidently she was to have been Razul's final fling before he settled down to the serious business of marrying someone suitable and acceptable, like Fatima, who came with gilt-edged fatherly approval. Musical wives like musical chairs.

Presumably they were now heading back to the palace... Well, he needn't think that he was going to lock her up there to moulder away until the end of the summer! Nor need he fondly imagine that when he descended from the Olympian heights of his outraged pride *she* figured on featuring on the entertainment list for his final fling. To put it equally bluntly, he had no hope!

The trip in the helicopter was short. Bethany alighted, her beautiful face set like pale marble. Only then did she realise that she was not where she had expected to be. She was surrounded by beautiful terraced gardens which were quite unfamiliar. Tamarisk and palm trees stood tall above lush slices of green grass and rioting tropical flowers. 'This isn't the palace...'

She turned but saw that Razul was still standing in the shadow of the helicopter. He was talking into a mobile phone, his intonation edged, his facial muscles clenched hard beneath his tawny skin. Whoever he was talking to, he did not appear to be enjoying the conversation.

Zulema answered her, 'The King's palace is only a short distance away, my lady. This palace is now the home of Prince Razul. It was where his mother lived. She died soon after the Prince was born. The King closed up this place, took his baby son and moved back to the old palace. It was very sad, for it is very beautiful, no?'

'No…I mean yes.' So Razul had grown up without a mother. Bethany crushed a tender green shoot of compassion in its tracks. What was that to her? she asked herself angrily, walking up a shallow flight of steps and beneath a carved stone entrance into a breathtakingly beautiful, marble-floored courtyard ringed by an arched cloister.

Dazzling panels of glazed tiles covered every wall. Water played softly in the silence, jetting down from a fountain set in the centre of a large pool. Beyond, yet another archway beckoned them into a magnificent hall the impressive width and length of a stretch of motorway.

Once in the hall, Bethany strolled through the nearest door into a large room, considerably surprised to find herself surrounded on all sides by antique furniture which would not have looked out of place in an English stately home.

'The Prince tells me that this is a drawing room,' Zulema informed her. 'We have lots of drawing rooms here.'

'Wonderful,' Bethany muttered rather weakly, and wandered across the width of the hall to walk into a highly traditional Arab reception room complete with sunken coffee hearth, heaps of cushions and the usual paucity of furniture. The same picture continued right down the length of that enormous hall—on one side, westernisation complete with elaborate furnishings and ornamental clutter, and, on the other, the simpler Islamic backdrop. It was peculiar, she reflected as she walked back outside again. Had the Western half been created for the purpose of entertaining foreign VIPs?

The sound of steps jerked her head round as she stood contemplating the fountain in the outer courtyard. Razul stilled several feet away, his suddenly screened dark eyes resting on her in much the same way as he might have regarded a grenade with the pin pulled out...very wary, coldly defensive, poised for a fight. And it disturbed her that she could tell exactly what he was feeling before he even opened his beautifully shaped mouth.

'Now you tell me why you did not leave when you had the opportunity,' Razul commanded.

Bethany's teeth gritted. 'Right now that is completely irrelevant.'

'Be warned that now you are my wife I will be less tolerant of your evasions.'

A shudder of raw resentment jolted through her. His wife... The unwelcome reminder was sufficient to send her temper rocketing again. Nor was she mollified by that stern intonation which implied that he was handing down a generous warning to a misbehaving child! She threw her vibrant head back, her emerald eyes flashing sudden fire. 'You run so true to type, Razul—'

'Explain yourself!' he breathed harshly.

Bethany loosed a laugh of scorn, thinking of how fast her aunt's adoring husband had changed his tune after their marriage. 'I'm well aware that the Arab male drops all charm and persuasion the minute he gets a wedding ring on a woman's finger. Then he feels secure. Then he feels he's free to be himself, master of his household and lord of all he surveys...and the much desired and courted bride becomes just one more possession to be used and abused according to his mood. Well, before you get totally carried away with that heady sense of being all-powerful, allow me to assure you that that ring on my finger means less than nothing to me!'

Razul stared back at her, and it was like standing in the centre of a swirling storm. Every poised line of his lean length was utterly still. And yet the fierce tension that emanated from him hit her in electric waves. His silence alone was a form of intimidation. Inside herself Bethany felt the compelling force of a temperament that was stronger by far than her own, and in immediate rejection of that disturbing suspicion she wrenched off the ring on her finger and sent it spinning into the pool. It vanished in one tiny splash.

The charged silence began to feel like a swamp that she was trying to wade through—heavy, unyielding...

'That ring is the symbol of a farce!' Bethany condemned, furious that she sounded defensive.

Razul was rigid and very pale. He appraised her with hard dark eyes as cold as a wintry night. 'Your manners are appalling and you have a temper as unruly as that of a spoilt child. You lash out blindly, careless of the insults you offer. I suspect this comes from a lifetime of regarding no counsel but your own, but you are foolish indeed if you believe that I will endure such displays. Retrieve that ring,' he ordered.

Furiously flushed and outraged by his censure, Bethany glared back at him, breathing fast. She was so mad that she wanted to jump up and down on the spot.

'Without it you will not enter my home,' Razul informed her grimly.

'Fine! I didn't want that stupid ring in the first place!' she slung back.

'No...you wanted me to treat you like a whore...but that hope could yet be fulfilled—'

'I beg your pardon?' Bethany gasped.

'With every offensive word and gesture you diminish my respect for you. I look at you and I ask myself, Was it for this woman that I have offended an honoured father?' Razul derided harshly. 'What should have been a day of joy has descended into a vale of tears, dissension and regret, and I have no patience left. Retrieve that ring or spend the night out here... Without it I will not recognise you as my wife!'

'And you think that matters to me?' Bethany blistered back shakily, her hands curling into fists.

'I believe that you should learn what it is like to be treated like a possession to be used and abused according to my mood. Only then, perhaps, will you appreciate that I have never treated you as a lesser being...until now.'

If he seriously thought for one moment that she was about to clamber into that wretched pool and get soaking wet, he had better think again fast! Bethany thought. She stood there like a stone statue as he swept off. She could see two guards standing just inside the door of the entrance into the palace; their presence was natural when Razul was within but, even so, rage engulfed her at the sight of them. She now had an audience. Her teeth ground together, murderous heat quivering through her. So he actually thought that he was going to teach her a lesson, did he?

How dared he stand there and tell her that she had appalling manners...how dared he? How dared he come over all superior and look down that arrogant nose at her with that aura of icy hauteur? Had she asked to be dragged out to Datai and married twice over? And if he had offended his father by marrying her was that *her* fault? The sun beat down on her unprotected head. She drew back into the shadows and finally dropped down onto her knees, which was damnably uncomfortable on that cold marble floor. I hate him...I hate him, she raged inwardly with real violence.

An hour passed painfully slowly. Who was the clever woman who hadn't got into the helicopter? Who was the clever woman who'd fondly imagined that she could reason with Razul...*control* him? Who had got up on her feminist soapbox and accused him of sins that he had not yet had time to commit...and who had put *this* blasted exercise in humiliation into his head in the first place?

She stood up again, stiff as a board, and tears of furious frustration scorched her eyes. Razul was the only person alive who could make her lose her temper to such an extent! Oh, to hell with it; she wasn't prepared to sit here all night and freeze and starve to make some stupid, childish point! And possibly throwing away the ring had been a little over the top, but what she had really been doing was letting him know that, when he had uttered those fatal words, 'I take another wife', as if wives were exchangeable commodities, she had experienced a powerful need to demonstrate that their marriage meant nothing to her either.

Down on her knees, she slid a hand into the pool and delved. It wasn't very deep and the water was crystal-clear, but could she see that wretched ring with the sun reflecting off the surface? Then a particularly bright glitter caught her eye near the centre. Her mouth compressed into a mutinous line. She stretched perilously across the surface of the pool and lost her balance, one knee sliding over the edge into the water, swiftly followed by the other. In a tempest of fury she picked herself up again, soaked to the skin by the splash, snatched at the ring and climbed out. She stalked, dripping, into the palace, leaving a trail of tiny puddles in her wake.

He's dead, Bethany swore to herself. He may still be walking around but he is dead! If he wants war, he has got war.

He didn't know you didn't want to marry him, a little voice whispered. She crushed it but the voice was remorseless. You wrecked his wedding day, you embarrassed him with his sister and brother-in-law, you insulted him all over again.

Her nose wrinkled as the tickly sensation of tears

threatened. All of a sudden Bethany felt that she was at her lowest ebb of all time. So why didn't you get into that helicopter? she asked herself desperately.

And the answer came back loud and clear—simple, straightforward and yet devastating to her pride. The threat of never seeing Razul again had paralysed her and wiped out her self-discipline. The same sort of uncontrollable attraction which had made such a mess of her mother's life, and threatened to do the same to her aunt's, had found another victim in her. Maybe that self-destructive streak ran in her genes like poison, for this time she hadn't had the strength to walk away from Razul… He had pulled her in too deep and too fast, drowning her in the desperate force of her own hunger.

And that was her own fault, she conceded miserably. To protect herself she had refused to allow men into her life, but that self-chosen isolation had not prepared her to deal with Razul. Yet the biggest enemy she had was not him, but what lay within herself.

He was the ultimate forbidden male, the epitome of her most secret fears: phenomenally handsome, just like her father, incredibly charming, just like her father, polished at making extravagant gestures, just like her father, highly successful with women, just like her father. A truly killing combination of the worst possible male attributes. So how could she possibly *want* a man like that? What was wrong with her that she could see all those things and still not be able to switch off this terrible, weak craving?

She stood shivering in a strange room with blind eyes while Zulema ran a bath somewhere close by. Shell-shocked by a sense of her self-betrayal, Bethany hovered while Zulema helped her out of the wet, clinging caftan. Like a sleepwalker she sank into a warm bath. Abstractedly she rubbed at her arm, feeling a slight ache above her wrist.

'You like something to eat now, my lady?'

Bethany emerged from her punishing self-absorption to find herself garbed in a diaphanous white silk nightdress. As she looked down at herself uncomfortably and noticed the way her pale skin gleamed through the whisper-fine fabric, a hectic flush lit her cheeks. 'No, thanks…'

'You should not be afraid, my lady,' Zulema whispered soothingly.

Bethany blinked. 'Afraid of what?'

'Of Prince Razul…'

'I've never been afraid of a man in my life!' But even as Bethany loosed a shaky laugh of scorn she knew that she was lying. Razul had already tied her up in terrifying emotional knots, and only his sheer, appalling persistence had forced her to acknowledge just how far out of control she was. She had actually been prepared to offer him an affair…on her terms, on her ground, at her speed…but that hadn't been enough for Razul. Razul wanted total, absolute surrender. *Never*! she swore to herself fiercely.

'When a man comes to his woman for the first time it is natural for her to feel a little nervous.' Zulema gave her a shy, teasing smile. 'But on this night many women will sigh with envy and dream of taking your place in the Prince's bed.'

Bethany stopped breathing altogether and sent an incredulous glance in Zulema's direction, but the little maid was already backing out of the room. Then she shook her head in mute disbelief and breathed again. Of course Razul wasn't *coming* to her! This was not going to be the average wedding night, but then Zulema was blissfully unaware of the circumstances of their marriage and of the current level of animosity between them.

Restively she lifted one of the books that she had brought with her to Datar—a nineteenth-century travelogue on the desert way of life. It contained some extravagant, even laughable errors, illustrating the writer's misinterpretation and ignorance of Arabic customs and superstitions. But had she been any less arrogant or any more fair in her response to Razul? Anxiously she hovered, suppressing the suspicion that she had always behaved in a downright unreasonable fashion with Razul—wanting him…and yet hating him for her own weakness…

When the door opened she spun round with a frown of surprise and saw him. A stifled hiss of shock escaped her and momentarily she was paralysed. His brilliant dark gaze crossed the room, closed in on her, and then wandered over her scantily clad figure with a kind of deeply appreciative intensity which filled her with a fiery mix of furious resentment and embarrassment. She snatched up the robe that Zulema had left across a nearby chair and held it in front of her like a defensive barrier.

'What do you want?' Bethany demanded shrilly.

Sudden, unexpected raw amusement flashed through Razul's tawny eyes as he strolled closer. With an indolent hand he removed the golden *iqual* and headcloth, baring his dark, luxuriant head of hair. 'You need to ask?' he murmured lazily.

'What do you think you're doing?'

'What do you think I am doing?' Razul turned the question back on her without hesitation.

He was undressing, but Bethany refused to believe the evidence of her own eyes. 'I thought this was my bedroom—'

'Tonight it is ours.' Razul framed the words softly.

'I am not sharing this room with you,' Bethany informed him flatly.

'You will.' He shifted with innate, fluid grace to survey her. 'You are my wife.'

'Technically speaking—'

'I am not technically minded.' He shrugged off the black, gold-edged cloak with complete calm.

The breath shortened in her throat. 'Morally—'

'And what could you possibly have to say on that subject?' Razul interrupted with sudden, slashing derision. 'Or do you forget that only this morning you offered me the freedom of your body without the commitment of marriage?'

Flames of hot pink burnished Bethany's cheeks. 'I was…confused this morning—'

'Correction…you were desperate, and allow me to tell you what would have happened if I had agreed. Once you were safely back in England you would have shut me out again and discovered a hundred reasons why we could not be together!'

'That's not true—'

'Your retreat stops here…now…tonight,' Razul spelt out with silken menace. 'And you made that decision for yourself when you chose not to go home. I told you I would marry you if you stayed, and I have no need to justify my presence here on my wedding night. You are my bride—'

'No…I want to get an annulment when I go home!'

'That is one fantasy destined to go unfulfilled. Think again,' Razul advised, with a blaze of anger in his magnificent eyes. 'Or think of me as your lover and not your husband… At this moment I do not care, but be assured that the games you play are at an end. Tonight you will lie in my arms and we will make love.'

Bethany trembled with furious disbelief. 'If you think that I would allow you to use me like that, you're in for a severe shock!'

Razul dealt her a look of shimmering intensity that burned up the distance that lay between them. 'I think it is not I who will be shocked.'

'You said that marrying me was a stupid, witless mistake!' she threw at him incredulously.

'A mistake I have to live with until the end of the

summer, and if I have to live with it you will live with it too!' Razul informed her with compelling emphasis.

'That is a totally unreasonable attitude to take!' Bethany seethed back at him.

'I am not feeling reasonable. Why should I be? You are no longer deserving of any special consideration from me. In honour I married you, and how am I repaid?'

'I didn't *want* to marry you!' Bethany reminded him hotly.

'Then why in the name of Allah did you not get on that helicopter?' Razul raked back at her in an intimidating roar.

'I...I—'

'I knew that would silence you...' Razul slung her a sizzling glance of splintering derision. 'But do not think that I do not know the answer to that mystery. I *know* what was on your mind!'

Bethany had turned very pale. 'How could you possibly know?'

'I know your arrogance—'

'*My* arrogance?' she queried, scarcely believing that he could accuse her of such a fault.

'You thought you could make me play your game. You believed that you could have everything your own way. But what lay beyond that piece of self-deception?' Razul demanded with contempt. 'The truth that you would go to any lengths to avoid. Your desire for me is stronger than your pride, stronger than your prejudices and stronger than any hold you now have over me...because *I* would have let you go!'

As he forced that unwelcome truth on her her teeth clenched and she went white. It was as if that half-hour of decision time out in the desert had been a contest between them—a battle of wills in which he had triumphed, and he was not about to let her forget that.

'So do not seek to punish me for your vacillation, for

I gave you your freedom and you turned your back on it,' Razul reminded her with savage impatience. Smouldering golden eyes whipped over her and his expressive mouth twisted. 'And why do you still cringe behind that garment? You look ridiculous! I am not so stupid that I imagined a woman of your age and background would still be a shy virgin!'

'I think you're very stupid,' Bethany hissed, flushed scarlet by outrage and chagrin, but she was not about to drop that robe and stand revealed in an almost transparent nightdress, no matter how ridiculous he thought she looked!

'In that you are probably right.' A tide of fierce emotion clenched his startlingly handsome features. 'I should have been true to my own ideals. I should not have sought to make allowances for your less principled society. I had to overcome certain cultural reservations before I could ask you to become my wife, knowing that I would *not* be your first lover—'

'Did you indeed?' Bethany quivered on another energising gust of rage. Yet she received a grim satisfaction from the realisation that he was unaware of her inexperience. 'And how did you know that?'

His sensual mouth compressed. 'I am well aware that you shared your apartment with a man the year before we met. I learned that in England.'

Danny, one of her colleagues, temporarily finding himself without a roof over his head, had begged for her spare room, and she had acquiesced purely and simply because he was the only male friend that she had ever had…and he was gay. 'But Danny—'

'I do not wish to hear about that other man.' Razul dealt her a furious glance of reproach, his tension palpable. 'And had you not roused such bitter hostility within me today such unjust feelings would not have occurred to me, nor would I have referred to them.'

'But I'm so glad that you did! I can quite understand

your reservations,' Bethany responded acidly, seeing the weapon that he had put within her reach and ready to use it if it held him at bay.

'I am not a hypocrite. I would not demand from you a standard which I cannot claim for myself. And, in the temper you have put me in, it is probably fortunate that you are not untouched,' Razul told her with controlled savagery as he impatiently began to unbutton his shirt.

A golden wedge of muscular chest sprinkled with curling black hair appeared between the parted edges of the shirt. Bethany turned away, her heart suddenly thumping madly inside her chest, her colour high as she dug her arms into the robe he had derided. 'If you're staying here,' she informed him in a voice empty of all expression, deliberately chosen to deflate any expectations that he might have, 'I shall be sleeping elsewhere.'

Without warning a pair of powerful arms closed round her from behind. 'No.'

'Please remove your hands from me.'

'No.'

'Razul—'

'I am done with being a gentleman,' he asserted, hauling her back into the hard heat of his tall, powerful body.

'If you don't let me go I will walk out of here tomorrow,' Bethany swore shakily, hot tears suddenly lashing her strained eyes as the evocative scent of him washed over her, but with every ounce of her remaining self-discipline she struggled not to surrender to her own weakness. 'And when I get home again I swear I will talk to the Press!'

In response to the worst threat that she could think of making, Razul went satisfyingly rigid. 'You would not do that—'

'I would!' she lied frantically, her throat closing over. 'And why not? Didn't you say you were prepared for a diplomatic incident? Well, I'll give you one!'

Razul slid his hands down to her hips and snatched

her off her feet in one dauntingly strong movement. 'Then tomorrow you go nowhere!' He headed for the door and wrenched it open before she could even catch her breath. 'Nor any other day!'

'What the heck are you doing?' Bethany gasped, thoroughly disconcerted by the tempest of fury that she had unleashed.

He strode off down the dark corridor.

'Razul...put me down!' Bethany ordered.

He kept a tight grip on her as he took a set of stairs at speed.

'Razul—'

'Close your mouth!'

'I'll scream!'

'Why not? In every tight corner you scream. Other people talk, you scream.'

'I just don't want to get any more involved with you...can't you understand that?' Bethany suddenly demanded in a voice an octave higher. 'I don't want to be married...I don't want an affair either! I just wish I had never met you!'

'Coward,' Razul jeered, thrusting wide some sort of a door with holes in it.

There was a metallic clang as it swung shut. 'How dare you call me a coward?'

'You have a streak of yellow down your backbone so wide I could find you in the dark!' Razul flashed back.

'It's not cowardice, it's common sense!' Bethany retaliated in outrage.

'And your cowardice took you all the way to Canada the last time...but not this time,' Razul informed her from between clenched teeth. 'As my wife you will have as much freedom as a criminal on parole, and you can thank my father for that. He never recovered from the humiliation of my mother's desertion. The female members of my family are the only women in Datar who cannot leave the country without a visa signed in triplicate by their husbands or fathers! To think that I should live to be grateful for such a medieval law!'

His mother's desertion? His mother had walked out on his father? Before she died? Well, obviously before she died, a dry little voice pointed out. Bethany cleared her swimming head of the irrelevancy. 'Put me down!' she demanded again.

Astonishingly he did so, only for it to become clear that that had been his intention in any case, for, a split second later, lights illuminated their surroundings. Bethany stole a dazed glance over the exotic splendour of the vast room they stood in. A simply huge bed hung with elaborate hangings stood in state on a marble dais. Her attention wandered over to the vibrant colours of the swirling murals.

She tilted her head, the better to interpret those pictures, and then flags of scarlet burned her cheeks. The act of love between a man and a woman was depicted in a series of graphic but highly artistic illustrations which she was severely embarrassed to look at in Razul's presence.

'For an anthropologist you are astonishingly prudish.' Razul surveyed her as though he had just learnt something fascinating about her.

'Where are we?' she enquired uncomfortably.

'My harem…did I not promise to bring you here?' Razul sliced back softly. 'Truly I honour you, for no European has ever seen these rooms.'

'And exactly why have you brought me down here?' Bethany snapped, infuriated by her inability to foresee what Razul might do next.

'Until you faithfully promise me that you will remain until the end of the summer, I will keep you here.'

Bethany turned to fix shattered green eyes on him, and any desire to ask him if he was serious was quashed by the unyielding set of his strong features. She swallowed hard and staunchly reminded herself that this had not been one of the most ego-boosting days of Razul's gilded royal existence, and, on those grounds, she was generously prepared to make certain allowances for his temper. 'That is a quite barbaric concept but I am convinced—'

'But surely only what you would expect from me?' Razul cut in grimly. 'As this day dawned you called me a barbarian and it is true that you unleash that side of my nature.'

'Only in the middle of an argument,' Bethany protested breathlessly.

'No...in argument with you I have subdued my natural instincts,' Razul told her, with a harsh laugh. 'I have quelled my temper, bitten my tongue and restrained my passion on your behalf. In an effort to gain your trust I have withstood the most base insults ever offered to me and I have forgiven you over and over again. I have also tolerated screams, tantrums and an attack of cold feet which would have driven most men to commit murder! But I tell you now that I will do it no more...my generosity is at an end.'

That sounded incredibly threatening. With difficulty, her colour high, Bethany cleared her throat in the claustrophobic silence. 'And what is that supposed to mean?'

'I will not lie down to be walked on by any woman!' Razul spat out at her with ringing bitterness. 'So, if that is what it takes for a liberated woman to accept a man, you will never find me acceptable!'

'I wasn't aware that I was—' she began in bewilderment.

'From now on I will be true to my own instincts,' he interrupted. Fierce emotion had clenched his facial muscles taut. 'I was conceived in the heat of the desert sun and I was born a true son of the sands, for I have nothing of my mother in me. No ice runs in my veins, no cool calculation controls my need for you. I know what I want. I know what I feel. I want to lock you up and hold you in purdah as my forefathers kept their women for their eyes alone. You *make* me feel like that!'

Glittering golden eyes scorched into hers with such ferocious intensity that she took a clumsy step backwards. 'Less than fifty years ago we would not have had this problem. I would have claimed you and taken you to my bed the same day I first saw you. I would have suppressed your rights with immeasurable pleasure! You would have known then that you belonged to me heart and soul. You would have been *honoured* to bear my ring on your finger—'

'You wouldn't have lived long enough to put it there!' Bethany asserted in a shattered rush of defiance, her emerald-green eyes spitting sudden fire.

'No?'

'No!'

Razul unleashed a slow, burning smile of sheer sensual threat and strolled fluidly closer. 'Then prove to me that you are not a coward. Prove to me that the same desire that flames in me does not flame in you... Come here, lie in my arms...reject me then,' he challenged.

'No bloody way!' Bethany gasped with heartfelt sincerity.

'Chicken,' Razul derided softly, stalking her across the depth of the room with the innate expertise of a natural predator.

CHAPTER SEVEN

'STAY away from me!' Bethany shrieked as she found herself backed up against the bed.

Razul stilled six feet from her and began to remove his clothing with slow, measured cool. 'You will not say that to me again. It is yourself that you fear, not me. Surrender may injure your pride but you will gain from the experience. A woman who denies her own womanhood is not complete—'

'I've never heard so much rubbish in my life!' Bethany watched his clothes dropping to the floor with her heart in her mouth and an unfamiliar clenched sensation gripping her stomach. She shivered violently. 'Don't you dare come near me!'

'Truly it takes a man among men to face such a wedding night.' Razul threw aside his shirt with an alarming air of purpose. 'But you will find that I am equal to the challenge,' he swore. 'And I have not descended to the intolerable humiliation of doing women's work to ingratiate myself into your bed as my predecessor did!'

'Excuse me?' Bethany mumbled dazedly, only half her mind functioning, as a superb golden torso straight out of her most embarrassing and secret fantasies emerged in reality. Her helplessly mesmerised gaze locked onto broad shoulders, powerful pectoral muscles and the pelt of black hair hazing his broad chest which dipped down over a flat, taut stomach into a silky furrow...and? Looking away was the hardest thing she'd ever done.

'That grovelling excuse for a man you allowed into your home and bed three years ago!' Razul gritted with a flash of white teeth. 'I heard the jokes about him. Your housewife, they called him, and laughed about how he cleaned your apartment and cooked your food and waited on you hand and foot...'

For a split second Bethany focused on what he was talking about. Danny's cooking had been out of this world, but his constant need to tidy up around her had in the end driven her batty because she had begun to feel like a lodger in her own home. Evidently Razul had missed out entirely on the one fact that had made Danny an acceptable temporary guest...his sexual orientation.

'But that...that...' She made the mistake of looking back at Razul, and what she had been going to say went clean out of her head again. Her startled gaze fell on narrow hips, long, lean, darkly haired thighs, and the shockingly visible thrust of male arousal displayed by the black briefs which he was in the very act of removing. Bethany froze and closed her eyes but somehow just a fraction too late, her innate shyness suddenly coming into unexpected conflict with a lowering surge of positively adolescent curiosity, which was duly punished. Dear heaven, she reflected dazedly, planting a hand to steady herself on the edge of the bed as her legs gave way, were all men *that*...?

'I will not emasculate myself to curry favour with you,' Razul informed her with wrathful intensity. 'But I will give you pleasure such as you have never known before in that bed, and we will see then which you prefer...man or wimp.'

Wimp, she decided helplessly, deeply shaken by her first view of a rampantly aroused male, and yet, on another level, quite beyond her comprehension, she felt all hot and sort of quivery deep down inside. Her fingers clenched convulsively into the bedspread beneath her as she fought for a window of reason in the blankness of her mind.

'I realise you're angry with me...'

'Release in the wondrous glory of your body will dispel all anger,' Razul said thickly, suddenly right there in front of her, determined hands peeling the robe from her shoulders, trailing it off and tossing it aside before she even knew what he was doing. 'And be assured that when the dawn breaks you will still be in my arms, as befits my bride.'

Before she could even part her lips, Razul gathered her up into his strong arms, but he threw back the bedspread and laid her down in that bed with surprising gentleness. Instantly she crossed her arms over her breasts, horribly self-conscious about the scanty nature of her attire. As Razul gazed down at her from beneath dense black lashes that were longer than her own her heartbeat went haywire, her breath catching in her throat. Absolutely overpowered by that molten gold appraisal, she lay there, held strangely still and captive by a feeling much more powerful than any she had ever experienced.

A slight frown-line drew his winged brows together. He stroked a forefinger mockingly over the back of one of her hands. 'Why do you seek to hide yourself from me?'

Bethany lowered her eyelids. It took an enormous effort of will to close him out but it helped, it really did help, to get her brain back again. Her teeth ground together as she became even more rigid. 'I don't want this…'

'Have I frightened you?'

'Of course not…I am just trying to be the voice of reason here!' she gasped, whipped on the raw by the suggestion.

'Close your mouth again,' Razul suggested very gently. 'But open your eyes…'

That could well be fatal. It terrified her that he might know that too…that when she looked at him she had the resistance of a sex-starved teeny-bopper, and that the simple knowledge that he was lying beside her without a stitch of clothing on was quite sufficient to reduce her normal composure to the consistency of jelly. 'Don't take this any further,' she advised shakily.

'What did this man do to you?' Razul demanded with sudden, growling ferocity.

Involuntarily her lashes flew up in astonishment, trapping her into searing contact with his blazing gold eyes.

'You are terrified... If this man has hurt you I will seek him out and kill him with my bare hands!' Razul seethed with naked violence.

'I am not terrified,' Bethany protested, her pride stung. 'I am simply trying to prevent you from doing something we will both regret!'

Razul leant over her like a tiger about to spring, black fury engraved on his strong features. 'What did this man do to you?' he demanded again.

'Nothing, you bloody idiot!' Bethany screeched back at him, losing all patience. 'He was gay!'

Razul stilled, his ebony lashes dropping low. 'Gay?' he whispered in a dazed tone.

'Right... Now that we have that complication out of the way, is it possible that you could think of the ramifications of consummating this ridiculous marriage?'

'Gay...' Razul said again.

'A man who does not feel attracted to women,' Bethany supplied bitingly in her desperation.

With a deeply disturbing air of relaxation Razul settled fluidly back down on his side and propped his chin on the heel of one shapely hand to survey her furiously flushed face and her still tightly crossed arms. The compressed line of his mouth abruptly slashed into a shimmering smile of unholy brilliance. 'Truly I am a bloody idiot...'

'What are you smirking at?' Bethany hissed as she began to sit up.

A strong hand reached out and met her shoulder to press her inexorably back down again. 'Would you like

me to switch the lights out? Would you feel less shy?'
Razul murmured wickedly.

Her teeth clenched. 'I am not shy! I am merely attempting to save us both from a dreadful mistake...if
you would only listen to me.'

'I listen...' He smiled again.

That smile literally clutched her with icy fingers of
dread...it made her heart pound insanely. 'We have both
agreed that this marriage was a mistake...right?'

'Wrong—'

'And in the light of that mutual agreement... What do
you mean *wrong*?' Bethany grasped his word belatedly,
her voice petering out to an unsteady halt.

Huge green eyes were entrapped by scorching gold
ones. She stopped breathing, and without warning every
inch of her taut body was poised on the edge of a sensual
anticipation so intense that it made her head swim.

Razul murmured something in Arabic and slowly lowered his dark head, brushing his mouth softly across the
tremulous curve of hers. She quivered violently as he let
the tip of his tongue intrude between her lips, and she
could feel the desperate force of her own craving threatening to break through and sweep away all rational
thought. It petrified her. She lifted a hand and pressed it
against his shoulder, felt the heat of his satin-smooth
skin at the same time as he gathered her close, spearing
his fingers into the tumbled fall of her vibrant hair.

Her heartbeat hit another terrifying peak as the heat
of him enfolded her and the pressure of his firm mouth
became inexorably more insistent. He employed his
tongue in a glancing foray deep into the tender interior
that she would have denied him, and her muscles jerked,
a burst of shuddering pleasure catching her up in its
tormenting grasp and making every sense scream with
sudden frustration.

Her hands sank into the glossy thickness of his hair,
holding him to her as the pulsebeat of desire thrummed

her every tensed muscle. What are you doing? a voice shrieked somewhere in the depths of her blitzed brain, but she was powerless against that voice as the dam wall of her own resistance cracked, unleashing all the hunger that she had suppressed for so long. An incoherent moan sounded low in her throat as he turned up the heat in that ruthless kiss and with erotic mastery emulated a far more intimate possession. Her temperature rocketed, driven sky-high. Hot, drowning pleasure gripped her.

'Razul...' she mumbled thickly as he released her reddened mouth.

With a shimmering smile he brought her hands down from his hair and pressed his lips gently to the centre of each palm. Her dazed eyes clung to his as he brushed the narrow straps of silk from her taut shoulders, and she made a sudden movement of panic as reality threatened to break through the spell that he had cast over her.

But he crushed her mouth under his again and the hunger came back in a blinding wave that drove all before it. When she surfaced, like a novice swimmer who had dived too deep, her breasts were bare, rising full and swollen with shamelessly engorged pink nipples. Razul closed a restraining hand over hers as she attempted to cover herself from his heated appraisal.

'Do not be ashamed...rejoice in your beauty as I do,' he urged huskily. 'Your hair holds the glory of the dawn and your skin the pristine glow of a white camellia.'

As she lay there, feeling her whole body strain towards him, her breath caught in her throat.

'Pure...without flaw.' Razul curved reverent fingers to one quivering mound, and her stomach clenched and her teeth gritted, her eyes closing on the bite of intolerable sensation as his thumb rubbed across an achingly sensitive nipple.

He cupped her breasts, shaped them, explored them with expert hands and then dropped his dark head to engulf a straining pink bud in the heat of his mouth, letting her feel the graze of his teeth and the sensual stroke of his tongue. Her heart hammered, all control torn from her as her back arched, a fevered moan wrenched from her as a current of electric excitement coursed through her. All of a sudden she was burning alive on a rack of tormenting pleasure and sinking ever deeper into its thrall.

She couldn't stay still. Her nails dug into the smooth sheet beneath her and then fluttered instinctively up to him, biting into his shoulders, snaking up into his hair, until, with a stifled groan, he took her mouth again with a passionate urgency that consumed her, a strong thigh sliding between hers as his fingers splayed across the quivering muscles of her stomach.

He bent his head to her breasts again, covering her already fevered flesh with hot, hungry kisses. He moved and wrenched at the silk barrier wrapped round her slender hips, smoothing a caressing hand along the silken stretch of one thigh, tracing the length of that trembling limb to the tangle of fiery curls which shielded the very heart of her. A shocked sound parted her lips as he found the source of the most unbearable ache of all.

He leant over her, one hand clenched in her tumbled hair as her head moved restively back and forth on the pillow. Her eyes flew wide, glazed with passion. He looked down at her like a lithe dark conqueror, his glittering golden eyes locking with hers as he pressed his knuckles skilfully to the most agonisingly sensitive spot in her entire thrumming body and murmured roughly, 'Now tell me that you did not imagine this the very first time you laid eyes on me. Tell me that you did not see yourself lying under me, your body on fire for my possession…'

A kind of appalled awareness flooded Bethany, memory dragging her back two years in the blink of an eyelid. She remembered time stopping dead as he'd walked towards her, devouring her with that burning gaze as if she were already *his*, as if he only had to look to possess, as if all her life she had been waiting for that one moment…and for *him*. And she had had a vision—an instantaneous, utterly wanton vision—of him throwing her down on a bed in the heat of passion and forcing her with every erotic inducement in his repertoire to surrender to his sexual dominance. That image had been so shattering, so intense and so utterly terrifying that it had taken her an entire twenty-four hours to recover from the encounter.

'I…I—' she gasped.

'One look and you wanted me—'

'No!'

'Instantly, desperately, unforgettably,' Razul gritted, scorching her with his savage golden gaze. 'You felt what you had never felt before. A sexual recognition so powerful, so consuming that we both saw the same thing—'

Her lashes fluttered on suddenly wild and furious eyes. 'No—'

He moved an expert hand, like a torturer bent on interrogation, and she cried out loud, unable to stifle that helpless moan of intolerable pleasure or to prevent the immediate jerk of her unbearably responsive body. 'Admit it,' he intoned with a feral flash of white teeth and the kind of awesome tenacity which terrified her.

'You bastard!' she sobbed in an explosion of frustration and emotional stress. 'All right…all right… yes…yes…*yes*!'

Having triumphed, Razul dealt her a sizzling smile in reward for her surrender and lowered his lean, hard length to hers again. He pressed his mouth hotly to the tiny pulse flickering madly above her collar-bone. 'You are my woman—'

'No—' she panted in despair.

'And if I had lifted you up and kissed you breathless

instead of trying to communicate in my very poor English you would have fallen at my feet—'

'*No!*' she moaned in anguish, furious with him—so furious that she was on the brink of explosion but she couldn't harness that energy into attack, couldn't control the shivering, tormented reaction of her body and the clawing need that he had mercilessly kept at boiling point.

'Yes.' With a husky laugh he ran the tip of his tongue down the valley between her heaving breasts then smoothly changed direction to encircle the engorged peaks that he had already caressed to throbbing sensitivity. He made her gasp and writhe while he sent his fingers travelling teasingly along the smooth stretch of one inner thigh, charting every tiny clenching muscle and following them to the very heart of her.

Her hips jerked wildly under the onslaught of that exploring hand. It felt as if every atom of her fevered being was centred there, and every caress drove her a little bit crazier until she was clutching frantically at him, finding his provocative mouth again for herself, desperate for any contact she could get, desperate for the agony of hunger attacking her to be assuaged.

'I will try not to hurt you,' Razul murmured raggedly. 'But you are very tight and it has been so long for me…'

He had driven her to such a pitch of excitement that she was completely out of control. Nothing mattered, nothing impinged on her fevered state but the devouring need for that intolerably aching emptiness to be filled. He slid between her parted thighs and raised her up to him with strong hands, and the hot, hard surge of his manhood thrust against her softness. She gasped and stiffened, lashes flying up on fearful eyes.

'Don't tense,' he grated rawly as he sought an entry to the moist welcome he had prepared for himself.

'Please…' And she meant to say 'don't', but her lips wouldn't form the word. She was so excited, so unbearably aroused that the first thrust of his slow invasion wiped out her ability to talk or think.

He arched lithely over her, the hair on his chest abrading her taut nipples, and ravished her mouth before he plunged home into the very heart of her, and the sharp pain froze her in shocked rejection. As she cried out he released her lips and stared down at her, his golden features clenched by the strain of the control that he was imposing on his own fierce desire, but his eyes were as vibrant as flames as they swept over her with possessive pride. 'Now you are truly mine, *aziz*,' he intoned with savage satisfaction.

On the outer edge of pain she was sucked back down into a well of hot sexual excitement. The feel of him inside her, stretching her, filling her, was so intolerably intimate and pleasurable that she whimpered deep in her throat. In reaction he shifted again, penetrating deep with a groan of answering hunger. And then the last scrap of self-awareness fell away from her as he began to move in her, possessing her with long, powerful strokes that enforced his dominance and her surrender.

She was overwhelmed by her own shattering response, caught up in his stormy rhythm, her breathing fractured, her pulses rising to screaming pitch as her heart slammed against her ribcage with his every fluid movement.

The primal drive to satisfaction took over, making every skin-cell sing as he drove her to a frenzied climax of savage passion. Her body jerked like a rag doll's as the explosion of heat started deep down inside her and then splintered through all of her, devastating her, blinding her, deafening her, leaving her stunned by sheer pleasure. And, as she wrapped her arms tightly, instinctively round him and clung through the quivering aftershocks, the most shattering truth of all came to her while all her defences were down... You love him; you've always loved him.

It was like falling into a great black hole without

warning. Reality hit Bethany hard. Nothing had ever shaken her as deeply as that head-on collision with the seething emotions that she had fought and denied to the last ditch.

She loved him but she had repeatedly assured herself that she was only suffering from a foolish infatuation, but foolish infatuations did not last this length of time nor cause such continual pain and conflict. Razul was everything she shouldn't want in a man when she had never wanted a man in the first place. She should have hated him on sight! And she had tried to hate him—oh, yes, she had tried—but she had failed so completely that she had refused to face her own failure.

She was still fathoms-deep in shock as Razul rolled over onto a cool spot in the vast bed, carrying her indolently with him. In the thick silence, imprisoned in the circle of his arms, she listened to the soft rasp of his breathing and the still accelerated thump of his heart and trembled, convinced that if she tried to get up her legs would fold under her, equally convinced that if she made a single evasive move he would haul her back to him like a rebellious child, because now she knew and he knew who was *really* in control...and that reality was like a hot iron searing her sensitive flesh. Love had got inside her and made a nonsense of her efforts to protect herself.

But how could she have known that he would use that wanton sexual hunger of hers as a weapon against her? She *should* have known, she told herself painfully as she recalled the controlled dark fury and outrage which her rejection of her wedding ring had provoked. Razul had decided to put her in her place and, lo and behold...and this was not a surprise...her place was flat on her back in his bed. And she saw now that there had been absolutely no way that Razul would have allowed her to sleep alone, not after the way she had behaved, not when *this* had been what he had wanted from her all along.

Her eyes stung fiercely. For the first time in her adult life she felt weak and inadequate. She had never needed anybody since childhood, had never allowed herself to need anybody, but Razul had *made* her need him. He had got beneath her skin and blown her every defence sky-high.

'Forgive me for hurting you,' Razul sighed.

Her teeth ground together as she recalled his primal satisfaction at that instant of sexual possession. She attempted to shift out of the incredible intimacy of his embrace. His arms tightened. Her eyes flashed and she lifted her head. 'You enjoyed it,' she condemned.

He tautened, paled and dealt her a look of such sudden flashing fury that her stomach turned over. 'I did not enjoy hurting you,' he countered in fierce rebuttal. 'But I took natural pleasure and pride in your purity. I have never lain with a virgin before. I did not expect to find you innocent, and that you should give me such a gift on our wedding night meant a great deal to me. I will not apologise for that.'

'I wish I'd slept with a hundred men!' Bethany snapped, her colour high.

'But you didn't,' Razul murmured with a slumbrous satisfaction that he did not even bother to try and conceal. 'You waited for me.'

'I did not wait for you!' she blazed.

'The question is academic now. Why, after the joy we have shared, are you again attempting to fight with me?' he enquired almost teasingly.

He was so gorgeous. Black hair, golden skin, stunning eyes and a mouth as wicked as it was innately sensual. Suddenly it hurt to look at him and feel the instant leap of her own possessive pleasure in him. She was in torment, emotions surging tempestuously inside her. Love at first sight. She had never believed in it and yet it had happened to her. She had fallen head over heels in love with him the first time she'd seen him and she should have known it—she should have known it long ago!

She had been in agony for him at that college dinner when he hadn't been sure of what cutlery to use, and at each course he had watched her covertly and she had made something of a show of picking up the right utensils purely for his benefit. And when she had found it quite impossible to shoot him down in flames until the bitter end, because she was so painfully conscious of that fierce pride of his, she should have known *then* that Prince Razul al Rashidai Harun had a hold on her far stronger than any infatuation.

She could have wept now for her own blind stupidity. Had she acknowledged her own feelings, she was bitterly convinced that she would have had the strength to get on that helicopter.

'Bethany...' he prompted, shifting lithely beneath her.

She quivered, abruptly registering the hard thrust of his masculinity against her thigh. That shook her. She knew all about the mechanics of sex but she hadn't believed that he could be aroused again this quickly.

'And now you go silent.' A caressing hand curved to her sensitive jawbone. He smiled at her—the sort of megawatt-brilliant smile which clenched her heart and sent every alarm bell jangling. 'And you look so worried but also very sexy.'

He ran a fingertip lightly along the lower lip swollen by his passionate kisses, and she collided mesmerically with smouldering green eyes, felt her pulses leap. With his thumb he prised her lips apart and softly invaded the tender interior, and in shamed disbelief she felt a surge of heat quicken between her thighs.

'Forget the world outside these walls,' Razul instructed huskily. 'This is our world and nothing can threaten you here.'

Nothing but him. The acknowledgement pierced her deep. 'Razul...'

He leant closer and allowed his tongue to penetrate just once between her parted lips in a darting, highly erotic assault which made her every skin-cell tingle. 'I want you again.'

'N-no!' she gasped strickenly, snaking away from him as if she had been threatened with violence.

He tugged her back to him with easy strength. 'Would I hurt you?'

A tide of scarlet washed over her cheeks as she connected with the concern in that clear, candid gaze. 'Yes...' she lied shakily.

'There are many ways of making love—'

'And I don't want to know about them!' Bethany asserted feverishly, on the edge of panic.

Razul angled a highly amused smile at her. 'But you will. Come on...we will go for a swim—'

'A swim?' she echoed, in a daze.

'If I am to restrain my hunger for you, *aziz*, the equivalent of a cold shower becomes a necessity.'

'Oh...go ahead,' she said with helpless enthusiasm.

He threw back his handsome dark head and laughed uproariously. Before she could ask him what he found so funny, he sprang out of bed and swept her up into his arms in one powerful motion. 'We share everything from this night on,' he assured her.

'I do not need a cold shower.'

'But you deserve one, *aziz*. Were it not for my recollection of the ecstasy you found in my arms, I would now feel most deficient as a lover.'

'You're a perfect ten. Don't worry about it,' Bethany bit out acidly. 'Now will you please put me down? I am not one of those women who go all weak at the knees at the superiority of male muscle-power!'

He lifted her higher and ravished her tender mouth in a hot, hungry surge that left her dizzy and wildly disorientated. 'Now that *does* make you go weak at the knees,' he told her without skipping a beat, lashings of raw amusement in the wolfish grin curving his firm mouth. 'A perfect ten?' he mused. 'But who do you compare me with? Did you fantasise about me as well?'

'I have never had a—'

'What a little liar you are…stubborn, aggressive, sharp-tongued… It is as well I did not marry you in the hope of honeyed sweetness and flattery.'

'You married me to get me into bed!' Bethany spat back at him.

'But I didn't have to.' He smoothly disconcerted her with that cool rejoinder. 'I could have taken you to my bed in England but I chose not to put your powers of self-restraint to the test… You should be grateful—'

'*Grateful*?' she gasped, with clenched fists.

He gave her a sardonic glance. 'You would have failed the test. I could have taken you the first time I kissed you.'

Enraged, Bethany took a swing at him and a split second later her overheated body was plunged into cold water. Spluttering and splashing and gasping in shock, she recoiled against the tiled wall of the pool for support and clawed her dripping hair out of her eyes.

'I will not allow you to strike me. While you are my wife you will treat me with respect.'

In the moonlight he was a dark golden silhouette, standing barely waist-deep in the lapping water. '*While you are my wife*', she registered furiously. Always the time limit—not that that mattered a damn to her, for loving him did not close her eyes to the impossibility of a more lasting relationship between them. On the other hand, she bitterly resented his arrogance in believing that he could take what suited him from the institution of marriage and deviously cast aside what did not.

'Not only do I not believe in marriage, I do not feel like your wife and I do not want to be your wife,' she spelt out hotly. 'I do not feel *honoured*…I feel used.

Those ceremonies were a mockery and you needn't think that putting a ring on my finger blinds me to that fact.'

Razul moved towards her. 'So you feel *used*,' he grated rawly. 'But then what can tenderness mean to you? Only something more to despoil as you seek to despoil everything we share, with your narrow, closed little mind and your selfish, smug sense of superiority!'

Her whole body had turned icy cold and the angry colour had drained from her cheeks. 'I do not feel superior,' she whispered strickenly, devastated by the dark fury that she had unleashed.

'But you give me your body and nothing else. It seems I am not worthy of anything more. If our marriage truly means nothing to you, I was wrong to make you put that ring on again.' He caught her to him, splayed her fingers and wrenched off the slender band. He sent it spinning into the water in a gesture of vehement repudiation. 'It will lie there for eternity, for you would have to come to me on your knees for me to allow you to wear it again!'

It was crazy, but the minute he took that ring from her she wanted it back with a passion as strong as his repudiation. Narrow-minded, selfish, smug, she recited inwardly, her throat thickening with tears. Was that really how he saw her? That hurt; that really hurt.

'But I need no ring on your finger to licence me to enjoy what is already mine.' Before she could even guess his intention, Razul planted firm hands on her hips and lifted her up out of the water onto the edge of the pool.

'What are you doing?' she gasped.

'What *I* want to do,' Razul informed her rawly, pressing her knees apart with his hard thighs as he sank his hands beneath her to hold her in place. 'If you believe that I have used you, then I might as well commit the sin.'

She sank her unsteady hands into his thick, silky hair,

emotions that were at powerful variance with her spoken rejection threatening to tear her in two, until he took her mouth with passionate urgency and with that one act drove every rational thought from her head.

CHAPTER EIGHT

BETHANY shifted in the comfortable bed and shivered convulsively with cold. Her arm was throbbing. She ached all over, she ached in places she hadn't even known she could ache, but, strangely, she felt drowsily detached from her physical discomforts and her mind was disorientatingly awash with a flood of erotic imagery.

She was remembering the hot, drugging glory of Razul's mouth on hers, the phenomenal speed at which her treacherously eager body had quickened to melted honey. She was remembering that savage joining as he'd sunk into her over and over again, remorselessly driving her to a pitch of excitement far beyond her wildest fantasies. She was remembering her own wanton ecstasy when he'd chosen to ditch all control and cool...and was shrinking inwardly from the shame of her own weakness.

Yet she was too honest to deny that she had gloried in that sensual intimacy and rejoiced in his hungry need for her and that, most of all, she had loved falling asleep in his arms, knowing that he was there in the night and feeling wonderfully secure in that sense of no longer being alone.

So, it had begun, she sensed wretchedly. This was what love did to you. It levelled your pride and betrayed your principles. It made a sane woman behave insanely. Her mother was an intelligent woman, but intelligence had not once prompted her to break away from her destructive marriage.

No, her mother stayed the course, apparently hooked

on the pain and humiliation of possessing a wandering spouse. 'He's my husband and I love him,' she had told her daughter in staunch reproof in the days when Bethany had still been naïve enough to think that she should interfere. Escape to university had been a blessing, and in burying herself in her studies and carving out her career Bethany had gradually let the ties of home wane to their current level of occasional letters.

With a weak hand she tugged at the sheet, trying to warm herself.

Had she really protected herself all these years just to fall flat on her face for a male who was a sexual predator like her father? The kind of man who stoked his inadequate ego with female flattery and surrender, who made an art form out of lying and who was loyal to nothing but his own self-interest. But that *wasn't* Razul, she conceded grudgingly, her head aching fit to burst.

It was laughable to think of Razul as inadequate. In the ego line, he was as tough as old boots. He was also fiercely loyal to his family, not to mention being possessed of a nasty habit of brutal candour that was frequently grossly unwelcome to Bethany's ears. In fact, if there was anything you least wanted to hear about yourself, Razul was most likely to break the bad news, presumably in the hope that you would admit the flaw and work hard to eradicate it.

But not one of those virtues made him any less of a predator, Bethany reminded herself painfully. Indeed, that powerful character made him even more dangerous, for she saw now that it was that innate strength and tenacity of purpose which she found so very attractive. He was the only man who had ever stood up to her, the only man who had ever managed to penetrate her defensive shell…and the only man ever to surprise her by constantly doing the unexpected, refusing to fall into the neat little pigeon-holes into which she had scornfully slotted all men from an early age.

So now she knew why she loved him. But that didn't blind her to the knowledge that all Razul wanted from her was that wild sexual oblivion which he had introduced her to last night. Only he wasn't prepared to admit that openly, was he? Presumably, if he did, his own moral scruples would take a battering. Marriage was much more respectable than an affair—which he could not possibly have got away with in Datar—but their marriage was *still* only a temporary affair.

It was becoming an effort to think, she registered, twisting her head back and forth on the pillow, her mouth as dry as a bone as she fought to concentrate. Her arm gave an unbearable twinge as she moved it, and with an effort, for she felt very weak, she pushed back the sheet and surveyed it with a curiously detached sort of interest. It was swollen and angry-looking, particularly puffy round the plaster covering Fatima's scratches. Blood poisoning, she decided, and she was probably running a temperature, which explained why she was feeling so cold.

She heard a door open. Had it been locked? She recalled his threat to lock her up and throw away the key and smiled with helpless amusement. She loved his drama, too. Her mind was wandering, she noted with faint irritation—she needed a doctor.

Razul appeared in her field of view, fully dressed in an exquisitely tailored dove-grey suit. In Western mode today. He looked devastatingly handsome but he shimmered a little indistinctly round the edges, as if she was suffering from some form of visual disturbance. She wondered dimly why he was carrying a laden tray complete with flowers, because he had the distinct attitude of someone who didn't know what to do with it.

'You are awake…are you hungry?' he enquired very stiltedly, hovering quite a few feet away and looking staggeringly awkward. 'I have brought breakfast.'

Doctor, she reminded herself, grateful that Razul would be rock-solid in a crisis.

He cleared his throat in the silence. 'Naturally you are awaiting an apology.'

Was she? Why was she expecting an apology? She couldn't imagine, and continued to observe him with glazed green eyes from the depths of the great, shadowy bed.

'I regret my behaviour last night,' he delivered, an arc of colour accentuating the strong slant of his cheek-bones and the brilliance of his dark, troubled eyes. 'I have no excuse to make for myself. I lost control. I lost my temper. I have never done this before.'

She just couldn't concentrate at all. Doctor, she thought again. 'I need a doctor,' she told him weakly.

'A doctor?' He frowned uncertainly at her.

She pushed the sheet down from her aching arm. 'See?' she pointed out.

The tray dropped with a thunderous crash of smashing china. She blinked in bemusement as Razul suddenly came down on the bed beside her in what could only be described as a flying leap. A flood of volatile Arabic rent the charged silence. He grasped her fingers in a death grip and stared down at her, immobilised by shock. Pan-ic, sheer panic, she registered in astonishment, and then he dug out a mobile phone, but his hand was shaking so badly that he evidently hit the wrong numerals, because he cursed viciously and had to start again. Nor was the call that he eventually managed to make distinguished by any princely form of cool.

'Sorry to be such a nuisance,' she sighed in what she hoped was a soothing tone.

He said something in his own language in response, his English obviously failing him. He groaned something in a tone of anguish as he snatched up her nightdress and began to feed her into it. Then he bundled her very gently into first the sheet and then the bedspread and swept her up, wrapped like an Egyptian mummy. About there, she slid into a feverish state of unawareness.

The next time Bethany surfaced she was in a dimly lit room in one of those beds with rails round it and a drip was attached to her arm. She felt terribly hot and uncomfortable, and she didn't want another thermometer stuck in her mouth and said so loudly. She heard Razul speak and heard a female voice literally snap back at him, which struck her as unusual, and if only it had not been too much effort to do so she might have looked just to see what was going on.

The time after that, she wakened up as if she had been sleeping. Her arm was no longer painful but she felt incredibly drained. The same voices were still talking. She shifted position with a faint mutter over the weakness of her muscles and opened her eyes. Laila was standing over the bed on one side of her, Razul at the foot, and there was more than a suggestion of acrimony in the air.

'There you are,' Laila said with satisfaction to her brother. 'I told you she was only asleep...as did Mr Khan.'

Bethany frowned in astonishment at Razul. He looked as though he hadn't shaved in a week and had been sleeping rough. A thick blue-black shadow of stubble covered his aggressive jawline. His eyes were bloodshot, his suit crumpled, his tie missing.

'How are you feeling?' he enquired tautly, ignoring his sister.

'How long have I been here?'

'Almost two days—'

'The longest days of my life,' Laila groaned. 'Please tell him to go home, Bethany, before I am tempted to commit a crime still punishable by death...an assault on his illustrious person—'

'You will not speak to me like that!' Razul bit out, making Bethany flinch.

'No human being can go that long without sleep and expect to retain a sense of proportion...and what has happened to your sense of humour?' Laila demanded.

'You expect me to laugh when my wife has been on the brink of death?' he asked incredulously.

'Your wife has not been on the brink of death. She has been *quite* ill but not seriously ill. Now will you please go home before I am reduced to ignoble strategy? You know as well as I do what will happen if I inform our father of your current state of exhaustion. One tiny hint that his beloved son is not rejoicing in robust health and he'll *order* you home.'

'I am staying with my wife. While she is unwell, this is my place.'

'Please go home,' Bethany muttered, feeling horribly guilty for causing dissension between brother and sister, and even more dismayed by the news that Razul had not slept in forty-eight hours.

His facial muscles clenched hard. His dense lashes screened his strained, dark-as-night eyes but she couldn't help feeling that he was reacting as though she had stabbed a knife into his back. His strong features harshly set, he withdrew a step. 'If that is your desire...'

As the door closed on his departure Laila groaned, 'You should have wrapped that up a bit. Now you've offended him and it's my fault. Ahmed would be cringing if he heard me speaking to Razul like that, but for heaven's sake...I'm twenty years older, I've lived most of my life in London and I keep on forgetting that my kid brother will one day be our king. I always had a big mouth,' she muttered wearily, 'but he's been acting like an idiot since you were brought in—'

'An idiot?' Bethany echoed weakly.

'He was in a blind panic. First of all he wanted to take you to London because he wasn't convinced we could offer a sufficient standard of care. I told him he really would have something to worry about if you had to wait that long for treatment. Then he wanted to fly in specialists. Then one of the junior staff…a young *male*,' she stressed witheringly, 'accidentally came in here, and Razul went through the roof and threatened to take you home if you could not be adequately chaperoned and protected from such an appalling invasion of your privacy. He has not left your bedside for a moment.

'He has not eaten, he has not slept and there are four guards standing outside that door… Any minute now I expect the arrival of an official food-taster!'

Bethany stared back at Razul's sister, wide-eyed. 'Oh, dear…' she mumbled.

'Oh, dear, indeed.' With a rueful smile Laila sank down on a chair. 'Now, I can understand that he's been worried sick about you, but I don't understand why he's been behaving as though it was his fault that you were ill!'

Bethany dimly remembered that apology. A sudden attack of conscience had undoubtedly prompted his extraordinary behaviour. Her heart sank like a stone. She would have felt wonderful if she could have believed that his behaviour had stemmed solely from genuine concern and worry about her well-being.

'As if it could be. You had bad luck, that's all. How did you get those scratches anyway?'

'Fatima—'

'Does Razul know that?' Laila gasped.

Bethany nodded, locked into her own miserable thoughts.

Disconcertingly, Razul's sister burst out laughing. 'That piece of news makes everything I have endured worthwhile,' she declared with renewed energy, and stood up again to press a button on the wall by the bed. 'Your specialist, Mr Khan, will want to check you over. Are you hungry yet?'

'No—'

'Please try to develop an appetite,' Laila teased. 'If you don't, Razul will import your Dubai cook…and then the next thing you know all our rich patrons will expect to do the same. Actually I'm very glad you are here.'

Bethany gaped at her.

'What Razul does, everyone else does,' Laila supplied cheerfully. 'If he had flown you to London for treatment, our reputation as a hospital would have sunk without trace!' She turned from the door and grinned widely. 'I am also depending on you to give birth to the first royal baby within these walls, but *please* let us make a pact to sedate Razul in advance of the big event, because I will surely strangle him if he starts trying to tell me what to do in my delivery room!'

A royal baby? In mute shock Bethany lay very still. Laila was under the impression that this was a *real* marriage. Of course she was. Why should Razul let his whole family know that she was only a temporary aberration? There was no necessity when he knew that by the end of the summer she would be gone anyway. But his father knew the truth, she suspected. Presumably that was the only reason why he had allowed Razul to marry her in the first place.

Well, King Azmir needn't worry himself, and Laila was destined to disappointment this time around. Razul hadn't run any risk of making his new bride pregnant. Even in the midst of wild passion in that pool, now she came to consider the fact, Razul had not taken any chances. He had carried her back to bed and protected them both from any possibility of her becoming pregnant.

And why the heck should that hurt so much? It was only confirmation of what she had known from the start. They had no future together. So why, when Razul employed a little common sense for a change, should that common sense feel like the ultimate rejection? She ought to be delighted that he had not risked such a development. Why was her mind now throwing up embarrassingly twee little pictures of Razul in miniature?

Her nose wrinkled as her eyes burned. She grimaced, furious with herself. A long time ago she had known that the one real drawback of the celibate life that she had planned would be never, ever having a child of her own when she loved children.

As she loved him...hateful creep that he was, she thought bitterly, turning her convulsing face into the pillow and absolutely despising herself for giving way to her emotions. Just to think of Fatima and him *together* made her stomach heave. The woman was a maniac! And not one single word of criticism had Razul uttered when Bethany had told him who had inflicted those scratches.

Of course, it didn't matter to him that Bethany had suffered grievously at that woman's hands. That nasty piece of work with no control over her temper and murderous impulses was very probably going to be the mother of his children.

All of a sudden Bethany wanted to die and leave him so miserable and so tortured by guilt that he would be totally useless as a husband!

'I understand that you are not eating very much,' Razul remarked tautly.

'I'm just not very hungry.' In the twenty-four hours it had taken him to show up again and visit her, Bethany had sunk deep into her misery, and when he had walked through the door looking as grim and tense as she felt it had been the last straw.

'I can understand that...' he breathed in an even tauter undertone. 'But you must be sensible.'

The silence was oppressive. She turned her face to the wall. He *deserved* Fatima, she decided wretchedly, trying to hate him, but somehow that only made her own pain bite all the deeper.

'I made a mistake in bringing you to Datar,' he conceded heavily.

Bethany went rigid, and emerged from the tumbled cloud of her veiling hair with a frown.

'I believed I could make you happy...for a while anyway,' Razul framed even more tightly, ferocious tension in every lean, hard angle of his features. 'I know now that that was very arrogant of me...and stupid—unforgivably stupid. I allowed my passions to carry me away. I have never wanted a woman as much as I wanted you. You were my dream... In the name of Allah, I sound like an adolescent boy!'

With a harsh laugh of angry embarrassment he strode restively over to the window. 'I was naïve enough to believe that we could have this special time together and that it would cost you nothing. I had so little time left. I have no freedom of choice. I *have* to marry and father children. I am thirty. That is quite an age to still be single in my position...'

'Yes,' she whispered unsteadily, absolutely ripped apart by a depth of honesty that she had not expected to receive.

'You were my dream...' she reflected on a tide of almost unbearable pain; if only she had been. He had exquisite tact. What he was really saying was what she had known all along. She had been his sexual fantasy, the desirable conquest who had refused to be caught, becoming even more highly desired as a result. He had wanted one last fling with a woman who was not of his world—a strong, independent woman who would scarcely fall apart at the seams or make a fuss when it was over—and he had never at any stage contemplated that one last fling turning into anything more meaningful or lasting.

'If it were not for my family I would have you flown

back to England, for that is what you must want now,'
Razul intoned almost jerkily. 'But for their sake I ask
you to stay for a little while longer. The too sudden
departure of my bride would cause them severe embarrassment.'

Bethany did not dare look at him. The thought of being transported home immediately filled her with horror.
Yet it was cowardly to want to put off the inevitable.
'This special time together'...why couldn't she have
been the type of woman who could accept that? And
suddenly, finally, she understood why she had not accepted it.

She had wanted more—all along she had wanted
more, even when she'd been fighting with him and telling him that she didn't believe in marriage. She had had
her dreams too, even if she hadn't acknowledged them.
She had wanted him for ever, she had wanted him to
love her, she had wanted him to prove to her that marriage could work between them against all the
odds...and that was immeasurably more naïve than anything he had expected, she conceded painfully. Cinder-
ella gets her prince, the ultimate fairy tale...who would
ever have believed that prosaic Bethany Morgan could
harbour such a dream?

'What is your decision? I must know,' Razul
prompted very quietly.

Thank heaven for his fear of embarrassing his family,
she thought. 'I'll stay,' she said unevenly, and fished
around for a reasonable excuse. 'I can do my research.'

'Of course...your research,' Razul said flatly.

But that wasn't all she planned to be doing, Bethany
decided with an abrupt flash of decisiveness which startled her. Right now Razul had the impression that the
end of the summer couldn't come quickly enough for
him. He had had enough. He had been disappointed.
He felt that he had made a fool of himself. He had
given up on his *dream*. Well, she wasn't planning to give

up on him that easily. If she was about to spend the rest of her life hopelessly in love with another woman's husband, she was going to have some worthwhile memories to take home with her! Right now he was *her* husband and the way Bethany felt—and she felt incredibly vindictive—Fatima was always going to feel second-best, and Razul was going to be languishing after his first wife for the rest of his days!

'I've been thinking a lot since I've been lying in this bed,' Bethany informed him in an impulsive rush, and there was considerable truth in the admission. Deprived of Razul for twenty-four hours, she had had time to come to terms with her feelings.

'You never stop thinking,' Razul said grimly, as if it were the worst possible offence that a woman could commit.

'My research means so much to me but it's terribly inconvenient that I don't speak Arabic,' Bethany sighed. 'You see, my research assistant *did*. That was why I picked him, and I realise that you're probably very busy but I was wondering if we could make a trip together—'

'A trip?' The apparently compulsive view beyond the window which he had been glued to suddenly lost his concentration. He swung back to her.

'Into the desert. So that I could get a real feel for the nomadic way of life. Of course, I would want the experience to be authentic—'

'Authentic?' he questioned, studying her with an obvious effort to conceal how stunned he was by the suggestion that she had just made.

'Basic and back to nature…just you and me against the elements without a cohort of guards and servants. They would rather get in the way of authenticity, don't you think?' she queried less confidently.

'But you would be alone with me,' Razul pointed out very drily, his black lashes very nearly hitting his cheekbones as he surveyed her with compelling intensity. 'I had not thought you would wish to be subjected to such unwelcome intimacy.'

Bethany took a deep breath, her cheeks hotting up to scarlet as she studied his feet. 'When did I say it would be unwelcome? It's not as though I hate you or anything like that.'

A silence had never been so thunderously loud in her ears.

'You would trust me not to touch you? I am not sure I could withstand the temptation of being alone with you.' It sounded as if admitting that physically hurt him.

'I was hoping not...' Bethany licked her dry lips as the silence got even noisier and her face got even hotter. She was beginning to wonder if she was quite sane. She had the feeling that he was wondering too. Green light...then red stop-light, she recalled, writhing with mortification.

'You were hoping I would *not* withstand temptation?' he framed raggedly.

Dumbly she nodded, silenced by shock at what she had just told him.

Razul gave her the fright of her life. He groaned something volatile in Arabic and grabbed her out of the bed, drip and all, just as the door opened.

'What on earth are you doing?' Laila enquired in disbelief.

'I am taking my wife home,' Razul announced aggressively, as if he was expecting a fight. 'I will take a nurse too.'

Laila was struggling to keep her face straight. 'Honeymooners. You make me feel every year of my age.'

As his sister left to make the arrangements Razul enveloped Bethany in a smouldering golden scrutiny that entrapped her. 'I will make this the happiest summer of your life,' he swore passionately.

And a shard of pain as sharp as a sliver of glass tore at her. The end of the summer loomed like a fate worse than death. Why did Razul have to keep on mentioning it? It was like pouring salt on an open wound, but then there was no point in avoiding reality, she reminded herself painfully.

CHAPTER NINE

LATE afternoon, Razul strolled across the grass towards her, fluidly graceful in his desert robes but wearing that slight frown-line between his aristocratic brows which told her that he was about to be difficult.

'You are usually taking a nap at this hour,' he reminded her, tawny eyes sweeping over her where she reclined in the shade of the trees with a book.

'I'm feeling as fit as a fiddle.'

'You still look pale…and strained.'

Bethany bowed her head. Only a week ago she had dropped her defences, burnt her bridges and thrown herself at Razul's head. Never in her worst nightmares had she imagined sacrificing her pride to such an extent. And with what result? she asked herself, with the furious and bewildered resentment which had begun to rise in her over the past week.

For some reason, Razul had gone from that brief instant of seeming jubilance at the hospital into a cool, distant mood. He was extremely polite and remarkably attentive. He brought her flowers and books and visited her several times a day, but he might just as well have been a gracious host calling in on an ailing house guest for there was nothing more intimate in his attitude towards her.

'When are we going into the desert?' she murmured bluntly.

'Perhaps next month when the temperatures begin to fall. You could not tolerate the current levels of heat—'

'I am quite sure I could—'

'But then you do not know what you are talking

135

about,' Razul incised with steely cool. 'And you will surely allow that I do? At this time of the year the desert is a furnace, and to undertake such a trip would be utter madness.'

Bethany set her teeth. 'You can have your own tent…if that's what's worrying you!' And then the minute she'd said that she wanted to crawl under the recliner and cringe. But the most deeply humiliating suspicion had begun to torment her. After she had transformed herself from an exciting challenge into a positive pushover at the hospital, had it then dawned on Razul that he no longer found her madly desirable? Was he now cursing the situation in which he found himself, longingly wishing that he could get rid of her and fervently embrace Fatima without delay?

Involuntarily she glanced up, and caught the feral gleam in his golden eyes and the grimly amused twist of his sensual mouth. 'Does your bed become lonely?' Razul drawled slumbrously.

She flushed to the roots of her hair.

'I am become a sex object. I do not find this role entirely unfamiliar. Other members of your sex have viewed me in this light. But you are my wife—'

'Temporarily!' Bethany lashed back, awash with furious embarrassment at the fact that he could read her so easily.

'And though I have no desire to be offensive—'

'But you do it so well, don't you?' she spat, fit to be tied.

'I am not your stud.'

'I beg your pardon?' Bethany was so outraged that she could hardly get the words out.

'You would like it very well if I came to your bed every night in silence and departed equally silently by dawn. You could have the physical pleasure without yielding me a single glimpse of your inner self. I will not be used in such a fashion. When you learn to talk to me, I will share your bed—'

'I don't want to talk to you…I don't want you in my bed…in fact I wish you'd take a running jump off the nearest cliff!' she launched at him, quivering all over with raw mortification.

'But I know that none of this is true,' Razul delivered with gentle emphasis. 'You simply cannot bear to be thwarted. Were you never disciplined as a child?'

Bethany's mouth fell open.

'I ask,' Razul murmured smoothly, 'because I threw such tantrums once…but I *was* disciplined. It did me a great deal of good.'

Bethany clasped her hands together tightly and slowly counted to ten.

Razul sank down fluidly into a chair opposite her. 'I would like a cool drink.'

Bethany lifted the iced jug beside her and proceeded to pour.

'And I do not wish to have it thrown at me.'

'Really?' Bethany breathed dangerously.

'I would hate to subject you to the indignity of being dumped in the nearest pool. Rumour of your paddling experience in the fountain on our wedding day has already spread beyond these walls.'

She went scarlet and counted from twenty to fifty in the simmering silence.

'That your temper matches the fire of your hair is no longer any secret.'

The count made it to a hundred at supersonic speed.

'Now what would you like to talk about?' Razul drawled with outstanding cool and a gently encouraging smile.

'Methods of torture and death,' she bit out shakily before she drew in a deep, sustaining breath and could bring herself to look at him again. 'You make me so mad sometimes,' she conceded, with a rueful groan.

'At least I do not bore you as my father bored my mother.'

'You said she left him before she died,' Bethany recalled abruptly.

His expressive mouth twisted. 'She is not dead.'

She frowned in astonishment. 'But Zulema told me—'

'I assure you that she is very much alive—the socialite wife of a prominent French politician and the mother of two other adult children.'

'Did your father divorce her?'

'She divorced him on her return to her family. My father was too proud to admit that he was a holiday romance which soured...thus the false report of her death.'

Bethany was fascinated. 'A *holiday* romance?'

'Laila's mother had died, leaving my father a widower with four daughters. He met my mother in Paris,' Razul explained calmly. 'She was young and rich and spoilt and she thought it might be fun to marry an Arab prince. My grandfather was still on the throne then—'

'Are you telling me that your mother was French?' Bethany interrupted helplessly. 'Christian?'

'Yes. Scarcely a problem. Over a third of the population of Datar is Christian,' Razul reminded her gently.

She had forgotten that fact. A century ago a large number of Christians of the Coptic faith had migrated from Egypt and begun settling in Datar. Their presence had led to a greater degree of religious tolerance and a smoother passage into a more secular society than was possible in many other Muslim countries. But she was stunned to learn that Razul was part French and, as if he understood her astonishment, he gave her a wry look.

'I resemble my father, not my mother.'

'How long were they married?'

'Longer than she desired for she became pregnant the first month. She left Datar when I was two weeks old.'

'Your father wouldn't have allowed her to take you with her,' Bethany assumed.

'She had no wish to do so. A half-caste child would have been an embarrassment to her. It was much easier for her to remarry without me in the picture.'

Half-caste? Bethany felt quite sick at the expression. 'Was that what your father told you?'

'You are keen to put all blame upon my father's shoulders,' Razul sighed, his dark eyes revealing his exasperation. 'He was deeply in love with her—an older man, perhaps not very wise to the ways of Western women but most vulnerable to so crushing a rejection, and that I, too, should be rejected inflicted the deepest wound of all.'

Bethany had flushed. But picturing that right old misery of a tyrant, as she had always imagined him, as a vulnerable, relatively unsophisticated older man, unceremoniously dumped by his bored young wife, took some doing. 'Have you ever had any contact with your mother?'

'Once. I went though my father warned me that it would be foolish.' His lean fingers tautened round the glass he held and he gave a rueful laugh. 'A skeleton rising from the grave could not have inspired more horror than I did. She does not like to remember that there was ever another marriage or another child because her husband does not love those of my race. In my presence she swore her servant to secrecy about my call.'

'What a hateful thing to do to you!' Bethany exclaimed hotly, appalled that any mother could have faced her son with such a repudiation, most particularly a son who, in spite of her desertion, had still retained sufficient generosity to seek her out.

'You sound as though you actually care, *aziz*.'

Bethany froze; her gaze collided with compellingly intense dark eyes and she glanced away at speed, guarding her heart, guarding her tongue. 'Of course I do. I wouldn't want my worst enemy to go through an experience like that!'

'I did not suffer so much,' Razul countered drily. 'I had a father who loved me and, by the time I was three, a stepmother who raised me as though I were her own child. I also have two younger sisters whom you would have met had our marriage not been arranged at such speed. Both are married and living abroad.'

'So you are the only son.'

'Which may explain to you why my father is so embarrassingly protective of me. Laila did not joke. I sneeze in his presence and he turns pale,' Razul revealed with wry exasperation. 'I have often wished that Allah had blessed him with more sons.'

'His *beloved* son,' she recalled Laila saying. It had not occurred to her then that Razul was in fact the only son that King Azmir had. Six girls and one little boy, who must have been more precious then gold-dust from the hour of his birth, but equally that same circumstance must have placed an enormous weight of responsibility on Razul's shoulders to be the perfect son and fulfil all expectations. Her hazy image of her father-in-law had taken quite a beating: not an old tyrant where his son was concerned, but, by all accounts, a loving, indeed over-protective father.

'My father began developing his famous distrust of the Western world after his marriage failed. He was unreasonably embittered by the experience. For that same reason I was educated here in Datar...'

Bethany almost groaned out loud. 'And then the one time he let you go to the West—'

'I met you.' Razul drained his glass and set it aside. A bitter curve twisted his firm mouth. 'And when the rains come and you leave he will say... No, I will not think now of what he will say.'

No doubt there would be an entire week of joyous celebration at the old palace and convivial relations would be fully restored between father and son. 'Of course…he didn't want you to marry me.' She had to force herself to say that out loud.

'He did not.' Razul made no attempt to duck the issue.

'So why did you *do* it?' she whispered helplessly, understanding better than most the incredible courage it must have taken for Razul to defy his elderly parent. Arab sons honoured their fathers. Arab sons were expected to regard paternal wishes as absolute rules to be obeyed without question.

'I have already told you why.' Perceptibly Razul had withdrawn from her again, his hard-boned features harshly set.

'You wanted me that much?' Bethany persisted unsteadily.

'Do you think I make a habit of kidnapping women and springing sudden marriages upon them?' A shadowy glimmer of his beautiful smile briefly crossed his mouth. 'I hear you have already inspected the stables…can you ride?'

The change of subject was so swift as to leave her breathless. 'Ride?'

'I ride at dawn every day when it is cool. Tomorrow, were you willing, I would take you with me. The desert is a place of wondrous beauty at that hour…I would share it with you.'

'Not much point in us sharing anything, is there?' Bethany muttered tightly, suddenly attacked on all sides by a tidal wave of bitter pain.

'Because you will leave?' Razul rose to his feet. 'Defeatist as always, *aziz*. If I can live with this knowledge, why cannot you? And why should I wish to settle for some empty charade of a relationship in the time that remains to us? I want the gold, not the gilt. I will not devalue what we might have together as you would devalue it. We will do more than share a bed before you return to your world.'

Bethany breathed in deeply and leant back fully to take in all six feet two inches of him as he stood with complete poise in the brilliant sunlight. 'Ten days ago nothing I could say or do would persuade you to leave me alone,' she reminded him fiercely.

'Ten days ago, even one week ago, I was foolish enough to believe that your attitude to me was...shall we say...warming, softening, *thawing*?' Razul queried with galling amusement. 'But when I visited you here in your sickbed I learnt my mistake. We have discussed the weather although there is nothing to discuss. Does not a hot sun rise with every dawn? We have also discussed your reading matter, your research and world politics.'

'Have I been boring you?' Her face was as hot as hellfire at that crack about the weather.

'You are far too intelligent to be a bore and your observations and opinions are always of interest to me,' Razul retorted gently. 'But, while you evade every personal subject and are scrupulously careful to show no more real interest in me than you might show in a stranger passing by you in the street, I feel we are still in a phase of courtship—'

'C-courtship?' Bethany slid upright, no longer able to bear the simple fact that he was looking down at her—both mentally and physically. He was driving her clean up the wall.

'You treat me neither like a lover nor a husband. You deny me all intimacy...except when you look at me.' His dark appraisal mocked her with an all-knowing sexual awareness that burned her right down to her toes. 'But, if I had to learn English to communicate with you, you too must learn the language which I desire to hear.'

'You want it *all* don't you?' Revenge, she thought bitterly. So much for the violins that he had played at the hospital when he had talked about her being his dream! He knew that if he touched her she was his...as much his as if he had a brand on her backside, she reflected furiously. But that wasn't enough to satisfy him—oh, no, indeed, he wanted to sneak inside her head as well and prise out her every secret so that his control was absolute.

'Have you ever doubted it?'

'Well, what do you want to know?' Bethany slung at him with a scornfully elevated brow. 'I have nothing to hide,' she declared.

'Really, *aziz*.' His tawny eyes danced with infuriating amusement. 'Are you so desperate for me that you must stun me with so immediate an offer?'

Bethany spread her hands in an arc of screaming frustration and then she caught his irresistible smile and began to feel foolish. 'You know how to send me up now, don't you?'

'I should have resisted the temptation...but then you take yourself so very seriously. You have accused me of so many ridiculous things. I look back in laughter now on my two hundred concubines, my other wife, your view of me as a potentially violent man...and more recently still the assumption that I am a sort of Jekyll and Hyde, who will turn into a monster within hours of wedding you,' Razul enumerated, and his mouth twisted. 'If I could not laugh I would be in deep trouble.'

Bethany swallowed convulsively. Now that he had reeled off all her accusations like that she was severely embarrassed by his tolerance. 'I'm sorry but...well, there was some justification for my suspicions.' She lifted her chin. 'My aunt was married to an Arab and she had a pretty ghastly experience. But I'm quite sure you are aware of that, since you had me investigated.'

A frown-line had drawn his fine brows together. 'I was not aware of it. The investigation only embraced your life over the past year, nothing more,' Razul stated very quietly. 'I too felt that I was intruding upon your privacy and sought only the information that you were free of any entanglement with another man.'

'Oh.' It was Bethany's turn to be disconcerted.

'Your aunt?' he prompted as they began to walk along a stone terrace under the trees.

Bethany's aunt was only seven years older than she was. She had been a frequent visitor in her older sister's home throughout Bethany's childhood. When she had been nineteen and studying for her degree, Susan had met an Iranian engineer at a party. Faisal had been utterly charming and seemingly as much in love with Susan as Susan had been in love with him. Their whirlwind romance had ended in marriage...*ended* in more ways than one.

'It was a *disaster* right from the start,' Bethany told Razul with stark emphasis. 'From the moment they were married he changed. He treated her like a prisoner. He objected to her clothing, her make-up and her friends. He accused her of flirting with other men. He tried to stop her going to her classes. He didn't even like her visiting her family. He turned against us too. In the end he was knocking her about and she was terrified of him... She had to go to the police.'

'And you cite this to me as evidence of a cultural gulf?'

'Wasn't it?' Bethany snapped.

'Surely such men exist within every culture? They are emotionally inadequate, irrationally jealous and possessive and they invariably turn to violence, do they not?' Razul drawled quietly.

Her tongue snaked out to moisten her dry lower lip. She was really quite devastated by a line of argument that she had never acknowledged before, because of course such men existed in every culture.

'He was a sick man and a dangerous man. It is fortunate that your aunt escaped him before he did more serious damage. But what was your family about in allowing so young and inexperienced a girl to marry a foreigner about whom they knew nothing?'

'He seemed so romantic,' Bethany said gruffly, recalling how reluctantly impressed even she had been by Faisal. 'He seemed absolutely devoted to her.'

'It must have been most disturbing for you to witness the aftermath of such a marriage.'

'Disturbing' barely covered it. Susan on their doorstep night after night, her haunted eyes swollen, face drawn, weight falling off her, all her youthful energy drained away by stress and misery and growing fear of Faisal's threats. It had been a nightmare period. But Razul was right, loath as she was to admit it. Susan could well have married one of her own countrymen and ended up in the same predicament.

'It was,' she agreed rather woodenly. 'But Susan did go on to get her business degree and she emigrated to Canada soon afterwards. She's actually a director in an international company now.'

'Has she remarried?'

'No.' Bethany almost laughed at the idea. 'She's very ambitious.'

'Your role model?'

Bethany flushed, thinking of the long talks she had had with Susan when she had fled to Canada two years earlier. Her aunt had hailed her as a virtual heroine for walking away from so dangerous and impossible an attraction. Susan had never regained her trust in the male sex. She was still very bitter about her two-year nightmare with Faisal, and for the first time Bethany fully acknowledged how deeply affected she herself had been by that same nightmare.

Faisal's apparent adoration of Susan had impressed her so much. The young Arab had seemed strong and caring, his relationship with her aunt before their marriage—in Bethany's adolescent eyes—seemingly the very essence of romance. Scarred as she was by growing up in the atmosphere of a bad marriage, Bethany had nonetheless been touched and delighted to see two people really loving each other. She had been absolutely shattered when that relationship had failed as well. It had seemed to her then that there was no such thing as a trustworthy or reliable man.

Bethany bent her head, admitting, 'I do admire what Susan's done with her life since that awful period.' But she was no longer sure that she could admire her aunt for allowing that one, admittedly ghastly experience to turn her off *all* men.

'Some women manage to combine both career and marriage,' Razul murmured.

'Superwomen, you mean...baby under one arm, vacuum cleaner under the other and a mound of work they bring home every night from the office!'

'Servants do make a difference. My sister Laila has managed this combination most successfully,' Razul pointed out. 'As soon as their youngest child began school she embarked on her medical training.'

'How on earth did she manage it?'

'Strong will and Ahmed's support.'

Involuntarily Bethany grinned. 'I have this feeling that Ahmed jumps every time Laila snaps her fingers.'

'This is true,' Razul conceded with a pronounced air of reluctance. 'But he is a skilled and most kindly man, somewhat in awe of my sister even after all these years. She has broken many taboos in our family and he is very proud of her achievements. They have a very happy marriage, a true partnership—'

'I wasn't criticising Ahmed,' Bethany broke in uncomfortably, wondering why he was labouring the point of his sister's blissfully happy marriage and successful career to such an extent. If anything it made her feel inexcusably and meanly envious.

'There must be a certain amount of compromise in all relationships between men and women.'

'And I know who usually does the compromising,' Bethany muttered with the cynicism of habit. 'The woman.'

'You know that is not always true.'

'Well, it's true more than it should be,' she countered, thoroughly irritated by the persistent way Razul contrived to put her in the wrong and make her sound like some man-hating feminist…like Susan? she asked herself uncomfortably, seeing much that she had refused to see before. Perhaps her aunt had become her role model because she had not been able to respect her own mother for the treatment she withstood from her father.

'Are you telling me that there are no women who take advantage of men?'

Her teeth gritted. 'You don't give up, do you?'

'You need to be challenged, for you are very stubborn.'

Involuntarily her gaze connected with his brilliant dark eyes and her heart skipped an entire beat, her mouth going dry. 'And you are not?'

'This is not a competition to see who can be most inflexible.'

Still looking at him, Bethany felt a prickling of heat twist low in her stomach. She could feel her entire body tense with physical awareness. Her breathing fractured, a sudden stirring heaviness swelling her sensitive breasts beneath their fine covering, pinching her nipples into painfully tight little buds. She watched his stunning eyes shimmer gold and trembled, her heart pounding.

'Do not look at me like that,' he breathed raggedly.

Bethany smiled with a new, sensual consciousness of her female power and waited. She was not one whit discomfited by her own response when she saw it mirrored in him. On this level, she thought helplessly, they were equal. 'Why not?'

With a muffled groan he reached out and pulled her to him, sealing every inch of her to the hard, lean muscularity of his male heat and strength. Her senses swam. Instinct took over. As his mouth came down on her softly parted lips a long sigh of satisfaction escaped her and a wanton thrill of excitement jolted her from head to toe, leaving her dizzy and disorientated and clinging to his broad shoulders to stay upright.

When he set her back from him the shock of separation was sharp. She focused passion-glazed eyes on him in bewilderment. He steadied her against the wall behind her and withdrew a fluid step, studying her with grim intensity.

'You learn quickly.'

'You're a good teacher.' A hectic flush lit her fair complexion as she registered his withdrawal. Suddenly she felt unbearably humiliated.

'But I was too impatient. I taught you the wrong things,' Razul murmured very quietly, and reached for her clenched hand, smoothing out her taut fingers and cradling them in his.

Scorching tears had flooded her eyes. She bowed her head, immobilised by her devastating weakness. She wanted him so much. It was as if there were a clock ticking inside her where her heart should be. She couldn't think, couldn't be rational about the concept of losing Razul, but she could feel the time they had left sliding remorselessly through her fingers like silky grains of sand. The inner strength she depended on was fast buckling into a kind of fevered desperation in which she told herself that she knew what she was doing, when she really didn't know at all.

'I want to show you something.' Retaining a purposeful grip on her hand, he trailed her back indoors with enthusiasm and drew her into one of the reception rooms. A basket sat on the priceless carpet. 'It is for you.'

She crouched down and lifted the lid, already knowing what she would find within—another kitten, a rolling ball of Persian fluff with bright eyes, the twin of the gift he had given her two years earlier.

'You kept the female,' he commented. 'This one is male.'

'Yes. Thank you. He'll be great company for her...when they finally get around to meeting,' she managed stiltedly.

The pedigree kitten danced across the rug, swung an ambitious paw at the strap dangling from the basket lid and fell over in comical confusion. Yet she didn't laugh; in fact her throat closed over.

A matching pair, male and female. He probably thought that she would let them breed. It would not occur to him that she might have had the female doctored and that this was one little male who would not become a father. Her cat was barren, just as her mistress would be, she reflected, gripped by a sudden stab of pain. No kittens, no children—and although it was a ridiculous comparison to make it brought home to Bethany as nothing else could have done that she would never, ever have a child of her own, because if she couldn't have Razul she would have nobody.

'You are thinking of the British quarantine rules,' Razul registered harshly.

She heard that harshness but was too distressed by her own emotional turmoil to question it. 'He'll be quite grown-up by the time he emerges from six months of confinement and comes home to me,' she mumbled tightly.

'Please excuse me...I have some calls to make.'

His abruptness disconcerted her. She sprang upright, painfully reluctant to see him leave her. 'Do you have to make them right this minute?'

'For what would you ask me to remain?' Razul angled a chillingly impassive glance over her. 'No doubt it is your wish that I make arrangements for the cat to be put into quarantine now?'

'No…yes…oh, I don't know.' Hurt by his visible reluctance to stay with her and wretchedly conscious of the ice in the air, she heard herself ask, 'What have I done…what did I say?'

The merest sliver of gold showed beneath the lush screen of his lashes. 'Nothing of import.'

Yet the silence stretched and buzzed like a razor-edge, honing her nerves to screaming point.

Awkwardly she cleared her throat. 'Did your father live here with your mother?'

'Is that not obvious?'

East on one side of the hall, West on the other. A his and hers set of rooms which were unmatched to a degree that might have been farcical had it not been the evidence of a bitterly divisive gulf which had never been bridged. 'I gather nobody compromised in that relationship?'

'My mother had no desire to go what she called "native".'

Bethany winced visibly.

'You flinch, but were you any more generous on our wedding day?' Razul condemned.

She paled and then swung her head up again with pride. 'You didn't give me enough time to adjust…you *have* to know that!'

His lion-gold gaze shimmered. 'What I know is that that half-hour waiting in the desert was the longest thirty minutes of my life,' he admitted in a growling undertone. 'Having undergone that, I was determined that we would marry without further delay.'

'Because I tried to run away…or because I seem to have this problem with you when it comes to making up my mind?' She worried ruefully at her lower lip, her wide green eyes unguarded and vulnerable as she stared back at him. 'The first four days I was here I lurched from one shock to the next, barely knowing *what* I was thinking or feeling. Everything happened so fast; I couldn't control it and I've never been in a situation like that before. It was unbelievably unnerving...'

'But not giving you time worked for me,' Razul responded without apology.

Yes, with hindsight she could see that it had. He had kept her on the run, emotionally and physically. He had battered down her defences and allowed her no breathing space and that constant pressure had been more than she could withstand.

'It would not have worked for me in England,' he continued with cool emphasis. 'There you would have closed doors in my face, taken the telephone off the hook, run away somewhere where I couldn't find you. And even here, now as my wife, you place outrageous barriers between us—'

'But I'm not your real wife, Razul!' Bethany reminded him, stabbed by an inescapable surge of bitterness. 'I'm only here on a temporary basis. You seem to forget that.'

'How *could* I forget it when you hold that belief between us like a drawn sword?' Razul demanded with a blinding flash of seething condemnation.

'What did you expect?' she retorted painfully.

Golden eyes flared over her in a shockingly sudden storm of dark fury. 'You play dangerous games in the name of pride,' he condemned. 'Allow me to make certain facts clear. We will not meet again after you leave. Our time will be over and there can be—indeed, there *will* be—no turning back for I will be married again within months. That was the promise I made to my father. I also gave my word that I would not contact you again, although I now see no room even for temptation on that count...your cold heart does not tempt, it repels!'

Caught unprepared, Bethany was stunned by the pain that his words inflicted on her. Every scrap of colour drained from her face. She swallowed convulsively, couldn't even suck air into her lungs, she was so devastated by what he'd flung at her. Her *cold* heart…she would have given ten years of her life to possess such a gift at this moment, to have the enviable power to detach herself from her pain.

But anger came to her rescue as nothing else could have done. Bringing her to Datar had been an act of unsurpassed cruelty and she blamed Razul absolutely for the torment that she was suffering now. It would have been better by far had she never known what they could have together. No, she *didn't* believe that old chestnut about it being better to have loved and lost than never to have loved at all!

She threw her fiery head back and fixed glittering green eyes on him, bitterness consuming her like a fire raging out of control. 'Do tell me what sort of second wife you are looking forward to receiving…' she invited with shrewish sweetness.

Razul froze in shock, his golden eyes veiling to darkness. 'That I will not discuss with you—'

'Why not? Heaven knows, you have been so disarmingly frank about everything else! So go on, *tell* me. I really would like to know!'

A silence of savage intensity now thundered between them, vibrating with her challenge and his wrathful incredulity.

'She will be a very good wife by my father's standards,' Razul gritted rawly, breaking that terrible silence with a suddenness that shook her. 'If I am ill-bred enough to raise my voice, she will beg to know how she has offended me. She will not answer me back. She will greet my every opinion with admiration and agreement. She will never come to my bed without invitation. She will spend her days dressing up in Western fashions, watching television, shopping and gossiping with her friends. I see her now,' he breathed with merciless bite. 'Beautiful, indolent by nature and not very well educated, but she will give me children.' A slight tremor fractured that final phrase.

Bethany had closed her eyes and turned away. She was devastated, her bitter fury quelled by shocked disbelief at the fact that he had actually answered her, called her sarcastic bluff with a candour that was savage. In a daze she stood there, heard him leave the room. The kitten scrabbled at her feet playfully, and as her knees gave she sank clumsily down on the beautiful rug and watched the tiny creature frolic innocently around her without really seeing its antics.

The deep-freeze effect of shock slowly receded, and her mind began to work again. She'd heard Razul describing his second wife not with pleasure...*no*, not with pleasure but with barely concealed revulsion. He did not want a not very well-educated wife, content to gossip and shop and watch TV and treat him like a god who could do no wrong. That might be his father's standard of a good wife but it was not Razul's. *That*, she realised dazedly, had not been his dream.

Tears of released stress suddenly stung her aching eyes. She had wilfully misunderstood what Razul had been telling her from the beginning. He had told her that he had no freedom of choice and she hadn't listened. He had told her that his father did not want him to marry her and she hadn't listened properly to that either.

In King Azmir's eyes she was not an acceptable wife for his only son and nothing was likely to change that fact. The old boy might be a fond and over-protective father but the only way Razul had been able to win his consent to bringing Bethany here had been by promising that it would only be a temporary alliance. It had been one last chance for them to be together before he did his filial and princely duty by marrying some brainless bimbo and settling down to produce children.

Not *his* choice; not *his* dream. How could she have been blind enough to believe that Razul would go to such extraordinary lengths merely to get her into bed? She remembered his panic when he'd realised that she was ill, and his distress at the hospital, and the tears fell faster than ever. Maybe it wasn't quite love but Razul really did care about her and he had never tried to hide the fact even when she was being more of a nightmare than a dream.

She covered her face with splayed fingers and sobbed with noisy helplessness as she thought of that ring lying at the foot of the pool. He had been trying to show that he respected her, that even if the marriage couldn't last it didn't mean that it had to be a mockery.

His father was a horrible, mean old man, rotten with prejudice and as cruel as some Dark Age medieval tyrant, she thought wretchedly. Just because *he* had made a mistake and had been humiliated and hurt by Razul's mother, he had decided that Bethany was unacceptable, unsuitable and not even worthy of a meeting or a chance to prove that she could be the right wife for his son. It was just as well that he was suffering from ill-health. At that moment Bethany decided that, if she could get close to the old misery guts, the sheer shock of hearing her opinion of him would finish him off altogether!

As she rooted around blindly for a hanky one was planted helpfully into her hand. With a start she opened her reddened eyes and focused strickenly on Razul as he crouched down on the carpet beside her. 'Go a-away!' she sobbed, cursing the sneaky silence of his approach.

'I have upset you.'

Her teeth gritted as another sob shuddered through her. 'Why sh-should you think that?'

'I have never seen you cry before.'

'What did you expect after saying what you did?' she flared at him on the back of another howl.

'You drove me to it,' he grated unevenly.

'That's right…b-blame me!'

He pulled her into his arms and she went rigid. But

the achingly familiar scent of him washed over her and her resistance broke with dismaying abruptness. She buried her face against his shoulder and struggled for breath.

'I should not criticise you for being the woman you are,' Razul whispered, not quite steadily. 'For if you were not the woman you are I would not want you.'

She sniffed. 'That's perverse.'

'Then I am perverse...what does it mean?'

She very nearly laughed. 'Stubborn, contrary.'

'We are both these things.'

'Quick-tempered, aggressive?'

'These too.'

This time she did let an involuntary gurgle of laughter escape her. 'A match made in hell?'

'No...never that, *aziz*. Although I cannot face the end of the summer, I will hold these weeks with you in my heart for ever.'

Any urge to laugh was instantly banished. Bethany horrified herself by bursting into floods of tears again. She had never been more miserable in her life. He smoothed her hair back from her brow and muttered soothing, incomprehensible things in Arabic as if he were trying to calm a distressed child, and she had the lowering feeling that he was totally at a loss as to what to say or do. For what was there to say? she thought tragically. Like it or not, the end of the summer would come.

'You are exhausting yourself,' he murmured, but she had the oddest suspicion that he was actually quite cheerful about the fact, which was, of course, a quite ridiculous idea in the circumstances and one more symptom of her seemingly ingrained need to find fault with him, she scolded herself fiercely.

'I want my ring back,' she mumbled.

'You did not want it before.'

'I'm not crawling for it either!' she asserted jerkily into his shoulder.

'I have never wanted you to crawl,' Razul sighed. 'Only to give us this chance.'

Her throat threatened to close over again. Dear heaven, why did he have to keep on saying distressing things like that? If she cried any more she would be suffering from dehydration! She drew in a deep breath to calm herself. 'I will.'

'You will have changed your mind again by tomorrow—'

'No, I won't...I *promise*!' she told him frantically, clutching at him with feverish hands while the kitten settled into the folds of her dress and went to sleep, having given up on the hope of receiving any attention from either of them.

'But what has brought about this change in you?' he demanded.

'The thought of you with another woman...you idiot!' Bethany sobbed, wanting to kick him just as much as she wanted to cling to him. Did he need everything spelt out?

'You are jealous?'

'Of course I am...do you think I have the feelings of a stone?' she accused in disbelief.

'Occasionally I have thought this,' he admitted gruffly, holding her so tightly that it was an effort for her to breathe, and no use at all for her to go stiff with outraged pride and attempt to peel herself away from him, because he was infinitely stronger than she was.

She subsided again, too exhausted by her emotional breakdown to continue a struggle against an embrace that she was thoroughly enjoying. She rubbed her cheek against his shoulder, comforted by the hard, warm feel of him. A strange sense of peacefulness was creeping over her, along with a bone-deep tiredness. She stifled a yawn.

'Am I allowed to carry you to bed?'

'Absolutely.'

He smiled down at her, and even on the edge of sleep she felt her drowsy pulses speed up and her heart accelerate. 'Unfortunately I am dining with my father tonight.'

She tried not to let her facial muscles freeze but it was hard. Although very possibly she did not have the right to censure King Azmir's decision. Her tempestuous emotions had drained away, leaving room for a little intelligent reflection. Maybe she was a genuinely unacceptable wife for Razul. Razul was half-French. He was not wholly of Arab blood. It was very possible that a British wife and the son who might eventually be born of such a union would not be acceptable to the people of Datar as the family of a future ruler. It was a thoroughly depressing suspicion but a realistic one.

Exhausted as she was, it was nonetheless hard for her to get to sleep. She was thinking helplessly of the empty, narrow life she would return to in England. The idea stirring at the back of her mind was madness, sheer madness, she told herself...or was it? She had to have *something* if she had to face that future without Razul, and lots of women managed to raise a child alone. But to deliberately bring a child into the world without a father... But then what else would she ever have of Razul? she asked herself fiercely.

She wanted his child, *his* baby. Was that so wrong? He would never know. What he didn't know couldn't hurt him. Two months...two months in which to become pregnant by a male scrupulously guarding against the possibility. It was a tall order but not an insuperable challenge, she decided, pitting her wits against the problem and coming up with one or two possibilities which made her smile to herself as she finally drifted off to sleep.

CHAPTER TEN

WHEN Razul saw Bethany walking across the stableyard towards him, his brilliant smile hit her like a shot of adrenalin in her veins. Crawling out of bed in darkness suddenly felt worthwhile. He caught her hand in his and introduced her to the inmate of every stable on the block before finally drawing her over to a doe-eyed mare whom Bethany cheerfully petted.

'You like horses,' he murmured in a tone of discovery.

'Very much, but I've only ridden a few times in recent years,' she confided. 'So I'll be a little rusty.'

'Did you have a pony as a child?'

It was an unlucky question. Her beautiful face shadowed and stiffened. 'Once…briefly. She was a real little beauty too. I had one wonderful season on her with the pony club.'

'I sense that I have roused an unhappy memory. Did an accident take her from you?'

Her mouth compressed and she shrugged. 'No…my father took her from me. He said he was only loaning her out to a very good friend for a week or two but I never saw her again.'

'He sold her?' Razul frowned with immediate sympathy. 'Perhaps the expense had become too much?' he suggested.

Bethany uttered a wry laugh and swung herself up agilely into the saddle, wishing very much that she had kept her mouth shut. 'No, it wasn't that. The very good friend was an actress he was chasing at the time. She had a little girl too. He wanted to impress her with an

158

extravagant gift, and why go the expense of buying another pony when he could take mine?'

Razul surveyed her in clear disbelief. 'You are not serious?'

'Look, he bought the pony in the first place. Can we drop this subject?' she said tautly.

'No, we cannot. Could your mother not prevent him from such an act?'

She expelled her breath in a charged hiss. 'My mother has never tried to prevent my father from doing anything in her life...and if it was unpleasant she just ignored it. At the time she pointed out that it was his pony, not mine.'

Before he could press her further Bethany moved off, directing the glossy little mare at the gates that led out of the stableyard. Beyond the walls she reined in, her troubled thoughts put to flight by the view before her. The sun was a great globe of rising fire, sending shimmering ribbons of glorious colour trailing across the dawn skies. Fingers of light fell on the sands, turning them peach and scarlet and gold, dancing off stark outcrops of rock and casting mysterious shadows. The desert landscape, so brutally drained by the merciless heat by day, had an eerie and glorious beauty at sunrise.

'You were right,' she marvelled as Razul drew level with her. 'It looks fantastic at this hour.'

'I could show you beauty here at any hour,' he asserted with immense pride and confidence.

His world, his heritage, and he was so much a part of it—as untamed as a land at the mercy of harsh elements that could not be controlled. She searched his hard profile with softened eyes and an aching understanding. 'You didn't like the English climate much, did you?'

'It was a change...but it was very cold. Come on,' he urged.

But she took her time in following him on that gorgeous Arab thoroughbred he rode. The sleek stallion raced across the sand, rider and horse enviably fluid and at ease. She liked watching him and smiled, feeling like a burden when he came back to her. He looked guilty too. 'I forgot that you had not ridden for a while.'

And he wouldn't take off again on his own, no matter how often she told him that she was perfectly happy to pad along at her own unexciting speed until she found her confidence again. Eventually she stopped telling him, for she could hardly help noticing that he was in a wonderfully good mood, that quick, spontaneous smile breaking out with quite devastating frequency. She couldn't take her eyes off him. He cast a spell over her and no longer did she feel threatened by that. Tomorrow, next month, indeed the end of the summer, suddenly seemed a lifetime away. One day at a time, she promised herself.

'We will breakfast outside and I will make coffee for you,' Razul announced on their arrival back at the palace.

'The proper way?'

He grinned. 'The *only* way.'

Taking time out from the quick shower that she had promised herself, she headed down to the old harem quarters, stripped down to her bra and briefs on the edge of that ancient marble pool and climbed in.

'Great minds...'

She spun round and her cheeks flamed pink as she saw Razul smiling down at her from the side of the pool. Tugging off his gleaming riding boots, he went in still clothed. 'Have you seen it?'

'No joy yet.'

'It's a big pool,' he sighed ruefully.

She started to giggle, and once she started it was very difficult to stop.

'I could buy another ring,' he suggested hopefully as he waded through the water.

'I want that one,' she insisted, sitting down on the

steps and hugging her aching ribs. 'Another one wouldn't be the same.'

'Well, then, don't sit there being lazy!' Razul shot at her in exasperation. 'Help!'

So she searched too, but it was Razul who literally struck gold with a relief that was highly entertaining. He snatched it up, grabbed her hand and threaded it on her finger with a lack of romantic ceremony which nearly sent her off into whoops again. He looked down into her laughing face and his stunning eyes flared golden in the sunlight, an expression of such intense hunger stamping his strong features that she blinked up at him in sudden stasis.

'You are so very beautiful...and so very undressed,' he murmured thickly.

As the sweep of his appreciative appraisal took in the flimsy bra and briefs which were all that interrupted his view of her gleaming body, only then did she actually recall that she was half-naked. Her cheeks warmed at the awareness but she made no move to cover herself. Indeed there was a wicked delight, she discovered, in standing there in the glow of his very masculine admiration.

He lowered his tousled dark head and pressed his mouth against the corner of hers, teasing, playing. The front snap of her bra gave beneath his deft fingers and her breath caught. In sensual shock she watched her breasts spring free, wantonly bare and full, her pink nipples pouting into taut buds even before he raised a hand to touch her.

'Don't you dare stop...' she whispered shakily.

He laughed softly, found her mouth and tasted her as if they had been apart for a century and he could not believe the joy of finding her again. Her knees wobbled beneath the onslaught. She strained forward, the throbbing tips of her swelling breasts rubbing with delicious friction against the wet roughness of his polo shirt, and he caught her to him with suddenly impatient hands, pinning her to him as he strode up the steps out of the water and swiftly to her bedroom.

The tip of his tongue flicked against the roof of her mouth, twinned hotly with her own in a highly erotic assault that made her senses swim. She dug her hands into his thick hair and kissed him back wildly, all the pent-up passion of her fiery temperament bent on entrapment.

It was like setting a torch to a bale of hay. With a savage groan he lifted her high against him and curved her thighs round his lean hips. Electrified by that primitive response, she did it again. He reacted with quite devastating enthusiasm.

He brought her down on the edge of the bed and ripped off his polo shirt.

She rested back breathlessly on her elbows, excitement snaking through her in a shameless surge, an even greater excitement than that which she had experienced on their wedding night for it was infinitely less one-sided. This time there was no fear of the unknown and no terror of her own responses, only an aching, tender need for his pleasure to match hers. She wanted to tell him how much she loved him without saying it out loud.

So she rammed back her own shyness and curved forward to unsnap the waistband of the skin-tight riding breeches he still wore. The palm of her hand rested against the hard, swollen bulge of his manhood as she struggled with the zip in sudden embarrassment over her own lack of expertise.

'I will die of frustration,' he swore, with a sound between an agonised groan and reluctant laughter, and then his patience gave and he brushed aside her inept fingers, dealing with the problem in one second flat.

She flung herself back on the bed like a willing sacrifice, every tiny muscle taut with helpless anticipation. Razul surveyed her with slightly dazed eyes, as if he was not quite sure that this was really happening to him, but he dispensed with the shrunk-fit breeches with remarkable speed and fervour, hauled her back to him and kissed her breathless.

He captured an urgently sensitive nipple in his mouth and her whole body jerked, a stifled gasp dragged from her as an arrow of clawing heat flamed through her, making her hips rise and her thighs tremble. Her own response was shatteringly intense. Her restive hands skimmed in torturous circles over the smooth skin of his back and then sank into his hair tightly as her temperature rocketed.

A hot fever of excitement seized her as he wrenched off her briefs. Never in her entire existence had she dreamt of wanting anything as desperately as she now wanted him. Her heart was slamming against her ribcage, the blood pulsating wildly through her veins. As he caressed an engorged pink bud with the flick of his tongue and the teasing graze of his sharp teeth, he found the most sensitive spot of all with skilful fingers and made her jerk and quiver and moan, thrown helplessly out of control, her teeth clenched, her throat extended as the hot wire of sexual tension tightened and tightened until she was convinced that she was in mortal torment.

'Now…now!' she pleaded.

'I must—'

Her glazed green eyes collided with smouldering golden ones; she felt him begin to pull away and then she remembered—remembered what he must not be allowed to do. 'No need…it's safe,' she gasped unevenly, hanging onto him with both hands in case he didn't get the message.

'Safe?' he groaned uncertainly.

'Absolutely…' Hoping to take his mind off the idea altogether, she lifted herself up to him and found his gorgeous mouth again for herself, and so enjoyed that rediscovery that she quite forgot why she had deviously embarked on it.

The fierce heat of him burned her as he spread her thighs. She was at a pitch of excitement beyond bearing and, at that first driving thrust, cried out in ecstasy, her eyes closing, her head falling back. Then he was moving on her and in her, answering a need as old as time with the hard, primal force of his sexual possession.

Her response was mindless, drugging in its completeness. There was nothing but him and the wildly torturous drive for satisfaction, and when one final electrifying spasm of delight pushed her over the edge she gasped his name and went spinning off into hot, quivering ecstasy. He shuddered violently over her and climaxed with a hoarse shout of pleasure.

They subsided in a damp tangle of limbs. She was in heaven, didn't ever want to descend to earth again. A tidal wave of love and tenderness flooded her, making her eyes sting. She curved her head into his strong brown throat and a long sigh escaped her. 'I have never felt so happy,' she whispered dazedly because it really did feel so strange.

'Nor I.' He released her from his weight and rolled over, pulling her with him so that she lay sprawled on top of him. '*Safe*?' he queried lazily.

Bethany tensed, not having been prepared for so immediate an enquiry.

But Razul was not tense. Indeed he was totally relaxed. He skimmed a teasing forefinger along her sensitive jawbone. 'I feel I should warn you that what I suspect you regard as safe is not a remarkably reliable method of birth control.'

'I'm on the Pill,' she lied.

'The contraceptive pill?' he questioned incredulously, and closed his hands on her forearms to tip her up so that he could look at her. 'But why would you be taking such a precaution?'

'S-skin problems,' she stammered, flushing scarlet.

'Your skin is flawless.'

'I got a rash,' she said defiantly.

'You should not take such medication for only a rash.'

'What is this…the third degree?'

'I think you should consult Laila…I will mention—'

'Don't you *dare*!' Bethany cut in, aghast. 'Is nothing sacred?'

'Your health is.' He dealt her a wry look of reproof.

Her colour fluctuated wildly. All of a sudden she felt horribly guilty for setting out to deceive him. She dropped her head again. He thrust an arrogant hand into her tumbling hair and tilted her reddened mouth up, his breath fanning her cheek as he caressed her lips tenderly with his. 'You are a very precious woman,' he told her gently. 'I would protect you with my life. Do not deny me the pleasure of looking after you.'

Nobody had ever wanted to look after Bethany before. Nobody had ever been too bothered about what might happen to her. Razul might as well have put a hand on her heart and squeezed it. She was unbearably touched and unbearably saddened too. To meet with such tender caring and know that she would lose it again tortured her, but she closed out that awareness with all the strength that was the backbone of her character. One day at a time, she reminded herself fiercely.

'It troubles me that you have had no communication with your parents since our marriage,' Razul remarked wryly.

A finger of tension prodded Bethany's lazily reclined body. Her brows pleating, she looked out over the desert from the vantage point of their cliff-top eyrie. With canvas walls on three sides, the structure was a highly realistic replica of a traditional Bedouin tent, and it was permanently sited on the edge of the palace gardens. Rich carpets, fabulous cushions and a coffee hearth distinguished its cool interior. Over the past weeks she had learnt to appreciate how very much the desert was still home to Razul. This was where he came to relax towards the end of a long day and recoup his energies, disdaining all the many magnificent rooms in the palace.

Conscious that he was patiently awaiting a response, Bethany shrugged uneasily. 'We're not close.'

'That is something of an understatement,' Razul remarked after a sizeable pause, and passed her a tiny cup of coffee. 'For an Arab, the family is everything. It is the very foundation of our culture and such strong loyalties impose often painful decisions and duties.'

Her face shadowed. Was their lack of a future the most painful duty he had ever faced or did she deceive herself? Since that day she had cried in his arms Razul had not made any reference to the subject of their eventual parting. Not once had he again revealed the smallest hint of tension or concern on that point.

The past three weeks had been the happiest weeks of Bethany's life, yet to maintain that glorious contentment she had had to suppress rigorously every thought of what tomorrow might bring. Was Razul following the same unspoken rule or was it simply that he had already reached a stage where he could think of her leaving without emotion? Was indeed their whole relationship just some pleasant little fling which he could calmly accept as having an inevitable end?

'Bethany?' he prompted.

'Oh, my family.' She grasped his meaning abstractedly, her fingers tightening tautly round the cup as she struggled to repress her fears. 'Well, I have a slight relationship with my mother and a non-existent relationship with my father, and that really doesn't bother either of them.'

'I find that hard to believe.'

She gave him a rueful smile. 'I suppose you do. Let

me explain. My mother believes that having me almost wrecked her marriage—'

'But why?'

'My father's first infidelity coincided with my birth. If you knew him you would understand why. He has to be the centre of attention, and naturally a new baby interfered with that need. But, looking at his track record over the years, it's obvious to me that he would have been unfaithful anyway.'

'He was persistently unfaithful?' Razul studied her face with a frown.

'He was forever walking out for some other woman.' Bethany shrugged again. 'And then he would roll home again and Mum would greet him with open arms. As I got older and understood what was going on I hated him for the way he treated her. It took me a long while to appreciate that, in accepting his behaviour, Mum was and *is* a willing victim. He's a very attractive man... physically,' she adjusted grimly. 'But he just uses her. She's his port in every storm.'

'Do you still hate him?'

'If I think about him at all, I guess I'm ashamed of him,' she admitted. 'He's got nothing but that surface charm to recommend him.'

'I had no idea that you had endured such a childhood,' Razul sighed.

'It wasn't that bad,' she said ruefully. 'It's just that I was never very important to either to them. My father isn't interested in children. If I'd been an absolutely adoring daughter like his absolutely adoring wife, maybe it would have been different, but, you see, I couldn't hide the way I felt about him...I couldn't pander to his ego as my mother did and I made him uncomfortable and resentful. He doesn't like me. Frankly, when I left home for university it was a relief all round.'

'I am sorry that I questioned your lack of contact with your parents. I did not understand the circumstances. But

I wish I had known these things sooner. I would have better understood your resistance to me.'

'I wish I still had some of that resistance.' She was sinking helplessly into the depths of those dark, intense eyes which were trained on her.

'I do not wish it,' he responded with very masculine amusement, reaching forward fluidly to deprive her of her cup. 'This is how it should be between lovers.'

'Lovers,' she repeated inwardly, stifling an odd little stab of pain. Funny how Razul never, ever referred to her now as his wife or to himself as her husband, or, indeed, in any way to the fact that they were actually married. Funny how those surely deliberate omissions could now fill her with a sense of rejection and deep insecurity and, no matter how hard she tried, an ever present awareness that she was living on borrowed time.

He leant over her and her heartbeat thundered so wildly that she was convinced he would be able to hear it. Brilliant golden eyes flamed over her with primitive satisfaction, and she trembled, feeling the spreading languor of desire constrict her breathing and flush her skin. The level of awareness between them now was so intense that he only had to look at her or she at him and the heat surged, closing out everything else.

'Allah has truly blessed us with passion.'

A tide of hotter colour embellished her cheeks; her guilty conscience stirred as she shamefacedly recalled a certain three days just over a fortnight ago when they had not got out of bed at all except to eat, and he had no doubt come to the conclusion that he had been blessed by an absolutely insatiably passionate woman. And admittedly he did make her feel insatiable, but she had the sinking, horrible suspicion that Razul would be appalled if he were ever to find out that she had had a rather more scientific purpose for ensuring that he stayed in that bed those particular days, and that even now she was anxiously waiting to find out whether or not all that passion had metaphorically borne fruit.

'You are very quiet.' He skimmed a blunt forefinger along the ripe curve of her lower lip. 'What do you think of?'

Her guilty conscience attacked her, releasing a sudden, dismaying cloud of uncertainty. Had she made a very selfish decision in trying to become pregnant? If Razul ever found out he would totally despise her for it. Was it fair to bring a child into the world without a father and without a father's knowledge simply to give herself some comfort? It seemed to her now that it was anything but fair, and what would she tell that child when it grew old enough to ask awkward questions? That she had deprived him or her of his birthright and heritage?

'What is wrong *aziz*?' Razul frowned down at her.

He called her 'beloved'. Ever since she had discovered from a smiling Zulema what that particular word meant she had hugged it jealously to herself and tried not to think that Razul might use it as casually as some men used such endearments in English. She looked up at him with swimming eyes, studied that hard-boned, sun-bronzed face which was so terrifyingly dear to her, and her awareness of her own deception bit hard. He had been so honest with her from the beginning.

'Nothing—'

'That was not nothing which I saw in your eyes,' he incised. 'You are becoming homesick?' His usually level drawl fractured on the last word.

Home? She didn't have a home, she decided wretchedly. She had a cat in a cattery and three bonsai trees being lovingly looked after by her neighbour. Nowhere was ever going to feel like home again without Razul. 'No.'

'I think you are not telling the truth—'

She read the fierce tension stamped into his lean features and it frightened her. She could not bear to talk about losing him, had become an utter coward where that subject was concerned. It was as if talking about it would somehow bring the time closer and kill the happiness they did have. Now reacting to the sudden turmoil of her emotions, she reached up to him, smoothing unsteady fingers across his high cheek-bones and pressing her lips passionately, desperately to his with the tears still damp and stinging on her cheeks.

For a paralysing moment Razul was tense and savagely unresponsive, and then, with a hungry groan, he caught her to him with strong hands and ravished her soft mouth with hot, hard insistence, and it was a relief when she felt that wild, wanton need fill her with a drowning sweetness that locked out her ability to think.

But there had been something disturbingly different in their lovemaking, she thought dimly in the aftermath. Certainly her own heightened emotions had lent a painful and yet immensely greater depth to her response, and just as she was striving to work out exactly what had been different she was shocked back into full awareness by what happened next. Razul literally thrust her away from him, sprang up and began to dress.

The tension in the air was so thick that it brought her out in a cold sweat. The silence was unbelievably oppressive. Sitting up, Bethany drew her discarded dress against her, suddenly agonisingly unsure of herself. 'Razul?'

'This is how you would say goodbye to me. You still think of the end of the summer, do you not?' he demanded fiercely.

Bewilderment gripped her as she focused on the muscles rippling on his smooth brown back as he tugged on his shirt. 'What are you trying to say?' she whispered.

He swung round, his bronzed features a frozen mask but tension emanating from every aggressively poised line of his lean, powerful body. 'You still think of leaving...I see it in your eyes!' he grated.

'How can I help thinking about it?' Bethany was plunged into a vortex of all the pain that she had struggled to hold off for weeks and she lowered her head to conceal her anguish.

'I can no longer live with this hangman's rope swinging above my head. It is intolerable. You are like a curse upon me!' Razul bit out with an embittered savagery that cut her to the bone. 'But I will no longer endure this curse. I am leaving you.'

She was in so much shock that she could barely hear him. A *curse*? She was a curse? He was *leaving* her? But it's not time yet, she wanted to scream at him in torment, and she wasn't ready yet, not prepared, not able yet to face that severance. 'You are leaving me?'

'I should have thrown you onto that helicopter!' Razul seethed back at her. 'It would have been wiser to end it then than now.'

'And now you're running home to Daddy,' Bethany mumbled thickly, helplessly.

An expression of such naked and incredulous outrage flashed across his strong, dark features that she was transfixed. 'You are not *fit* to be my wife,' he murmured with chilling emphasis, his self-discipline asserting itself with an immediacy that cruelly mocked her own loss of control.

And then he was gone, and she was left sitting there staring into space, sick with pain and completely at the mercy of it.

CHAPTER ELEVEN

BETHANY lurched nauseously out of bed like a drunk and only just managed to make it to the bathroom in time. After she had finished being horribly ill she sank down in a heap on the floor and sobbed her heart out.

Razul had been gone a week—the worst week of her life—and she didn't know what she was supposed to do next. She didn't want to go home. She didn't want to stay. Most of the time she just wanted to die. In any case how could she even *get* home without that visa signed in triplicate which he had mentioned? She couldn't even leave Datar without his permission. Her teeth ground together at that humiliating awareness.

For seven utterly miserable days she had lurched between hating him and loving him, but it was extraordinarily hard to hate someone whom you missed more with every passing hour.

And she was pregnant. She had got her wish and right now there was a lot of repetition of that old adage about being careful about what you wished for washing around in her mind. Her breasts ached and her stomach heaved every morning, and somehow there was no joy in the discovery that she was expecting the baby of a male who had rejected her on the cruellest, most inexcusable terms. She had thought that she *knew* Razul and in the space of minutes had been forced to face the fact that she did not know him at all!

He had been wildly infatuated with her but now that had burnt out. Once her mystery and challenge had gone, the pleasant little fling had run its course. After all that specious talk about her being precious and *beloved* he

172

had rejected her and gone home to that hateful, vicious, nasty old man, and she now saw very clearly the resemblance between Razul and his hateful father. She had let herself be used and this was her reward and it served her right, didn't it? But, unsurprisingly, lashing that hard reality home to herself only made her feel more wretched than ever.

It was a couple of hours later that Zulema came to tell her that the Princess Laila was waiting for her downstairs. 'Tell her I'm not well,' Bethany instructed, and then groaned, recalling that Razul's sister was a doctor. 'No, tell her I'm very sorry but I don't want to see anyone right now.'

Zulema's dismay was unhidden. 'This will cause very grave offence, my lady.'

Her mistress reddened, recalling Laila's kindness to her while she had been in hospital. It wasn't Laila's fault that her brother was a creep of the lowest denomination or that Bethany was still incomprehensibly and insanely attached to that same creep. In fact, maybe she could mention that visa problem to Laila and employ her as a go-between.

Laila stood up as soon as she entered the room. 'You will be wondering why I am here.'

'Yes.'

'You look unhappy.' Laila surveyed her pallor and shadowed eyes with grim satisfaction.

'All I want now is to go home,' Bethany stated tightly.

'But if you are pregnant you cannot possibly go home,' Laila said very drily.

The assurance with which the older woman made that statement shattered Bethany. She found herself staring back at Laila in wide-eyed dismay. How on earth could she know or even suspect such a secret?

Razul's sister gave a humourless laugh. 'Bethany…you cannot walk into a chemist in the centre of Al Kabibi and purchase a pregnancy test and expect it to remain a secret. Naturally you were recognised, naturally such an interesting purchase was eagerly noted and discussed—'

'Discussed?' Bethany repeated strickenly.

'Our family may not suffer from the embarrassing intrusion of television crews and tabloid reporters in Datar but then our people have no need of such devices to know what we do. This is a small country and Datari society rejoices in a most effective form of the bush telegraph. The chemist will have been on the phone to his wife as soon as the door shut behind you, and she will have phoned all her friends while he was phoning his friends to share this exciting titbit, and within days everybody who is anybody hears of your interesting purchase. Had you wanted to maintain secrecy, you should have called me.'

Bethany's legs wouldn't hold her up any more. Wordlessly, clumsily, she sank down on the chair behind her.

'I gather the test proved positive.' Laila sighed. 'Razul must be told.'

'*No!*' she gasped in horror.

'Well, if you do not tell him I will,' Laila informed her with flat impatience. 'It is none of my business that you have driven my brother from you. I do not like you for it but the fact that you may be carrying the next heir to the throne of our country overrides all other considerations, and if you do not accept that fact you are indeed a very foolish woman!'

Bethany was paper-pale and furious. 'I did not drive your brother anywhere! He left *me!*'

Laila looked angrily contemptuous. 'I am aware that *you* want to leave him. He told me that—'

'He was lying!'

'My brother does not tell lies—'

'But then you don't know the promise he made to your father, do you?' Bethany slung back with abrasive bitterness as she rose to her feet again.

'I do know that he promised that if the marriage didn't work out he would remarry without argument or fuss.'

'But you don't know that our marriage wasn't a real marriage, do you?'

'What on earth are you talking about?' Laila enquired impatiently. 'Did not my brother wait two years to win my father's permission to marry you?'

'But only temporarily, because that's all your father would agree to...and what does that matter anyway now?' Bethany demanded unsteadily. 'Razul has walked out on me—'

'Temporarily? What nonsense are you talking? Razul loves you. *Everyone* in Datar knows how much Razul loves you!' Laila asserted with complete exasperation. 'In the end everyone also supported his right to choose his own bride, and you were a very popular choice because you are from the West. Many find this glamorous and also encouraging proof of Datar's new liberal image.

'It is true that my deeply pessimistic father was stubbornly set against such a marriage, but only because he was afraid Razul would be hurt as he was hurt...that you would find our culture impossible to adapt to and that the marriage would end in divorce as his did.'

Bethany licked her wobbling lower lip, frozen to the carpet by shock. 'Razul doesn't love me—'

'Of course he blasted well loves you, you stupid woman!' Laila shot at her with raw impatience. 'And now he's undergoing the tortures of the damned listening to my father miserably bemoan the fact that he ever agreed to him marrying you! What the hell do you think it is like for Razul right now? His romantic, fairy-tale marriage has gone down the tubes so fast he feels a complete failure, and he feels he's let the whole family down by marrying you, *and* he's got my father muttering "I told you so" at every available opportunity...so don't you dare talk about— leaving him!'

A strangled sob punctuated Laila's last words. She

turned away, visibly fighting to conceal her distress. Bethany was reeling with shock. Was it possible that she had somehow misunderstood Razul about the temporary nature of their marriage? She so badly wanted to believe what she was hearing that she was dizzy.

'I am sorry to have called you stupid...' Laila said stiltedly, having firmly reinstated her usual self-command. 'But I love my brother very much and I cannot bear to see him in such pain.'

'I love him too,' Bethany managed in a wobbly voice. What had he said? Something about being unable to live with this rope hanging over his head? But he had always behaved as though he didn't expect her to stay...hadn't he? But then that didn't necessarily mean that he didn't *want* her to stay, did it? It might only suggest that he was very insecure about her feelings for him...

'Then what the heck is going on between the two of you?' Laila demanded blankly. 'I don't understand.'

Ten minutes later Bethany was rigidly seated in Laila's chauffeur-driven Mercedes. 'If your brother shoots me down in flames,' she warned shakily, 'you do understand that it will be my turn to call *you* a very stupid, foolish woman?'

Laila laughed with amusement. 'That is an opportunity you will be denied.'

Bethany wished she had that confidence. Could Razul have left her because he believed *she* was planning to leave *him*? That pride—that incredible pride of his, she recalled painfully as her fingers knotted tightly together on her lap.

'Ah, my father's secretary,' Laila announced, waving an imperious hand in the echoing foyer of the old palace as Mustapha trod towards them looking most reluctant to respond to that gesture. He avoided looking at Bethany altogether.

'Mustapha will take you to my brother,' Laila informed her.

Mustapha turned pale, his jaw-line stiffening. 'I regret to say—'

Laila murmured something low-pitched and brief in Arabic. Whatever it was, it had an extraordinary effect on Mustapha. His compressed mouth fell wide, and he flushed and shifted from one foot to the other in clear perturbation.

'Yes, indeed,' Laila sighed. 'If I were you, I would endeavour to circumvent such instructions. I would practise true diplomacy.'

It suddenly sank in on Bethany that Razul had already given instructions that if his wife should show up she was to be shown the door again. She began turning on her heel, white with furious humiliation, but Laila caught her arm and hissed in a fierce undertone, 'Do not be foolish, Bethany. My father is furious with you. This is his command. As far as he is concerned you have ditched his beloved son and a whipping three times a day would be too good for you!'

With a smile of reluctant amusement Mustapha inclined his head to Bethany and politely asked her to follow him. But what possible point was there in even approaching Razul if King Azmir was still so bitterly hostile to her? Her heart had sunk like a stone.

In silence Mustapha escorted her deep into the bowels of the palace. He halted outside a courtyard, ducked his head as if to check that it was unoccupied, and murmured, 'Please wait here, my lady. I believe Prince Razul is with his father.'

The courtyard contained a very elaborate and large conservatory. Unable to stay still, Bethany wandered into it and was astonished to feel the temperature-controlled cool of the interior, and even more astonished to lay eyes on the glorious collection of bonsai trees displayed on a series of ornamental plinths within. She focused first on a miniature forest of pine trees, and then, reached out a reverent hand towards an ancient-looking and gnarled Acer barely thirty inches tall, quite dumbstruck with admiration.

'Do not touch!' a harsh voice rapped out at her.

Bethany very nearly leapt out of her skin. She spun around and only then noticed the elderly man seated in a chair by a bench in the far corner. Clad in an old apron, with a pair of scissors clenched in one hand, he almost stared her out of countenance, so visibly infuriated was he by the interruption.

'I'm sorry. I should have known better but it looked so beautiful...you see, I have some at home. They're my hobby.'

The fierce dark eyes narrowed fulminatingly. 'Bonsai trees?'

'Yes. I'm so sorry I interrupted you. Please excuse me.' A rather ghastly suspicion was beginning to cross Bethany's mind. Those dark, deep-set eyes, those level brows...

'I do not excuse you.'

The rather ghastly suspicion was decidedly confirmed by that tone of hauteur. Bethany stilled, the colour draining from her cheeks.

'You are the wife of my son,' he pronounced through compressed lips. 'Why do you come here?'

Bethany tried and failed to swallow the constriction in her throat. 'I...I wanted to see Razul—'

'Why should you want this?' King Azmir demanded harshly.

Her eyes burned, her tongue cleaving to the roof of her dry mouth.

'Why?' He repeated the question with grim emphasis.

Bethany hovered, tears of stark pain suddenly welling up in her eyes. 'Because I love him!' she finally bit out, thrusting her chin in the air.

He frowned at her, clearly taken aback by the announcement.

'And I believe I could make him happy...that is if he wants me to,' she adjusted unevenly.

'Then why are you not making him happy?'

'I would rather discuss that with him,' Bethany said stiffly.

Her father-in-law shook his head in exasperation. 'I do not like my son to be upset.'

'If you will excuse me for saying so, your son is very well able to look after himself,' Bethany murmured.

'Not when he marries a woman he cannot persuade to stay with him,' he retorted brusquely.

'I will stay.'

'Then why is he here and not with you?'

'I thought I couldn't stay. I thought that you...wouldn't accept me as his wife,' Bethany stated tautly.

'Do you not think that that is a most peculiar belief to hold when I agreed to the marriage?' he pointed out rather more gently.

'But that's nonetheless what I believed.'

'Is my son's English so poor?'

'In certain moods he is not the soul of clarity,' she muttered tightly.

Her companion studied her for several unbearably long seconds, and then he threw back his head and laughed with rich appreciation. 'Tell me about your trees,' he invited.

In a daze she began to do so and then he moved a silencing hand. She followed the path of his gaze and went rigid when she saw Razul standing in the doorway, his dark features frozen with incredulity.

'Take your wife home, my son, and borrow a dictionary,' his father urged him, with a wry look of amusement.

A tide of dark colour obscured Razul's hard cheek-bones, which were more prominent than they had been a week earlier. His lips parted and then, as he clearly thought better of comment, compressed into a bloodless white line. He inclined his head then strode back out of the conservatory. Hurrying in his wake, Bethany could barely keep up with that long, ferocious stride. They were out of the palace in five minutes flat and she was out of breath.

'A car will convey you home,' Razul informed her.

'Are you coming too?'

'No.'

He very badly wanted to know what had passed between her and his father but she sensed that torture would not have driven him to request an explanation. He wouldn't even look at her. She searched that coldly clenched profile and decided that it was not imagination which made her think that he had lost weight since she had last seen him. A Mercedes drew up.

'I'm sorry I insulted your father,' Bethany confided in a rush.

'We have nothing more to say to each other.' He turned fluidly on his heel.

'I'm pregnant,' she revealed dulcetly as she slid into the waiting car and slammed the door. The car drew off within seconds.

She glanced back over her shoulder. Razul was standing where she had left him, wearing an arrested expression of extreme shock. Well, whatever happened, she had had no choice but to tell him, and no doubt it was just one more messy complication, she reflected miserably, and, moreover, a complication that *she* was wholly responsible for creating. How stupid she had been—how unutterably stupid. Razul regretted their marriage now and she would just have to take that on the chin. However, her attempt to apply common sense to their problems only confused her more, for she could not imagine what could possibly resolve the situation that they were now in.

She was feeling a bit dizzy when she got back to the palace, so she went to her room. She had barely lain down when the door went flying open. Zulema stole one startled glance at Razul's furious face and scurried out past him at speed. Pierced to the heart by that dark fury, Bethany closed her burning eyes.

'Tell me that what you said is not true,' Razul breathed rawly.

'I'm afraid it is and it's all my fault. I suppose you want to strangle me and right now I want to strangle myself,' Bethany whispered with painful honesty. 'I lied to you when I said I was on the Pill. I deliberately set out to get pregnant, and I did feel bad about deceiving you, but not bad enough until it was too late—'

'Why did you lie?' Razul broke in roughly.

'I wanted a baby,' she muttered painfully.

'Without a father?' he gritted with contemptuous distaste. 'I have read about such women in your newspapers.'

'Well, I wasn't one of them! I wanted you too,' Bethany confided miserably. 'And if I couldn't have you the baby was the next best thing. I just don't know what came over me. It was a crazy, stupid thing to do. I knew you didn't want me to become pregnant.'

'I assumed *you* would not want to become pregnant.' Razul sounded desperately strained. 'Nor would I have risked such a development, not with the lesson of my own childhood behind me.'

Shock was settling in on him hard. She knew how he felt. Her own head was whirling in ever more torturous circles, for she could see no easy way out for either of them. She guessed that if she had a girl it would be all right for her to leave, but suppose she had a boy? And why did his father have to accept her when it was too late to make any difference? How much had his hostility towards their marriage contributed to Razul's rejection of her?

'You said…you said you wanted me too,' Razul remarked rather unsteadily.

'Yes,' she said equally unsteadily. 'My timing is very off, isn't it?'

'How deep does this wanting of me go?'

Her nose wrinkled. 'Miserably deep.'

'I need the dictionary.'

'I love you…all right?' she flung at him with sudden defensive aggression, her anguished eyes flying wide.

'But you are most unhappy about it, and no doubt if you are unhappy about it for long enough you will soon overcome such unwelcome feelings altogether and feel a strong sense of achievement,' Razul assumed with dark fatalism.

Bethany sat up. 'Is that what you're hoping for?'

'I am sure it is what you are hoping for—'

'And since you are always so sure that you know what I want, how could you possibly be wrong?'

'I already know that you have good reason to have little faith in marriage. I also know that you are devoted to your career. I cannot blame you for these facts. But last week, when I believed we were happy and that there was hope for us, I was devastated to realise you were *still* thinking of leaving me—'

'Razul…you left me with the impression that I *had* to leave at the end of the summer…no matter how either of us felt!'

'That is not possible. I was entirely honest with you,' Razul countered tautly.

'I believed that your father had only agreed to a temporary marriage between us,' Bethany spelt out. 'For heaven's sake, who was it told me on our wedding day that he would divorce me at the end of the summer and take another wife?'

'But this was when you'd accused me of deceiving

you into marriage and made it clear that you wanted
your freedom back and I said nothing that was not the
truth,' Razul defended himself. 'I promised my father
that—'

'You would remarry *if* our marriage failed?' At his
frowning nod of assent she was ready to explode. 'You
know something, Razul? You embarked on our marriage
with so much pessimism you deserve everything that's
gone wrong!'

'It was not pessimism. I did not believe that I had
much hope of you staying with me—'

'Pessimism,' she said again.

'And naturally I had to be frank on this subject with
my father—'

'Instead of keeping your mouth shut…you turned him
right off me, didn't you? And you kept on saying things
to me like "one last chance to be together", and you
mentioned the end of the summer with such frequency
that it became firmly fixed in my head as the date of my
expected departure!'

His lean hands were clenched into feverish fists. 'Naturally I had to prepare myself for that departure—'

'But I didn't want to depart…I wanted to stay,' she
whispered vehemently.

'Your career—'

'Stuff my career!' she raked at him, out of all patience.

Breathing fast, he studied her with painful but silent
intensity.

'Just why were you so convinced that I would leave?'
Bethany pressed furiously. 'Was it because that was
what you really wanted to happen?'

His strong jaw clenched hard. 'I did not feel I could
offer you enough to make the sacrifice of your other life
worthwhile,' he proffered in a stifled and driven undertone.

All the anger in her was instantly doused. She could

not doubt that sincerity. She lowered her fiery head, and there was an enormous lump in her throat. She blinked back tears. If he saw them, his pride would be savaged.

'All you have to offer me is yourself,' she managed gruffly. 'And that is enough for me. I happen to love you a lot. I can't even imagine my life without you now, and you know...I don't even know whether that pleases you or not.'

'It pleases...it overwhelms,' he muttered unevenly.

The silence went on endlessly. She heard his breath catch, listened to him swallow convulsively.

'Does that mean you love me?' she finally dared to ask.

'I have always loved you,' he said thickly. 'Surely you know this well?'

'Oddly enough, no, because you never quite got around to mentioning it,' she mumbled, then looked up, and her impressionable heart spun like a merry-go-round as her gaze collided with the deep, inner glow of those burning golden eyes trained compellingly on her. 'I honestly believed you had struck this devil's bargain with your father that meant we could only be together for a little while.'

'I was prepared to accept a little while if that was all I could have.'

'I have a lifetime to offer.'

'And a baby,' Razul remarked abstractedly, as if that fact was only now sinking in. 'This news astonishes me. I can hardly believe it.'

'You're not even a bit annoyed that I lied the way I did?'

'How could I be?' A blazing smile suddenly drove the last evidence of strain from his lean features. He strode across the room, came down on the edge of the bed and breathed with unhidden emotion, 'What greater proof of your love could you give me than to desire my child?'

'True,' she agreed, giving up on a seemingly unnecessary need to appear remorseful.

'I thought you knew how much I loved you. I thought my love was embarrassingly obvious,' he confessed in a sudden surge of explanations. 'What did you think I was telling you in the hospital when I said that you were my dream?'

'I thought it was only—well...sex.' She flushed as she admitted it, finding fault with her own cynicism.

'In truth I am severely challenged being this close, to restrain my desire for you,' Razul murmured, with a rueful quirk of his sensual mouth. 'But nothing less than love would have driven me to lure you out here and browbeat you into a marriage within days. All I wanted was the chance to prove that I could make you happy—'

'And you had to fight your father for that chance—'

'I fell very deeply in love with you two years ago.'

Her eyes swam. 'I couldn't admit that I felt the same way. I was too scared.'

'My father was pressing me to choose a bride when he heard rumours about you. He confronted me and I told him that you are the one I love.'

'You are the one'... She rested her head against a broad shoulder and tightened her arms around him.

'The only woman I would ever love, the only woman I wanted to marry. He was profoundly shocked. He reasoned, he threatened and then he gave in with very bad grace and forecast disaster—'

'Misery loves company,' Bethany slotted in, but she was shaken by the awareness that he had fought for her, risking...indeed expecting to suffer ultimate rejection and his father's righteous censure.

'I am miserable no longer. And I do not even have to work out a subtle approach to the subject of having children. You have done it all for me.' With a glittering smile of slumbrous amusement Razul pressed her down onto the pillows. 'Three solid days in bed... I admire such strong commitment to a goal as much as I revelled in your passion. And this week—it has been the longest, most agonising week of my life.'

'Did your father say "I told you so"?'

'No…he was morosely sympathetic, which was worse. He asked me how he could blame me for making the same mistake that he did.' Razul grimaced at the memory.

'Didn't he ever want to meet me?' Bethany asked tautly.

'You were to meet after our wedding, but you were in such a mood, how could I risk it?'

Guilty recollection supplied her with a memory of the strained phone call that Razul had been engaged in when they'd arrived back here the day of the wedding. 'I'm sorry, but I was in shock.'

'He was too… The marriage was not to take place for some weeks but I lost my nerve to wait.' A faint line of colour had accentuated Razul's hard cheek-bones. 'I should have waited,' he conceded. 'I should have had more patience.'

'I'm not sure patience would have worked with me,' she admitted. 'But why did you stop mentioning the fact that we were married?'

'I believed that constantly reminding you that we were man and wife was making you feel trapped. I wanted you to see that we could be truly happy. But how will you manage without your work?'

She thought about it and smiled. 'I shall probably start writing books…but not right now. Maybe you find it hard to accept but I was a workaholic so long simply because there was nothing else in my life, and now there are lots of other things I'd like to take time out to enjoy.'

'Will you find occasionally entertaining foreign dignitaries very boring?'

'No.'

'My father does not like to be troubled with these

duties unless the guests are personal friends. Further-more, many men bring their wives these days and my father is not accustomed to such gatherings.'

'I think I could quite enjoy myself playing hostess. It would beat the hell out of watching TV and gossiping,' she said wickedly. 'Was it Fatima who was lined up to take my place?'

Razul frowned. 'That is a joke in very bad taste,' he scolded with mock sobriety. 'No. My father did once consider Fatima when she was younger but as time revealed her character he changed his mind, and when she took you out into the desert and assaulted you—' his strong face clenched hard '—he was quite appalled, as was I. She has agreed to marry a Saudi prince and I understand she is quite content. It was only ambition which made Fatima throw herself at me... I have never been more embarrassed in my thirty years of existence than I was that day, and that you should witness such a scene—'

'And misinterpret it in the most unkind way—'

'Cruelly unkind.' But he smiled that heart-stopping smile, and he took her mouth with drowning sweetness.

A loud knock landed on the door. With searing impatience Razul sprang off the bed. He had a short exchange with whoever had interrupted them, but when he turned back from the door he was smiling with amusement. He was holding the exquisite bonsai tree she had admired at the old palace.

'Such a gift from my father quite takes my breath away,' he confided. 'These trees are like his children.'

'You'd better give it back fast. All the leaves keep falling off the ones I have at home!' she admitted. 'They're hanging onto life by a slender thread.'

'Even better. He loves to instruct.'

'I'm frightened to death of him!' she gasped.

'But you must have impressed him deeply.' Razul

gathered her back into his arms. 'Import the dying ones. They will be a challenge to him.'

He kissed her again.

'You know…I really do love you,' she whispered, glowing with contentment.

'But not enough to take me with two hundred concubines,' Razul lamented.

'You've got your hands full with me,' Bethany told him sternly.

'This is true…this is wonderfully true,' he agreed, covering her soft mouth again with his, drinking in her response with glorying pleasure. 'You divinely precious woman…I have one small confession to make…'

'Hmm?'

'The helicopter waiting to take you to the airport that day…had you climbed aboard it, it would have suffered mechanical breakdown and failed as a means of transport.'

Her lashes fluttered.

'I had decided that half an hour was not long enough for you to make such a serious decision.'

'You had no intention of letting me go!' Bethany registered in a daze.

'I will never let go of my dream.'

Winding her into the strong circle of his arms, Razul suited his passionate embrace to the assurance, and the rising thunder of her heartbeat and the hot race of her pulse made her quite forget what she had been about to say. Instead she luxuriated in the wonderful feeling that she had finally come home.

Initially a French/English teacher, **Emma Darcy** changed careers to computer programming before settling into marriage and motherhood and a community life. Creative urges were channelled into oil-painting, pottery, designing and overseeing the construction and decorating of two homes, all in the midst of keeping up with three lively sons and the very social life of her businessman husband, Frank. Very much a people person and always interested in relationships, she finds the world of romance fiction a happy one and the challenge of creating her own cast of characters very addictive. She enjoys travelling and her experiences often find their way into her books.

Emma Darcy lives on a country property in New South Wales, Australia. She has been successfully writing for Mills & Boon® since 1983, and has written more than sixty novels, which have been published worldwide.

WHIRLPOOL OF PASSION
by
EMMA DARCY

CHAPTER ONE

SHE would do it, Ashley decided. So what if it was a stupid, irresponsible idea! No one would ever know about it. No one that mattered. She was half a world away from home, and answerable to no one as far as her own personal financial position was concerned. If she lost the money, it wouldn't drastically affect her life, but if she won . . . to help Sohaila into a happy marriage would give her more satisfaction than anything had given her in years.

Common sense told her she was clutching at straws. The odds against her winning the amount Sohaila and Ahmed needed were undoubtedly astronomical, but Ashley was fed up with being sensible. At least trying something positive was better than remembering the misery on her friend's face.

Ashley knew that kind of misery all too well, the deadening sense of futility that came with fighting something that couldn't be beaten. She would never forget the despair of those last months of her marriage, trying to face up to what couldn't be faced, suffering Damien's pain with him, knowing she could do nothing to help except be there. And in the end her being there had eaten away his will to live. She had been no help at all.

Ashley dragged her mind off those torturing memories and glanced at her watch. She had seen the advertisement in the hotel elevator often enough to know that the casino opened at nine p.m. It was now almost eleven, late enough for the gambling tables to be in full operation.

This was a once-in-a-lifetime experience, Ashley thought grimly, as she searched through her clothes for something suitable to wear. She had never been inside a casino, and the rather unsavoury glamour attached to such a place was a little unnerving. Not to mention the fact that she was totally ignorant of games of chance. What she needed was something classy but inconspicuous, and her choice fell on the long-sleeved black dress she had bought at Harrods in London.

Despite its modest style, it was the most deceptively sexy dress Ashley had ever worn, and she hesitated a moment before pulling it on. She had had a few discomforting experiences in Egypt, fending off the unwanted attention of the local men. But there was nothing to fear in this hotel. The Cairo Sheraton was a perfectly safe harbour for foreigners. It was not as if she was wandering abroad. The casino was only six floors below her own.

Ashley loved the rich sheen of the black silk brocade. She had loved the elegant lines of the dress from the moment she had first tried it on. The sleeves were slightly puffed at the shoulder line to add featured interest to a bodice that was starkly sculptured to the generous swell of her breasts and clung to her body long enough to emphasise her narrow waist and the feminine curve of hip before slicing to a V-line across her stomach. The skirt was artfully pleated on to the V, accentuating the hip line, then narrowing to just below the knee.

Sheer black stockings and black patent leather high heels were the perfect complements, and Ashley piled her long tawny-blonde hair into a gleaming loose chignon on top of her crown to set off her fashionable attire. She touched up her green eyes with a subtle make-up, added a blush of colour to her cheeks, and carefully applied her favourite coral-red lipstick. Then, ready to face any critical eye, she slid the cheques she needed into her evening bag and took the elevator to the second floor.

Casino—the discreet gold lettering at the side of the doorway brought a twist of uncertainty to Ashley's stomach; but the lure of quick money, big money, the kind of money Sohaila needed, drew her feet to take the decisive step inside.

The moment she entered the plushly carpeted lobby Ashley feared she had badly miscalculated her timing. There was no noise; no hum of conversation nor clink of glasses to suggest a crowd of carefree gamblers. The darkly panelled walls enclosed an almost funereal hush, which was emphasised by the subdued lighting.

The impulse to turn tail and forget the whole idea was stilled by the interest of the two men behind the reception desk. Some perverse pride insisted that she go on, and she adopted an air of studied nonchalance. She could pretend she was looking for someone and walk out again in a few minutes if the situation didn't suit her. There was no need for panic.

'Your nationality, *madame*?'

The question startled her. Was there some special procedure necessary before being allowed into a casino? She looked blankly at her inquisitor until her nervous gaze caught the sign—'No Egyptians may go past this point'.

'Australian,' she replied with a smile of relief.

The man smiled back at her. 'May I wish *madame* good luck?'

'Thank you,' she breathed, then walked quickly on, feeling the speculative gleam in the dark eyes behind her.

Her spine crawled uneasily. Sohaila had told her that the morals of any unescorted Western woman were suspect in Egypt. Apparently there were women who came here precisely for the purpose of having a sexual fling. Their reputation tarred everyone else. Ashley considered this dreadfully unfair, but there was nothing that could be done about it.

When Sohaila had explained the situation, Ashley had been shocked, and yet she could understand the attraction of Egyptian men. They were spectacularly handsome, with their beautiful dark eyes and brilliant smiles. Under different circumstances she might have appreciated the admiration that had caused her discomfort, but Ashley could never think of sex without remembering Damien.

She shuddered and concentrated her mind on her present purpose—to help Sohaila towards the happiness that she herself had been denied.

A tingle of excitement warmed her as she paused at the top of the steps which led down to the gaming-room. It was not as large as Ashley had expected, containing only three roulette tables and two others where card games were being played. All the tables had drawn their measure of players even though they were not yet crowded.

No one took any notice of her and she instantly understood the lack of noise. All concentration was focused on the fall of a card or the spin of the roulette wheel. Gambling was obviously a lonely, intense occupation, not even superficially social.

The croupiers made their calls in low voices. The click of playing chips being placed or removed was the dominant language being spoken. Ashley noted with wondering curiosity that the faces around the tables were completely impassive, showing no joy at winning or disappointment at losing. It seemed incredible that the money meant nothing. Was it bad form to show emotion?

An abrupt movement at the roulette table directly below her caught Ashley's attention. A bulky man in a fawn suit spun the seat of his stool around and heaved himself off it, leaving an inviting vacancy. Ashley did not want to take up a playing position yet, but the space did give her a clear view of what was happening. She moved down the steps and stood behind the stool. The croupier gave her an encouraging nod, but she shook her head and kept her distance.

'Would *madame* like a drink?'

One of the silent-footed waiters was at her elbow. 'Yes. A gin and tonic please,' she decided quickly, feeling in need of some extra fortitude in this strange atmosphere. The drink was swiftly brought and Ashley opened her bag to pay the man.

'No charge, *madame*,' he informed her quietly, and as she glanced up, startled, he discreetly added, 'All drinks in the casino are free.'

'Oh! Thank you,' she rushed out, grateful that her lack of *savoir-faire* had been so tactfully corrected.

She nursed her drink, feeling rather guilty about accepting it when she wasn't playing. But she intended to, she promised herself, as soon as she knew what to do.

A betting card gave Ashley all the information she wanted. A maximum of a hundred dollars on a straight-number bet returned three thousand five hundred, but the odds against any one number coming up were too prohibitive, and she would need three wins on those to collect the amount Sohaila and her fiancé needed. On the black market, ten thousand American dollars could be changed for eighteen to twenty thousand Egyptian pounds. With that extra amount the pair could buy the apartment they wanted and start their marriage without the dreaded in-laws breathing down Sohaila's neck and dictating how her life should be lived.

However, Ashley did not have the heart of a gambler. Her more cautious eye was drawn to the even-money bets; black or red; odd or even; 1-18 or 19-36. She could place a thousand dollars on those and all she had to do was win ten more times than she lost.

Of course, no bet was safe. Common sense reminded her of that. Ashley watched the play for over an hour, recording the result of each spin of the wheel on her card. She found that black or red often came in a three or four sequence before changing. Sometimes it went longer. However, the very essence of gambling was its unpredictability, so she couldn't rely on these patterns continuing for any length of time. If she was going to hazard the thousand dollars, it was better to do it now before she lost her nerve.

Her heart accelerated with nervous excitement as she walked purposefully towards the money-changing counter to convert her traveller's cheques into the American dollars necessary to buy the chips. The face of the man behind the grille held a bored expression. Ashley wondered just how many thousands of dollars passed over this counter each night.

Her hand shook a little as she picked up the hundred-dollar bills and crammed them into her black, beaded evening bag. She took a deep breath to quell the slight flutter in her stomach, then turned back towards the tables.

The flowing white robes of the Arab caught her eye. Pristine white. Clearly of the finest linen. Most of the Egyptians wore the long dress-like *galebaya* with a turban or skull-cap on their heads, not the more graceful head-dress that this man wore.

But then he couldn't be Egyptian. Not here. Perhaps he was a Saudi, or from the UAE, or Kuwait or Bahrain. Whatever he was, he held a posture of command and authority which was impressive.

He stood at the top of the steps where Ashley herself had paused. Something that Sohaila had told her clicked into her mind. The thick twisted *'iqal* that fastened the Arab's head-dress was made of golden cord. Ashley had never expected to see it worn, and certainly not at close quarters. Only people of royal blood were allowed to wear it.

Ashley stared at him in fascination. He was not exactly handsome, nor even particularly attractive. The eyes were too deeply set in their sockets, the nose too hawkish, the mouth too full-lipped, but somehow the sharp cut of his cheekbones and the hard thrust of his jaw stamped him with an impression of power that was aggressively masculine. He literally emanated the kind of charisma that would always force attention.

He surveyed the room below with a slow, careless arrogance, almost as if he was considering if it was worth the waste of his time to enter. With an abruptness that caught Ashley by surprise, the dark gaze stabbed straight at her, fastening on her with such a searing intensity that it made her skin burn with self-awareness.

An uncontrollable surge of defiance fired her own gaze straight back at him. It was a sexual challenge that was totally instinctive, without thought or reason, fracturing the numbness that had characterised her reaction to men since Damien's death.

Danger prickled down her spine, but for some unaccountable reason, Ashley found the sensation delicious. She felt herself vividly alive in a way she hadn't felt for over three years. Perhaps it was her decision to gamble a thousand dollars away tonight that made her feel reckless. Or perhaps it was a rebellion against the Arabic assumption that Western women were immoral. In any event, she'd be damned if she would lower her eyes in modest rebuttal of the blatant desire in his. Let him think what he liked; it wouldn't do him any good.

What made her do it, she didn't know. Nor did she stop to question the mad impulse. She walked towards the gaming table with a roll of her hips, deliberately flaunting her body in front of him. Some fiercely awakened devil relished the gleam of lust it brought to those dark, flashing eyes that raked her from head to foot.

A satisfied little smile tilted his lips, giving his mouth an extraordinary sensuality. And a twist of cruelty. Ashley's heart pumped an alarm which she sternly repressed. It was exciting her too much, the way he looked at her. She could not tear her eyes away from his. It was exhilarating to make this arrogant Arab look at her like this.

A thrill of power danced through her veins and she exulted in playing with fire, uncaring of what might happen next. She had never expected to feel the thrall of sexual awareness ever again, but it was pulsing through her now with a force that insisted upon being savoured to the full.

He did not move. He watched her all the way with unswerving intensity, and Ashley was more physically conscious of herself than she had ever been in her life; conscious of the silk of her stockings brushing between her thighs; conscious of the rounded thrust of her breasts pressing into the fabric of her dress; of her delicately pointed chin tilted high above her long, golden-tan throat; of the tendrils of tawny hair dangling down her smooth cheeks; of the weight of the long, thick, sun-streaked tresses piled high on her crown; and she knew that her clear green eyes were no longer their usual cool. They were flirting with the ignition of volatile passions.

She had never been a tease, and never wanted to be. It was crazy, what she was doing, flagrantly inviting trouble, but she could not stop herself. Not even a quivering sense of disloyalty to Damien acted as a deterrent. Somehow this man was drawing a reaction from her that set every nerve in her body vibrating with exultant, primitive life, and not once in her twenty-eight years had she felt anything like it.

She judged the most tantalising moment of imminent confrontation, then swung her back on him, and in an elegant movement, slid her bottom on to the still vacant stool at the roulette table. She could feel the dark eyes burning along the row of covered buttons that ran down the curve of her spine, and she had a mad, hysterical urge to laugh. She felt free, free in a way she had not felt since Damien's illness had destroyed their relationship and driven him to take his own life.

The croupier smiled at her and Ashley returned a dazzling smile that quite startled him. He raised his eyebrow questioningly, but she shook her head, too dizzy with wild sensation to concentrate on betting right now.

The wheel was turned. The man on her right lost the last of his chips and left his stool. He had been sitting just around the corner of the table from her. As he moved, Ashley heard a faint rustle of cloth behind her and her heart leapt into her throat. She knew who it would be. Even before she caught a glimpse of his white robes from the corner of her eye, she knew it had to be the Arab.

Her whole body tingled with an electric awareness as he took the place vacated. She wanted to look at his face, wanted to see if the desire was still in his eyes; but she no longer dared. He was too close, too dangerously close if she was to keep some control of the situation. She had been unbelievably mad to challenge such a man. How

she was going to defuse the situation was still
beyond her, but sanity insisted that she give him
no more encouragement.

A wad of hundred-dollar notes was carelessly
thrown upon the table. The croupier checked and
rechecked them, then slid them down the money-
slot. Ashley counted the twenty-five-dollar chips
pushed towards him. There were forty. A thousand dollars.

The darkly tanned hands curled around the
chips. Strong hands, with long, supple fingers.
They placed half the chips on black, the other half
on odd.

Ashley sat absolutely still, her gaze inexorably
fixed on those very deliberate bets. Black and odd.
Was that because of her dress and her behaviour?
She had no doubt that it was a statement of some
kind, designed to gain her attention.

Well, he wasn't going to win it that easily,
Ashley determined. She relaxed as the sense of
power rippled through her once again. He could
do whatever he liked—she did not have to respond
to anything he did. Yet caution whispered that a
man who bet a thousand dollars on a mere whim
could not be taken lightly.

She removed the betting card and pen from her
evening bag, and was pleased to see that her hands
were still steady. The tourneur set the roulette
wheel in motion. Other players kept placing their
chips until the croupier called, 'No more bets,
please.' A few moments later the ivory ball
clattered into its final resting-place.

'Fifteen.'

Black and odd. Ashley made a note of it on her card. The brown hands reached out and took the winnings, letting the original bets stand. A gold signet ring on his left index finger winked teasingly at her, but she did not look at him.

In what seemed like a gesture of careless contempt for any system of betting whatsoever, he tossed the chips on to the numbered pattern of squares on the table, and showed no interest at all in where they fell. The croupier shifted some that had scattered outside the betting area, raising his eyebrows at the Arab as he moved them to the closest square. He received no audible reply.

Obviously money meant nothing to him, Ashley thought with a touch of envy. And resentment. These blood-royal Arabs could throw it around like so much confetti. For people like Sohaila and Ahmed it meant the difference between a marriage that was independent of their families and one that would be torn with dissent.

The wheel was spun.

'Thirty-three.'

Black and odd won again. The Arab had the luck of the devil. Some of the chips had fallen on thirty-three, others on the line-bets around the number. Stacks and stacks of chips were pushed down to him. Again he left the original stakes on black and odd. All the others he had won he placed in front of Ashley. His hand gestured an invitation.

'Play with these, *mademoiselle*. Perhaps they will

give you the courage . . . to commence betting.'

His voice was low and pleasant, but the challenge implicit in his words goaded Ashley into a reply. Mentally harnessing all the nerve she possessed, she slowly tilted her face, and lifted her gaze to his. His face was close enough for her to see the lines of ruthless purpose stamped on it, and the eyes . . . they were the eyes of a man who could kill if it were necessary, or take forceful possession of anything he wanted.

And he wanted her. He did not give a damn about the wedding ring on her finger; could not know she was a widow. The man was amoral, a devil who meant to take what she had so recklessly offered, and he meant to take it tonight. There was no mistaking his intent. Nor the undiluted lust burning in those dark, brilliant eyes.

It raised no fear in Ashley, but rather injected a burst of adrenalin through her veins that heightened a compelling sense of contest. She could feel the tentacles of his will reaching out to dominate her and the excitement of locking her own will in battle with his was more than she could resist.

She smiled and returned the French address that was more common in Egypt than any English form. 'Thank you, *m'sieur*, but I don't need those chips any more than you do. I pay my own way.'

Ashley did not wait to see his reaction. She opened her evening bag and tossed her thousand dollars on the table, copying the nonchalance he himself had displayed. His low laugh played havoc with her pulse, but she steeled herself against any crack in her calm composure. He could not win with her unless she let him.

The croupier took her money and served her with the same number of twenty-five-dollar chips he had given the Arab. Ashley ignored them, disdaining to place a bet until she was ready. The wheel was spun. The Arab did not make any other bets, apparently content with those still placed on black and odd.

'Twelve.'

Red and even. He had lost. Ashley barely repressed a grin of triumph as the croupier scraped her adversary's chips back to the roulette bank. The run of blacks had ended. She waited for the Arab's next move. Without any hesitation at all, he placed a five-hundred dollar stack of chips on both black and odd. He was going to lose again. She felt as sure of that as it was possible to feel sure of any gamble. He would lose and she would win. It had to come up red again. By the law of averages . . . but there was no law of averages in gambling, she reminded herself.

Nevertheless, logic was a weak voice at this heady moment. She craved action. Successful action that would show this man that she was no weak-hearted woman. With every appearance of complete sang-froid she placed the thousand dollars worth of chips on red, but her heart raced faster than the wheel as it spun the ball towards its ultimate destination. It seemed to go on for an eternity before the ball lurched from the rim into a pocket. Ashley waited for the call; she could not bring herself to try and look at the wheel.

'Seventeen.'

Black and odd. She stared disbelievingly as the croupier placed the winning marker on the number. Black . . . and odd. She had lost, lost the lot. A thousand dollars. She had told herself she could afford to lose it, but she hadn't really expected to. Not all of it, not on the first spin. It had been utter madness to do what she had done. Madness! All motivated by stupid pride . . . and the challenging presence of the Arab.

She hadn't even thought of Sohaila and the money that was still needed to buy the apartment. The Arab had taken over her mind. It was all his fault. If he hadn't . . . No, she couldn't lay the blame at his door. She had chosen to play against him. She had gambled and she had lost.

'A brave plunge, *mademoiselle*,' came the soft, insidious voice, the challenge in it subtly muted to a note of provocative approval. 'All or nothing. I like that.'

Ashley still felt shaken by the suddenness of the loss, but she turned towards him, opening her hands in ironic self-deprecation. 'Reckless folly! It's the end of the game, *m'sieur*.'

'No. I can't allow it.' He smiled and it was the most dangerous smile Ashley had ever seen. Even the white gleam of his teeth seemed to radiate a confidence that undermined her own. 'You haven't got what you came for,' he added with a flat certainty that Ashley immediately wanted to shake.

'Then I must leave without it,' she tossed at him carelessly.

'What were you trying to win?'

Ashley raised mocking eyes to meet his. 'Only ten thousand dollars. Nothing else, *m'sieur*.'

'How totally foolish!'

The scorn in his voice made Ashley blush. No point in trying to explain a shattered dream, or a quixotic desire to help someone else to a better life. No point in telling him it was all done in the name of love. His cold ruthlessness would never understand such sentiments.

She rested one hand on the table as she levered herself off the stool. Strong, warm fingers covered her own, dark on golden-tan. It was a fascinating juxtaposition and for one wild moment Ashley wondered what it would be like to have his whole body covering her own, what it would be like to be possessed by a man who exuded so much raw power. His fingers curled around hers, sensing her moment of weakness and playing on it.

'I must go,' she said thickly, having to force herself to fight the physical magnetism he was exerting.

'Not until you have what your heart desires, *mademoiselle*. That takes total commitment. I'll show you how to do it.'

'No...I...' Her voice was swallowed up by the mad temptation to give in and be shown whatever this man could show her.

'Think of a number, any number on the table,' he commanded softly.

'Don't be absurd,' she whispered, but there was no conviction in the way she said it.

'Tell me your number.' His voice was hypnotic.

'You can't do it!'

He merely smiled. The need to challenge him swept her again.

'Twenty-three.'

'So be it.' His eyes were predatory and chilling. He picked up a bundle of chips and looked hard at the tourneur, as if he could direct the turn of the wheel by the sheer power of his will.

'You can only bet a maximum of a hundred dollars on a number,' Ashley stated defiantly. 'Even if twenty-three comes up, you will only win three and a half thousand dollars.'

'If twenty-three wins, it will be red. I place a thousand dollars on red. Another thousand on odd. Five hundred dollars on the column, five hundred on the range of numbers from twelve to twenty-four, and another thousand on the numbers nineteen to thirty-six.'

Her mind whirled through the figures as he calmly placed the bets. He was laying out over four thousand dollars. If the number did come up the return would be eight and a half thousand dollars, plus the stakes. Nearly thirteen thousand dollars in all!

The wheel was set spinning; the ivory ball revolved around its perimeter. Ashley could not drag her eyes away from the Arab. It was madness; he couldn't win. It was a crazy, flamboyant gesture, doomed to failure.

The croupier cried, 'No more bets, please.'

The brown hand tightened its grip on hers as the ball tumbled towards its final destination. A faint smile touched the croupier's mouth.

'Twenty-three.'

Ashley stared disbelievingly as the winning marker was placed on the number. Piles and piles of chips were pushed down the table to rest directly in front of her. Her mouth went dry.

'It's yours,' the Arab murmured in his low, seductive voice. 'To do with as you wish.'

Ashley snapped out of her mesmerised daze. She had read of oil-rich Arabs handing over fantastic gifts to people who had won their favour for some reason or other, but Ashley believed that such gifts had to generate a sense of obligation upon the person who received them. There was at least a subtle pressure for goodwill in any future dealings.

If she took what he was offering her now, it would almost certainly imply an acceptance of him and all that he was. And Ashley wasn't prepared to do that . . . was she? Nothing could be more certain than that he only wanted one kind of relationship with her, and that was purely physical.

Her eyes lifted and met his with fiery pride. 'You misunderstood me, *m'sieur*. The money means nothing to me. I merely wanted to help out a friend.'

He shrugged. 'Take it. Your pleasure is mine.'

'No. Your pleasure is not mine, *m'sieur*.'

He raised a sardonic eyebrow. 'You play with words, *mademoiselle*, but your actions are far more eloquent.'

Ashley couldn't deny it. Even now her body was reacting to him; the touch of his hand, the wicked promise of his eyes. But she couldn't just walk off with him and share his bed, no matter how deeply tempted she was. It was totally irresponsible, dangerous and stupid.

Self-respect warred with the desire he had planted in her and somehow emerged the shaky victor. She lifted her chin in pointed disdain and forced a proud scorn into her voice. 'And you, *m'sieur*, are gambling again, and this time on impossible odds. You have lost, and the game is over.'

'I do not gamble, *mademoiselle*. And I always win.'

A gleam of hard ruthlessness brought a sharper intensity to his eyes, and Ashley felt pinned by them. She nodded towards the table, needing to rock his arrogant assurance. 'If you don't gamble, *m'sieur*, what do you call those bets you placed just now?'

A slight twitch of his lips drew her attention to their suggestive sensuality. 'Perhaps I wanted to play at being ... your God. Perhaps you struck a chord of compassion in me. What does it matter? I want you to have the money you came for. Take it. It's yours.'

She could not accept that there were no strings attached to it. No one gave away sums of money like that on a mere whim! And the way he was looking at her ... devouring her. Not even for Sohaila could she take that money. It would mean a surrender to his will, and Ashley was frightened to think where that might lead.

'You misunderstood me,' she repeated vehemently and snatched her hand from his.

He was too potent, too mesmerising. If she stayed with him any longer she might be persuaded into some further madness she would surely regret. The only sane thing to do was escape as quickly as she could. Without uttering another word, Ashley swung on her heel and marched off up the steps.

CHAPTER TWO

ASHLEY made her escape from the casino and was a few metres down the corridor when she heard him behind her.

'Come back!'

The soft call made her step falter. She turned, seduced from her intention by the sheer magnetism of the Arab's presence. His hand was stretched out to her, inviting her return.

'You are no coward!' he continued even more seductively. 'Why do you run away before we have barely brushed the surface?'

Impossible even to pretend misunderstanding. Ashley needed all her will-power to resist the tug of his powerful attraction. 'We inhabit different worlds, you and I,' she cried in a desperate attempt to drive a wedge of cold reality between them.

'The meeting-place is here and now.'

The meeting-place for what? A mingling of their flesh? It could never be of minds. His way of life, views on social issues, customs ... all so different. Alien to everything that had formed her life. 'No, it's not possible,' she insisted, and forced herself to turn away from him and keep walking.

He followed her, his pace unhurried but undeterred by her rejection. The soft thud of his footsteps pounded in Ashley's ears, but she did not turn round. She strode along the corridor towards the elevators, doing her best to hide her inner agitation. She walked stiffly, trying hard to negate the sexual promise she had suggested before, but her body was pulsing to the possibilites that had simmered between them.

As great as the temptation was to explore those possibilities, Ashley could not contemplate doing so. She was here in Egypt on a mission of enormous responsibility, negotiating with high-level officials in government. She had won their respect and she wasn't about to lose it by plunging into an affair with an Arab who was probably well known to them.

It appalled her that she could even want to do such a thing. She had never indulged in casual sex, not before her marriage and certainly not since. The idea of a purely physical relationship without any emotional ties whatsoever, without anything in common but a mutual need . . . it ran counter to everything she believed in. There had to be something more. It was wrong, this desire she felt. It had to be terribly wrong.

Almost in a panic at the attraction the Arab was still exerting, Ashley jabbed her finger on the up-button for an elevator, then whirled around to face him, forcing a frosty dignity she was far from feeling.

'Please go back. Your chips will be stolen if you leave them lying on the table unattended.'

The dark gaze probed the fearful confusion in

her eyes. 'No one will touch them. They are safer there than in any Western bank.'

'I don't want you with me,' she blurted out, denying the feverish pumping of her heart.

He stepped towards her. Ashley shrank back, hard against the wall, frantically willing the elevator doors to open and provide her with a ready escape. He lifted an arm, placing his palm flat on the wall near her ear.

'I'll scream if you touch me,' she whispered shakily, her breath constricted in a throat so tight that she could barely swallow.

His face came closer, his eyes commanding hers with relentless purpose. 'You want to taste me as much as I want to taste you.'

There was time for her to turn her head aside. His mouth approached hers with a slow deliberation that taunted the throb of need inside her. She could not stop her lips from quivering in anticipation. It was recklessly wanton of her to concede. He was dangerous. But somehow the arguments her mind conjured up didn't sound as good as tasting what this man was offering.

All the frustrations of the day curdled the last bastion of common sense. She had wanted a decision out of the Egyptian officials on the jewellery of the Pharaohs. She had wanted to help Sohaila. Nothing had worked out right. And now she wanted . . . craved to know whether this strong desire she felt was a wild fantasy, or fact.

His hand moved from the wall and curled around her throat, caressing the intense tension that held her motionless. His thumb tilted her chin. His mouth took possession of hers, ruthlessly pressing the desire that tore through her belly and drained the strength from her legs.

His kiss was merciless, smashing through every inhibition with an aggressive eroticism that had all of Ashley's senses reeling into chaos. All thought of resistance was driven from her mind, lost in a whirl of sensation that peaked into passion when he swept her body hard against his. Her whole being vibrated in wild response to his. She was utterly helpless to stop him from doing anything he wanted with her.

Ashley didn't want the kiss to end. It was as if she had been starving, and she could not bear the feast of sensation to be taken away. A little animal cry of need dragged from her throat when his mouth withdrew, and he rubbed his cheek against hers as if in loving comfort for her distress. His harsh breathing fanned her ear with a tingling heat that grew more intense when his warm lips brushed close to her lobe and whispered his triumph.

'You cannot deny what we have.'

The softly spoken words dropped into the whirlpool of her mind and formed chill ripples of sanity that lapped at the edges of her senses, forcing an acknowledgement of reality. No matter that this man was filling needs and desires that had lain dormant for years; it was still madness to succumb.

She did not even know his name. And what

manner of man was he that he should kiss her like this, here where anyone might come along and see them? The lateness of the hour was the only reason why they had not yet been interrupted.

With slow, seductive sensuality his mouth trailed kisses around her temples, down her cheek, and her head turned instinctively to the command of his lips. The shreds of her will-power were hopelessly weak. How they drew the necessary strength, Ashley never knew. Even as she tore herself out of his embrace, the shock of loss left her shaking.

He caught her easily. His hands flashed out and encircled her wrists, pinning them effortlessly between her breasts as he dragged her back to him. Alien, her mind screamed, as her frightened eyes flashed a confused appeal to the dark, hawkish face that stared so demandingly at her.

'Why do you fear the pleasure I can give you?'

Was it pleasure? Her whole body was a tremulous mass of shrieking nerve-ends. What he could do to her was no fantasy, but she couldn't let it go on or she would lose all control. 'I don't fear it,' she insisted, but the words were furred with a tumult of conflicting emotions.

He laughed softly. The black ruthlessness in the depths of his eyes still had the power to shake her to the innermost parts of her body and mind. She knew she had to escape him if her life was not to be inexorably changed. What had already happened sent a flush of shame to her pale cheeks.

But even as her mind feverishly reasoned

against him Ashley could feel what little strength she had mustered draining away. Her gaze flicked despairingly to the elevators. They were notoriously slow in responding to a call. And if one did come right now, would this man even hesitate to accompany her up to her room? How could she stop him?

'I wish to go free, *m'sieur*,' she said, doing her best to inject a calm, reasonable tone into her voice. 'If you don't release me now, I shall yell for help.'

One black eyebrow rose in amused disdain of her words. In sheer panic, Ashley tried to drag her hands out of his hold. The sharp movement caught him by surprise and his grip slipped to her fingers before closing hard to prevent her escape.

'Please . . .' Ashley whispered, hoping to reach some spark of humanity in him.

His eyes looked into hers, dismissing the plea and probing straight to the need that pulsated within. 'You cannot go free, any more than I can. The bond is already forged and you cannot escape it.'

Ashley tried to laugh at his arrogance, but no sound came forth. Her stomach was tied in knots, twisting to the tug of his presence. Self-survival depended on her getting away from him. She swallowed hard, desperate to work some moisture into her arid throat.

'You are wrong, *m'sieur*. I've had all I want from you and I don't need you for anything more,' she said harshly, driven by his forcefulness to be cuttingly blunt. He had stirred her out of sexual apathy, but she simply couldn't allow any further intimacy between them.

He smiled that slow, dangerous smile, his eyes glinting with a mockery that was edged with supreme confidence. 'Your need matches mine and I see no peace from it.'

He lifted her hands and pressed a kiss into each palm and, although his grip on her had gentled and she could easily have snatched her hands away, Ashley simply stared at him in helpless thrall, her arms weak and utterly useless as the warmth of his kisses tingled down her veins.

'Shall I prove it to you again?'

Once more he gathered her close. The experience of his previous kiss ravaged Ashley's will to resist, and when his mouth took hers she surrendered to his will with a wanton abandonment that cared for nothing but his possession. She had lost all sense of self by the time the elevator doors slid open beside them.

'Come with me now. We will learn all there is to know about each other.'

His arm was pulling her towards the compartment when a thread of sanity finally struggled through the web of dependence he had woven with his kiss. Horror billowed through Ashley's mind. In blind panic she tore herself out of his grasp and ran for the great marble staircase that led to every floor of the hotel.

'Stop!'

The sharp command stabbed at her heart, but

Ashley did not stop. She knew what he could do to her and it terrified her. Her legs felt like jelly as she pushed them up the steps. Her whole body seemed to be shaking out of control. She paused to catch her breath on the next landing and flung a frightened look down at him.

He had started after her. He was directly below her on the opposite side of the stairwell. Even that distance did nothing to mitigate the searing power of the dark gaze that pinned her there, clutching the brass banister in a convulsive need to feel some barrier between them.

'No! No!' she cried, her voice shrilling in hysterical need to deny what she had so very nearly done. Then, driven by the spectre of such madness, she clattered on up the stairs, wishing she could take her high heels off and hitch up her narrow skirt. But he was watching her and she didn't dare stop again.

She had bolted up three floors and there were still three more to be negotiated when the realisation suddenly struck her that all he had to do was stand in the stairwell and watch her and he would see what floor her room was on. The staircase spiralled around itself so it was possible to see right up to the roof. She felt certain that whatever means he employed to find out her room number, he would do it. She had to think how to avoid that happening.

Trying the lifts was no good. They took too long to come. She kept on running up the stairs until the blood was pounding through her head and she felt dizzy from the effort. She was between floors when she heard the swish of opening elevator doors just above her. If only she could reach it before they closed again. Her legs felt leaden, but she pushed them as hard as they could go. She was panting from the exertion, almost exhausted when her feet tottered on to the carpeted landing.

'Please . . .' The appeal was a bare whisper, and the man to whom she made it didn't understand. She gestured despairingly towards the elevator doors, but they were already closing behind him. It was too late.

The man said something, but there was a buzz in her ears that made his words indistinguishable. She shook her head and tried to catch her breath. The floor seemed to be spinning. 'I need help,' she gasped, frightened that she was going to faint. If she collapsed, the Arab would catch her and . . . wild, unreasoning panic scrambled her mind. She took a couple of unsteady steps.

The man grasped her arm. 'I'll get a doctor straight away.'

'No!' She looked up at him, too physically distressed to explain. There was concern in his eyes. It was a nice face, she thought, before it started swimming in front of her. She could feel the blood draining from her own and, just as her knees started to buckle, an arm came round her shoulders and another lifted her off her feet.

Her head dangled on to the broad shoulder of a pin-striped suit. A respectable, civilised suit that somehow comforted her as the man carried her along a corridor. Her torso felt as if it was wound around with hoops of steel, and a painful stitch was tearing through her abdomen. She needed to speak, but her throat was so terribly dry and the effort to do anything was too great to make.

They came to a halt. The man bent over and slid his arm from beneath her legs so she could stand up. His other arm supported her tightly against him as he fished in his pocket for a door-key. A wave of apprehension brought strength enough for Ashley to grasp some control of herself.

'I need your help,' she blurted out, 'but . . .'

He flashed her a dry, little smile. 'There will be no trouble, *mademoiselle*. I'll call a doctor for you immediately I get into my room.'

'No.' She pushed back against the door-jamb, not knowing whether to trust him or not. One nerve-shattering experience with a man was more than enough for one night and, while she still needed a means of escape, to throw herself out of a frying pan into a fire was absolute idiocy.

He shrugged his shoulders. 'I have nowhere else to take you. If you need help . . .'

His accent was heavily French. Ashley searched his face, trying to read his motives. She looked into blue-grey eyes that held the saddest expression she had ever seen.

'Of course, the door will remain open while you are here,' he asssured her. 'You may leave whenever you please.'

He could be trusted. She was suddenly very sure of it. 'Thank you,' she breathed, relieved that she had stumbled on a haven of safety.

He opened the door. She slid from the door-jamb and he caught her around the waist, steering her to the nearest armchair and lowering her into it.

'Thank you.' Her voice was even shakier than her limbs. Reaction was setting in and, fearful that the Arab might still find her, she blurted out, 'If you don't mind, I'd rather have the door closed.'

He shot her a sharp, assessing look, then moved to do her bidding. Having secured her safety he walked straight over to a side-table on which stood a bottle and a set of balloon glasses.

Ashley watched him open the bottle, then swept her gaze around the room, realising for the first time that he had brought her into one of the luxurious corner suites of the hotel. They were in a spacious sitting-room, its windows obviously overlooking the Nile as well as the square at the end of Tahrir Bridge. The furnishings were in restful shades of blue and green, and the work-manlike desk in one corner was spread with papers, suggesting that her host was in Cairo on business.

Her eyes returned to him in sharper appraisal. He was a tall man, over six foot, broad-shouldered but slim-hipped, and her recollection of a hard chest and strong muscular arms suggested he kept himself fit. His face was not young, nor was it old. It wore a settled maturity that placed him around forty, and from the lines of stress she had seen around his eyes Ashley surmised they had not all been easy years. The stylishly cut dark hair held a lot of grey.

He put down the bottle and carried a glass over to her. 'You could probably do with this,' he said, pressing it into her hand and waiting until her tremulous fingers had curled securely around it before straightening up. An enigmatic smile curved his mouth. '1906 Grande Champagne Cognac.'

'It's ... very kind of you,' Ashley murmured, suddenly feeling ill at ease with the situation. While he had certainly helped her escape from the Arab, it struck her forcibly that she didn't know this man's name either, and here she was accepting his hospitality.

She watched him warily as he drew another armchair closer to hers and sat down. He did not fully relax, but perched himself forward, elbows on the arm-rests and the fingers of one hand stroking the other.

The blue-grey eyes observed her keenly. 'You have some colour in your face now. Are you ill, or ...'

She shook her head. 'No! I was ... very ... stressed. I didn't know what to do ...' She looked at him helplessly, at a loss to put into words what had happened.

He nodded and his eyes crinkled sympathetically. 'So you have a problem. Tell me what it is and I will see what I can do to solve it.'

'A man ...' Heat flooded through her at the memory, and she took a sip of cognac in the hope of calming herself.

'You were molested?' the Frenchman asked softly.

The smooth richness of the cognac slid down her throat and she sucked in a deep breath to steady her fluttering pulse. 'No. No ... not exactly. I ...' Shame and her own sense of guilt would not let her accuse the Arab of taking advantage of her. 'It was the situation. It got beyond my control. I ... I had to run away.'

She lifted agonised eyes, only to find him frowning down at the glass she held in her hand. His gaze flicked sharply up to hers. 'I was wrong to call you *mademoiselle*. You look so very young, I was deceived. But why wasn't your husband with you at this time of night? Is he without eyes, without soul?' He rose to his feet with an expression of disgust. 'I shall ring him at once to come for you.'

The old grief dragged at her heart. 'I'm alone, *m'sieur*. My husband ... my husband is dead.'

And she remembered the torment in Damien's eyes and the despair in his soul, and she bowed her head in terrible shame for what she had done this night. Tears welled into her eyes. How could she have acted so? How could she have let that Arab get to her like that? It had been her body and the futility of wanting to satisfy all her needs that had tortured Damien into that final self-destruction.

The glass of cognac was prised out of her grasp, and through a blur of tears she saw the Frenchman looming over her. He knelt beside her chair and gently wiped her cheeks. 'Love is without mercy. It destroys everything,' he said grimly, then in a softer, more soothing tone, 'You must not weep for what is for ever gone. We will talk of other things.'

He released her hands and straightened up. His fingers brushed her cheek in a kindly gesture of encouragement. 'I don't even know your name.'

The voiced echo of her own thoughts brought a tremulous smile to her lips. 'Nor I yours.'

'Louis-Philippe de Laclos.' He gave a slight bow as he added, 'At your service.' Again his smile held a faint twist of irony, as if he expected nothing from life, least of all any pleasure.

'My name is Ashley Cunningham,' she replied, intensely grateful for the generous service he had already performed for her tonight.

He gave her a startled look, then shook his head in a bemused fashion. 'How extraordinary!'

'Why?' Ashley asked in surprise.

He gave an eloquent shrug and dropped back into his chair. His eyes roved over her features with a kind of speculative appreciation. 'I was talking to Sohaila Sha'ib this morning. MISR appointed her as my personal assistant the last time I was in Egypt, and when I saw her, naturally I stopped to pass civilities. She told me she was working with you and seemed very pleased with the assignment.'

Sohaila! Ashley rubbed at her forehead as her mind whirled. The coincidence was more extraordinary than Louis-Philippe de Laclos knew.

This whole disastrous night had started with
Sohaila, the Egyptian girl's misery and Ashley's
desire to help her. Then the meeting with the Arab
and his offer of the money ... Ashley shuddered
and forcibly dragged her mind off that insane
encounter. It seemed strangely ironic that her
rescuer was also connected to Sohaila.

'She mentioned something about a jewellery
collection.'

Ashley grasped the prompt, needing to shift her
mind on to more tangible things. 'I've been trying
to organise one of the greatest collections of
Egyptian jewellery ever assembled.'

'The jewellery of the Pharoahs?'

'Oh, much more than that. There's the collections of King Farouk. The Nubian silver from
Aswan. The masterpieces of the Bedouins. But the
Pharoahs' jewellery would certainly be the centre-
piece around which the others revolved ...' She
gave a weary shrug. 'That's if the Egyptian
authorities will ever come to a decision about it.'

'And why can't they make up their minds?'

Ashley hesitated, but the interest in his eyes
seemed genuine, not merely polite. Her own
enthusiasm for the concept crept into her voice as
she continued.

'To pay for the display will cost a great fortune.
In order to finance the collection, the jewellery
company I work for wants to sell reproductions,
ranging from thousands of dollars to millions. And
there's the rub, I think. It's the commercialisation

that seems to worry the officials I've been talking to.'

Her eyes narrowed with determination. 'Our aim is to design and sell a fabulous range of jewellery—the Egyptian Collection—directly inspired by what I've seen here. My drawings are nearly complete. We'll cover everything from the most elaborate collars to the smallest trinkets, and I'm certain it will be successful because the pieces are so ... magnificent, so flattering to women. The Egyptians, however, wonder if we are not taking advantage of them in some devious way, even though they get a commission on everything we sell. They see the advantages in such a worldwide display in every major capital in the world ... yet still they hesitate.'

'Undoubtedly. They always do,' Louis-Philippe said with a grimace. 'They've become wary of letting anything out of the country, and it's understandable. Egypt has been plundered of so much of its treasure. That's why the restrictions are now so tight.'

He went on to describe his own experiences of working in Egypt. Ashley took further stock of the man as he talked of the difficulties in raising finance for excavations. He had been involved with many of the most productive sites that archaeologists had uncovered over the last twenty years. The cost of such long-term and labour-intensive projects had to be prohibitive. Ashley decided that Louis-Philippe de Laclos had to be on talking terms with the Rothschilds and the Rockefellers of the world.

But at least he was of her world, not like the Arab, and it was reassuring to have a calm, sane conversation that dealt with things she could comprehend. She almost felt normal again.

When the subject of antiquities lagged, she asked Louis-Philippe if he was organising some new dig. He shook his head and spoke of some restoration work in which he was presently involved. His voice used a curious range of intonation, from enthusiasm to almost a half-hearted diffidence, which suggested an ambivalent attitude towards the project.

'Isn't it going well?' she asked when his talking trailed into a heavy sigh.

His gaze lifted reluctantly and again Ashley thought they were the saddest eyes she had ever seen. His hand made an empty gesture. 'I promised myself some time ago that I would never return to Egypt. Then I made an excuse. I told myself I was needed here, but only the money was needed. I shouldn't have come.'

'Why not?' Ashley prompted curiously.

He threw her a glance that was full of self-mockery. 'They say whoever drinks from the Nile must return and taste it again. Maybe that's true, but ...' he paused and there was no humour at all in the grim smile that thinned his mouth '... along with its fascination comes too many other frustrations. The differences of race, culture, religion ... and other things ...' he shook his head '... impossible.'

The image of the Arab welled instantly into

Ashley's mind. 'Yes,' she whispered as a convulsive shiver ran down her spine.

Louis-Philippe looked sharply at her. Their eyes met and locked, and some indefinable understanding, something totally instinctive leapt between them so that they were no longer strangers apart, but people who shared the same knowledge on a level that was deeply hidden from everyone else.

'It's been good of you to give me your company for so long,' Ashley said impulsively.

'Not at all.' He smiled. 'It can be lonely in a foreign country.'

'Yes,' she agreed, pushing herself out of the armchair. 'It's very late.'

He rose swiftly to his feet. 'You must allow me to escort you to your room.'

He took her arm and Ashley did not protest the gentlemanly offer. It was almost three o'clock and although she was no longer afraid that the Arab might still be in the hotel, the security of another man's presence was very comforting. Louis-Philippe de Laclos was the type of man she should be responding to. He was kind, courtly, a real gentleman. Not like the Arab at all.

They met no one until they reached Ashley's floor. One of the room-service boys was waiting at the elevators when they stepped out. Ashley saw nothing suspicious in his presence. She did not even notice that he did not take the elevator that she and Louis-Philippe had just vacated. She was not aware that he watched them to her room, watched her press a grateful kiss on Louis-Philippe's cheek, and then took to the staircase with a hurried, stealthy step.

CHAPTER THREE

WHEN her wake-up call came in the morning, Ashley responded sluggishly, her body groaning in protest at having its rest cut short. Then the memory of last night's devastating encounter with the Arab slid into her mind and she groaned out loud.

Her abandoned response to his powerful sexuality made no sense at all. Even when she was married to Damien she had never felt so . . . so taken over. Absolutely mindless! A shaming frustration crawled through her body, sharpening the memory to a point where Ashley was goaded out of bed to seek active distraction from the feelings the Arab had aroused.

She pulled on her dressing-gown and strode out to the balcony of her room. Normally she enjoyed the view of the city stretching out to meet the desert, but this morning she winced at the noise of the traffic with its continual honking of horns, and not even the more peaceful traffic on the Nile River drew her interest.

From this height, Cairo looked like any bustling city of the modern world, but that was an illusion that had been very quickly dispelled with closer acquaintance. Two and a half thousand years ago, a Greek historian named Herodotus had written that if all the countries in the world did everything one way, then in Egypt they did it the opposite; and it still held true.

Ashley felt she had weathered the culture-shock rather well, but the whole social structure still appalled her. The restrictive rules by which women had to live were an affront to any intelligent person, yet even Sohaila accepted them, despite her rebellious stance over the marriage issue.

A knock on her door heralded the delivery of breakfast. Ashley moved swiftly through the room to admit the service-waiter. He set the tray on her table, waited for the inevitable *baksheesh* tip, then smilingly took his leave.

The continental breakfast reminded her of the strong French influence still evident in Egypt, and of the remarkable man who had been her saviour last night. Just the thought of Louis-Philippe de Laclos soothed her sense of discontent. He was a true gentleman; the kind of man she could really admire and respect.

Perhaps she would run into him again, since they were staying in the same hotel. They were both alone. She might even ask him to dine with her, as a thank-you gesture for his kindness. She would be safe with him ... safe from the mind-shattering passion aroused by the Arab.

She had to forget that experience and the feelings it had stirred, and the best way to do that was to concentrate on her work. A glance at her watch showed her that she had lingered too long over breakfast. She would be late for her appointment with Sohaila at the museum if she didn't hurry.

She quickly changed into her favourite cotton two-piece. The comfortable gored skirt and the tunic with its loose, three-quarter length sleeves were ideal for the Egyptian heat, and the bright floral pattern in red and yellow and green always gave her a buoyant feeling. She strapped on yellow sandals, and snatched up her hair brush.

There was no time to twist the long tresses into a tidy top knot. She slid side-combs into the thick waves above her ears, dashed on some lipstick, snatched up her travel-bag and sketch-folder, then scooted along to the elevators, hoping she wouldn't have too long to wait for one to come.

For once Ashley was lucky. Two minutes later she was on the front steps of the hotel and the commissionaire was waving up a taxi for her. The shiny black Mercedes surprised her. Most of the taxis in Cairo were old Volvos, scratched and dented from the daily dodgem antics of the city traffic, but she had seen a fleet of Mercedes taxis at the Meridian Hotel, so this one didn't raise any question in her mind.

The commissionaire opened the back passenger-door. Ashley was too street-wise now to step inside before an agreement had been reached on the fare. 'I want to go to the Egyptian Museum,' she said very firmly, and raised a couple of fingers in the air. 'Two pounds.'

To Ashley's relief the driver nodded, and did not bother with the usual haggling. She climbed in, feeling quite pleased with herself. A firm voice was obviously the trick to forestall argument. The commissionaire closed the door and the car moved off, smoothly joining the stream of traffic leading on to Tahrir Bridge.

Ashley relaxed into the plush leather seat,

thinking how nice a change it was from the dusty velvet upholstery in the older taxis. The whole interior of the car was spotlessly clean too, which was an even more pleasant change. She had almost become used to the prevailing dust and dirt.

One of the problems in Cairo was that it hardly ever rained, so the streets were rarely washed clean. But that didn't excuse the rubbish that was heaped up everywhere. A clean-up programme was badly needed. It was a terrible shame, the way some things were just let go. There were so many beautiful things in this city, like the gorgeous poinciana trees . . .

Ashley's attention drifted to those blooming along the bank of the Nile, and she was too late to stop the driver from taking a wrong turn down to Garden City. She leant forward and tapped his shoulder. 'The Egyptain Museum. It's not this way. You have to go back through Tahrir Square,' she explained in irritation. If he thought he was going to take her for more than two pounds, he could think again. She wasn't a green tourist.

The driver nodded, but he didn't turn back. Ashley was about to tap him again when she realised they were in a one-way street. She settled back with a sigh of exasperation. The whole damned traffic-system was a maze of one-way streets, and once the wrong one was selected it was the devil of a job to get back on course again.

She checked her watch. It was already ten o'clock. She was going to be late and Sohaila was always punctual. That was something the Egyptian authorities had got right, Ashley thought on a sigh of general vexation. Sohaila worked for MISR, the government agency which kept tabs on Ashley's work in Egypt, and from the very beginning she had been a goldmine of information, knowing precisely where to find what Ashley wanted, and capable of giving her all the background detail she needed. They had very quickly formed a good working relationship, and over the weeks they had spent together, a close friendship had grown between them.

Ashley wished she could have won the money last night. It would have been marvellous to hand it to Sohaila this morning and see excitement replace the dull misery in the lovely expressive eyes. If only she had had the luck of the Arab! He had boasted that he always won. Well, he hadn't won with her, Ashley thought, but it had been too near a thing to feel anything but a hollow triumph.

The Mercedes slowed down and the driver pulled over to the kerb. They were nowhere near the museum. With a stab of annoyance Ashley leaned forward to instruct the driver again, but just as she was about to speak the passenger-door was opened and a man in Arabic dress pushed into the seat beside her, slamming the door behind him.

Ashley's heart did a quick somersault, but it wasn't the Arab of last night. 'This is my taxi. You get out this minute or I'll call the tourist police,' she blustered angrily.

The man was completely unmoved. Hard, dark eyes gave her only a cursory glance as the Mercedes moved off again.

'Stop!' Ashley cried out, but the driver took no notice of her. Fear fluttered through her stomach.

She turned back to the Arab. 'You have no
right ...'

'Calm yourself, *madame*,' he said in precise
English. 'No harm will come to you. The Sheikh
requires your presence. That is all.'

'That's all!' Ashley heard her voice climb to a
shrill note and quickly sucked in a deep breath. Her
heart hammered around her chest. The Sheikh!
The Arab with the golden corded *'iqal*. He was
having her abducted. Right off the steps of the
Sheraton Hotel!

Fool! Fool! Fool! she railed at herself for not
realising that such a man would never accept
defeat. She should have been anticipating some
follow-up to last night's confrontation. Hadn't he
said she couldn't escape him? And this was his
answer to her vehement rejection. He was not
giving her any choice in the matter. He was taking,
with ruthless disregard for her right to make her
own decisions. And where did that disregard stop?
Would it stop at all?

CHAPTER FOUR

ASHLEY tried her utmost to stave off panic. The situation would have been incredible if it wasn't so horribly real. Abducted! In broad daylight!

'He can't get away with this!' she cried in outrage, and turned to the Arab beside her, her voice rising in bitter protest. 'There are laws in this country!'

The response she got was even more nerve-shattering. 'The Sheikh is beyond the law, *madame*. You are honoured to be asked . . .'

'Asked! I wasn't asked!' Ashley almost shrieked.

'That is immaterial.' The black eyes he turned to her held no grain of sympathy for her plight. 'Please do no attempt anything foolish. It would be my duty to restrain you. The Sheikh does not want you hurt in any way, so there is no need for you to be concerned. Relax, *madame*. Our journey will not be long.'

It was impossible for Ashley to relax. The memory of the man's air of ruthless power was all too vivid. Hadn't she even thought last night that he was capable of killing to get what he wanted? She had been the worst possible fool to have challenged such a person.

The Mercedes was halted by traffic and Ashley lunged for the door handle, desperate to escape.

She pressed it frantically, but the door did not open.

'The locks are power-controlled, *madame*. Please do not distress yourself. It will change nothing.'

The words beat on her fevered brain like inexorable drums of doom. The man beside her might not wish to use force, but he was certainly strong enough to subdue any struggle she might put up. The wisest course was probably to sit back and concentrate hard on the streets they were passing. If she could memorise the route, it might be of some use to her.

Her eyes darted from side to side, picking up every landmark possible. She did not recognise anything and did not know where they were until she spotted the distinctive minaret and huge walls of Ibn Tulun's Mosque, built over a thousand years ago, and still the largest mosque in Cairo. They had to be near the medieval part of the old city, not so very far from the business centre, and only half a kilometre from the Australian and British embassies.

Minutes later, the Mercedes turned into a narrow street, hardly more than an alley, compelling the driver to slow the car to a crawl. He threaded a path between the buildings before entering a gateway. Ashley caught only a glimpse of a formidable, two-storied stone building, bisected at ground level by the cobbled road.

The car drew to a halt in front of the steps which led into a side-entrance of the building. The driver got out, opened the door on her side, then stood guard next to it.

This private cul-de-sac gave Ashley no possible chance of escape. With a despondent sigh, she allowed herself to be handed out, and then followed the Arab into the entrance hall of the building. It was perfectly clear that putting up a fight could only end in her being hurt, perhaps badly.

The two men, one on each side of Ashley, took her along a screened corridor to a central courtyard. Resistance seemed futile, but beyond the fear that Ashley felt was a mounting anger against the man who had ordered this outrageous action, this violation of her right as a person to make her own choices.

They mounted a flight of stairs, at the head of which were a pair of double doors. One of the men flung them open, and gestured for Ashley to proceed. She entered a huge *qa'ah*, or reception room, which took up two floors of the building. At either end were two great *liwans*. The galleries along both sides were fronted with *mishrabiyyah* screens, an arabesque wooden filigree behind which anyone could watch the activity below. In the centre of an ornate marble floor was a beautiful mosaic fountain.

A woman appeared, garbed in the traditional black gown, her face covered with a veil. The Arab addressed her in a tone of command. 'Escort *madame* to the harim and see that she has refreshments.' Then he turned to Ashley. 'I trust

you will be comfortable there, *madame*. The
Sheikh will attend you as soon as he is free.'

He pronounced the word sheikh in the Arabic
way, with a guttural 'k', harsh and discordant, yet
Ashley heard the subservience in his voice and
could see the respect in his manner. It was the
goad that spurred anger beyond fear. She had no
reason to respect the man who had forced her
here; and subservience was the last reaction he
was going to get from her. How dared he think he
could place her in his 'harim' in this overly exotic
place?

There was no point in being passive any longer.
If it meant getting hurt, then that was better than
tamely waiting on any Sheikh's pleasure. The two
men turned to leave, and the woman-servant took
Ashley by the arm.

'Oh, no, you don't!' Ashley cried striking the
restraining hand away and stepping out of reach.

The men halted and looked back at her in
surprise. The woman hesitated a moment. Instinctively drawing on all her experience in Egypt,
Ashley threw her head up haughtily, assumed an
expression of command and stamped her foot. She
slapped her hands vehemently together and
shouted '*La! La! La!*' which was the Arabic for
'no'.

The woman stared at Ashley in mesmerised
uncertainty. Having won this momentary advantage, Ashley turned to the men, and yelled her
orders. 'Go to your Sheikh immediately! Tell him
I will not be put in anyone's "harim". And if you

so much as try it, I promise you'll all get more trouble than anyone ever bargained for.'

She sucked in a quick breath and continued the tirade with barely a pause. 'And if it's pleasure he wants, I doubt that it will serve his purpose to have me bruised and beaten, so you'd better not lay a finger on me. In fact, I'm walking out of here right now, and don't you try to stop me. You go and tell your master that!'

Ashley started walking towards the door. The men glanced at each other, apprehension and indecision reflected in their expressions. 'Go! Go!' Ashley yelled at them, gesticulating wildly in the hope it might help.

Suddenly the woman snatched hold of Ashley's upper arm and tugged at it, not very hard, but insistently. It was more than Ashley could tolerate. For all her bravado she was trembling inside, and her reaction to this form of coercion was instant and violent. She shook herself free and pushed the woman away with all her strength.

Taken unawares, the woman stumbled backwards, lost her footing on the edge of the fountain and collapsed with a cry into a spray of water. Ashley stood paralysed on the spot, wondering what would happen to her now. A gabble of Arabic broke forth from the men, louder than the wail of distress from the fountain; but the sound that shook Ashley most of all was the soft, male laughter echoing down from behind the *mashra-biyyah* in the galleries.

Her head jerked up, eyes darting around the

meshed screen, her mind leaping into even more feverish turmoil. He had been watching her; enjoying the fact that she was powerless to escape him this time, and amused by her attempt to assert her independence. Ashley seethed over her impotence, and wildly vowed that she would make his triumph over her a bitter one. She would fight him with every weapon at her disposal.

The laughter suddenly stopped. Terse commands followed in Arabic, but Ashley's knowledge of the language was too sketchy to understand them. She was sure of only one thing. They were not meant for her well-being.

The woman hurriedly waded out of the fountain, gathering up her wet skirts and wringing the water from them as she did so. She bowed to Ashley and scuttled off to an exit at the back of the room. The two men also bowed, then took a more dignified exit through the double doorway. The doors closed behind them with an ominous clang.

For a moment she was alone, but Ashley did not doubt that the Sheikh was on his way to her and any attempt to use either exit would be thwarted. At least she had shown him she had a mind of her own and would not be tamely installed in any damned harim'!

However, that small victory was little consolation to her as she thought how she might be tamed after the way she had reacted to him last night. She had to do something more concrete to protect herself from him.

She forced herself to move, so that he would not

find her waiting like a mesmerised rabbit. She skirted the fountain, trying to put more distance between herself and the door she expected him to enter by. If she kept the water between them he couldn't touch her. Unless he forced his will on her in the fountain. Ashley shuddered.

Her eye caught an ornamental scimitar hanging high up on the end wall. The downward turning handle was elaborately carved and studded with gem-stones. The long blade curved wickedly upwards in its scabbard. It was exactly what she wanted.

This Arab sheikh was not the kind of man to call for help in a confrontation with a woman. It would be beneath his pride. So perhaps she could hold him at bay with this weapon, or at least make some stand that would induce him to think twice about what he was doing. Driven by a sense of urgency, Ashley leapt upon an adjacent divan, and reached up to lift the scimitar out of its holder, hoping that the blade was not entirely useless.

The ease with which it ran from its scabbard surprised her. Light flashed from the blade as she stepped down. A few testing slashes gave her a feel for the perfect balance, and Ashley no longer had any doubt that she held a very formidable weapon. For the first time this morning she had some control of the situation.

'Take care. That sword is said to have belonged to Salah al-Din. It's made from the finest Damascene steel, the best the world has ever known.'

Ashley wheeled around to face her tormentor. 'It means I'll run you through with it before I'll let you get away with this!' she fired at him.

He laughed. He was just as she remembered him, the amused arrogance on his face barely lightening his air of ruthless purpose.

'I don't care who you think you are,' Ashley bit out angrily, determined not to be intimidated by his manner, 'but as far as I'm concerned you're not above the law, and I'll defend myself to your death.'

There was a fleeting glint of admiration in his eyes before his face sobered into hard command. 'You have courage. I respect you for it, if for nothing else. However, you obviously do not understand your position. I can do with you as I wish. And I will. The sword means nothing.' He paused so that his next statement would have its maximum effect. 'The law cannot touch me. In this country I have diplomatic immunity.'

He walked around the fountain as he spoke, approaching her with all the confidence of a man who knew he was untouchable. His smile was cruel. 'Whereas you, Mrs Cunningham, would bring upon yourself a most unenviable fate if you injure me in any way. A far more disagreeable fate than any you'll meet here with me.'

Ashley gulped, but defiance still spat off her tongue. 'When it's known what you have done to me you will be expelled from the country. The authorities will . . .'

'Perhaps,' he shrugged. 'But it will be worth it!'

'Why are you doing this to me?'

His eyes mocked her. 'You are an intelligent woman. A clever woman. Or you would not have been sent here by the firm of Dewar and Buller to negotiate with the authorities over a collection of jewellery. Such a mission requires some finesse in judgement. It would be a very stupid, self-defeating move to use that sword *madame*. Give it to me and I shall return it to where it belongs.'

He stepped up against the point of the blade. Ashley held firm, all too aware that any retreat would show weakness. He pressed forward, letting the sword prick his chest and a drop of blood stained the pure white cashmere of his tunic. Their eyes locked, his challenging, hers frantically defiant.

'Or use it as you wish,' he said quietly.

Whatever the rights or the wrongs of the situation, Ashley knew she could not hurt or kill the man in cold blood. And his logic was impeccable. He had shaken her resolve with each point he had made. The fact that he had learnt so much about her in so little time confirmed his position of power, and the inside of an Egyptian jail would leave her with no options at all.

When he reached for the sword, Ashley did nothing to stop him from taking it. She was defeated, and they both knew it. Her fingers felt nerveless as she loosened her grip. He balanced the sword in both hands, and again his mouth curved into that cruel smile. His black eyes stared into hers, completely merciless.

'What a pity that you are not as fine a work of art as the sword. Or as constant. This blade can cut the finest silk with a mere stroke.'

Ashley blazed defiance back at him. 'And you're just like it—a relic from the past! The twentieth century hasn't even touched you.' She swept a contemptuous gaze over the rich, Ottoman furnishings of the room. 'You even live like some great Khan of long ago.'

He gave a sardonic laugh. 'This house was restored and furnished by an English general who fancied the surroundings of oriental splendour while he exercised his more sophisticated pleasures with Nubian boys. But, of course, you would not find that kind of behaviour at all reprehensible, would you?'

Ashley was shocked and confused by his savage counter-attack. 'Yes, I would,' she insisted, instinctively rising the the taunt.

His mouth curled again. 'You surprise me, Mrs Cunningham. Don't you take your pleasure when and how you please, without regard for anyone but yourself?'

Ashley was so stunned by the accusation that he had turned away before she found wits enough to form an answer. 'That's not true,' she croaked, her throat completely dry from a resurgence of fear. If he believed that of her, she didn't have much chance of persuading him to let her go free.

· He ignored her, returning the sword to its position on the wall with a careful reverence that suggested it meant more to him than anything she might say.

Ashley swallowed hard. She only had words left to defend herself. 'You have no right to judge me like that. How dare you assume . . .'

'I don't assume.' He turned, a taut grimness sharpening the hard planes of his face. 'I know! Cairo is one of the meeting places of the world, and in my position I have information available to me that is not available to others. I now know that you're a married woman, but you have no sense of fidelity. Last night you wanted me. Only fear stopped you.'

He paused, and an acid note crept into the flat, emotionless tone. 'You went straight from me to another man. After some considerable time, enough time to satisfy your . . . needs, he returned you to your room, where you gave him a loving farewell before he left. The man was not your husband.'

His indictment of her behaviour was like a series of punches that almost knocked Ashley off her feet. She rallied slowly, attacking him in blind self-defence. 'So this is the justification for your actions, is it? I hurt your monumental ego, so you resort to force to get what you want.'

'I took a short-cut, yes. A quick means to an end, but the end will not require any force, will it, Ashley? I would not want to use it, and I will not have to.'

The absolute assurance in that soft, personal taunt sent a shiver of uncertainty down her spine.

The memory of her response to him last night throbbed between them, undeniable. And he was evoking a response in her even now, just by looking at her with that mocking challenge in his hard, black eyes.

Her long neck stiffened as his gaze raked the rippling silkiness of her hair to where it fell loosely over her shoulders. When his eyes dropped lower, her breasts tingled with awareness, their nipples jutting hard against the flimsy nylon bra and cotton tunic. A trembling weakness invaded her thighs and by the time he returned his gaze to hers, Ashley was dredging desperately for the strength to fight his devastating effect on her.

'You think you know everything, but you know nothing!' she snapped at him.

'Is it easier for you to deceive yourself than to see the truth?'

'You haven't got the faintest inkling about what kind of person I am,' she retorted hotly.

'I don't care!' he said with a savagery that silenced her, and desire blazed from his eyes, so fiercely intense that it engulfed Ashley, shrivelling every line of defence in her mind.

He stepped forward and curved his hand around her cheek and chin. His voice dropped to a low, riveting note of passion. 'I don't care if you've had a thousand men, because they haven't had you, Ashley. They haven't reached inside you and twisted your gut so that you can't think of anything but the man who's possessing you and how that feels. And I intend for you to feel that. With me. I don't care what words you spout, because I know . . .'

His thumb moved, brushing slowly over her lower lip. '. . . I know that you will surrender to me, Ashley Cunningham. Body and soul.'

Her heart was thundering in her chest, wildly protesting the sheer sexual force of the man. Her mind groped desperately for something, anything to repel this insidious attack on the very core of her being. 'I loved my husband. I loved him,' she whispered with hoarse vehemence, the old pain swimming into her eyes. 'And he killed himself because he loved me. Do you think you could ever take his place in my heart?'

It gave her a fierce satisfaction to see the fire of passion recoil behind the narrowed blackness of his eyes. His hand tightened its grip around her face. His lips thinned in some inner conflict. She sensed the wave of violence that he fought back before he dropped his hand and turned away from her with a sharp, angry abruptness.

He paced across the room like a man driven with scourges, but when he wheeled around, his face was completely expressionless. 'So . . . you are a widow,' he said coldly.

'Yes.' She felt too depleted of energy to say more.

'Tell me how your husband died.'

A shudder ran through her and Ashley tried to control the revulsion she felt at his callous command. 'It's none of your business,' she replied flatly, fighting the tears that pricked at her eyes.

Pride insisted that she should show no weakness in front of him.

'Ashley, I am giving you the chance to explain yourself, and I will not brook defiance.'

Something inside her snapped from all the tension he had put her through. 'Go to hell!' she screamed at him, and the tears could not be contained any longer. They streamed down her face and she could do nothing to stop them. 'I don't care what you think of me,' she sobbed. 'I don't care what you do to me. Take what you want! It won't be much, I promise you. Just get it over with and let me go.'

He crossed the room in a few strides, grasped her upper arms with fingers of steel, and roughly shook her until her head was flung back and she sobbed helplessly.

'You cannot escape me like this,' he exploded in fury. 'This is one of your tricks. However much you say you loved your husband, he's dead. He's dead and you're alive, and I felt your heart beating with mine last night, so don't tell me it's lying in a grave with him.'

'You don't understand,' she choked out.

'Then tell me!'

Tears kept spilling down her cheeks as she flung the words at him. 'He had a . . . a wasting disease . . .' She couldn't say it. Her mind sheered away from that horror and tried another path. 'It was making his body . . . useless. He couldn't be the man he was. Not with me. We couldn't have children. It wasn't the pain that drove him to . . .

to end his life. It was . . . me. It was because of me!'

The terrible guilt which had burdened her heart suddenly burst from her. 'The sight of me tortured him. He wanted me to have a normal life . . . and we couldn't. Not any more. I wanted him . . . just to hold me. To let me hold him. But he hated not being able to . . . be what he was . . .'

She lifted agonised eyes to the darkly brooding man who had demanded so much from her, then plunged on to the last haunting grief. 'That last night . . . he kissed me. He kissed me all over. And when I went to sleep, he went out . . . and shot himself. So you see, I haven't wanted . . . any . . . not any man since . . . Damien died. And I certainly don't want you! I don't know why I reacted to you last night. I'm sorry. It was wrong. It was . . .'

'No!'

She lifted sad, empty eyes. 'I don't know you.'

His gaze was hard and insistent, but his hands gentled their hold, then slid up to cup her face. 'The Baron de Laclos. What about him?' he demanded.

'The Baron?' She felt too drained to think. The pain that had been dragged to the surface still clouded her mind. 'Do you mean Louis-Philippe?'

'The man you ran to last night,' he said harshly.

Her eyes were empty of interest and she replied with some difficulty, groping for the right words to explain. 'A . . . a friend. I was upset and he helped me. He showed me kindness when I needed it. He's a good man.'

A long sigh whispered from his lips and the harshness melted from his face. An ironic smile curved the strong, sensual mouth. 'A pity, perhaps, that I cannot be kind, but that wouldn't work for me, would it?'

Ashley couldn't follow his meaning. 'It never hurts to be kind.'

'Then will you be so ... to me?'

The soft appeal was so unexpected that it confused Ashley. She stared up at him, struggling to understand what this abrupt change of manner meant.

'Stay here as my guest.'

'And if I don't want to stay?' she pleaded.

He stroked her cheek in a softly mocking salute as he released her. 'I'm afraid I cannot give you any choice in the matter. Until the course has been run.'

CHAPTER FIVE

WHAT course? He was speaking in riddles. Or *was* he? Ashley lifted her hand to her cheek, unconsciously rubbing at the warmth his palm had left there. She felt drained. Her mind was sluggish, revolving in slow, heavy circles without grasping anything clearly. There was no longer any threat in his manner, and yet ... until the course has been run ...

He still meant to have her!

And she had nothing to fight him with any more. Nothing! With a little cry of despair she turned her back on him and forced her legs to carry her to the divan. She sank on to the cushions and slowly lifted bleak eyes to her nemesis.

'Why mince words? I'm not your guest. I'm your prisoner.'

He came and sat beside her, taking her hand and fondling it with a gentleness that surprised her. 'You will have the freedom of the house. There is no reason why you cannot be ... comfortable here. And you have my word that I will not take from you anything you don't wish to give.'

'I don't wish to give you anything!' she retorted bitterly. 'Let me have my freedom. There's no point in your keeping me here. I shall never forgive you for what you've done.'

His gaze dropped to her hand and his thumb pushed savagely at her rings, causing the diamond solitaire to dig into her middle finger. 'What's done cannot be undone,' he muttered, then lifted eyes that held a strangely moving intensity. 'I cannot let you go. You must accept that, Ashley.'

Her mind screamed no, even as her body turned traitor and yearned for a reawakening of the passion which had flared between them last night. Ashley tore her gaze from his, averting her head so that he could not reach her with those compelling eyes. The painful thump of her heart was reminder enough of the way he could affect her.

'I could never love you,' she whispered, then realised with jolting horror that the words concealed much that she meant to remain hidden.

For several long moments he made no answer, and his silence held a tension that played havoc with her ragged nerves.

'My name is Azir,' he finally murmured. 'Azir Talil Khaybar.'

A ripple of panic cramped Ashley's stomach. She did not want to know his name. Somehow it made him a person instead of a cruel, ruthless tyrant who would stop at nothing to get his own way. She had to remember that. It was impossible to yield to the temptation he was offering. That would justify what he had done to her, and she would never, never give him that satisfaction.

'Why do I disturb you so much?'

The soft question jangled her frayed emotions even further. She didn't understand it herself.

Why him? Of all the men she had met since Damien's death, why was it this man who had roused feelings that were shaming her even now?

'Look at me, Ashley!' he commanded.

She couldn't resist. Without any conscious volition, her head turned towards him, her inner conflict still mirrored in her eyes.

He reached up and removed the head-dress. His hair was black and straight, its thickness slightly rumpled. Somehow it made him look more human, not quite so invincible, but the glint of triumph burning in his black eyes warned her that any suggestion of humanity should be instantly discounted.

'I'm not a man who makes decisions lightly, or acts without a strong foundation on which to build. I've handled top-level negotiations for my country for many years.' He paused a moment to give emphasis to his coming words. 'We have something too strong between us to . . .'

'No!' she denied vehemently, driven by his certainty to strike an even more certain wedge between them. I could never be happy with a man who only wants me for . . . for physical gratification. You've given me a forceful demonstration of how little you regard the rights of women.'

'If I had no regard for you I would not be talking now, when every instinct I have is crying out with my need . . . for you.'

His gaze dropped to her mouth and again Ashley jerked her head away, biting her lips to prevent any tell-tale quiver. 'You'll get nothing from me,' she cried back at him. 'Nothing,'

'Time will prove or disprove that,' he replied, and the relentless purpose in his voice sent a cold chill down her spine.

In sheer desperation she pleaded with him. 'Let me go. I won't report any of this to the police if you'll just let me go.'

'That is impossible.'

He was hell-bent on the course of destruction he had chosen, and there seemed no way of shifting him from it, but Ashley still could not accept the inevitable end. She stared down at the richly woven Persian carpet on the floor. It pictured the Tree of Life. She grimly wondered where *her* life was heading now.

'You simply don't care how this will affect me, do you?' she observed, deriding herself for the futility of the words even as she spoke them.

'Perhaps I care too much,' he suggested softly.

She flashed him a look of scathing disbelief, but again she was caught and confused by the dark intensity of his eyes. 'You brought me here to violate me,' she accused, more from the need to remind herself of that fact than to recall it to his notice.

'Did I?' He let the question hang between them for several seconds before he added, 'You said you hadn't fully understood the desperation your husband felt. Obviously you're unaware of the effect you can have on a man. In his position, I would have done the same as he.'

He lifted her hand and pressed it to the

bloodstain on his tunic. The strong heartbeat under her palm seemed to vibrate through her own body and she recoiled from the contact as if she had been burnt, snatching her hand away and hugging it under her other arm. 'How dare you cite my husband in defence of your own actions?' she hissed at him. 'How dare you compare your . . . your lust to Damien's love?'

His face hardened. She sensed the firming of his purpose even before he spoke, but the words cut straight to her heart with devastating force.

'He's dead, Ashley. And on your own admission, you've been dead to any feeling too. Until we met last night. Don't tell me you want to crawl back into the grave with him.'

He rose from the divan, and with a sharp, angry gesture, paced away from her. When he wheeled around, his whole demeanour was one of arrogant command. 'As for what I dare . . . I dare anything that will keep you with me. You can fight me with whatever weapons you like, and for as long as you like—but I will not let you go.'

Shock drove Ashley to her feet. Her hands fluttered an appeal even as a protest leapt off her tongue. 'You can't mean . . .' She licked lips which were suddenly parched dry. 'You can't mean you want to keep me here . . . for ever?'

'You will live with me,' he said unequivocally.

She swallowed hard. 'You intend to imprison me in this house for the rest of my life?' Her voice came out as a frightened squeak.

'Of course not! I have to travel to many

different countries and you will come with me wherever I go. But for the present we stay here.'

'You can't do this!' she shrilled.

'It is an easy matter to have your passport re-registered with the police.'

Her mind clutched frantically at straws. 'The airport authorities ...'

'Do not look at my private jet.'

'The firm I work for ... who sent me here ... they'll ask questions ...'

'You will not be the first missing person who cannot be traced.'

'Why? Why?' she repeated helplessly.

'Because I want you,' came the relentless answer.

Ashley took a deep breath to ease the constriction in her chest. It was hard to believe what he was saying, yet he left her with no doubt that he meant every word. 'I'll fight you every inch of the way,' she promised him bitterly.

'Then so be it,' he retorted, his tone as Arctic as an immovable glacier. 'Perhaps by tonight you will have had time to re-assess the situation, and your mood will not be quite so intractable. I will have you shown to your room.'

He was already striding past the fountain before Ashley snapped out of her shocked daze. 'Azir!' she cried after him in total desperation.

He paused and turned an impassive face towards her.

Somehow she had to reach into him, show him the inevitable end to what he was doing. Her hands lifted in one more appeal. 'Can't you see how hopeless it is? There is too much that is different between us.'

Slowly he swung around and for once he showed her compassion. His voice dropped to a softer tone, begging her understanding. 'I am not a fool, Ashley. I see almost insurmountable obstacles that have to be overcome for you and me to be happy together. I know I will grieve people who are very dear to me because I choose to have you at my side. But I cannot . . . will not give up hope that what I want with you will be realised. Given time.'

She shook her head in helpless despair. 'It's not the kind of life I want.' Then, in bitter frustration at his immovable stance, she hurled more defiance at him. 'At the first opportunity I get I'll escape from whatever prison you try to keep me in, Azir. And I will not be put in your damned harim!'

'Do you think I want it to be like this between us?' he retorted fiercely, thrusting his hand out in angry supplication. 'What choice do you leave me?'

And while Ashley was still digesting his outburst of frustration, Azir wheeled away and strode to the end of the room. He flung open the door through which he had entered, and clapped his hands sharply.

'Heba!'

A young Egyptian girl came running. She wore a light blue yashmak, but her face was uncovered and on it was written an anxious desire to please.

She bowed to her master and then to Ashley.

'Heba, you will look after Mrs Cunningham. Show her to the Damascus Room. See to everything she wants or needs. I will be seriously displeased if you fail me in any way.'

He turned briefly to Ashley and the tone of voice was lethally matter-of-fact. 'You will find our security here more than adequate. I know how to guard my possessions. Don't waste your time in futile thoughts or actions, Ashley.'

Then he was gone, leaving her alone with the servant-girl. Ashley did not move. Fear was ballooning through her mind and it took every shred of will-power to contain it. A fit of hysterics was not going to help her out of this situation. She didn't know if anything could, but if there was any possible line of escape she had to find it.

'*Madame*?' The Egyptian girl gestured towards the door. 'It is this way.'

The way to the Damascus Room ... that was what the girl meant ... but was there a way out? And the girl ... could her sympathies be worked upon? Ashley's mind was working feverishly as she walked down the room. She forced a smile. 'Your name is Heba?'

The smile returned was full of ingenuous pleasure. 'Yes, *madame*.'

'It's a very lovely name. Have you been in service here very long?' Ashley quizzed, hoping the girl's sense of loyalty was not very deep.

Puzzlement flitted over the young face. The girl

could only be sixteen or seventeen. An impressionable age, Ashley hoped.

'I have always lived here, *madame*. My family
. . . we look after the house.' The smile lit up again.
'The Damascus Room is beautiful. You will like it
very much.'

Ashley sighed. It was highly doubtful that the
girl could be persuaded into any action that would
adversely affect her family, but it still had to be
tried if all else failed. Reserving comment, Ashley
followed Heba out of the *qa'ah*, along a corridor,
up a flight of stairs, and along another corridor.
The house was a veritable maze and it was obvious
that finding her way to an exit was not going to be
easy without help.

In some other situation, Ashley would have
found the Damascus Room fascinating. The
lacquered walls and ceiling with their gilding and
intricate patterns deserved closer study, as did the
ornate carving of the Islamic furniture. The rugs
on the floor were stunningly beautiful and every
fabric in the furnishings was a richly woven work
of art. But Ashley moved straight to the window,
sweeping the curtains aside without any regard for
the heavy silk.

Beyond the glass was an iron grille, barring her
way to freedom. The fear billowed anew and
Ashley fought it down. 'Are all the windows in the
house barred, Heba?' she asked, straining to keep
her voice steady.

'Yes, *madame*. It is for safety. No one can get

in, except through the doors.'

Or get out, Ashley thought despairingly. And such grilles weren't at all unusual in Cairo. She had seen them on a lot of private houses, as well as official residences. 'How many doors are there? I mean, for coming to or going from the house.'

'There are the entrance doors where you came in, *madame*, and the door to the kitchens. But these are always guarded. The Sheikh ... he is a very important man. He has to be protected,' she added in a tone of reverence.

And there would be no way past his hand-picked guards, Ashley concluded. For a few moments she was swamped by the hopelessness of her position and it took an enormous effort to pull herself together. She couldn't afford to give in to despair. That would only sap her will to fight, and fight she had to, or accept defeat ... a whole life of defeat as a second-class citizen in Azir's world. A prisoner of his will and desires.

She turned back to the girl. 'Heba, I would like a cup of tea. Is that possible?'

'Of course, *madame*. Anything you want is possible. It is the Sheikh's orders. I will go and get it for you.'

Left alone, Ashley paced the floor, driving her mind to look at the possibilities of rescue. However remote they were, it was better to think positively than allow fear to take over. And even worse than the fear was the insidious fascination ... the temptation to even think that she might like what this man intended to do to her. That had to be blocked out of her mind at all costs. She had to concentrate all her efforts on escaping.

It was now almost midday. Would Sohaila have gone to the hotel looking for her when the appointment at the museum had not been kept? Sohaila would have been puzzled, hesitant about pursuing enquiries in case Ashley had been called out on other business. Even if she had gone to MISR and reported Ashley's absence, would anything be done? Undoubtedly the Sheikh would have covered that contingency, anyway. He had known all about why she was in Egypt.

The Australian embassy? Would anyone there remark on her failure to keep up contacts? Not for a few days. If then. They probably wouldn't act until an enquiry came from her firm in Sydney, and it could be weeks before anyone back home would be disturbed by her continued silence. She might not even be in Egypt by the time someone started looking for her.

No one even knew that she had met an Arab sheikh. A man . . . that was all she had told Louis-Philippe de Laclos last night, and their acquaintance was so slight that the Baron de Laclos would not find her disappearance notable. A rueful smile flitted over her mouth. A Baron, no less. Born and bred a gentleman. But there was no hope of his helping her out of this situation.

Ashley shook her head despondently and slumped down on the bed. A double bed. And tonight . . . the hell of it was, she wasn't sure that

Azir Talil Khaybar wouldn't get exactly what he wanted from her. When he had kissed her last night she had had no control over her reaction. None at all. And even this morning he had still evoked a sexual awareness that she didn't understand—or want.

Somehow she had to keep warding him off. He didn't want to use force and Ashley didn't think he would. He had promised . . . but how much did a promise mean to such a man? If she didn't weaken as he expected her to, would his pride demand some redress?

Ashley's frenzied thoughts were interrupted by Heba's return with a tea-tray, set with Spode china. For one treacherous moment Ashley wondered how she would like being the cosseted mistress of a man who could afford Spode china and a private jet, but her soul instantly rebelled against the physical servitude that would be demanded of her. She could not give in to him tonight. If she could hold out . . . an opportunity for escape had to come. Had to!

Once again Ashley quelled an upsurge of panic and set herself to winning the Egyptian girl's confidence. She poured out her cup of tea and, under the guise of natural interest in her surroundings, she proceeded to question the girl about the plan of the house. Heba was only too happy to tell her all about it; the wonderful library, the English dining-room, and all the other rooms, including the 'harim', which was not what Ashley had imagined at all.

'That is the room for the Sheikh's wife,' Heba explained, 'so she can do as she pleases. It is where she would meet and talk with her lady guests, just as the *qa'ah* is where the men guests are entertained.'

Ashley's sense of outrage returned in full measure. Azir Talil Khaybar was not only abusing her, but also his wife! Ashley hadn't even thought about whether he was married or not. He had swamped all normal thoughts with an intensity of feeling that had blotted out the possibility of there being any other woman in his life.

'Where is his wife?' Ashley asked, the outrage suddenly deflating into a hurt, hollow feeling.

Heba looked surprised at the question. 'The Sheikh is not married.'

Ashley felt bewildered. 'But you said that the harim . . .'

'I only meant that is its traditional purpose,' Heba explained.

Ashley was conscious of a very positive feeling of relief. Not that Azir's single status changed her position at all. She was still his prisoner.

'If you would like, I will show it to you,' Heba suggested eagerly. 'We are in the women's quarters of the house so we will not disturb anyone, and it is a very beautiful room.'

To Heba, every room in the house was very beautiful. Ashley doubted that the girl could see any fault in anything that the Sheikh owned, or did. However, there might be some advantage in seeing the layout of the women's quarters, so

Ashley quickly agreed to the girl's suggestion.

The 'harim' was luxurious with its rich sofas and armchairs, elaborately carved coffee-tables and magnificent Persian rugs. Excited by being able to show off such splendour, Heba started to giggle as she demonstrated that a corner cupboard was not a cupboard at all, but a secret room from where the ladies could watch the men's entertainment below in the *qa'ah*.

It barely measured six foot by six, but it contained two upholstered stools and the *mashrabiyyah* screen allowed a good view of any activity below. Ashley looked across at the gallery on the other side of the *qa'ah* from where the laughter had come this morning. 'What's over there?' she enquired.

'Oh, that is part of the men's quarters,' was the dismissive reply.

'I'd like to see everything,' Ashley pressed.

Heba retreated in some fluster. 'No. No! It is not permitted. You may only see the women's quarters.'

And so much for the freedom of the house, Ashley thought bitterly.

Heba beckoned her out of the secret room and hastily shut the door, her young face stamped with concern over whether she had committed an indiscretion in revealing its existence. She gestured to a table on the other side of the 'harim'. 'Would you like to sit here, *madame*? It is nice for lunch. You can see the roof garden.'

Through grilled windows, Ashley observed, but

she accepted the suggestion. Poor Heba was weighed down with the responsibility of trying to please her; and it was better than looking at a bed, which reminded her all too forcefully of what might happen tonight.

Lunch was savoury meatballs and rice, cooked in the Egyptian style, and accompanied by the usual elaborate salad. Ashley had no appetite for any food, but she mananged to force some of it down. The time was rapidly coming when she would need all her strength.

It did not sit well on her churning stomach. A clammy perspiration beaded her forehead, and she had to ask Heba to take her to the bathroom. The girl was distressed when Ashley finally vomited, apologising profusely and wringing her hands as if she was frightened of being blamed for the sickness.

It had nothing to do with Heba or the food. The emotional turmoil caused by this morning's traumatic events was taking its toll, but it seemed futile to explain that. Heba would not understand and Ashley felt too physically drained to try talking about it. She didn't even protest when Heba steered her back to the Damascus Room and insisted she lie down.

The girl fussed over her, washing her face and arms with iced water before running from the room in order to bring back some new remedy which might help. The application of smelling salts nearly choked Ashley before she realised what was being offered. Another meal was prepared and brought to her, but Ashley could only wave it away uneaten.

Heba's desperation and terror concerning the welfare of her charge finally communicated itself to Ashley, but nothing she could say or do appeared to calm the girl. Heba was frantically worried that there might be something seriously wrong, and continued to fuss until Ashley could bear it no longer.

'Heba, please ... just go away and leave me alone!' she demanded irritably.

But Heba would not go. She had to stay by her mistress. That was the order of the Sheikh.

It was the last straw! However helpful and pleasant Heba might be, there was no way Ashley wanted a maid in constant attendance. Orders be damned! She wouldn't stand for it no matter what the Sheikh said.

Ashley rose from the bed to do battle, but was distracted from her purpose by the arrival of her suitcases from the Sheraton Hotel. Heba immediately wanted to unpack them. The sight of those suitcases containing all the evidence of her presence in Egypt gave Ashley an even greater incentive for rebellion. To have them unpacked meant an acceptance that she would be staying here, and Ashley could not concede that. Not yet. Not ever, she thought with a grim ferocity that speared from her eyes as she turned on Heba.

'Don't you so much as touch those suitcases!' she cried vehemently. 'I want you out of this room, and you will stay out until I call for you.

Now go! Go! Or so help me God, I won't be answerable for the consequences.

The girl sprang to her feet with a cry of fear as Ashley advanced upon her. She did not wait to see what Ashley's intentions were, but ran for the door and scuttled out, hastily closing it behind her.

The violent upsurge of temper left Ashley feeling more exhausted, and she lay back down on the bed and closed her eyes, wishing for a sleep from which she would never waken; then wearily chided herself for the thought. Death was so terribly final. Even life with the Sheikh had to have some value. If she slept now, surely she could regain the strength to fight him again. Maybe he would leave her alone and not press his desire if she rejected him forcefully enough.

But what if he ignored her protests? If he simply swept words aside and took direct action ... kissed her and ... oh, God! She would surely get pregnant. It was the fertile period of her monthly cycle. If a child was conceived ... a baby ...

To have her very own child ... the old yearning swept through her, tugging at her heart, obliterating fear with a desire that was as old as time. If she stayed with him ... if he gave her a child ... a child ... Ashley clutched on to the thought. It gradually soothed away the turmoil, letting her drift into a peaceful, heavy sleep.

CHAPTER SIX

OUTSIDE the door of the Damascus Room, Heba waited until all sound of movement ceased, then nervously crept back into the room, gently tucked a mohair rug around her strange new mistress, and watched over her in deep concern for several hours.

Agitated by Ashley's stillness, the girl finally felt driven to report all that had happened to her master, whose dark frown did nothing to lighten her fear that she had done something terribly wrong. But when he finally noticed that she was hopping from foot to foot in sheer nervousness, he gave her a kindly smile.

'You have done well to tell me of this, Heba. For the present let her sleep on. It will be good for her. Later, I will come and see for myself.'

Heba flashed him a relieved smile, gave a low curtsy, and hurried back to her post beside Ashley's bed. When it became dark, she switched on one of the lamps so her new mistress would not be alarmed when she awoke. The light was dim and soft, too weak to disturb a sleeper.

Ashley was lifted into half-consciousness by the featherlight touch on her cheek. Her skin tingled from the caress, forcing an awareness through her mind. A more pervasive sensation brought her fully alert as fingers grazed over her jawline and down the long column of her neck to rest on her shoulder. Other fingertips brushed her temple, stroking tendrils of hair back from her face. Her heart leapt into a violent pumping action, and only an urgent command from her brain kept her from opening her eyes.

It was him. She didn't have to see to know it was only his touch that could stir this chaotic reaction. And she was so hopelessly vulnerable. Ashley willed herself to keep absolutely motionless, to pretend she was still asleep, so that he might go away and leave her alone. She wasn't ready to face him . . . she needed time . . . time to get herself under control.

The frantic necessity to keep her breathing even, to make the slow, regular inhalations of the sleeper, required the most intense concentration. If even one involuntary gasp escaped her, he would discover her ploy and take instant advantage of her apparent passivity.

His hand played soothingly over her brow, then so lightly over her eyes that Ashley was barely aware she had been touched. He brushed the hair away from her ear, his fingers straying delicately around the rim before he caressed the lobe. Exquisite sensation squirmed through her body, melting the defensive shield she had tried to create.

A hot flush of blood seeped through to the outermost layer of her skin; every hair on her body prickled with sensitivity. Surely he must be aware of what he was doing to her, aware that she could not be asleep. He was playing a silent, seductive cat-and-mouse game that she couldn't possibly win, but still she stubbornly clung to the pretence of sleep, postponing the inevitable, which was too frightening to face.

His hand dropped to her throat. Somehow Ashley controlled the desire to swallow, the desire to give up this hopeless charade. All he had to do was feel the artery throbbing in her neck with each pulsation of her heart to know that her body was responding to him with wanton eagerness.

For one wild moment Ashley wanted to believe that the way he was touching her could only be the product of loving tenderness; that it was not just lust, but a deep caring for all her needs. But reason forced her to discard that madness. It insisted that he only wanted to gratify his needs ... to own ... to dominate.

The hand on her shoulder slowly swept down towards her breast. Ashley could feel it poised, wanting to go further, yearning to touch her in a way only one other man ever had. If he did that to her when he thought she was asleep, she would pluck his eyes out. But the hand went no further, returning from where it had come.

Perhaps he knew she was awake and he was deliberately torturing her. The warmth of his breath fanned her cheek. It was a moment of acute terror. She knew what would come next. The effort to remain immobile made her hands go clammy. He was going to kiss her, and she did not know how she would get past the test.

Then she knew she didn't want to!

She could feel his presence so close to her that he

could only be millimetres away, and her mouth craved for the same erotic invasion of last night's kiss. The masculine scent of his body excited her, and through her mind ran a burst of exhilaration, tipping her inexorably towards surrender. She could feel her lips parting ever so slightly in blatant invitation. She was ashamed that she could participate so eagerly in her own seduction, in her own downfall, but did it really matter . . .? If there was a child . . .

The confusing tumult of thoughts was brushed away by the faintest touch of his lips against hers, tantalisingly sweet. She could not stop the shudder of pleasure that swept through her, the rampant need, the clawing expectation of more pressure that made her whole body ache for intimate contact; his weight and strength enveloping her, sinking into her, possessing her.

And then he was gone. She felt the mattress lift with his withdrawal, could not understand how this could be happening. Her body cried out in anguish for the promise of fulfilment.

Relief came like a crawling snail, leaving its path of shame as she recognised the narrowness of her escape. Perhaps he still believed that she was asleep. She didn't dare raise her eyelashes. She could feel his gaze on her, sense the desire he was repressing. It was so strong that every nerve in her body was still twitching in response.

He moved away, but he did not leave her. The soft fall of his footsteps told Ashley he was pacing up and down the huge rug near the window. He stopped at the far end, paused there for a long

time, and the tension emanating from his presence
drove Ashley to risk a covert peek at him.

He was dressed in white, but they were western
clothes, the tailored trousers revealing a taut,
masculine physique that exuded virility. The loose
shirt of white silk was opened almost to the waist,
giving her a glimpse of black curls sprinkling the
darkly tanned skin. The sudden, urgent desire to
touch him there, over the heartbeat she had felt
this morning, was so strong that it shook Ashley to
the very core of her being.

His head was bare and turned slightly towards
the window. For the first time, Ashley was struck
by the noble cast of his face. It was strong,
commanding in its very strength. But it was not
stamped with arrogance tonight. The interplay of
expressions ranged from uncertainty to grim
frustration.

That he should even feel hesitant about the
course he had chosen astonished Ashley, but
clearly he was in conflict. His gaze suddenly
swung back to her and the black eyes were burning
with pent-up need. He moved, and Ashley's heart
pounded with alarm at the thought that, despite
the dim light, he might have seen the tiny flicker
of her eyelashes dropping shut.

He stood beside her for what seemed an
eternity. She heard him sigh, then in an abrupt,
decisive movement he left the room. Ashley could
hardly believe it, even with the soft click of the
door being shut behind him. She remained still for
a long time, not daring to accept that he really
meant to leave her alone.

Eventually she plucked up enough courage to open her eyes and look at her watch. It was almost ten o'clock. She had slept close to eight hours. Would he come back again when he was sure she could no longer be asleep? If so, Ashley could no longer delude herself that she would fight him. He only had to brush his lips against her own and she would give in to him.

She squirmed restlessly under the mohair blanket, all too appallingly aware of her susceptibility to his attraction and despising herself for it. She couldn't lie here like a sitting duck, waiting for him to fire a final arrow into her heart. And he would come back. She had seen the need eating into the incredible control he had maintained. It had to surface soon, sweeping aside every other consideration.

Ashley tossed the blanket aside and sprang to her feet, driven to take some course of defensive action. A visit to the bathroom was necessary, anyway. Her skirt and tunic were crumpled, but she dismissed the impulse to open her suitcases and change into fresh clothes. It might be a petty and futile act of defiance, but at least it would show him that she was not resigned to staying in this damned house!

She splashed water on her face and regretted that she couldn't brush her hair. The mirrored walls of the bathroom did nothing for her morale, so she made a quick exit. A shudder of apprehension ran through her as she contemplated a return to the Damascus Room. She took the opposite direction, hurrying along the corridor, frantically thinking there must be some place she could hide, some place where she couldn't be immediately found.

However stupid the idea was, Ashley did not have any others to act on, so she pushed on, discarding one room after another until she reached the 'harim'. Did the Sheikh know of the secret room?

Of course he would, Ashley berated herself. But he might not know that she had been shown it. Driven by the need to keep away from him as long as possible, to hide herself from him, Ashley opened the cupboard door and stepped into the tiny gallery.

The voice from the *qa'ah* below almost caused her to trip over a stool. The hard, distinctive tone of it rang in her ears like some inescapable echo. But then another voice spoke and hope leapt in her heart. It hardly seemed possible. How could it be so? She crept to the screen and looked down. She had not been mistaken. it was him! Louis-Philippe! The Baron de Laclos. And he was facing the Sheikh with an imperturbable air of authority.

Amazement quickly melted into relief. All she had to do was cry out to him, begging his help. No matter what Azir said, she was sure Louis-Philippe would take her side. He knew enough about her to realise that she would not spin such an outrageous story. But as she drew breath, he spoke, and the words were so shocking, the tone so chilling, that Ashley froze into horrified silence.

'The war in Algeria taught many of us the more barbaric methods of interrogation. Few men can remain loyally silent when a knife is biting into their naked flesh. So don't blame your chauffeur! He had to tell the truth. So I know you had Ashley Cunningham abducted. I know she is here.'

The silence that followed simmered with antagonism. Ashley held her breath. She was watching some deadly conflict, a contest of wills that diminished her own plight. The two men stood some considerable distance apart, as tense as two gladiators in the ring, assessing each other, waiting ... waiting like coiled springs for a glimmer of vulnerability before rejoining battle.

'The Algerian war taught many lessons,' Azir finally answered, his tone laced with bitter contempt. 'How to kill helpless women and children ...'

The Baron de Laclos did not flinch. The accusation made no impression on him whatsoever. His face remained completely impassive, his gaze steadily fixed on the blazing black eyes of Azir Talil Khaybar.

'You know I did my utmost to prevent the massacre of innocent lives. You know I was court-martialled for disobeying those orders. Blame your father for using the villagers and putting their lives in jeopardy ...'

'They were prepared to lay down their lives to get the French out of their country,' came the fierce retort. 'What right did you have to subjugate the Arab people and take their land?'

'We could argue that question all night. We've already fought a war over it. It achieves nothing. I've long since lost all interest in politics. What-

ever you think of my . . . participation . . . I paid for
it. And I paid for your father's freedom. You know
he owes his life to me. That's what I've come for.
I'm calling in the debt.'

Ashley had recognised the ruthlessness in Azir
Talil Khaybar at first sight, but she had not even
sensed it in Louis-Philippe de Laclos. She stared
down at him, trying to match the gentle man she
had met last night to the man she saw now. A
deadly determination was graven on his face, and
the sad, grey eyes were unrelenting steel.

'No!' The word exploded from Azir's throat,
harsh and violent.

Louis-Philippe's mouth thinned in contempt.
'A man of honour would not deny me.'

'Ask for any other of my possessions and you
can have it. Our family pays its debts,' Azir
retorted with cold, stinging pride. 'Take whatever
you want, Frenchman.'

'A life for a life, Azir,' came the relentless
demand. 'Have the girl brought to me. That's all I
ask.'

'We no longer keep slaves,' Azir replied, his
voice dropping to a low rasp. 'She is not mine to
give.'

'Nor yours to take,' Louis retorted sharply.
'You had her abducted, Azir, and she wasn't a
willing victim. It was you she ran from last night,
you who put the fear in her eyes . . .'

'And me she wants!' The words hung in the air
between them, vibrating with suppressed
emotion.

'Then let her tell me that,' was the quiet, but

equally lethal reply.

It was a simple matter for her to call out, to end the confrontation being enacted below her, but Ashley still hesitated. The elemental clash of character, the raw revelation of feelings that throbbed beneath the surface of their masks, held her spellbound. Was Azir's desire for her so strong that he valued her above all his other possessions? She waited, her heart pounding in her ears as she strained to hear his reply.

'She is asleep,' he said in a low, dismissive tone. 'And I will not have her disturbed.'

'Take me to her!'

'No! Come back tomorrow.'

The concession astonished Ashley until she realised how many hours there were before tomorrow. Was he gambling that he could tie her to him with his lovemaking? Or was he playing for time to remove her from Louis-Philippe's reach?

The grey eyes narrowed. 'I will not leave this house without her, Azir.' The flat, unequivocal statement held relentless purpose.

'Then either you will have to kill me . . . or I will have to kill you.'

The low, vibrant words echoed and re-echoed through Ashley's mind, but still she couldn't believe that they had been spoken. It was not until Azir strode down the room and drew the sword of Salah al-Din from its scabbard that the reality was stamped home. The scream that tore from Ashley's throat reverberated around the huge two-storeyed room.

'No-o-o! No-o-o!' She beat at the *mashra-*

biyyah screen with frenzied hands.

'Ashley!'

She saw Louis-Philippe's face turn up to her, but her frantic gaze sought Azir's.

'Stop it! You can't do this!' she cried, in desperate fear of the ruthless will behind the sword.

He lifted a grim face to the gallery where she stood shaking with terror. His eyes burned with fierce command. 'Then tell him you will stay with me. Tell him now, Ashley, and send him away.'

'No!' Louis-Philippe barked the counter-command. He strode down the room to where Azir held his position and came to a halt with barely a yard between them. 'You won't get her by force, Azir. We both know that if you kill me, you'll lose, anyway. My death will hang like an albatross around your neck, and she'll never look at you without seeing it.'

'Oh, God!' Ashley sobbed, and forced her voice to a scream. 'Please stop it! Both of you!' Again she beat on the screen in helpless frustration, too terrified to move in case something happened while she tried to find her way down to them.

Light flashed from the sword. It wavered in Azir's hand. She saw the tortured heave of his chest under the white silk of his shirt. His head suddenly jerked up, his gaze probing the screen behind which she stood, and the conflict that raged within him was written on his face. Pain, such as she had never thought to see in him, flowed up at her, wound around her heart, pleading, demanding recognition.

'Ashley!' It was a hoarse, driven cry. 'Say it! Say you want to stay with me!'

'I can't,' she sobbed, torn beyond bearing. 'Don't do it, Azir. Please . . .'

She could not look at his face any longer. Her gaze dropped to the sword in his hand. She saw the clenched grip tighten, saw the blade swing as if to strike, felt horror strangling her throat. Then the sword was arcing through the air, clattering on to the marble floor, tipping into the fountain. And all the breath in her body was released in a tortured sigh.

Some automatic process set her feet moving. Shock still glazed her mind, but her legs pounded along the corridors, down the flight of steps, through the passageway that led to the *qa'ah*. She burst open the door at the back of the room, ran on past the fountain and threw herself against Louis-Philippe de Laclos, sobbing with relief that he had not been injured. A strong arm came around her, hugging her tight. A hand gently stroked her hair. 'It's all right, Ashley. We can go now. It's over.'

The soft murmur ravaged her heart. It was over. She was free, yet every instinct screamed that she would never be free of this day . . . this night. A terrible uncertainty ripped through her mind.

A harsh, soft laughter echoed through the *qa'ah*. 'It's not over. It will never be over. But my father's life is now repaid, Frenchman. From here our paths go separate ways.'

The dull finality in Azir's voice hurt Ashley in some indefinable way. She turned, pulled by a need that she didn't stop to question. But the pained black eyes passed over her without recognition, and the harsh, arrogant face was carved in stone.

'Go! You have chosen,' he said in a flat monotone. 'May you find your happiness.'

This last was a bare whisper as he set off, leading the way to the double entrance doors. Louis-Philippe dropped his arm around Ashley's waist, half-supporting her as he pushed her into walking the length of the room. Azir opened the doors, barked orders in Arabic, then stood back for them to pass.

Ashley was intensely, frighteningly aware of his taut body, so rigidly motionless as Louis-Philippe steered her to the top of the steps which led down to the courtyard. Her feet faltered, stopped, turned, drawn by a power beyond her control.

The hurt was so bad, she had to try and explain. 'It wouldn't have worked, Azir,' she said softly.

He looked at her then, the black eyes seeing straight into her soul.

'You should have listened to your heart, Ashley. I did.' And with that bleak utterance he turned and walked back up the room to the fountain. Just before the doors swung shut, Ashley saw him stoop to retrieve the sword of Salah al-Din.

She shivered, remembering the way he had pressed into the tip of the blade this morning . . . so sure of himself, so sure of her. A hand grasped her elbow and she dragged her gaze up to the sad, blue-grey eyes that had softened in concern for her.

'Ashley, we must go now. He is strained to the limits of control.'

'Yes. Yes, of course,' she murmured distractedly.

Louis-Philippe took her at her word, steering her away and lending his strength to her tottering footsteps. No one stopped them. Even when they stepped outside, down the steps to the cobbled cul-de-sac, the guards there stood respectfully aside and waved them on to the gateway.

She stubbed her toes on the rough roadway and loked down at them dazedly, having forgotten that her feet were bare. Her sandals were still lying beside the bed in the Damascus Room. And not only her sandals! She stopped dead, the churning sense of loss deepening into panic. She plucked wildly at Louis-Philippe's arm.

'We've got to go back. All my things are here . . . money, passport, my folder, everything . . .'

He shook his head. 'You can't go back! He would never let you go again. You saw what it cost to buy your freedom this time!'

He was right. She knew he was right. But a wild hysteria clawed up her throat and spilled off her tongue. 'You don't understand! I haven't got anything! All the sketches I've done . . . my airline tickets . . . my passport . . . how do I even get out of the country?'

Louis-Philippe's arm tightened around her. 'They can all be replaced. I will look after you. Whatever you need can be bought tomorrow.'

Again he carried her along with him, sweeping her out to the narrow, unlit street where a car stood waiting in the darkness. He bundled Ashley into the back seat, followed her in, slammed the door and threw a curt command at the driver. The car accelerated away, and only then did Ashley realise that tears were trickling down her cheeks.

She couldn't stop them. There were too many emotions welling inside her, needing some release. And the ache in her heart . . . why did it ache so?

CHAPTER SEVEN

AN arm curled around Ashley, and Louis-Philippe gently tucked her head on to his shoulder. He pressed a clean handkerchief into her hand. 'We'll soon be back at the hotel,' he murmured.

Ashley tried to mop up the tears but her eyes kept overflowing. 'I ... I haven't even thanked you. It was so much. So ...'

'It was only a matter of knowing how to proceed,' he said dismissively. 'Once I knew it was Azir ...'

He did not finish his thought, and Ashley could not find the will to pursue the matter further. The traumatic scene with Azir was still too close, too raw, too laden with pain. She sensed that Louis-Philippe didn't want to talk about it, and neither did she.

'It will never be over.' Azir's words hammered through her heart. But what else could she have done? Azir had demanded an impossible choice from her ... hadn't he? How could she have stayed? Louis-Philippe had risked his very life to rescue her, and she had been frantic to escape Azir. There had been no other choice. None. She shivered at the memory of his touch on her skin ... the look in his eyes ...

'You're suffering from shock,' Louis-Philippe

murmured, hugging her more closely to him for warmth. 'We're almost at the hotel.'

Indeed, within a few moments the car was slowing to a halt at the front entrance of the Sheraton. Louis-Philippe helped her out, then whisked her up the steps and through the lobby where people were still milling around the shops and food-bars.

'Ashley! Ashley!'

Sohaila's beautiful young voice floated through the reception area, totally distinctive in its accent. Ashley's head jerked up in time to see her friend come flying across the room, her black curls bobbing, her lovely face lit with excitement. She threw her arms around Ashley and hugged her close.

'You're safe! You're safe! Oh, Ashley, I was so worried for you. When the Baron found out what had happened, I thought I would never see you again.'

The Baron ... and Sohaila ... and Ahmed, Sohaila's fiancé, looming up behind her ... Ashley didn't understand any of it, but she was relieved to see her friend, to feel her life moving back on to familiar rails.

Sohaila drew back, falling naturally into the mannerisms that Ashley found so endearing. Her whole body moved as she spoke, an expressive lift of her shoulders or wriggle of her hips; the delicate gestures of her fingers and hands; the lovely almond eyes flashing white as she rolled her irises.

'I did not know what to do when you didn't come to the museum, so I came here and asked for you and they said you'd checked out, which I felt couldn't be right. And then I saw the Baron and he . . .' Her eyes flashed to the man behind Ashley, and they shone with admiration. 'He found out where you were.'

As if recollecting herself, her gaze returned anxiously to Ashley. 'There was nothing I could do, you understand. The Sheikh . . . his power and prestige . . . not even MISR could act against him without the President's authority.'

The flat statement of fact shook Ashley. Despite Azir's claim of diplomatic immunity, she had not realised that only the President of Egypt would dare move against him. Yet Louis-Philippe de Laclos had done precisely that!

Her gaze lifted wonderingly to the enigmatic man who had so many hidden depths. Even now his face was shuttered, slightly stiff as if he had once more donned a mask, retreating behind it to the weariness of soul that had been so eloquently expressed last night.

'Sohaila, you have seen that your friend is safe now,' Ahmed stated pointedly. The finely drawn cast of his handsome features emanated disapproval, and it was plain that he did not like his fiancée's attachment to these foreigners.

A deep flush burned over Sohaila's beautiful olive skin. 'Ahmed, Ashley needs my help,' she pleaded.

He took in Ashley's dishevelled hair, the

pinched paleness of her face, the crumpled clothes and bare feet, then shot a cynically knowing look at the Frenchman.

'Perhaps you can help Ashley tomorrow, Sohaila,' Louis suggested quietly. 'You can safely leave her in my care tonight.'

'Yes. Yes, of course. I'm sorry, I ...' She faltered and turned pained eyes to Ashley. 'I'll come in the morning.'

Ashley squeezed her hand. 'Thank you for all you've done. For caring enough to ...'

'Oh, Ashley!' Tears blurred the luminous, dark eyes and once again Sohaila hugged her close. 'I'm happy you are safe,' she whispered huskily.

Her friend's affection moved Ashley deeply. The abduction today had probably cast her in the role of a fallen woman by Moslem standards. Condemnation was written on Ahmed's face as he stood sullenly beside them.

Ashley quickly disentangled herself from Sohaila's embrace and flicked an appeasing look at her friend's stern fiancé. 'It was good of you both to wait. I appreciate it very deeply.'

Ahmed took Sohaila's arm and said a curt goodbye for both of them. As the two Egyptians walked away, the hand on Ashley's elbow tightened its grip to a painful clench and she looked up at Louis-Philippe in mute protest. His face wore a grim tightness and she caught a glimpse of some intense emotion in his eyes before he glanced down at her.

'I'm sorry. I find it difficult to tolerate such rudeness.'

'He was probably tired . . .'

Louis-Philippe relaxed and lifted his arm to curl comfortingly around Ashley's shoulders. An ironic smile softened his mouth as he added, 'Perhaps you're right. The tyranny of culture creates a chasm we cannot cross.'

An elevator opened its doors behind them, and Louis-Philippe steered her into it. Ashley felt discomfited by the awkward parting from Sohaila and Ahmed, but it was only a tiny addition to the depression that weighed on her heart.

Louis-Philippe had summed the truth up in a few words. It couldn't have worked with Azir, no matter how deep the attraction. The culture difference was too daunting. She leaned tiredly against Louis-Philippe, intensely grateful for his support and understanding, and when the elevator reached his floor, she accompanied him to his suite without the slightest hesitation. The sense of kinship she had felt with him last night was even stronger now.

They didn't talk much, both of them preoccupied with their own thoughts, and both of them automatically respecting the other's silences. Louis-Philippe ordered a meal which neither of them showed much interest in. He organised a room for her on the same floor as his corner suite, just along the corridor so that she could easily call on him if she felt nervous about anything. He had given his word to Sohaila that he would take care of her, and he did.

'Why?' Ashley asked at one point. 'You hardly know me, Louis.'

He gave his sad, ironic smile. 'Perhaps an old-fashioned sense of chivalry. Sohaila asked me to help her. You asked me to help you last night. And the war in Algeria left its scars.' He paused and shot her a sharp, probing look. 'But Azir didn't act without reason, did he, Ashley?'

'He had reason,' she admitted. 'But he had no right to take me like that. And I could not have been happy with that kind of life.'

'Yes. That is always the bottom line. And force can't get you what you want. Not what you really want,' Louis-Philippe murmured. He sighed and startled Ashley by adding, 'Still, I can sympathise with Azir.'

She looked askance at him, remembering the ruthlessness he had displayed tonight and wondering what he really wanted.

He shrugged. 'How much longer do you need to be in Egypt, Ashley?'

'Only a week or two if I could get a favourable decision out of the government.'

'Perhaps I can help you. I have some little influence that might ease the way. If you like, I shall talk to some people tomorrow and ...' He paused as he saw her puzzlement. 'It is better finished, is it not? For you to go home and forget this?'

'Yes. Yes, I suppose it is,' she agreed. She had been too long in this foreign country. She was even causing trouble between Sohaila and Ahmed, not helping her friend at all. 'Thank you, Louis. I would be grateful for any help I can get from anyone.'

He nodded. 'I'll let you know. Would dinner tomorrow night be convenient?'

'Yes. Thank you.'

'It is sometimes . . . invigorating . . . to be of use.'

Their eyes met in understanding and there was nothing more to say. Louis-Philippe saw Ashley into her new room and they parted sympathetic friends.

Ashley was woken by a porter's call the next morning. Azir had returned everything to her; the two suitcases, her handbag containing her passport, money and airline tickets, and the sketch folder that represented so many weeks of hard work. There was no accompanying note. No message.

Ashley told herself she should feel relieved. Azir had accepted her choice. She would never see him again; it was finished. But no relief came. The aching sense of loss she had felt at parting with Azir intensified, raising tormenting questions in her mind.

Would she have been unhappy with him? He had reached into her, touching depths she had never recognised in herself before, awakening desires to a more vibrant life than she had ever known. She had craved for his touch, craved to feel . . . everything!

Madness, she told herself once again, but it did

not take the ache away, and Ashley felt thoroughly miserable as she unpacked her suitcases and changed into fresh clothes. She forced herself to eat breakfast in the wan hope that food might fill the void, but it didn't.

She put a call through to Louis-Philippe's room and informed him that all her belongings had been returned. 'So I can get straight on with my work,' she concluded, and thanked him once again for the support he had offered.

Louis-Philippe had certainly given her the right advice—wrap up her business in Egypt as quickly as possible and get back home, away from all things foreign. She was going mad here! The idea of gambling her money away should have been warning enough.

By the time Sohaila arrived, Ashley was ready to go to the museum and get on with her work. The Egyptian girl was clearly relieved that everything had apparently returned to normal.

'Are you sure you're all right, Ashley?' she asked anxiously.

'Of course,' Ashley assured her with a smile.

An embarrassed flush crept into Sohaila's cheeks. 'I am sorry that I had to leave last night. I did not think . . . like Ahmed . . .' She floundered, her hands gesturing an anxious apology.

'I understand, Sohaila,' Ashley said in soft sympathy. 'I hope I didn't cause you any trouble with your fiancé.'

Sohaila shrugged and her mouth tightened into a stubborn line. 'It does not matter. I can think for myself, can I not?'

'Well, I'm certainly glad you did yesterday,' Ashley said lightly, wanting to dispel the slight awkwardness of the moment. 'If you hadn't spoken to Louis I would have been in terrible trouble. I'm immensely grateful to you, Sohaila.'

The colour in Sohaila's cheeks ebbed and flowed. 'He is a wonderful man . . . the Baron. So kind.'

'He certainly is,' Ashley agreed warmly. 'He's even offered to help me get the permission needed for the jewellery exhibition. Isn't that marvellous?'

'Yes,' Sohaila agreed, but her enthusiasm was shadowed by some other, indefinable emotion.

'What's the problem, Sohaila?' Ashley asked bluntly. 'You're not yourself at all.'

The expressive mouth turned down into a self-mocking grimace. 'I was thinking you will be leaving our country soon, Ashley. And I will miss you.'

'I'll miss you, too,' Ashley sighed, then linked her arm with her friend's and forced a cheer-up smile. 'But I'm not gone yet, so let's enjoy today.'

Once at the museum, they went straight to the north wing which housed the Tutankhamun galleries. Nearby was the Jewel Room which contained the pharaonic artefacts from many dynasties, and it was here that Ashley had seen the bracelets she wanted to sketch. Sohaila found them both chairs and they settled down to work beside the showcases.

The cylindrical bracelets had the most immediate eye-impact with their designs of winged
scarabs and sun-disks and the cartouches of the
kings; all gold inlaid with lapis lazuli, cornelian
and green felspar. Ashley did not doubt their
selling-power, but she was fairly certain that the
daintier type of hoop bracelet which had been
found on the mummy of the high-priest
Pinudjem would have even more buyer appeal.

The last seemed to be the forerunner of today's
charm bracelet. From two small rings near the
clasp fell a number of tassels, some ending in lapis
lazuli pendants in the form of hexagonal pyramids; others were strung with beads which
supported gold flowerettes formed by six con-
joined petals. The workmanship in the flowerettes
was exquisite, and Ashley marvelled over it as she
sketched.

Sohaila's incredibly detailed knowledge of the
relics of Ancient Egypt allowed her to tell Ashley
the meaning of every design in the jewellery.
Invariably, she added entertaining stories about
the people who had worn the pieces. When Ashley
thought some detail was particularly relevant, she
would get Sohaila to write it out. In this way each
piece acquired its own fascinating history.

Time passed all too quickly. Ashley skipped
lunch, but sent Sohaila off to have something to
eat in the museum cafeteria. Her friend had been
gone some ten minutes when Ashley felt the man's
presence. Even as she berated herself for the
wildness of her imagination—it could not be him,

it was all over, he would never see her again—her gaze was drawn from her sketch-pad and pulled towards the archway at the other end of the gallery.

Azir stood there. He was clothed as she had first seen him, as formidable now as he had been then, and Ashley's reaction was instant and over-whelming. Her mind crackled with hot, frantic explosions of thought. A quiver of electric excitement ran through her body; catching her breath, cramping her heart, and digging a queezy hollowness in her stomach.

He stepped forward, the dark eyes devouring her in a way that was a violation in itself. Ashley forced herself to stand. The folder slipped from her nerveless hands, spilling the contents over the floor. The light sound of her pencil hitting the stonework seemed to reverberate throughout the room.

'You must not be frightened of me, Ashley. You have nothing to fear. You never did. Although I understand why you do not see it that way.' His voice was quiet, the tone tense.

Her hand instinctively crept to cover her heart, which had burst from its constriction and was pounding its wild agitation against the wall of her chest. 'Why . . .' The word was a graceless croak. She swallowed convulsively and tried again. 'Why are you here? I thought . . . when you sent back my bags . . . I never expected to see you again.'

The muscles in his face tightened; his eyes darkened with a ravening hunger that tore at her own feeble composure. 'I could not live with myself if I did not try to make some reparation for the wrongs I have done you ... for the terrible mistake in judgement that I made ... and for the pain I gave you.'

Reparation! The word shattered the wanton hope that had fluttered through Ashley's mind. 'Oh, please ...' she begged, swamped by a wave of intense humiliation. She had to send him away before he realised his power over her. Sheer despair lent strength to her voice. 'There's no need to say or do anything. I don't want ...'

'Will you not hear me out, Ashley?' he interrupted softly.

The request tugged at her heart, and she could not refuse him, no matter how hard it was to keep some grain of self-possession in his presence.

He paused only a moment or two, then continued with a quiet deliberation that projected a strong emotional impact into every word. 'I had no right to take anything from you. Not your possessions ... nor your freedom. My blind desire to keep you with me overruled every other consideration. Even humanity.'

His mouth twisted into a bitter grimace of self-contempt. 'I deluded myself! Even when I knew ... Heba told me how distressed you were ... I still clung on to the belief that ... I had to be right.'

'And ... and now?' Ashley asked, driven by her own need for a solution that would allow her to meet him in some acceptable way.

'And now ... I accept the consequences ... and

I hope . . . make some recompense for the pain I caused you.'

He walked towards her and every nerve in Ashley's body twanged with an expectation that was impossible to control. She couldn't move. Her legs almost gave way when he stooped at her feet. But it was not to touch her.

For the first time she noticed he carried a parcel, carelessly wrapped in brown paper, and fastened with twine. He threw it aside on the chair she had vacated, then turned his attention to the sheets of sketches that had scattered on the floor. He retrieved them all with meticulous care, replacing them one by one in her folder. With the task completed, he lifted the parcel and slid the portfolio under it.

When he straightened up he was barely an arm's distance away, and Ashley felt she was being sucked into the dark whirlpools of passion that were his eyes. His voice fell softly, yet struck chords of recognition that quivered in response.

'You called it lust, Ashley. Perhaps it is, but I don't believe it. Never before in my life have I ever experienced such an instant, compelling attraction for a woman. When I first saw you, it was as if my whole being leapt in excitement. And with every second that passed, I grew more certain that my life could never be complete without you. I can control lust. I could not control what I felt for you.'

His hand reached over and took hers, reinforcing his words with a gentle stroking that was more compelling than any possessive grip.

'You will never comprehend the violence of my
rage when I believed you had forsaken me to sleep
with the Baron de Laclos. The thought that under
the beauty of your face and body lay the
wantonness of a whore ...'

'No!' Her own anguish of spirit forced the
denial. She was not a whore, and yet with Azir ...

His other hand lifted to stroke her cheek in
tender apology. 'You think I don't know that
now? That I am not deeply shamed by what you
told me?'

It was madness, utter madness, but the urge to
nestle her cheek into the warm palm of his hand
was so primal she almost gave way to it. Her skin
heated and quivered under the light touch, and
the despairing appeal in his eyes tore at her heart.

'I was deranged by what seemed to be irrefut-
able evidence that you were not the woman I
wanted you to be. I despised myself for still
wanting you, yet I could not rid myself of the need
to have you with me. And then I found I was
wrong. That I had deceived myself. And you made
it ... abundantly clear that I had destroyed any
chance I had of your staying with me of your own
free will.'

The lingering finger-touch trailed from her
cheek, his hand dropping reluctantly to his side.
'Not only that,' he added bitterly, 'but I'd
condemned myself so much in your eyes that I had

no hope of your agreeing to see me again if I let you go.'

The memory of his cold callousness as he ordered her imprisonment stung Ashley into a reply. 'You didn't give me that choice, Azir.'

His eyes mocked her. 'Ashley, there was only one course left to take and I took it. You couldn't think any worse of me, and I hoped, in time, I could persuade you that . . .' He stopped, and his expression hardened. 'Given the same circumstances I would make the same decision again. The miscalculation was in overestimating your . . . reaction to me, and in underestimating your attachment to the Baron de Laclos.'

That shook Ashley out of the draining weakness which had almost betrayed her. Azir's remorse might be genuine, but there was no ignoring the intrinsic ruthlessness in his character. It would lead to utter self-abasement if she gave in to him. He had left her in no doubt that he wanted to own her body and soul. Did she really want a relationship that demanded so much of her that she was left with no identity of her own?

'I must make my own decisions, Azir,' she said defensively, frightened by his power over her, and all too aware of his ability to sweep aside all the normal safeguards of the law. 'I won't have that right taken away from me.'

Something dangerous glittered in his eyes. His fingers closed more firmly around her hand, re-asserting the physical link between them. 'The decision you made last night ... was it the right one, Ashley?'

Confusion swirled through her mind. His thumb caressed her wrist and it was impossible to concentrate on anything else. Her whole body was prickling with sensual awareness, aching for the resolution only he could give her.

Had she made the right decision? There was no other she could have made at the time, and yet ... the tumult of emotions he aroused in her ... the intensive desire he could evoke just by looking at her ... if she confessed what she felt, he would sweep her away. And then ... could she live his life? Be content as his mistress?

'Ashley ... answer me!'

The urgent pressure of his voice ... his hand ... his eyes probing into her ... taking her over ... leaving her no other existence except as his possession.

'Yes! Yes, I made the right decision,' she cried, almost panting from the effort needed to deny him.

And another, different cry trembled on her tongue as his eyes dulled and he released her hand. Every instinct clamoured to recapture his attention, his touch, uncaring of the consequences. He turned and started to walk away, and the clamour of her mind increased, drowning out the voice of reason.

'Azir!'

He stopped abruptly, then half turned, his face totally expressionless. Ashley's mind went into a spin, frantically reaching for a way that could make their relationship work.

'It was partly my fault . . . the way I acted at the casino. I don't blame you for . . . for thinking the worst of me.'

There was no reaction from him. He simply waited patiently for her to continue, his dark gaze fixed unblinkingly on hers, hard and unreadable. Ashley groped for a resolution that would allow her time to consider what a future with Azir might mean to her.

'I . . . I don't think badly of you. Now that we understand each other better, couldn't we meet . . . as friends?'

'No, Ashley.' There was a wafting quality of sadness in his voice. 'We can never be friends. You and I can only be lovers!'

The temptation to give in and fling herself at him was almost irresistible. The prospect of being totally immersed with him held its own compelling fascination, but Ashley could not quite set aside the practical reality that to love this man would necessitate her throwing off attitudes and beliefs she had held all her life.

Slowly she shook her head in negation.

'I could not be content with anything less,' he said softly. 'Between us, it has to be all or nothing.' And with that flat ultimatum, he turned away and walked on towards the archway through which he had entered the room.

Ashley searched her mind for anything to keep him with her longer, to prevent this final retreat

away from her. There was nothing. Her gaze
darted abstractedly over the display cases ... the
jewellery that had seemed so important to her ...
just meaningless objects. Her folder of designs ...
the parcel!

'Azir!' She snatched it up as if it was a lifeline.
'You've forgotten your parcel!'

He paused for just the briefest moment, flung
the words over his shoulder at her. 'No! That is
yours. I hope it gives you the joy you expected of
it.' And then he was gone.

Ashley sank down on Sohaila's chair, too bereft
to organise any rational thought. A deathlike
drum kept hammering on her heart. Azir had gone
... gone ... and gone with him was the last chance
of their becoming lovers ... the last chance of
knowing, of experiencing what it might have been
like if she'd had the courage to grasp all ... instead
of nothing.

Sohaila's hands gripped her shoulders tightly,
her lovely almond eyes dilating in alarm. 'Ashley!
Ashley! Are you all right?'

'Yes, of course,' Ashley replied automatically.
'Why wouldn't I be?'

'The Sheikh's guards blocked off the room.
They would not let me enter. I feared ...' Her
arms went round Ashley's shoulders, hugging her
in comfort and relief.

'It's all right. I'm fine. Truly.' The words
tripped out; stupid, empty words.

Sohaila anxiously searched her eyes. 'He didn't
hurt you?'

'No. He never meant to,' Ashley answered dully. But she had just hurt him, and herself, and that truth could not be dismisssed so easily. She sucked in a deep breath and forced a smile to relieve Sohaila's mind. 'He just wanted to say he was sorry for yesterday, and to give me this.' She picked up the parcel from the chair and was surprised to find it was quite heavy.

'What is it?' Sohaila asked, unable to restrain her curiosity.

'I don't know. Azir said it was mine. Something that was left behind, I guess.'

More for the sake of something to do than out of curiosity she began to unwrap the parcel in a half-hearted and desultory fashion. She frowned over the protective layers of tissue papers, and with a spurt of impatience tore them aside. The sheer magnificence of the gift left her gaping in astonishment. Because it was a gift. Ashley had never owned anything like it before in her life.

The jewellery-box was similar to that found among the treasures in Tutankhamun's tomb; exquisitely carved wood, inlaid with turquoise and gold. It had to be incredibly expensive, and Ashley wondered if this was what Azir meant when he spoke of making reparation for the pain he had caused her. She unfastened the catch and lifted the lid.

The neat stacks of American currency stared back at her. They were all one hundred dollar bills. Ashley did not have to count it. She knew exactly how much would be there. Ten thousand dollars.

The amount she had wanted to win at the roulette table in the casino. And Azir's last words to her echoed through her mind—'I hope it gives you the joy you expected of it'.

Sohaila's gasp of astonishment hardly impinged on her consciousness. Ashley's heart was a lump of cold stone. Azir was paying her off, making complete restitution for whatever he had done to her, expiating his mistake of judgement, driving the final nail into her coffin of need.

'He must love you very much!'

Sohaila's quiet words astonished Ashley. She looked at the girl for the first time since she unwrapped the parcel. The dark irises were rolled back in her head with amazement, her hands still thrown up in the air in surprise. The fingers gesticulated in emphasis as she repeated. 'He must love you. To give you such a present . . .' The words trailed away as she searched for adequate words to express what she felt.

Ashley patted her friend's arm with a mixture of affection and sadness. 'No, Sohaila,' she said, and each word was a stab of pain as she dragged out the truth. 'It's not so. Azir doesn't love me. This isn't even a present for me. He knows I don't want the money. It's for you.'

CHAPTER EIGHT

SOHAILA stared at the money, then back at Ashley, her eyes widening in shocked denial. She shook her head vehemently. 'No, Ashley! How can it be so? The money has to be for you. The Sheikh does not even know me.'

Ashley ignored her. She hastily rewrapped the box and rose to her feet in a burst of purposeful energy. 'We can't talk about it here. Come back to the hotel with me and I'll explain.'

Sohaila was full of puzzled protests, but Ashley determinedly steered her out of the museum and into a taxi. There might not be any joy in it for her right at this moment, but Ashley felt a bitter satisfaction in knowing that someone was going to get some happiness out of all this mess, and that someone was going to be Sohaila.

At least her friend could have the future she wanted. As for her own future ... that was a bigger, darker question mark than it had ever been, and she couldn't bear to contemplate it. Ashley was intensely grateful that she had one action in hand that could be counted as a positive achievement.

Once inside her hotel room, with privacy ensured, Ashley re-opened the box and tipped its contents on to the bed. 'It's all yours, Sohaila! Ten thousand American dollars! And it was won at the

119

roulette table in the casino downstairs. That's where I met the Sheikh.'

'You were gambling?' Sohaila gasped, still hopelessly bewildered.

'All in a good cause,' Ashley retorted firmly. 'And that cause was to win enough money so that you and Ahmed won't have to wait any longer to get your apartment. You can get married now, Sohaila! There'll be no in-laws breathing over your shoulder. No economic problems. You can start your marriage free and clear. It's all yours.'

Shock and pain drained the colour from Sohaila's face. She backed away, putting out a trembling hand as if to ward off the gift. 'No,' she whispered in a strained, hoarse voice. 'It's all wrong. I cannot take it.'

Ashley had expected some confusion from Sohaila initially; eventually delight and happiness at what the gift entailed. She had certainly never anticipated the horror in her reaction. It could only be due to the large sum of money involved.

'I want you to have it.' Ashley insisted firmly, anxious to put her friend at ease, and resolve the matter before Sohaila's negative attitude locked her into a position from which she could not retreat with dignity. 'I only went to the casino to help you. I have no need of the money. Azir helped me win it. Even he knew that it was to help a friend, not for me. I want you and Ahmed to be happy.'

Tears welled into the lovely dark eyes and Sohaila shook her head in hopeless distress. 'I cannot . . . I cannot marry Ahmed.'

'What?'

The tactless squawk made Sohaila turn away. She burst into heart-rending sobs. Clearly there was something terribly wrong, and it wasn't the money. Ashley gently drew the girl into her arms and tried to soothe her convulsive weeping.

'Why? After all these years of waiting?'

The words when they came were so incoherent that it took Ashley some time to understand them. 'I ... don't ... love ... him.'

She suddenly recalled Sohaila's strained manner this morning. And Ahmed's sullen air of disapproval last night. Had they argued about Sohaila's friendship with her? Was she the unwitting cause of this wretched misery? The thought worried Ashley so much that she had to speak.

'Sohaila, have I caused any trouble between you and Ahmed?'

'No ... I am sorry ... for losing control. I just ... cannot help myself, Ashley,' came the halting reply.

'Come and sit down on the bed and when you're ready, we'll talk about it. Maybe I can help.'

'No ...' Sohaila sobbed despairingly, but she sank on to the bed at Ashley's urging and tried to mop up the tears with the tissues handed to her.

'Sohaila, you must tell me. There can't be anything so terribly wrong that it can't be fixed up.'

A paroxysm of grief shook the girl, and she cried uncontrollably as Ashley put her arms around her in comfort and concern. As best she could, Ashley tried to soothe her, letting Sohaila cry out the tormented passion that drove her to such despair. Gradually the racking sobs quieted, and she drew away from Ashley's embrace, hunching over in self-conscious shame.

Ashley took her hand and squeezed it in affectionate encouragement. 'Sometimes it's good to cry, Sohaila. It releases all the pent-up feelings that we can't carry around any longer. And talking about them can help, too. Don't feel shy with me. Aren't I your friend?'

She nodded, then slowly lifted her tear-stained face. Her inner anguish still shimmered in the reddened eyes as she struggled to explain. 'I tried ... I tried to break off our engagement twice, Ashley. Once when I was seventeen—and again just before I graduated from the University. Both times my family put such pressure on me ... the shame ... the disgrace ... the humiliation. If I didn't honour the contract with Ahmed, no one else would want me anyway. My parents made my life such a misery ...'

She sucked in a deep breath and let it out on a shuddering sigh. 'I thought about leaving the country ... leaving everything. But you see ... I would not belong anywhere else. In the end, I decided I would do my best to make Ahmed a good wife. But I put it off as long as possible. That is why I insisted on having our own apartment before I would allow him to consummate the marriage.'

Her gaze wavered away and she dropped her head, shaking it sadly as she dragged out the core of her pain. 'Then three years ago . . . I fell in love with . . . with another man. So foolish and stupid! I didn't know what to do. There was no one I could talk to. No one who would understand what I felt, and not condemn me. Yet how can I be a good wife to Ahmed, when I love another man?'

Compassion stabbed through Ashley's heart. Her friend, trapped by custom into a relationship she didn't want, and loving . . . 'What about the man you love, Sohaila? Does he love you?'

She gave a sigh of utter misery. 'No! There was never any chance of that. He is an important man and I . . . he would not even see me as a woman to love. He was always nice . . . kind . . . that is all.'

The wretched yearning in Sohaila's voice convinced Ashley beyond a doubt that her friend was not in the grip of any shallow infatuation. 'Are you sure there's no chance with him, Sohaila? He might not have spoken because you were betrothed to someone else.'

Pain and the blackest of despairs looked back at her. 'It's Louis-Philippe! The Baron de Laclos. So you can see how hopeless it is, Ashley.'

And she did see. She could offer no consolation, no help. There was none. Louis-Philippe might be kind and chivalrous, but she had twice heard his opinion about cross-cultural relationships, and each time it had been delivered with negative overtones. She had no doubt that he liked Sohaila. Anyone who had worked with her for any period of time would have to grow fond of her. But Sohaila was right. Louis-Philippe would not see her as a woman to love.

And Ashley suddenly understood Sohaila's misery two days ago. That was when she had seen Louis-Philippe again after three years and known that she still loved him. It was savagely ironic that Ashley had gone to the casino that night in the hope of solving the problem of the marriage to Ahmed.

Sohaila's head lifted and her lovely eyes reflected the bleakness of her future. 'It was very kind of you, Ashley, to want to help us . . . to want to help me. And I am grateful to you. It makes me see where I am, what I have to do, no matter what my family says. I will have to break with Ahmed. I cannot continue the way I am going. I must be fair to him. At least he will be able to find someone else. There will be no disgrace on him.'

Ashley was well aware that an unmarried girl was considered a burden on the family in Egypt, and what Sohaila was proposing to do would probably make her a social outcast. It seemed so terribly unjust. And of what practical help could Ashley be? She would be going home to Australia soon. No wonder Sohaila had said she would miss her! Just when the Egyptian girl most needed a sympathetic friend . . .

The solution flashed into Ashley's mind like a lightning bolt. With Sohaila's ability and degrees, she could earn a good living anywhere in the world. Ashley snatched up her friend's hands, urgently pressing for her full attention.

'Sohaila, would you consider emigrating to Australia? I know my parents would sponsor you if I asked them. With your skills there would be no trouble getting a job. And you could come and live with me,' she suggested eagerly.

For a moment the sad, brown eyes lit with a glimmer of hope, but painful uncertainty quickly overshadowed it.

'Why not?' Ashley pressed. 'Is it such a frightening idea? If your family is going to make your life a misery, why stay on with them? You would be free to do anything you like in Australia, and you'd have no trouble making new friends in Sydney. I promise you, you wouldn't be lonely.'

Sohaila's gaze remained downcast and there was no discernible change of expression on her face. 'Ashley, you are so very good. Kind and generous to a fault. But I cannot make a decision now. Not until after I have done what I must.'

'I understand,' Ashley sympathised. 'Just remember you can count on my support, Sohaila. At any time. Are you going to speak to Ahmed tonight?'

She nodded.

'If either he or anyone else gives you a bad time, Sohaila, you walk out and catch a taxi to the hotel. Come up to my room. You're not alone any more. I'll be here for you.' Ashley suddenly remembered her dinner-date with Louis-Philippe and quickly added, 'If I'm not here, 'I'll leave my room-key at the reception desk for you. And think about coming with me to Australia. Will you do that?'

Uncertainty and need quivered over Sohaila's face. 'Thank you for caring so much, Ashley. You have given me the courage to do what I should have done twice before. I have never had someone who . . .'

The tears welled up again, but they were tears of relief, and the two girls hugged each other with deep affection. Ashley had tears in her own eyes when Sohaila finally took leave of her and went bravely off to face the consequences of her decision.

Love is without mercy, she thought despondently. Louis had certainly been right about that. Damien's love for her . . . Sohaila's love for Louis-Philippe . . . and Azir's obsession with her—could it be called love? Could what she was feeling for him be called love?

Whatever it was, Ashley could not push it aside. If it was only desire, it was the strongest desire she had ever known. She wished for the courage to turn her back on every other consideration and take what Azir had offered.

It slowly dawned on Ashley that she had given that precise advice to Sohaila—to turn her back on everything she had known and emigrate to Australia. It had been so easy to say . . . cheap talk . . . costing nothing. Why couldn't she herself find the same courage as her Egyptian friend, who was about to break with a tradition that carried far greater penalties than Ashley would ever have to suffer?

She stared down at the money that was still scattered over the bed. It was Azir's money. She might have chosen the number, but he had put up the cash for the winning bets. It wasn't right to keep it, not now that the purpose for which he had given it to her was no longer valid. If she returned it to him . . .

Her heart skipped a beat, then careered around her chest in a wild thrumming of excitement. Her mind churned with all the possible consequences of such an action. The force of her agitation drove Ashley to pace up and down the floor.

She was mad to consider it! Mad! She had taken on the responsibility of Sohaila's plight. The sketches and the negotiations for the jewellery collection still had to be completed. Impossible to shirk either responsibility!

Would Azir let her go if she went to him? If she showed . . . if she said she did want him, that she wanted to know . . . needed to know all there was to know about him, to the depth of every intimacy possible between a man and a woman. A wanton wave of heat swept through Ashley, fanning the desire that was driving impulse towards resolution.

Azir had said he wouldn't make the same mistake again. He wouldn't keep her if she didn't want to stay. Ashley was certain he had been sincere when he'd said it. The risk was worth taking, anyway. There were no guarantees in this world. Anything could be taken away at any moment. Like Damien. Like her own life.

She was twenty-eight years old, with nothing ahead of her except her working career. And what was behind her? A marriage that had ended in guilt and grief, overshadowing its initial happiness. And after that, three years that had been barren of any meaningful relationships. Azir was right. She did want to taste him. She wanted to taste the best that life had to offer, and maybe this was her one chance to do just that. It was like the money she had gambled. It might win or it might not, but if she did not try, she would never know.

Ever since Azir had first touched her she had been running like a frightened gazelle. Wasn't she adult enough, mature enough, courageous enough to take one big step into the unknown? When she had come to Egypt she had been completely confident that she could handle anything that was thrown at her. The magnitude of the job in organising the jewellery collection had not daunted her; it had been a challenge she had eagerly accepted. Why should she shrink from the challenge of meeting Azir half-way?

Her gaze dropped once more to the money on the bed. In a burst of feverish activity she snatched up the wrapping from the box, wound it round the wads of notes and stuffed it into her large handbag. A self-conscious flush burnt over her skin as she stripped off her clothes and raced into the bathroom. It had been a long, long time since she had shared her body with a man.

She took a quick shower, all too aware of the tingling anticipation building inside her. Most of her clothes had been crushed from being packed in the suitcases, but she found a pretty floral blouse that was wearable, and teamed it with her good white skirt that always survived any mishandling. She brushed out her hair, dashed on her favourite *Joy* perfume, applied a soft pink lipstick; then, breathing as hard as if she had run a ten-mile race, she grabbed her bulging handbag and set off, determined not to retreat into cowardice.

The elevator took an age to come, and when Ashley eventually arrived on the ground floor more time was lost as she handed in her key at reception and left a message for Sohaila in case of unforeseen circumstances. The commissionaire compensated somewhat with the speed he summoned a taxi for her—a battered old Volvo this time. Ashley settled herself in the back seat and nervously gave her instructions.

'Take me to the Ibn Tulun mosque, please. I will give you further directions when we get there.'

The driver nodded and careered off into the traffic, horn blowing continuously at the cars whose drivers had the temerity to contest his right of way. With a sinking feeling of regret, Ashley remembered she had been too impatient to haggle over the fare. It was too late now, and she resigned herself to paying two or three times as much as she should.

They turned off Tahrir Bridge and edged down to Garden City with the driver keeping at least two cars within millimetres of his own all the way. Why more accidents did not occur, Ashley did not know. As soon as they left the main arterial road, she was again lost in the maze of narrow winding alleys that passed for streets. She breathed a sigh of relief when she saw the tall distinctive minarets of the old mosque.

The detailed memorisation of her first trip served Ashley well. The taxi-driver obligingly followed her instructions and within minutes they were at the gateway into Azir's house. Two uniformed soldiers with machine-guns guarded the entrance, and Ashley was instantly reminded of Azir's position of power. Such soldiers regularly patrolled the embassies and most of the big hotels as well.

A wave of panic glued Ashley to the back-seat. What if Azir wasn't here? What if . . .

'Ten pounds!' The taxi-driver was grinning triumphantly at her.

Ashley pulled herself together. If Azir wasn't here she didn't want to be left without transport in this place. She opened her handbag and passed over the money without argument. 'Please wait . . . five minutes,' she commanded, well aware that she had overpaid the man.

'I wait,' he said, still grinning, delighted at the prospect of picking up some more easy money.

Ashley screwed up her courage and alighted from the taxi. The soldiers gave her an interested appraisal, but did not challenge her passage through the gateway. The Arab guards at the entrance to the house were more particular.

They demanded her name, the nature of her call, and requested her to wait in the small vestibule until her admittance was accepted by the Sheikh. Ashley was so relieved to hear that Azir was at home that she did not mind waiting, but as the minutes ticked by, her inner tension grew.

The Arab who had effected her abduction swept in on her, and Ashley's heart fairly thundered with apprehension, but his courteous manner and speech eased her overstretched nerves. 'Please follow me,' he said, 'I am your guide.'

He escorted her through the house to what she now knew to be the men's quarters on the other side of the *qa'ah*. 'This is the library, *madame*,' he informed her as he ushered her into a large book-lined room. 'If you will wait here, the Sheikh will join you in a few minutes.'

'Thank you,' Ashley murmured.

He bowed and left the room, quietly closing the door behind him. Ashley took several deep breaths in an attempt to calm her skittering pulse-rate. She needed something to steady her trembling legs, so she walked over to the richly polished desk and propped herself against it. There were a number of comfortable-looking armchairs but the idea of sitting down had no appeal. To face Azir ... to say what she had to say ... she had to be on her feet. But she wasn't going to run from it. Not this time!

The soft click of the door-handle triggered a heightening of all her senses. Her eyes took in every enthralling detail of the man who entered. He had discarded his robes. In his white shirt and grey trousers he could have been any sun-tanned man on the streets of Sydney, except that he was still Azir. No one else she had ever met exuded that air of absolute power. And as he stood there, his dark gaze devouring every telling nuance of her appearance, Ashley lost all sense of purpose, except that of pleasing him.

He did not approach her. Nor did he speak. He waited, utterly motionless, a wary tension in every

still line of his body. Ashley knew it was up to her
to break the silence. She had rejected him three
times, and the memory of those rejections brought
a plunging loss of confidence. What if he rejected
her offer? What if he looked at her in contempt?
What if he said it still wasn't enough for him?
How would she bear the humiliation of being
refused?

'The money . . .' The words burst forth before
she realised she had spoken them out loud. They
forced her to go on with other words of explanation. 'I had to come and return it. My friend . . .
I was wrong about her needing it. I thought it
would help her, but it wasn't the kind of help she
needed, so . . .'

There was no reaction from Azir. His face was
completely impassive. He didn't move or speak.

Ashley fumbled open her handbag and drew out
the package of notes. Her hands were shaking. He
didn't come forward to take the money. He didn't
even glance down at it. His gaze did not move
from her, as if he was waiting, willing her to say
something he wanted to hear.

Ashley's heart was pounding in her ears as she
turned to place the packet on the desk. She had to
say it, and she had to say it now. Her courage was
slipping away and this would be her only chance.
She stared down at the parcel of money and forced
herself to speak.

'Why I came . . . it wasn't only the money . . . I
want . . .'

Her voice dried up. Her head swam with the
buzzing urgency to choose the right words.

Everything sounded so cold and callous. Yet how could she express the turbulence of feeling he provoked? There was no other choice but to bluntly state what she felt. And she would face him as she did it!

Ashley lifted her head, straightened her back, then swung around to confront him. She met Azir's gaze with a proud defiance of any contempt he might feel for her. Her whole body was a quivering mass of vulnerability, but somehow she pitched her voice to a steady note of declaration.

'You were right, Azir. I do want you. And for the rest of the time I'm in Egypt, I want to be your lover.'

CHAPTER NINE

AZIR'S reaction was instant and explosive. The impassive mask split with sharp anger. A hard ruthlessness tightened his face, and an infinitely dangerous glitter flared into his eyes. His mouth thinned and curled with the cruel travesty of a forced smile.

'So you want me as your lover!' He threw the words back at her in a soft, ominous taunt. His hands lifted with slow, contemptuous deliberation, and began to unbutton his shirt. 'But only while you're in Egypt. And how long is that, Ashley? A few days? A week? A month?'

The light mockery gathered a vicious edge as he continued without giving her time to answer. 'I don't suppose it matters much. It's the satisfaction of the experience that counts, isn't it? Maybe the flesh of an Arab feels different. Maybe he does it a different way.'

He paused, one eyebrow raised in sardonic enquiry, but Ashley was too shattered to speak. The grain of truth in his interpretation of her words brought a scorching flood of shame to her cheeks. She had wanted to know what it would be like with him. She still did. She could not tear her gaze away from the hands that were steadily working down his shirt.

She wanted to say that it wasn't sexual

attraction that had brought her here, that there were other dimensions of feeling that he had stirred and left unanswered. But her mouth was completely dry, her tongue stuck to the roof of her mouth. The shirt was gaping open, revealing the muscular contours of a highly masculine chest; a sprinkle of tight black curls gave an intriguing texture to the darkly tanned skin.

'Would you prefer to undress me yourself?' he taunted, flicking his gold cuff-links through the cuff-openings.

The whip-sting in the observation forced Ashley's gaze up. The burning rage in his eyes stopped her heart in mid-beat.

'No? Then, let's not waste any more of your time.' He tore off his shirt and tossed it aside as he walked towards her, coiled menace in every step. He prised her handbag from her convulsively clutching fingers and hurled it into a corner of the room. 'You're not helping, Ashley. Do you want me to do everything?'

She was too stunned to move. His hands tore at the buttons of her blouse, impatient with her lack of response. 'Not ... not like this,' she croaked, finally forcing her voice to work.

'But this is all there is ... for you,' he retorted bitterly. 'But don't think I won't enjoy it, because I shall. I'll give you an experience you'll remember all your life.'

Her hands scrabbled up to snatch at his. 'Don't!' she begged, her eyes frantically pleading for understanding. 'You said we could only be

lovers. That's why I came. I want to know you.
To . . .'

'Oh, you'll know me, Ashley,' he promised,
with no abatement of his fury. 'You'll know me to
the very depths of your being before you leave
Egypt.'

He grabbed the two opened edges of her blouse
and pulled them down over her shoulders,
dragging her arms back and keeping them
imprisoned in the sleeves. To her intense humiliation, Ashley felt her nipples harden into knotted
peaks as the hot afternoon air wafted on to her
bared breasts.

'Please . . .' she whispered, her body already
quivering its expectancy, her eyes desperately
seeking some glimmer of mercy.

There was none.

'No?' he mocked, dropping the blistering heat
of his gaze to the tremulous fullness of her breasts.
'I'm not to give you what you want? But we're so
close, Ashley. Almost touching.'

He jerked her arms down, arching her back as
he moved forward, his thighs pressing hers against
the edge of the desk. The grip on her arms relaxed
enough for her taut nipples to brush the prickling
hair on his chest. Ashley gasped at the electric
current. He rolled her upper body from side to side
with a slow, deliberate, tantalising sensuality,
inching her forwards, making her breasts ache to
be crushed into the moist heat of his flesh.

And in spite of the hateful way he was using her,
Ashley could not stop the insidious rise of sensual
excitement. She almost groaned with relief when

Azir wrenched the blouse off her arms and caught her to him, crushing the breath out of her.

But there was no relief. One hand curved under her buttocks, pressing her lower body into his, working them both into a sexual arousal that was aggressively erotic. The hard thrust of him against her stomach excited Ashley beyond bearing, but he would not give her any freedom of movement. She could feel his heart thundering against her breasts and the heat of him soaked into her, melting any thought of trying to pull away. She wanted him, wanted him so much she didn't care what he thought of her.

'I could kill you for coming to me for this.'

The harsh whisper twisted her heart, but he gave her no chance to speak, to explain the need that had driven her here. Fingers threaded through her hair and dragged her head back. His face was contorted with violent emotion.

'I hate you for the way you're using me!'

'You don't understand!' Ashley cried, reaching up to hold his head still.

He looked at her with tortured eyes.

'I didn't meant to hurt you, Azir,' she whispered. 'I thought ... we could try.'

'Try!' The word hissed from his lips and his eyes narrowed into glittering slits. 'Well, let's see how you like it, Ashley.'

One iron-tight arm pinned her to his body, while his other hand tore at the zip fastening at the back of her skirt. He hoisted her up and dragged both skirt and panties down over her hips.

'No!' she cried, beating down at his shoulders in frenzied panic.

'Yes!' he swore, and laid her on the desk so he could strip the clothes from her legs.

Her limbs seemed to have turned to water. Her arms flailed helplessly in her struggle to get up, knocking the pile of money she had placed so neatly on the desk into the air. Hundred dollar notes fluttered around her. She kicked out with her legs that were suddenly, frighteningly free of all constriction, and they were caught and relentlessly parted.

'No! No!' she panted, shocked by the melting weakness that trembled down her thighs. She couldn't find the strength to lever herself up. Appalled by the terrible vulnerability of her open nakedness she tried to squirm sideways, but a hand instantly spread across her stomach, defeating the movement.

'Please . . .' The word sobbed from her throat.

He removed the constricting hand, but only to pull her towards him. Ashley suddenly saw the full, vibrant power of his manhood and knew there was no escape even before his hands curled under her buttocks and lifted her.

'Yes!' he answered, his voice harsh with raging purpose as he thrust inside her, plunging hard and fast to the very centre of her being, finding it, filling it, then asserting his possession with a fierce stroking that ripped all thought from Ashley's mind.

Waves of pleasure-pain billowed through her, ebbing and flowing to the cataclysmic rhythm of flesh crashing into flesh. And Ashley found herself revelling in the sheer violence of this savage union, abandoning herself to it with a primitive exultation, abetting it by curling her legs around Azir's lean hips, tightening the pressure, urging him even more deeply inside her.

Her fingernails dug into the palms of her hands from the sheer frustration of not being able to pull him down to her. Her head threshed from side to side as tension built into wild urgency. Her whole body convulsed with the jerk of Azir's ejaculation, and she sobbed as she felt his power drain into limpness.

It couldn't be over, she wouldn't let it be over! It wasn't enough, it had to go on. Even as he removed the support of his hands and slumped forward, Ashley clung on to him with her legs. Her body acted instinctively, contracting the muscles necessary to imprison him within her. His head snapped up, a startled cry tearing from his throat, and Ashley felt a fierce jubilation at taking him captive. He arched back as if in denial, but Ashley would not let him go. With savage, wanton deliberation she rolled her thighs around him, her eyes feasting exultantly on the throbbing pulse-beat of his heaving chest, the incredulous shake of his head.

'No!' he groaned.

'Yes!' she hissed. 'Oh yes, Azir. You won't have it all your own way.'

His eyes glittered down at her, but it was no longer the glitter of rage. 'Do it, then. Have your own way!' he urged, his voice furred with challenging desire.

Excitement rippled through her. She had control this time. She would torment him as he had tormented her with his aggressive dominance. She didn't have to use strength. Just a seductive manipulation that kept him as her possession. She teased him unmercifully, moving from side to side, pressing the heat of her body against him, letting him slide a little then drawing him back in.

His breathing broke into ragged little gasps. His fingers raked her hips, across her stomach and down her thighs. Then with a frenzied cry, he gathered her up into his arms and crushed her to him, hugging her with a pressure that almost broke her in half.

Her legs started to slide down, but the stirring force of his loins pinned her to him, spearing inside her with a potency that made her gasp. Slowly, almost lovingly Azir lowered her to the desktop, gently supporting her with his arms. 'Until you're satisfied,' he promised huskily, then drew back, his eyes glowing with a warmth that made her tingle to her fingertips.

Ashley no longer cared what he did to her. She closed her eyes and clenched her hands, wanting to capture every nuance of feeling. A shudder of pleasure swept through her as he pushed past her womb. Excitement quickened with each stroke, some swift and certain, others slow and searching, but all driving her inexorably towards an explosion of exquisite sensation. And still he pushed on, spilling her from one orgasm to another, setting her afloat on a billowing sea of erotic pleasure that drained all the strength from her body.

A sweet, heavy languor invaded her veins. She did not know when Azir finally spent himself. She felt his arm slide under her shoulders. Another hooked under her legs. And then he was lifting her, cradling her against his chest, carrying her. His mouth brushed over her temples, whispering soothing words that she didn't understand.

It felt right that his arms were around her, the moist warmth of his flesh pressed to hers. Somehow she managed to lift her own arm, and curled it around his neck to hug closer, snuggling her face into his throat, breathing in his earthy male scent, tasting him with the tip of her tongue.

He groaned, his step faltering for a moment, then hurrying on. Ashley didn't look to see where he was taking her. She didn't care; didn't care about her nakedness, didn't care what he had in mind; didn't care about anything so long as he kept her with him. She vaguely heard the swish of silk curtains being swept aside, then Azir was bending over, laying her down, and there was cool satin beneath her, soft pillows under her head.

She opened her eyes and feasted on the glistening animal strength of his body as he slid down on to the bed next to her. He propped himself on his side to look down at her and she felt herself drowning in the dark whirlpools of his eyes. Love, tenderness, want, need; impossible to define the depth of emotion that pulled her to him, offering her mouth to his. He took it softly, without passion, but with a slow, erotic intimacy that was a possession of another kind; a sweet, shivery mingling of touch and taste and belonging.

The kiss went on, and on, and on; more intensely satisfying than any other in Ashley's experience, and her body shivered its pleasure to the soft caress of his hand. He circled her breasts, caressed her stomach, pushed slowly down to her thighs, slid up between them and held her there, gently sealing his claim on her. A delicious warmth pulsed through Ashley, and with it came a welling of emotion that brought tears to her eyes.

'I didn't hurt you?' Azir asked anxiously.

'No,' she whispered, her heart filling with contentment at the deep caring in his voice.

He sighed and rolled on to his back, pulling her with him so that her body half straddled his; her leg falling between the two strongly muscled thighs, her hip pressing against his manhood, her cheek resting over his heart. With half his body exposed to her touch, Ashley indulged the desire to run her fingertips over the powerful combination of firm flesh and muscle.

She thrilled to the sensitised crawling of his skin, to the slight shudders that followed the feathery paths she made. His chest heaved with the thunderous pounding of his heart and his hand raked up through her long hair, fingers entwining themselves in the long tresses, convulsively tugging, releasing, rewinding.

'Stay with me.'

The taut whisper stilled Ashley's hand. She felt his whole body tense as he waited for her answer. Even the fingers in her hair clenched together.

She wanted to say yes, yearned to say yes, *needed* to say yes, but she could not. If she were to live with Azir, she might never want to leave him. Not for any appreciable time. The burning sensation in her heart was proof enough of that. And she had to leave him. A week—a fortnight at most—and her work in this country would surely be finished.

She was pledged to follow through on the jewellery collection back home in Australia. That was her job, the responsibilty she had taken on. And her other responsibilities could not be shrugged away, either. Sohaila had her promise for help and protection; and Ashley herself had accepted Louis-Philippe's help. To throw every other consideration to the winds, and shut herself into a cocoon of existence that only recognised what could be shared with Azir, would be totally selfish and self-defeating.

Even if she could turn her back on everything else, what would her life be like if she stayed with him? They couldn't make love all the time. They had both acted out of sheer need for each other, and yet ... that didn't seem to matter in this blissful aftermath of togetherness.

It hurt to speak the words that would separate them, but Ashley could see no other way. 'I can't, Azir,' she said quickly, regret flooding through every fibre of her being. 'It's impossible, no matter how much I want to,' she added with even more feeling, and the deep sincerity of absolute truth.

There was no sound from him, no movement bar the almost imperceptible fall of his chest as he slowly exhaled pent-up air from his lungs. Then, with a stiff carefulness, the fingers in her hair spread open and pulled free of the tangled strands. His body remained quite still beneath her, but he no longer held her in any way. The message was chillingly clear. No words had to be spoken. She was free to leave. Right now, if that was her choice.

Regret savaged her heart and she pushed herself up to beg his understanding. Her eyes met a dark reserve that deflected her plea before it was uttered. 'I have appointments to keep, people I must see. And a friend who needs me to stand by her,' she stated, as matter-of-factly as she could.

The darkness of his eyes seemed to intensify, but when he spoke his voice was completely empty of tone. 'If you stayed here with me, you could come and go as you please. A car and chauffeur would be at your disposal. I will provide anything you require. Does that satisfy you?'

Her hands lifted in appeal, then fluttered limply in a gesture of hopelessness as Azir stared fixedly at her, waiting in judgement. To him the issue was obviously clear-cut, but it wasn't. Far from it. Her mouth twisted into a rueful grimace as she struggled to explain.

'That's extremely generous of you ... and I appreciate your ... your kindness ... but ... it's just not that simple, Azir.' She glanced down at her watch, suddenly realising that she had no idea how much time had elapsed. It was almost six-thirty. 'I have to go back to the hotel,' she murmured, more to herself than to him, but his reaction was cutting and abrupt.

'I'll get your clothes for you.'

He was on his feet and walking away from her before Ashley recovered her startled breath. 'Azir!' she called after him, but he had already strode through the opening of the curtains beyond the foot of the huge four-poster bed with its high canopy.

He did not reply to her call.

For the first time Ashley really looked at her surroundings. The three walls around her were richly covered in green and gold wallpaper. There were no windows and the room was smallish, containing a minimum of furniture. Elegant lamps stood on the two bedside tables. There were three Regency-style chairs upholstered in gold velvet. The only exit was the wall of gold curtaining that faced her.

Ashley swung herself off the bed and tiptoed to the opening, apprehensive about what lay beyond it. She gaped in startled surprise as her gaze drank in the luxurious furnishings that comprised what was obviously a private sitting-room and study. The room was huge; and the bedroom where Ashley stood was but a convenient recess at the end of it.

Desks, tables, cabinets and chairs, were all fashioned from heavily lacquered bamboo and decorated with chinoiserie motifs. Gold-framed mirrors and paintings hung on the walls and a magnificent crystal chandelier fell from the tall ceiling. She remembered Heba's enthusiasm over 'the English dining-room' but Ashley could not imagine its comparing to the Regency grandeur of this room.

The contrasts in Azir's house were as confusing as the man himself. He spoke English with a marked Oxford accent, but there was no diminution of his Arabic heritage. He was born a sheikh and would never be anything else, although Ashley fancied he would assert the innate power of his personal authority in any society. But was he really as cross-cultural as his possessions suggested? Would Azir ever accept a woman as an equal, or would he only regard her as a possession?

The questions were still teasing Ashley's mind when he re-entered the room, wearing the clothes he had discarded. He carried her sandals and handbag, and she could see her skirt and blouse hanging over his arm. Ashley shrank back from the curtain, feeling a self-conscious shame in her nakedness. Only her husband had ever seen her like this. It hadn't mattered while she and Azir had been close, but now . . . she snatched up a pillow in an instinctive need for protection.

Azir swept aside the curtain, and dropped her belongings on the bed. 'I trust you'll find everything there,' he said coldly, and without even glancing at her, left her to dress alone.

A terrible hollowness burrowed through Ashley's soul. Surely she did not deserve to be treated like a whore that he had finished with! But it was her own fault, she reminded herself savagely. As he saw it, she was using him in the same way, wanting him as a lover at her convenience.

Yet how could she commit herself into his keeping when . . . no, it couldn't be done! Their backgrounds were too different to even contem-

plate the total commitment she would want to give
and be given.

Her hands trembled as she dragged on her
clothes and tidied herself as best she could. A
sickening regret weighed on her heart. But she
could see no way of recapturing the precious
intimacy they had shared.

It was some relief to find him waiting for her in
the sitting-room. He was propped against a
writing-desk, his arms folded, an impassive mask
fixed once more on his face. 'I've ordered a car for
you. It will take you back to your hotel,' he stated
tonelessly.

'Thank you,' she murmured, the words almost
choking on the rising lump in her throat.

His smile was a bitter twist of irony. 'You make
a very impressive lover, Ashley. In fact, I've never
had a better one. Please feel free to come at any
time. I can't guarantee I'll always be available, but
I'll do my best to accommodate you.'

His eyes slowly swept her from head to foot and
back again in a taunting reminder of every
physical intimacy there had been between them.
Never before in her life had Ashley felt so shamed
by her own words and actions. Pride urged her to
say she would not come back, not ever, but in her
heart she knew she would. She had to. She
couldn't bear not to.

Her legs felt like half-set jelly but she forced
them to cover the distance between them. Her eyes
met his, honestly and openly, holding back
nothing. 'It's not what you think, Azir. I don't

know where I'm going with you. I need time. Maybe . . .'

His hands came up and gripped her shoulders. She gasped as his fingers dug into her flesh, but any hurt was seared away by the fierce passion that blazed from his eyes. 'There's no . . . maybe . . . for me, Ashley. Did you feel any . . . maybe . . . when you gave yourself to me this afternoon? Did you?' he demanded with bruising vehemence.

'No,' she whispered, enthralled with the emotion that was bursting from him.

'It takes courage to give yourself completely to another person, Ashley. To love so much that it hurts to even think of being parted. You gamble with your life, because you know the dependence will be absolute and inescapable.'

He paused to drag in a deep breath, his eyes swirling with dark torment as they searched hers. His voice rasped between fierce conviction and urgent demand as he added, 'Do you have that courage, Ashley?'

What he appeared to be saying seemed so unbelievable that the air caught in Ashley's throat and choked her for a moment. A welter of confusing thoughts sprang unbidden to her mind. Was he really offering to share his life with her? Completely? Without any reservation?

She stared up at him in terrible conflict; her heart leaping with wild elation, her mind desperately dictating caution. Her hand rose spontaneously to touch the taut muscles along his jaw-line, begging his patience while her eyes pleaded for a stay in judgement. 'Please . . . Azir.

It's too soon. I don't know. I . . .'

'How much longer will you be in Egypt?' His voice was harsh, demanding, discordant.

'Between one and two weeks. I'm almost finished. There's Aswan . . .'

'Come back tomorrow,' he demanded.

'Yes!' she cried impulsively, driven into decision. Yet even as she spoke she remembered that Louis might have made some arrangement with the Egyptian officials. 'No, I can't,' she corrected swiftly.

The instant hardening of Azir's expresssion brought a stab of anguish. Her hands flew up around his neck, compelling him to listen. 'Please, Azir, you must understand. Tomorrow I've got the negotiations for the jewellery collection, and Louis . . . the Baron de Laclos . . . he is helping me, So . . .'

'You go back to him?'

The hissed ferocity of the words stunned Ashley for a moment. Azir was snatching her hands down before she realised what he was thinking, and then her chest heaved with furious indignation at the bitter accusation in his eyes.

'I told you he was only a friend. I would never have come to you this afternoon if my . . . my feelings were involved with him. If you don't know that, Azir, then you know nothing about me. You talk about love, but what about trust?' The turmoil he had put her through churned out more resentment. 'I've been as honest as I can be with you. If you can't . . .' The anguish in her heart left her shaking her head in miserable despair. 'I knew it was impossible.'

'No!' Before she could move Azir had stepped forward and swept her against him in a crushing embrace. 'Nothing is impossible! It is up to you!'

His hand raked up through her hair and dragged her head back. She had a brief glimpse of his despair, then his mouth was on hers, passionately seeking what had been lost in the war of words. And Ashley could not fight the need that rose instinctively to answer his. She surrendered to it without the slightest hesitation, feeling the same violent desire for emotional reassurance.

They were both shaken by the tumult of passion that raged between them, and for a long time after the kiss ended they clung tightly to each other, too drained to speak or move.

'Forgive me my madness,' Azir finally murmured, his cheek rubbing softly across his hair. His chest rose and fell in a long sigh. 'I know I have to let you go, Ashley. I know this in my head, but my heart keeps crying out for you, and over that I have no control.'

He gently withdrew his embrace and lifted his hands to gently cup her face, his eyes openly pleading his cause. 'You must come back to me.'

'As soon as I can,' she promised, her own heart swelling with a blind surge of unquestioning love.

'Then go now, Ashley. Before I do or say something more I will surely regret.' A rueful smile played across his mouth as he released her. 'And I hope your business goes well for you tomorrow.'

'Thank you,' she whispered gratefully.

Ashley wished she could say more. She felt that Azir was doing all the giving, but she knew that if their relationship was to work, it needed the time and the understanding she had fought for.

He gently drew her arm around him. 'I'll take you down to the car.' As they passed the desk he picked up a card and pressed it into her hand. 'Ring that telephone number at any time, and I'll send a car to bring you here.'

'Thank you, Azir,' she murmured again, and she walked through his house with him, not even noticing the odd mixture of cultures, conscious only of the extraordinary man at her side.

CHAPTER TEN

ASHLEY was barely aware of the drive back to the hotel. She leaned her head back on the cool leather seat and closed her eyes, focusing her mind on all that had happened between herself and Azir. From almost the first moment she had seen him, her life had no longer been her own, and now ... now she simply couldn't comprehend a life without him.

He hadn't wanted her just for sex. It was more, much more than that. Ashley was certain of that now. When Azir had abducted her he had said he wanted her at his side for the rest of his life, and he had surely meant it. His words and actions this afternoon confirmed that beyond a doubt.

Ashley winced as she realised the terrible hurt she had given him in suggesting they be lovers while she was in Egypt. She hadn't meant that their relationship had to end then, but she now understood why Azir had reacted so violently. To have offered his life to her and then to be seemingly told he was only wanted as a short-term lover ... the insult to his pride had been deeply wounding.

Could she truthfully and confidently give him the commitment he wanted? Not yet, common

sense insisted. But her heart kept urging that it
didn't matter where their relationship was heading, or what heartache the future had in store for
them, she could not turn her back on it, nor choose
any other path. She wanted to be with Azir more
than she wanted anything else, and somehow she
had to work everything else out so that it was
possible to stay with him.

Ashley was forcibly jolted back to reality with
the car's arrival at the Sheraton. A glance at her
watch told her she barely had time to shower and
change before facing up to Louis-Philippe for
their dinner-date. She hurried through the lobby
and felt a surge of relief when she collected her key
and the receptionist informed her that Sohaila
Sha'ib had not called.

It was difficult to wrench her mind off Azir as
she soaped her body under the shower. Just the
memory of that wild act of intimacy in the library
was enough to stir involuntary spasms of pleasure.
She even hoped that Louis-Philippe's talk to the
authorities had been unsuccessful, so that her
departure from Egypt would be delayed as long as
possible. And that really was totally selfish, she
chided herself. Dewar and Buller would not be
impressed with such a lack of concern for their
interests.

And Louis-Philippe wouldn't appreciate that
attitude either, particularly since he had gone to
the trouble of involving himself on her behalf.
Ashley tried to get herself into a more responsible
frame of mind, but even by the time she was

dressed and presentable, her thoughts were still skittering around Azir.

The knock on her door brought her thumping down to earth. She took a deep breath. Louis-Philippe de Laclos was a man she liked and admired and respected, and he deserved her full attention. And her gratitude. She opened the door and smiled a welcome.

He was dressed in a beautifully tailored, dark grey suit and looked every inch a man of class; handsome, distinguished, impressive, a man of strong character and deep compassion. Ashley did not have to wonder why Sohaila had fallen in love with him. Few women could fail to appreciate so many attractive qualities, and he carried an individuality that successfully crossed all barriers.

'You look positively radiant, Ashley,' he said approvingly. 'I'm happy to see that yesterday's experience has not caused you any lasting trauma.'

Ashley winced at the thought of admitting the truth. A new zest for life was leaping through her veins, but it was because she had gone to Azir, not escaped him.

'Come in for a minute, Louis,' she said quickly, swinging the door wide open and waving an invitation for him to enter.

'How was your day?' he asked with friendly interest, accepting her invitation without question.

'Rather eventful,' Ashley admitted. 'I just have to write a note for Sohaila and leave it at the desk with my room-key before we go to dinner. If she decides to come here tonight . . .'

'Sohaila? Why should she come?'

The sharp interruption cut Ashley's train of thought, then threw her into some emotional confusion. She could hardly confide Sohaila's problem to the man at the root of her friend's dilemma. 'It's . . . it's a personal problem. Nothing to do with work,' she explained distractedly. 'Sohaila might be in trouble, and if she is I want to be available to help her.'

'So do I,' Louis-Philippe muttered with startling intensity. He crossed the space between them with a couple of strides and took Ashley's hands in a grip that was strong and rough and urgent. 'Why should Sohaila come to you tonight? What trouble is there that I don't know about?'

Ashley was dumbfounded by the sudden change in his manner. It vividly recalled the coiled tension of last night when he had faced Azir in the *qa'ah*, ready to fight to the death if necessary. Grim purpose was stamped on his face, and the steely glint in his eyes warned that he would not be diverted from that purpose.

'Ashley?' It was a terse reminder that she hadn't answered him.

'Sohaila went home to break her marriage contract with Ahmed,' she blurted out.

'To break . . .' Shock and a curious conflict of emotions chased across Louis-Philippe's face. 'Why? After all this time?'

· The questions weren't really asked of Ashley. He had withdrawn from her both mentally and emotionally, searching, struggling for answers that he could fit together himself.

A wild hope took root in Ashley's heart. It hardly seemed possible, but if there was any chance that Sohaila's love for Louis-Philippe was not unrequited, now was the time to clear any obstructions from their path.

'Sohaila doesn't love Ahmed. She never did,' Ashley said pointedly, watching to see what impact the information had on Louis. 'Only family pressure has kept her tied to him all these years,' she added for good measure.

Pain and despair ravaged his face as he dropped Ashley's hands and turned away, shaking his head. 'She can't do it! They'll make her an outcast, a social pariah. It'll be hell for her. She won't be able to stand out against them.'

He paced the floor in extreme agitation, and suddenly broke into a torrent of voluble French, which was too fast for Ashley to comprehend with her scanty knowledge of the language. She got the very firm impression, however, that it was the type of patois used by soldiers when they are very highly stressed.

Excitement lifted wild hope into the realms of probability. With slow, careful deliberation, Ashley set about clearing the path. 'I'm going to help Sohaila emigrate to Australia if she wants to. She had no one to turn to before, but she has now. Don't doubt her courage, Louis.'

· He stopped in mid-stride, his head snapping back to her, his face appalled with the realisation that he had completely forgotten Ashley's presence. The strain to recompose his expression was evident, but within seconds he had brought himself under control. His hands even gestured an apologetic appeal as he spoke, but he could not quite strip his voice of the emotion churning through him.

'What I did for you yesterday, Ashley ... if Sohaila is in trouble I would have to do at least the same. She is ... very special to me ...'

Probability lifted into certainty and Ashley swiftly interrupted the spasmodic speech. 'Louis, we have been very frank with each other. Is Sohaila the reason you came back to Egypt? Do you love her?'

He grimaced at her bluntness, shook his head, then lifted eyes that were filled with helpless anguish. 'I would do anything for her, but ... Sohaila would never see me as a man to love. I am too old for her. More than twenty years older than her. And a foreigner.'

'Sohaila is deeply in love with you, Louis,' Ashley told him softly. 'It was seeing you again that forced her to realise she couldn't go through with the marriage to Ahmed.'

Still he struggled to contain the hope that Ashley had just held out to him, not quite daring to believe it after having lived through years of despair. 'Did Sohaila say that? Did she actually say ... she loved ... me?'

'Yes, she did. And cried her heart out because

she was sure you could never see her as someone you could love.'

A knock on the door froze them both for a moment. Then a sweet smile of satisfaction curved Ashley's mouth. 'If that is Sohaila, don't waste any more time, Louis.'

He muttered something in French, and the low, impassioned tone broadened Ashley's smile as she opened the door. Sohaila stood just outside, a suitcase in her hand, a look of frightened appeal working over her lovely face.

'You said . . .'

Ashley reached out and took the suitcase; then caught her hand, giving it a reassuring squeeze. 'I said I'd be here for you, Sohaila, and I am. Come in. You're very welcome.'

The stiff apprehension eased enough for Ashley to pull her friend inside. She quickly shut the door, aware that Sohaila might be flustered into a retreat once she caught sight of Louis in her room. In her distressed state of mind she might leap to any number of wrong conclusions.

'Sohaila . . .'

The soft call from Louis-Philippe carried an undertone of barely controlled emotion. Sohaila jerked around to face him, all colour draining from her face. Her mouth opened and closed. Her chest heaved as if fighting for breath.

'I . . . I am sorry,' she said stiltedly, then darted an anguished look at Ashley. 'Please, I do not want to interrupt you, I . . .'

'Sohaila!'

The urgency in Louis-Philippe's voice silenced her. Pain pinched her face, but she turned to him, squaring her shoulders and pasting a resigned dignity over her inner anguish.

He came forward and took her hands, his eyes glittering feverishly as he strove to contain himself. 'Do you know why I came back to Egypt?' he asked softly.

She lifted shy eyes to his and slowly shook her head.

His answer held an unmistakable throb of passion. 'Because you're here, Sohaila. Because I couldn't stay away. I had to see you one last time.'

The colour ebbed and flowed on Sohaila's face. She shot an agonised look at Ashley, desperately wanting to believe what Louis was saying, but afraid she was making some dreadful mistake. The words were too unbelievably wonderful to be fully credited on first hearing.

Ashley smiled her reassurance, then quickly picked up her handbag and room-key. 'I think you two have some talking to do in private. I'll come back later. Be happy.'

She felt like dancing down the corridor to the elevators. Louis-Philippe would surely look after Sohaila, and Sohaila would just as surely make Louis-Philippe happy. All the pain and suffering was over for both of them. In their case, love had triumphed against all the odds. The age difference, their nationalities, culture, religion ... all had been swept aside by the purity of their feeling for each other.

And so it could be for Azir and herself, Ashley thought with happy determination. Being together was more important than anything else. Her delight for Sohaila and Louis was suddenly compounded by the realisation that the resolution of their problems also relieved her of worrying about them any more. She was free to go to Azir. Tonight if she wished. And she *did* wish! So strongly that it was almost a pain of need.

The card Azir had given her was in her handbag. One short telephone call to him and a car would be instantly despatched to the hotel. Within half an hour she would be . . . but she couldn't just leave without first saying something to Louis and Sohaila. They would worry about her. And she had to give them some time to reach an understanding before breaking in on them.

The elevator arrived and Ashley rode down to the first floor. Half an hour should be enough, Ashley decided, and she could fill that time in having something to eat. She had gone without food since breakfast time, and the Sheraton's La Mamma restaurant was one of the most pleasant dining-rooms in Cairo.

A waiter led her to one of the window-tables and took her order. Ashley settled back in the comfortable cane dining-chair, her gaze drawing pleasure from the clean whiteness of the furnishings, the bright touches of green and lemon, the thriving indoor pot plants. Like the sun-room in her parents' home.

The thought slid into Ashley's mind and stuck,

giving rise to other, less comfortable thoughts. Her parents would be appalled by what she was doing! They would never understand how she could throw up her career to go and live with a foreigner. When she went back to Australia to finish up her job, she would have to make up some story to account for her return to Azir ... taking up the offer to work overseas, or something like that. The truth would hurt them and she loved her parents too dearly to cause them worry and pain.

Yet how could she keep deceiving them indefinitely? She had taken no precautions this afternoon, and neither had Azir. If a child had been conceived ... the thought brought a warm tingle of happiness and suddenly it didn't matter what anyone thought. It was her life. She wasn't getting any younger, and she wanted Azir above all else. Sooner or later her parents would realise that her happiness depended on him and they would come to terms with the situation. They might never approve, but they would not condemn.

Ashley was certain that Azir would never turn his back on her or any children they might have together. Marriage was another question altogether, and one that Ashley wasn't ready to contemplate. She knew so little about Azir's life and the world he inhabited that she couldn't imagine how she would fit into it. But somehow she would. Azir no more wanted to be parted from her than she wanted to be parted from him.

The waiter brought the meal she had ordered, but Ashley was too churned up with the decisions she had made to enjoy it to any great degree. As she finished the last mouthful, a glance at her watch showed that ample time had passed since she had left Louis and Sohaila in her room. Ashley signalled the waiter, signed for the meal and left the restuarant. With her heart thumping in excited anticipation, she took the stairs to the reception lounge, then headed for a telephone.

It wouldn't take her long to pack. Even less time to wish Louis and Sohaila all the happiness in the world and take her leave of them. Sohaila could have her room. There was no reason for her to stay here at the hotel any longer.

She dialled the number on the card. Any time Azir had said, but it was not his voice that answered her call. Ashley calmed a sudden attack of nerves, gave her name, and asked to speak to Sheikh Azir Talil Khaybar, desperately hoping that he had not gone out somewhere.

'Ashley?'

A smile spread through her, relaxing all the tension. 'Azir, I can come to you now if you'd like to send your car for me. I'll have my suitcases ready in about fifteen minutes.'

She heard a quick expulsion of breath, then, 'I'll come for you myself.' Swift, decisive, and the line disconnected before Ashley could say anything else.

Not that it mattered, she thought joyously, as she skipped over to a miraculously open elevator and pressed the button for her floor. Azir was coming for her. In barely a quarter of an hour she would be with him again.

Ashley gave a discreet knock on the door of her room before using her key to enter, but she had no doubt that Louis would observe all the proper conventions where Sohaila was concerned. Sohaila would expect it, and Louis would respect her deeply ingrained sense of what was right and wrong. Marriage was the only answer that would satisfy their needs.

A rueful smile touched Ashley's lips as she opened the door, but she did not regret giving herself to Azir. Nor did she believe that she had lost any respect in his eyes. Neither of them had had any control over what had happened, and it had smashed barriers that might have otherwise kept them apart. Besides, as Azir had stated this afternoon, their relationship could only be that of lovers. Ashley had accepted that.

Louis and Sohaila were sitting on the bed, Louis holding her as if she were the most precious and fragile work of art. They were so wrapped up in each other that they weren't even aware that Ashley had entered the room.

Ashley cleared her throat. 'Can I assume that you two now understand each other?' she asked drily.

Sohaila leapt to her feet and flew over to Ashley, hugging her in rapturous happiness before drawing back to express herself more volubly. 'How can I thank you, Ashley? You are such a wonderful, wonderful friend.' Her beautiful almond eyes rolled all around their sockets in trying to express the intensity of her emotion, and her hands flew into any number of eloquent gestures.

'Oh, perhaps you could name one of your daughters after me,' Ashley replied teasingly, and laughed as a bright red flush stained Sohaila's cheeks.

'If we are blessed with a daughter, we will do that, Ashley,' Louis said seriously, standing up and curving a loving arm around Sohaila's waist. 'We will always be grateful to you for bringing us together.'

Sohaila looked adoringly into eyes that had lost all trace of sadness. 'Louis is going to speak to my parents.' She dragged her gaze back to Ashley. 'He says he will smooth over all the trouble. But we will get married anyway,' she declared with triumphant defiance.

'And very soon,' said Louis.

'Good for you,' Ashley approved warmly, and kissed them both in benevolent blessing.

She had no doubt that Baron Louis-Philippe de Laclos would find a way to appease the Sha'ib family, but Sohaila's declaration of love and loyalty to the Frenchman was an assurance that nothing would stand in the way of their being together. Ashley hoped they would both understand her own decision.

'I've just telephoned Azir,' she announced. 'He'll be here in about ten minutes and I'm going to ... to live with him.' There was no point in mincing words, Ashley told herself sternly, and continued in a calm, steady voice. 'So you can have my room, Sohaila.'

'The Sheikh?' Sohaila's eyes widened incredulously.

Ashley nodded and turned to open her suitcases. 'I know you'll probably find it shocking, but it's what I want, Sohaila, and my life is my own to do with as I want.'

A touch on her arm drew her out of the wardrobe she had opened. Sohaila's lovely dark eyes brimmed with emotion. 'I know you could only be following your heart, Ashley. I would never think badly of you whatever you did. Ever,' she said with loyal fervour.

Ashley nodded, too choked to speak. She didn't know why it meant so much to her, but she was intensely grateful for Sohaila's support.

'Now let me help you pack,' Sohaila continued, showing her uncritical acceptance of Ashley's decision.

'Ashley, is there anything I can do for you?' Louis asked, a worried note in his voice.

She took a deep breath to clear the lump in her throat and shook her head. 'Did you get anywhere with talking to the authorities about the jewellery collection?' she asked belatedly.

'Progress has been made, but of course they did not commit themselves,' he said dismissively. 'I meant . . . what if you are not happy with Azir?'

She flashed him a smile to appease his concern. 'I'll face that problem when it comes—*if* it ever arises. Don't worry about me, Louis. I was frightened of Azir yesterday, but not any more.'

Louis nodded, but his concern deepened into a dark frown. 'I hope you understand what you're doing, Ashley.'

A tremor of fear ran through Ashley's heart. Was she risking too much?

'Louis . . .' Sohaila's lilting voice held a soft note of indulgence '. . . I do not think you understand how it is. Ashley would not go to him if she ever meant to leave. And the Sheikh . . . he cares very much, or he would not have come with the money this afternoon.'

Louis frowned in puzzlement. 'What money?'

'I will tell you later,' Sohaila assured him. 'For now you must wish Ashley happiness, not worry her with doubts.' A chiding smile curved her mouth. 'You know, Louis, sometimes you men make it very hard for us women.'

His answering smile begged forgiveness. 'I will learn from my mistakes. Ashley, I wish you all the happiness that you've made possible for me, and for . . .'

'. . . me,' Sohaila breathed gratefully.

And Ashley hugged their blessing to her heart, all too aware that happiness could be snatched out of one's grasp with a mere twist of Fate. She had lost Damien; Louis and Sohaila had very nearly lost each other. Determination swept all doubts aside. She was *not* going to lose Azir.

CHAPTER ELEVEN

ASHLEY had planned what she would say to Azir but, as in all their encounters, he took control the moment he arrived at her hotel room. His eyes blazed at her with a fierce possessiveness that seared away all coherent thought, and his kiss left her quivering with an excitement that blotted out every other consideration. A porter took care of her luggage and Azir swept her out of the hotel and into his car before Ashley recovered enough to speak.

'Thank you for coming,' she said huskily.

Azir's fingers threaded hers and gripped tight. He looked at her, and that one look cut staight through conventional speech even before he spoke. 'It was agony ... waiting for your call.'

His pain shamed her, reminding her of the times she had rejected him. 'I'm sorry. It won't happen again, Azir.'

'You will stay with me now?'

'Yes.'

Her answer was unequivocal, drawn from her by the intensity of feeling emanating from Azir. The moment was so charged with tension that Ashley postponed explaining the necessity of a return trip to Australia. She didn't even want to think about it. Azir's dark eyes were devouring her again, and the desire flooding through her veins weakened any sense of purpose beyond pleasing him.

When they arrived back at the house, Ashley was once more installed in the Damascus Room with Heba in fluttering attendance. The servant-girl was delighted that this time she was allowed to unpack the suitcases and see to all Ashley's needs. And when finally she was dismissed by Azir, the ensuing silence in the room throbbed with too much urgent anticipation to even think of words.

Their lovemaking was a raging tempest of desire, totally demanding and intensely satisfying. The violence of their need for each other gradually eased into a sensual tenderness that savoured their mutual possession in a slow, knowing celebration of absolute intimacy. For a long time they lay together in a silence of blissful harmony.

'Ashley ...'

The soft whisper of her name carried an undertone of need that stirred Ashley out of her sweet languor. Suddenly there was something different in the stillness of Azir's body, a tension in the prompting pressure of his fingertips.

'Yes?' she asked quickly.

'You accept now ... that we belong together?'

It was too dark for any telling expression to be seen on Azir's face, or in his eyes, but the tight cautiousness in his voice was warning enough that her answer was very important to him.

'Yes,' she said, with careless disregard of the consequences. It was the truth. Not even with

Damien had she felt such a deep sense of belonging. She no longer questioned why Azir should have the power to bind her to him, and there was no point in denying it. She took a deep breath and told him her decision. 'When my business here is finished, I will have to return to Australia for a short while to tie up my commitments there. But if you want me to, I'll come back and live with you, Azir.'

His fingers dragged up and down her back. 'If . . .' He breathed the word as if he hated it. He moved abruptly, heaving himself up to lean over her. 'Do not speak of "ifs" again, Ashley. Have I not made it clear what I want?'

There was anger and frustration in the way he kissed her, and Ashley's passionate response did nothing to soothe either emotion. 'How can you leave me?' he demanded, his breathing harsh and spasmodic as he continued, 'Do you not feel as I do? I say that you cannot go. I will not permit you to leave me.'

Shock squeezed her heart. She had not anticipated that Azir would try to force his will on her again. As she stared up at him in stunned confusion, he gave a groan of anguish and shook his head.

'No, I do not mean that. You are free to do what you like. But for your return to Australia, you must accept that I cannot let you go alone. Now that you have come to me, Ashley, I cannot bear to be separated from you. The thought of not having you constantly by my side . . .'

'You'll come with me?' she cried, relief heading the surge of happiness that washed through her.

'You don't object?'

The pained uncertainty in his voice brought a choking lump of emotion to Ashley's throat. She didn't care what her parents or anyone thought. 'I'd love you to come with me, Azir. I don't want to be separated from you either.'

His chest heaved as if he could no longer contain the emotion swelling his heart. 'I love you, Ashley. More than life itself. Won't you reconsider about only being my lover?'

Before she could reply, Azir continued, the words spilling from his tongue in passionate bursts. 'I want you, I need you, I love you. Please, my darling, I want you to think about being my wife. You tell me we are too different, that it is impossible. But that is not so, and I will prove it to you. Ask what you like of me, and if it's within my power, I will give it to you . . .'

Joy ripped away the shock. Ashley hadn't dared let herself hope for so much, but Azir surely meant what he was saying. He did not want her as his mistress, but as his wife!

'. . . You said you needed time, and I will not press you, Ashley.' He hurried on. 'I do not expect you to love me with the intensity I love you. Just give me the chance to show you that our lives can be melded together, and I will do all I can to make you happy. I need you so much, so . . .'

She reached up to kiss the words of love flowing from his mouth. He stopped the violent outpouring of emotion to take the sweet offering of her mouth with a passionate intensity that even more eloquently transmitted his need for her.

It was minutes later that he broke away from the thraldom of her response. 'You will think about it, then?' he demanded hoarsely.

'Yes. Oh, yes!' she breathed happily. 'I don't understand it. I still hardly know you. But I've never felt this way about a man before. I ...'

His hands trapped her face, stilling her speech as he struggled to accept the words she had spoken. 'Ashley ...' It was a plea, a wish, a clutch at a dream he had not dared believe in. His voice gravelled along the edge of hope. 'Oh, Ashley, do you really mean what you're saying?'

'Yes,' she said simply, giving him the most direct reassurance.

A cry of elation broke from his lips. 'Then it will be all right. You will see, my darling. I will make you so happy ...'

He rained passionate kisses all over her face, down her throat, and Ashley hugged him to her with a fierce thrill of possessiveness. However foreign and alien he had once seemed to her, he had brought her back to a life worth living and she loved him. She loved him!

On that sweet wave of certainty she spoke. 'I don't have to consider it, Azir ...'

'No!' The breath was squeezed out of her as Azir caught her to him in a crushing embrace. 'You can't deny me. We are meant for each other. From the first moment I saw you ... Ashley, you must have felt it too?' he cried despairingly.

'Yes,' she confessed. 'And I will marry you, Azir. That's what I was going to say.'

The expulsion of a tortured breath whispered through her hair, and then he was lifting his head and Ashley felt the exultation that soared through him. 'You will be ... my wife?'

A totally primitive satisfaction ripped through Ashley at the ring of ecstatic ownership in those last two words. 'Yes,' she breathed, knowing on every instinctive level that this man was her mate and there would never be another.

He touched her face, almost in wondering reverence. 'I have been waiting for you, wanting you all my life. I cannot describe ... you cannot conceive the despair I felt when I found out you were married. And when you left with the Baron ...'

She brushed his mouth with soft, silencing fingertips. 'I promise you I'll never leave you again, Azir. I'm sorry I hurt you so much.'

He took her hand and pressed her open palm against his cheek. 'No matter now. I promise that I will never give you cause to regret this, Ashley.'

She smiled. 'How could I? I love you.'

He kissed her with a worshipful tenderness that brought tears to Ashley's eyes. They trickled down her cheeks and Azir's mouth roved lovingly over her face, kissing away the salty stains, murmuring huskily against her skin, 'You must not weep, Ashley. I will always be by your side to look after you. I will not let anything come between us.'

She remembered his ruthlessness in pursuing her and did not doubt his claim. And she remembered also how he had tempered that ruthlessness, loving her so much that he would not make her unhappy by taking her freedom away. He had conceded her the right to choose, against his own interests, and she loved him all the more for it.

Whatever differences there were between them didn't matter. She believed, as Azir said, that nothing would come between them, nothing that could make her regret the decision she had made tonight. The commitment had been given, he to her and she to him, and when Ashley finally dozed off to sleep in the arms of her lover, she was absolutely positive that she was where she wanted to be. With Azir for the rest of her life.

CHAPTER TWELVE

THE next few days were the most exciting Ashley had ever experienced. She grew to appreciate what a multi-cultural man Azir was, with so many impressive facets to his character that she was almost in awe of him. Why he loved her, of all the women who had crossed his path, she couldn't imagine, but she was intensely grateful that he did, and he never left her in any doubt of it.

Each day seemed to bring them closer together, nearer to a perfect union of a man and a woman, closer to a total acceptance of each other for exactly what they were. Ashley could only shake her head in wonder whenever she recalled Azir's certainty that first night they had met. 'The bond is already forged,' he had declared, and he had been right. And the bonding grew stronger with every minute they spent together.

There were hours in every day when they had to be apart, Ashley to conclude her business, Azir on affairs of state. The rapture of finding each other, whether it was in the Chinese Room, or the Regency Room, or any other room, was like a reuniting of two separate streams of life which were totally diminished without the other.

As for her negotiations over the jewellery collection, once Azir heard of her problems, he immediately swung his influence behind her. Louis-Philippe had been helpful, but it was Azir who opened doors for her that would always be shut to foreigners. The negotiations had quickly progressed to the stage where her firm's proposals had been accepted in principle, and that virtually concluded Ashley's mission in Cairo.

It gave Ashley enormous satisfaction to send all the completed paperwork back to the company management in Australia. Mr Buller, who had been responsible for sending her to Egypt in the first place, would now handle all future developments. There was only the Aswan trip to be made for her portfolio of sketches to be completed also, but Ashley was reluctant to leave Azir, even for a few days.

However important she had once thought the Egyptian Collection to be, her work on it certainly didn't rate at all if it meant she and Azir had to be separated. She even contemplated asking Mr Buller to send a replacement for her, but in the end common sense prevailed. She had taken on a job and her own sense of reponsibility demanded that she finish it.

When she told Azir she should make the trip, he nodded thoughtfully then asked, 'How many days do you need in Aswan?'

'Three or four, I suppose,' she answered regretfully. 'I'll be as fast as I can.'

The dark eyes lit with delight at her eagerness to return to him. 'I will go with you, Ashley. My business here can wait. Our time together is far too precious to waste.'

Ashley flew into his arms, hugging him in happy relief. 'You're sure it will be all right? You mustn't let my work interfere ...'

'I will make it right,' he said, with an arrogant assurance that Ashley no longer resented. She had come to the conclusion that Azir could make just about anything happen if he set his mind on it. He really was the most extraordinary man.

'However,' he continued, his eyes searching hers in concern, 'I am not sure that it's a good thing, your giving up your work, Ashley. It has been part of your life for so many years. If you begin to miss it, you must tell me, and ...'

She laughed in sheer happiness. 'Oh, Azir! I doubt I will have time to miss it. I think running your homes in Paris and London and Rome and Washington will be a full-time job, not to mention being the wife of a very busy diplomat. And I'm going to love every minute of it.'

She kissed him to erase any possible doubt in his mind, and he smiled his contentment. 'As long as you are happy, Ashley. But remember, I will arrange whatever you want.'

Ashley didn't doubt that he would. There was nothing mean or selfish in Azir's regard for her. Her happiness was his first concern, and he proved it over and over again.

They flew to Aswan in his private jet and Azir devoted all his time to her, never leaving her side, and even taking a keen interest in the jewellery that Ashley pointed out to him as designs that were unique to this region. He insisted on buying her a silver bracelet that was a particularly fine piece of workmanship, and would have bought her more if Ashley hadn't vigorously protested.

The days passed all to quickly; bright, scintillating days of blissful companionship, and nights of long, passionate lovemaking. On their last night in Aswan, it was very late when their desire for each other was finally sated. Ashley awoke early the next morning, her subconscious mind restless with the knowledge that her work in Egypt was finally finished. They would be going to Australia soon. She hoped that her parents would welcome Azir when she introduced him to them.

Azir was still asleep and it was Ashley's first experience of actually seeing him in complete repose. Invariably he woke first in the mornings, and it was his loving caresses that drew her out of sleep. She was tempted to do the same to him, but there was a touching vulnerability in his stillness that gave her pause for thought.

There was one other matter that had to be sorted out before she left Egypt. Ashley had been putting it off, not wanting to raise an issue that might bring discord into the wonderful harmony of their own personal happiness, but she had to speak to Azir about Louis-Philippe and Sohaila.

Friendship demanded it.

Azir had been more than good to her. Nothing that could please her was too much trouble or too expensive. Ever since she had gone to live with him he had been showering her with an embarrassment of gifts. He was incredibly generous, but what she wanted to ask might test his generosity too far.

She loved Azir too much to hurt him. A sigh of sweet contentment whispered from her lips as her gaze travelled slowly over his firm, muscular body, and a smile curved her mouth as she noticed the curly thickness of his long, black eyelashes. She hoped their child would inherit them.

Ashley's hand crept over her stomach, hugging her secret pleasure in the knowledge that her monthly period was late. Only a few days late. Not long enough to be absolutely positive about a pregnancy. But in her heart Ashley was certain that a child had been conceived.

A vague sense of guilt flitted through her mind as she thought of Damien, who had so desperately wanted her to have his child. He had been a good and wonderful person, a truly loving partner, yet Azir had given her a joy in loving that she had never experienced before. There was no way Ashley could compare them, nor did she want to. Damien belonged to the past now, and there was nothing more she could do for him, ever. Azir was her present and her future, and Ashley was determined to make whatever adjustments were necessary to keep their life together happy.

But could Azir make the emotional adjustment necessary to accept Louis-Philippe's company? Ashley reached out a hand to touch him, then withdrew it, reluctant to disturb him when he looked so relaxed and peaceful.

Very carefully, she slid out of bed and padded over to the window that gave such a spectacular view of Aswan. She wanted to imprint it on her memory before she left, because she was quite sure there could be no place in the whole world that encapsulated so many contrasts.

Their rooms were on one of the top floors of the Oberoi Hotel on Elephantine Island in the middle of the Nile River. Below her, the gardens leading up to the hotel from the ferry wharf were lushly tropical, and the green strip of fertility along the banks of the Nile held masses of palm trees; yet the harsh backdrop of the sterile desert was a telling reminder of how precious water was in this ancient land.

Along the city-side bank of the river, a row of modern cruise-ships stood at anchor, waiting for their fill of tourists before beginning the journey down to the Valley of the Kings near Luxor. The island harbours held a fleet of *feluccas*, the sturdy, primitive sailing-boats that had been in service for many hundreds of years, their swift manoeuvrability still shaming modern technology.

On the west bank of the Nile stood the luxurious villas built by the Aga Khan; behind it like a lonely

sentinel in the desert his marble tomb; on the east
bank the poverty of the Nubian dwellings, and the
granite quarries that had provided the outer
casings for the pyramids of the Pharoahs.

Further up the river, although it was too far
away for Ashley to see it, was the High Aswan
Dam. Azir had taken her to look at it, intent on
explaining all the problems that had to be taken
into consideration with every step towards
modernisation in these third world countries.
Although the dam regulated the flow of the Nile so
that there was no more destructive flooding, the
valley no longer received deposits of rich silt, and
the soil was losing its fertility.

Ashley no longer worried about the differences
between her and Azir's backgrounds. Despite the
kind of contrasts in their lives that she saw spread
below her in Aswan, nothing could change what
they had together.

Ashley had been so deep in thought she hadn't
heard Azir get out of bed, and she gasped in
surprise when his arms slid around her. She
nestled back against him, loving the feel of his
warm, hard flesh pressing into hers. He trailed
little kisses over the curve of her shoulder and she
twisted her head around to smile at him.

'What were you thinking of?' he asked, rubbing
his cheek against hers with a sensual tenderness
that sent a warm ripple of pleasure right to her
heart.

'Lots of things,' she sighed, and turned around

into his embrace.

She looked up into eyes that searched hers intently. 'Going home?' he questioned.

'Home is where you are, Azir,' she answered, and kissed him with all the passionate conviction in her soul.

He clung on to their togetherness, his arms encircling her in compelling ownership. 'I thought you might have been a little homesick for Australia. And your family. When I meet with your parents, Ashley, I will assure them that I shall care for you always. They may or may not approve of me, but at least they will know I am sincere in my love for you.'

Happiness overflowed from her heart and her eyes sparkled their contentment. 'They will approve! How could they not approve when you make me so happy?'

He laughed. 'So when do you want to leave Egypt? I have already begun making arrangements to take temporary leave, but I need to have a date of departure.'

There was no time to think of a tactful way of approaching the question she wanted to raise. 'It depends on you, Azir. Sohaila and Louis-Philippe have invited us to their wedding. The marriage ceremony is to be held in a fortnight's time. I know you ...'

'If we attend the ceremony, you will stay in Egypt an extra fortnight. Is that what you are saying Ashley?'

Ashley sighed, feeling she was defeated before she had barely begun. 'I know that you and Louis-Philippe can never be friends, but Sohaila is very dear to me, and . . .'

'. . . and we will go to the wedding!' He frowned over the uncertainty he heard in Ashley's voice. 'Don't think of me as being some form of tyrant, Ashley. An Arab is not the same as a Western man. Our wives are our dearest possessions, partners in life, sharing everything. Marriage is for ever. Of course I will go to the wedding with you. I will always consider what you want, and give you all that it is possible for me to give.'

Ashley shook her head in wonder at the faultless generosity of the man she loved. She felt uniquely blessed that he loved her. 'Thank you, Azir,' she said with heartfelt gratitude. 'I realise what it must cost you, with all the enmity between your family and his. It's more than I ever expected . . .'

He smiled, his eyes caressing her in a way that made Ashley prickle with pleasure. 'Perhaps it is time to put enmity aside,' he said softly. 'We were born on different sides of the fence, born to fight one another, but I do not forget that my father owes his life to the Frenchman.'

The smile tilted into dry irony. 'The Baron is a man of courage and integrity. I'll grant him that. And now that we are no longer involved in battle over you, my love, I can view him far more tolerantly than I ever could before. It is even possible that we could come to understand each other, so I'm not averse to meeting him. Particularly since it pleases you.'

Ashley could not stop the wide grin that spread across her face. These two extraordinary men shared so much more in common than they would ever realise. 'I think you will like Louis, once you get to know him, Azir.'

He laughed. 'Perhaps. One thing is certain—I am obliged to him if going to his wedding will keep us a fortnight longer in Egypt. Now that we are being married there is much to be arranged, and I prefer to do it in a civilised manner.' His eyes gathered a gleam of possessive desire as he added, 'Not that anything would stop me from marrying you, or going with you to Australia. I have a terrible need for you, Ashley.'

'Now?' she teased, sliding her arms around his neck and swaying provocatively against him.

'Now,' he growled, and swept her back to bed where he made love to her for a long time, until they found a mutual peace in each other's arms.

They lay together, gently caressing in the soothing afterglow of total contentment. Instinctively responding to the need to share everything, Ashley snuggled closer as she prepared to tell her husband-to-be that she might be carrying his child.

'Azir . . .' she whispered, trying to contain her own excitement, and hoping he would be just as pleased as she was. 'I think you might have become a father.'

'I tried hard,' he agreed, and she looked up to see a triumphant grin on his face. 'I've been trying hard ever since you came to stay with me,' he confessed. 'I know you won't change your mind now, Ashley, but I wanted to be sure you would marry me one way or another.'

Ashley laughed out of sheer joy. 'Well, I think you succeeded on the first day, because I ...'

The grin went slack as he stared up in surprise, then gently pressed her back on the pillows, a whole range of emotions skating across his face. 'Ashley, you don't mean ... already?'

'Do you mind?' she asked, a chill of apprehension rippling over her heart as she saw the dazed horror in his eyes.

'You should not have let me make love to you so ... so violently,' he choked out. 'If we have hurt the baby ...'

She barely swallowed a bubble of laughter as relief swept through her. 'It can't possibly have hurt the baby, Azir.'

His relief was slower in coming. 'Are you sure?'

'I'm sure,' she said, very positively.

A smile of absolute pleasure lit his face. He caressed her lazily for hours, kissing her breasts and stomach, loving her for the mother she was going to be. Ashley lay in his arms, finding pleasure in giving pleasure, knowing that a whole new way of life was opening up for her ... the wife of a diplomat ... mother of a child ... perhaps of several children, if Azir wanted them. Clearly, the idea of being a father was very much to his taste.

She thought how strange it was that love could change so many perceptions, so irrevocably alter a person's life. Sohaila's and Louis-Philippe's also, not just hers and Azir's. So much had been changed since that first night when she had gone to the casino to win the money for Sohaila. And Azir had won it for her. She remembered her incredulous shock when the number she had chosen had in fact come up.

'Azir,' she said drowsily as his mouth moved adoringly down her body.

'Mmm?'

'You're a very lucky man!'

He moved his head sideways, and looked back at her consideringly. 'That is exactly so! I never thought otherwise.'

'You misunderstand me,' Ashley laughed back. 'I'm not so conceited as to think you're lucky to have me. What I meant was the first time we met. You remember?'

'How could I ever forget it?' His voice was deep with pleasant memories.

'You had the luck of the devil himself on that roulette wheel. I even thought so at the time. Particularly with that last bet on twenty-three. I thought you were mad to do it, but . . .'

She stopped, intrigued by the odd shift of expression on his face; a look of guilt, then remorse, and finally a touch of self-mockery. 'Ah, Ashley,' he sighed, then took the bit between his teeth and plunged on. 'Don't ever believe in that kind of luck.'

'But ... I saw you have it,' Ashley protested, puzzled by his reaction and assertion.

His mouth turned down into a grimace. His eyes begged her understanding. 'Sometimes in the diplomatic service it is necessary to make an impression. We have ways ... it's not really diplomatic to say what they are ... it costs a great deal of money ...'

'Azir, are you trying to tell me that ...?'

'My dearest darling, you must not question me! There are some things that are best not revealed. Believe me! All I'm trying to suggest to you is that you should never trust in luck.'

Ashley let the information filter through her mind. He had not won the money. She was quite certain of that. He had wanted her so badly he must have paid for whatever he won. She remembered what he had said at the time. 'I don't gamble. And I always win.'

And he had certainly won her, Ashley thought in another burst of ecstatic happiness. She wound her arms around his neck. 'Thank you for loving me, Azir,' she said fervently, and it was a prayer of gratitude for all he had done for her, and a paean of praise for the life ahead of them.

'How could I not?' he replied simply. 'We were made for each other.'

And Ashley knew he was right. Even when her mind had denied it, her instincts had recognised the truth. Whatever the odds had been against them, they had found each other, and the bond had been forged.

Sandra Marton had her first book published by Mills & Boon® in 1985 and is now the author of more than forty romance novels. Readers around the world love her strong, passionate heroes and determined, spirited heroines. When she's not writing, Sandra likes to hike, read, explore out-of-the-way restaurants and travel to far-away places.

The mother of two grown sons, Sandra lives with her husband in a sun-filled house in a quiet corner of Connecticut where she alternates between extravagant bouts of gourmet cooking and take-out pizza. Sandra loves to hear from her readers. You can write to her (SASE) at PO Box 295, Storrs, Connecticut 06268.

HOSTAGE OF THE HAWK

by

SANDRA MARTON

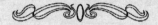

CHAPTER ONE

THE cry of the *muezzin* rose in the warm evening and hung trembling over the crowded streets of Casablanca. Joanna, listening from the balcony of her hotel suite, felt a tremor of excitement dance along her skin. Not that there was really anything to get excited about. While the hotel was Moroccan in décor, it was the same as hotels everywhere.

Still, she thought as she put down her cup and leaned her crossed arms on the balcony railing, it was wonderful to be here. This part of the world was so mysteriously different from the life she knew. She felt as if she had stepped back in time.

'Jo!'

Joanna sighed. So much for stepping back in time. Her father's angry bellow was enough to bring her back to the present with a bang.

'Jo! Where in hell are you?'

And so much for the mystery of Casablanca, she thought as she straightened and turned towards the doorway. She was used to Sam Bennett's outbursts—who wouldn't be, after twenty-six years?—but she felt a twinge of sympathy for whatever poor soul had made him this angry. Jim Ellington, probably; Sam had been on the phone with his second in command, which meant that Jim must have done or said something that displeased him.

'It's about time,' he snapped when she reached the bedroom. 'I've been calling and calling. Didn't you hear me?'

'Of course I heard you.' Her father was glaring at her from the bed where he lay back against a clutch of squashed pillows, his ruddy face made even redder by the pain in his back and his bad temper. 'Half the hotel must have heard you. I take it there's a problem?'

'You're damned right there's a problem! That stupid Ellington—he screwed things up completely!'

'Well, that's no surprise,' Joanna said pleasantly. She plumped the pillows, then took a small vial from the nightstand and dumped two tablets into the palm of her hand. 'I tried to tell you not to rely on him, that he was the wrong person to deal with this idiotic Eagle of the East.'

'Hawk,' Sam said grumpily as he took the tablets from her. 'Prince Khalil is called the Hawk of the North.'

'Hawk, eagle, east, north—what's the difference? It's a stupid title for a two-bit bandit.'

Sam grimaced. 'That "two-bit bandit" can end Bennettco's mining deal with Abu Al Zouad before it starts!'

'That's ridiculous,' Joanna said. She poured some orange juice into a glass and offered it to Sam. 'Abu's the Sultan of Jandara—'

'And Khalil's been harassing him for years, stirring up unrest and trouble whenever he can.'

'Why doesn't Abu stop him?'

'He can't catch him. Khalil's as sly as a fox.' Sam smiled grimly, then gulped down the juice and handed back the glass. 'Or as swift as a hawk. He swoops down from the northern mountains—'

'The mountains Bennettco wants to mine?'

'Right. He swoops down, raises hell, then escapes back to his mountain stronghold, untouched.'

'He's more than a bandit, then,' Joanna said with a little shudder. 'He's an outlaw!'

'And he's opposed to the deal we've struck with Abu.'

'Why?'

'Abu says it's because he's opposed to our bringing in Western ways.'

'You mean, he's opposed to our bringing in the twentieth century,' Joanna said with a grimace.

'Whatever. The point is, he'll do everything he can to keep Bennettco out. Unless we can change his mind, we might as well pack up and go home.'

'I still don't understand. Why can't Abu simply have Khalil arrested and—?' Her brows lifted as her father began to chuckle. 'Did I say something funny?'

'Have him arrested!' Sam's laughter grew, even though he clutched at the small of his back. 'Have pity, Jo! It hurts when I laugh.'

'I'm not trying to amuse you, Father,' Joanna said stiffly. 'I'm just trying to understand why this man isn't in prison if he's an outlaw.'

'I told you, they can't catch him.'

Joanna's brows lifted. 'In case you haven't noticed,' she said drily, 'Khalil can be "caught" this very moment at a hotel on the other side of Casablanca.'

'Yeah, yeah, I told that to Abu.'

'Well, then—'

'He doesn't want to cause an international dispute with the Moroccan government. This is their turf, after all.' Sam sighed and fell back against the pillows. 'Which brings us back to square one and that dumb ass Ellington. If only I could get out of this bed long enough to make that dinner meeting—'

'When we left New York, you made it sound as if this meeting were pro forma.'

'Well, it is. I mean, it should have been—if I hadn't pulled my back.' Sam's mouth turned down. 'I know I could have finessed the hell out of Khalil—and now Ellington's managed to make a bad situation worse.'

'I'll bet Ellington obeyed you to the letter, phoned your regrets about tonight's meeting, and said he'd dine with Khalil in your place.'

'You're darned right he obeyed me.' Sam glared at her. 'If he wants to keep his job, he'd better!'

'It's what everybody who works for you does,' Joanna said mildly, 'even if your orders are wrong.'

'Now, just a minute there, Joanna! What do you mean, my orders were wrong? I told Ellington to tell the Prince that something had come up that I couldn't help and—'

'You insulted him.'

'What?'

'Come on, Father! Here's this—this robber baron with an over-inflated ego, gloating over the fact that he's got Sam Bennett, CEO and chairman of the board of Bennettco, over a barrel. He's probably been counting the minutes until tonight's meeting—and then he gets a call telling him he's being foisted off on a flunky.'

'Don't be foolish! Ellington's my policy assistant.'

'It's a title, that's all, and titles are meaningless.' Joanna sat down on the edge of the bed. 'Who would know that better than an outlaw who calls himself a prince?'

'I already know we're in trouble, Jo! What I need is a way out.'

'Take it easy, Father. You know what the doctor said about stress being bad for your back.'

'Dammit, girl, don't fuss over me! There's a lot at stake here—or have you been too busy playing nurse-maid to notice?'

'I am not a "girl".' Joanna got to her feet, her gaze turning steely. 'I am your daughter, and, if you weren't so determined to keep me from knowing the first thing about Bennettco, I wouldn't have to ask you all these questions. In fact, I might have been able to come up with some ideas that would have gotten you off the hook tonight.'

'Listen, Jo, I know you have a degree in business administration, but this is the real world, not some ivy-covered classroom. It's Ellington who let us down. He—'

'You should have told Ellington to tell Khalil the truth, that your back's gone out again.'

'What for? It's nobody's business that I'm lying here like an oversized infant, being driven crazy by you and the hotel doctor!'

'Contrary to what you think,' Joanna said coolly, 'being sick isn't a sign of weakness. Khalil would have understood that he wasn't being insulted, that you had no choice but to back out of this meeting.'

Sam glared at her, then shrugged his shoulders. 'Maybe.'

'What did you plan on accomplishing tonight?'

'For one thing, I wanted to eyeball the bastard and see for myself what Abu's been up against.'

'And what else?'

Sam grinned slyly. 'He may resent us dealing with Abu—but I bet he won't resent a deal that has some under-the-table dollars for himself in it.'

A frown creased Joanna's forehead. 'You mean, Bennettco's going to offer him a bribe?'

'*Baksheesh*,' her father said. 'That's what it's called, and you needn't give me that holier-than-thou look. It's part of doing business in this part of the world. It just has to be done delicately, so as not to offend the s.o.b.' Sam sighed deeply. 'That was the plan, anyway—until Ellington botched it.'

'Have you any idea what, exactly, he said to the big pooh-bah?'

'To Khalil?' Sam shook his head. 'Ellington didn't even talk to him. He spoke to the Prince's aide, a guy named Hassan, and—'

'His first mistake,' Joanna said with crisp self-assurance. 'He should have insisted on speaking with the Prince directly.'

'He tried, but Hassan says Khalil doesn't deal with underlings. Underlings, can you imagine?' Sam chuckled. 'The only good part of this is imagining Ellington's face when he heard that.'

'What did Ellington say then?'

'The conversation was all Hassan's after that. He made some veiled threats, said if Sam Bennett wasn't interested enough to deal with Khalil man to man, Khalil wouldn't be responsible for what might happen.'

'That's insane! He can't be fool enough to think he can ride down on our crews with his band of cut-throats—can he?'

'Maybe—and maybe not.' Sam grunted with displeasure. 'Hell, this meeting was the key to everything! I just know that if I could have met face to face with this Khalil I'd have been able to convince him that Bennettco—'

'We still can.'

'How? I just told you, Khalil won't meet with Ellington.'

'But he might meet with me,' Joanna blurted.

She hadn't planned those words, but once she'd said them her heart began to pound. Sam's prideful stubbornness, Ellington's blind adherence to orders and the arrogance of a greedy bandit with a fancy title had set in motion a series of events that might make all the difference in her life.

Sam laughed, and Joanna looked up sharply.

'Right,' he said sarcastically. 'I'm supposed to send my daughter to meet with a barbarian. Do I look like I'm crazy, Jo?'

'Come on, Father. He's not exactly a barbarian. Besides, I'd be meeting him for dinner, in a fancy restaurant. I'd be as safe as if I were dining in my suite.'

'Forget it. The great Khalil doesn't deal with underlings.'

'Maybe he'd feel differently about someone named Bennett, someone with a vested interest in Bennettco.' Joanna looked at her father, her voice strengthening as her idea took shape. 'Someone who could identify herself as not just her father's daughter but Bennettco's vice-president.'

Sam scowled darkly. 'Are we back to that?'

'We never left it. Here I am, your only offspring, somebody who grew up as much in the field as in the office—'

'My first mistake,' he grumbled.

'Here I am,' Joanna said evenly, 'the only person who knows as much about business as you do, my university degree clutched in my hand, and you absolutely refuse to let me work for you.'

'You do work for me. You've been my hostess in Dallas and New York since you were old enough to carry on a conversation.'

'That,' she said dismissively.

'Yes, that! What's wrong with "that", for lord's sake? Any girl in her right mind would grab at the chance to—' Joanna's brows lifted and Sam put his hand to his heart. 'Forgive me,' he said melodramatically. 'Any *woman* in her right mind would be perfectly happy to—'

'Stanford Mining's offered me a job,' Joanna said softly.

'They did what?'

She walked to the bureau and leaned back against it, arms folded over her breasts. She'd never meant to tell her father about the offer this way; she'd planned on working up to it, using it as the final link in a well-conceived argument designed to convince him, once and for all, that she wanted more than to be a beautifully dressed figurehead, but she knew in her bones that now was the moment.

'The manager of their Alaskan operation is leaving. They asked if I might be interested.'

Sam's face darkened. 'My own daughter, working for the competition?'

'The key word is ''working'', Father. I've told you and told you, I've no intention of spending the rest of my life like some—some over-age débutante.'

'And I've told you and told you, I didn't work my tail off so my daughter could get her hands dirty!'

'I'm not asking you to let me work in the field,' Joanna said quickly. 'Even I know better than to expect the impossible.'

'Joanna.' Sam's voice softened, took on the wheedling tone she knew so well. 'I need you doing just what you've been doing, baby. Public relations is important, you know that. Having your name listed on the committee for charity benefits, getting your picture in the paper along with the Whitneys, Rockefellers and Astors—'

'You're wrong about the importance of that stuff, Father, but if it matters to you so much I can hold down a job and still manage all the rest.'

Sam gave her a long, hard look. 'Are you serious about taking the job with Stanford?'

Until this moment, she had only been serious about considering it—but now she knew that she would accept the offer rather than go on playing the part her father had long ago assigned her.

Joanna nodded. 'Yes,' she said, her eyes locked with his, 'I am.'

They stared at each other while the seconds passed, Joanna's emerald gaze as unwavering as her father's pale blue one, and finally he sighed.

'Do you really think you could get this guy Khalil to agree to meet with you?'

A little thrill raced through Joanna's blood but she was careful to keep her expression neutral.

'I think I could have a good shot at it,' she said.

'By telling him you're my daughter?'

'By telling him the truth: that you're ill but that this meeting is too important to miss. By telling him I'm your second in command, that everything I say has your full support and backing.'

Sam pursed his lips. 'That simple, hmm?'

Nothing was ever that simple, Joanna knew, not in business, not in life, and surely not in this place where custom vied with progress for dominance. But this was no time to show any hesitation.

'I think so, yes.'

She waited, barely breathing, while Sam glowered at her, and then he nodded towards the phone.

'OK.'

'OK, what?' Joanna said, very calmly, as if her pulse weren't racing hard enough so she could feel the pound of it in her throat.

'Call the Prince's hotel. If you can get past that watchdog of an aide, if Khalil will talk to you and agree to meet with you in my place, you've got a deal.'

Joanna smiled. 'First let's agree on the terms.'

'I'm your father. Don't you trust me?'

'You're my father and you raised me never to sign anything without reading it twice.' She saw a glimmer of a smile in Sam's eyes as she held up her fisted hand. 'Number one,' she said, raising her index finger, 'I get a vice-presidency at Bennettco. Number two, it's a real job with real responsibilities. Number three—'

Sam threw up his hands. 'I know when I'm licked. Go on, call the man. Let's see if you're as good as you think you are.'

Joanna's smile blazed. 'Just watch me.'

Her father reached out, took a notepad from the night-stand, and held it out to her. 'Here's the phone number. It's direct to Khalil's suite.'

Joanna nodded and reached slowly for the phone. She would have preferred to make this call from the other room instead of here, with her father watching her every move, but Sam would be quick to pounce on that as a sign of weakness.

'Good evening,' she said to the operator, then read off the number on the notepad. Her stomach was knotting but Sam's gaze was unwavering and she forced a cool smile to her face as she sank into the bedside chair, leaned back, and crossed her legs. The phone rang and rang. Maybe nobody was there, she thought—and at that moment, the ringing stopped and a deep voice said something in a language she couldn't understand, except for the single word 'Hassan'.

Joanna clasped the phone more tightly. 'Good evening, Mr Hassan,' she said. 'This is Joanna Bennett. Sam Bennett's daughter.'

If Hassan was surprised, he covered it well. 'Ah, Miss Bennett,' he said in impeccable English, 'I am honoured. What may I do for you?'

'Well?' Sam said impatiently. 'What's he saying?'

Joanna frowned at him. 'How are you enjoying your stay in Casablanca?' she said into the phone.

'The city is delightful, Miss Bennett, as I'm sure you agree.'

Joanna touched the tip of her tongue to her lips. 'And the Prince? Is he enjoying his stay, as well?'

'Dammit,' Sam hissed, 'get to the point! Is Khalil there, or isn't he?'

'Indeed,' Hassan said pleasantly, 'my Lord Khalil has always had a preference for this city.'

Joanna took a deep breath. Enough pleasantries. It was time to get down to business.

'Mr Hassan,' she said, 'I should like to speak with the Prince.'

Hassan's tone hardened. 'I'm afraid that is out of the question, Miss Bennett. If you have a message for him, I shall be happy to deliver it.'

Joanna's hand began to sweat on the phone. Her father was still giving her that same steadfast look and a self-satisfied smile was beginning to form on his lips.

'Give it up, baby,' he said quietly. 'I told you you couldn't pull it off.'

'Mr Hassan,' Joanna said evenly, 'I'm afraid you don't understand. I want to assure the Prince that the only reason for the change in plans is because my father is ill. As for Mr Ellington—I'm afraid he misunderstood my father's instructions. The Prince will be dining with my father's representative, whom he trusts completely and holds in the highest esteem.' Joanna looked at Sam. 'Vice-president Jo Bennett.'

'One moment, please, Miss Bennett,' Hassan said.

Joanna felt a rush of hope. She smiled sweetly at Sam. 'He's going to put the Prince on,' she said, and hoped that her father couldn't see her crossed fingers.

Across town, in the elegant royal suite of the Hotel Casablanca, Prince Khalil glared at his prime minister.

'What sort of man is this Sam Bennett,' he growled, 'that he asks his daughter to telephone me and beg on his behalf?' He folded his arms across his chest, his dark blue eyes glinting like sapphires in his tanned, handsome face. 'Bennett is worried,' he said with satisfaction as he leaned his hard, six-foot frame against the wall.

'Precisely, my lord. He must be ready to bend to your will or he would not have ordered a woman to act as his agent.'

'Only a fool would bring his daughter on such a trip,' Khalil said with disdain. 'The woman must have thought Casablanca would be an exotic playground in which to amuse herself.'

Hassan's grizzled brows lifted. 'Of course, my lord. She is, after all, of the West.'

Khalil grunted in assent. 'What does she want?'

'To speak with you.' Khalil laughed and Hassan permitted himself a smile. 'I told her, of course, that was not possible, and then she said Sam Bennett wishes tonight's dinner meeting to take place.'

'Ah.' Khalil's hard mouth curled with the shadowy beginnings of an answering smile. 'Bennett has decided he wants to keep our appointment now?'

'He is ill, sire, or so the woman claims, and wishes to send an emissary. I suspect it is an excuse he uses to save face.'

Khalil strode forward. 'I do not meet with emissaries, Hassan.'

Hassan dipped his head in respect. 'Of course, my lord. But her offer is interesting. The emissary is Joe Bennett, a vice-president of the company.'

Khalil's eyes narrowed. 'Who? I have never heard of such a person.'

Frowning, Hassan took his hand from the telephone and spoke into it. 'We have no knowledge of this person who would meet with Prince Khalil, Miss Bennett. Is he related to your father?'

'Mr Hassan, if I could just speak with the Prince—'

'The Prince does not speak with underlings, and he surely does not meet with them,' Hassan said coldly. 'If you wish to answer my questions, I will transmit the information to my lord. Otherwise, our conversation is at an end.'

'Jo,' Sam said, 'give it up. You're not gonna get to first base with this guy.'

Joanna swung away from her father. 'Jo Bennett is hardly an underling, Mr Hassan.'

'Jo,' Sam said, his voice gaining authority, 'did you hear me? Give it up. You took a shot and you lost.'

'Miss Bennett,' the voice in her ear said sharply, 'I asked you a question. Who is Joseph Bennett? Is he Sam Bennett's son?'

Joanna swallowed, shut her eyes, then opened them. 'Yes,' she said into the telephone, praying that the Prince would forgive the deception after she convinced him that there'd be enough money in this deal to make him happy, 'yes, that's right, sir. He is.'

'A moment, please.' Hassan put his hand over the mouthpiece again and looked at the Prince. 'The man you would dine with is the son of Sam Bennett.'

Khalil glared at his minister. 'A son,' he snarled, 'a young jackal instead of the old.' He stalked across the elegant room, turned, and looked at Hassan. 'Tell the woman you will accept a meeting with her brother. Perhaps my judgement is wrong. Perhaps the son has some influence on the father. At any rate, you can convey my message clearly: that I will not be ignored in this matter!'

Hassan smiled. 'Excellent, my lord.' His smile fell away as he tilted the phone to his lips. 'Miss Bennett.'

Joanna blinked. 'Yes?'

'I, Adym Hassan, Special Minister to His Highness Prince Khalil, will meet with your brother tonight.'

Joanna clutched the cord tighter. 'But—'

'Eight o'clock, as planned, at the Oasis Restaurant. As they say in your world, take it or leave it, Miss Bennett.'

'Jo?' Sam's voice rose. 'Dammit, Jo, what's he saying? He's turning you down flat, isn't he?'

Joanna hunched over the phone. 'Of course,' she said, 'eight o'clock. That will be fine. Thank you, sir.' She hung up the phone, took a deep breath, and turned to her father. 'You see?' she said briskly. 'That wasn't so hard after all.'

'He's meeting with you?' Sam said doubtfully.

Joanna nodded. 'Sure. I told you he would.'

Sam blew out his breath. 'OK,' he said, 'OK. Now, let's figure out how to get the most mileage we can out of tonight.' He looked at his daughter and a grin spread over his face. 'Not bad, kid,' he said, 'not bad at all.'

'It's not "kid",' Joanna said with an answering smile. 'It's Vice-President Jo Bennett, if you don't mind.'

Vice-President Joseph Bennett, she thought, and gave a little shudder. Things were going to get interesting when Special Minister Adym Hassan found out he'd been lied to.

Halfway across the city, Special Minister Hassan was already thinking the same thing.

'I am suspicious of Bennett's motives, my lord,' he said to Prince Khalil as he hung up the phone. 'But we shall see what happens. The woman's brother will meet with me tonight.'

Khalil nodded. 'Good.' He turned, walked slowly across the room, and stood gazing out the window as if he could see beyond the city to the hills that marked the boundary of his kingdom. Sam Bennett was a sly, tough opponent; it was more than likely his son would be the same. Too sly and too tough for Hassan, who was loyal and wise and obedient but no longer young. How could he let the old man meet with Bennett? If he'd learned one thing these past weeks, it was that dealing with anybody named Bennett was like putting a ferret in charge of the hen house.

Khalil spun away from the window. 'Hassan!'

'Yes, my lord?'

'I have changed my mind. I will meet with Sam Bennett's son myself.'

Hassan looked startled. 'You, sir? But—'

'There are no "buts", Hassan,' Khalil said sharply. 'Call down for some coffee and lay out my clothing.' He smiled tightly, the sort of smile that chilled those who knew him well. 'I promise you this, old man. One way or another, tonight will change everything.'

It was Joanna's thought, too, as she sat beside her father, only half listening as he droned on about tonight's agenda.

One way or another, she knew in her bones that her life would not be the same after this night ended.

Afterwards, she would remember how right she'd been.

CHAPTER TWO

WHAT did you wear to a dinner meeting with a Hawk of the North?

Not that she'd be dining with the great man himself, Joanna thought wryly as she peered into the wardrobe in her bedroom. Her appointment was with Hassan, Special Minister to Prince Khalil, although what a bandit needed with a minister was beyond her to understand. Their conversation had been brief but it had been enough to give her a good idea of what he'd be like.

He'd be tall and angular and as old as the hills that lay beyond the city. The skin would be drawn across his cheekbones like ivory papyrus. His eyes, pale and rheumy with age, would glitter with distaste when he saw her and realised that she was Joanna Bennett, for he lived in a world in which female equality was unheard of.

Joanna smiled tightly as she riffled through the clothing hanging inside the wardrobe.

How would she convince him to continue the meeting, once her deceit was obvious?

'Surely, the great Khalil wishes prosperity for his people,' she'd begin, 'and would not wish you to refuse to meet with someone who can provide it.' Then, as distasteful as the prospect was, she'd dig into her purse, take out the envelope with the numbered Swiss bank account her father had established, and slide it gently across the table.

After that, Hassan wouldn't care if she were a man, a woman or a camel.

Joanna glanced at her watch as she stepped from her taxi. Eight o'clock. Her timing was perfect. She put her hands to her hair, checking to see if the pair of glittery combs were still holding the burnished auburn mass back from her face, then smoothed down the skirt of her short emerald silk dress. She'd hesitated, torn between a Chanel suit and this, the one cocktail dress she'd brought with her, deciding on the dress because she thought the suit might make her look too severe, that it would be enough of a shock for the minister to find himself dealing with a woman without her looking like *that* kind of woman.

The doorman was watching her enquiringly and she took a deep breath, lifted her chin, and walked briskly towards him. She was nervous but who wouldn't be? Everything she wanted—her father's approval, the vice-presidency at Bennettco—hung on the next couple of hours.

'*Masa el-kheyr*, madam.'

Joanna nodded. 'Good evening,' she said, and stepped through the door.

Soft, sybaritic darkness engulfed her, broken only by the palest glow of carefully recessed overhead lighting and flickering candlelight. Music played faintly in the background, something involving flutes and chimes that sounded more like the sigh of wind through the trees than anything recognisable to her Western ear.

'*Masa el-kheyr*, madam. Are you joining someone?'

The head waiter's smile was gracious but she wondered if he would continue smiling if she were to say no, she wasn't joining anyone, she wanted a table to herself.

'Madam?'

Joanna gave herself a little shake. The last thing she needed was to get herself into an antagonistic mood.

'Yes,' she said pleasantly. 'My name is Bennett. I believe there's a reservation in my name.'

Was it her imagination, or did the man's eyebrows lift? But he smiled again, inclined his head, and motioned her to follow him. There was an arched doorway ahead, separated from the main room by a gently swaying beaded curtain. When they reached it, he drew the curtain aside and made a little bow.

'The reservation request was for as private a table as possible,' he said.

Joanna nodded as she stepped past him. A private alcove. That would be better. At least, she and Hassan wouldn't have to deal with—

A man was rising to his feet from the banquette. Joanna's eyes widened. He was thirty, perhaps, or thirty-five, tall, with a lithe body and broad shoulders contained within a finely tailored English suit. Her gaze flew to his face. His eyes were shockingly blue against his tanned skin. His nose was straight, his mouth full and sensuous. And he was smiling.

Joanna's heart gave an unaccustomed thump. Lord, he was gorgeous!

She smiled back, flustered, then turned quickly to the head waiter.

'I'm terribly sorry, but there must be an error.'

'Yes.' The man had spoken, and she looked back at him. His smile had grown, tilting a little with intimacy and promise. 'I'm afraid the lady is right.' His voice was soft, smoky, and lightly tinged with an indefinable accent. 'If I were not expecting a gentleman to join me—'

The head waiter cleared his throat. 'Excuse me, sir. I believe you said you were waiting for a Mr Joseph Bennett.'

'Yes, that's right. I am.'

'Then there's been no error, sir. This is the gentleman—uh, the lady—you were waiting for.'

Joanna's eyes flew to the man's face. They stared at each other in silence. This was Hassan, Minister to Prince Khalil? Oh God, she thought, as she saw his expression go rapidly from surprise to disbelief to fury, and she stepped quickly forward and shot out her hand.

'Mr Hassan,' she said with a big, determinedly cheerful smile, 'what a pleasure to meet you. I'm Jo Bennett.'

He looked at her hand as if it were contaminated, then at her.

'If this is an example of Western humour,' he said coldly, 'I should warn you that I am not amused.'

Joanna swallowed, dropped her hand to her side, and fought against the desire to wipe the suddenly damp palm against her skirt.

'It's not a joke, no, sir.'

Sir? *Sir*? What was going on here? Was she really going to permit this—this arrogant minister to a greedy despot to reduce her to a deferential schoolgirl? It was one thing to be nervous, but it was quite another to let the balance of power be stripped from her without so much as a whisper. Whether Mr Hassan liked it or not, they were here on equal footing. The sooner she reminded him of that, the better.

Joanna lifted her chin and forced a cool smile to her lips.

'I am Joanna Bennett,' she said calmly. 'And I can understand that you might be a bit surprised, but—'

'Where is Sam Bennett's son?'

'I'm his son.' Joanna shook her head. 'I mean, he has no son, Mr Hassan. I am—'

'You are his daughter?'

'Yes.'

'You are Joe Bennett?'

'Joanna Bennett. That's right. And—'

He swung towards the head waiter. 'Bring me the bill,' he snapped. 'For my apéritif, and for whatever the restaurant will lose on this table for the evening.' He snatched a liqueur glass from the table, drained its contents, slammed it down, and made a mocking bow to Joanna. 'Goodnight, Miss Bennett.'

Open-mouthed, she stared after him as he strode towards the beaded curtain, still swaying delicately from the waiter's exit, and then, at the last second, she stepped out and blocked his path.

'Just a minute, Mr Hassan!'

'Step aside, please.'

It was the 'please' that was the final straw. The word was not offered politely, but was, instead, tossed negligently at the floor, as one might toss a bone to a dog. Joanna drew herself up.

'And what will you tell Prince Khalil, Mr Hassan?' Joanna slapped her hands on her hips. 'That because you were narrow-minded, old-fashioned, petty and stupid—'

The dark blue eyes narrowed. 'I advise you to watch your tongue.'

'And I advise you to use your head,' Joanna said sharply. 'Prince Khalil sent you here to meet with me.'

'I came here to meet with Sam Bennett's son.'

'You came to meet with his emissary, and that is precisely what I am!'

A muscle knotted in his cheek. 'Whose idea was this subterfuge? Ellington's? Or was it your father's?'

'There was no subterfuge meant, Mr Hassan.'

His smile was swift and chill. 'What term would you prefer? Deception? Trickery? Perhaps "fraud" has a finer ring.'

'At the worst, it's just a misunderstanding.'

He rocked back on his heels and folded his arms over

his chest. 'Please, Miss Bennett, don't insult me with games of semantics.'

'I'm simply trying to explain why—'

'What sort of misunderstanding could possibly have led to your thinking I would even consider discussing your father's greedy plans for my country with you?'

His disdain, his contemptuous words, were like a bucket of iced water. Joanna met his harsh gaze with unflinching directness.

'Wrong on all counts, Mr Hassan. For starters, I did not wish to discuss anything with you. It was Prince Khalil I wished to meet this evening, remember? As for greed—it is not my father who's standing in the way of progress and betterment for the people of Jandara, it's your high and mighty ruler.'

Hassan's brows lifted. 'An interesting description of the Prince, Miss Bennett. Clearly, your father didn't send you on this errand because of your subtlety.'

Joanna knew he was right. Her words had been thoughtlessly spoken but to back down now would be a mistake.

'He sent me because I have his trust and confidence,' she said. 'And if my honesty offends you, I can only tell you that I see little value in not being as direct as possible.'

An unpleasant smile curled across his mouth. 'How readily you use the word ''honesty''—and yet here you stand, having lied your way into my presence.'

'I did no such thing! I am who I said I was, Jo Bennett, the vice-president at Bennettco.'

'And we both know that if you had identified yourself properly, this meeting would not have taken place.'

'Exactly.' Joanna smiled thinly. 'I'm glad you admit it so readily. You and the Prince would have turned your noses up at the very idea of discussing business with a woman.'

'Typical Western nonsense,' he sneered. 'A woman, taking a man's name, trying to pretend she can do a man's job.'

'I haven't taken anything,' Joanna said coldly. '"Jo" is short for Joanna. As for a woman trying to pretend she can do a man's job—I don't know how to break this to you, but women don't have to "pretend" such things any more, Mr Hassan. In my country—'

'Your country is not mine,' he said, his tone rife with contempt.

'It certainly isn't. In *my* country—'

'In Jandara, those who lie do not break bread with each other.'

Joanna glared at him. 'It isn't my fault you assumed Jo Bennett was a man.'

'I don't recall you attempting to correct that assumption, Miss Bennett.'

Anger overcame her. 'If I didn't,' she said, stepping forward until they were only inches apart, 'it was because I knew your boss would react exactly the way you are at the prospect of a woman representing Bennettco. No wonder my father's gotten nowhere all these weeks! Trying to deal with a—tyrant is like—like…'

The rush of words stopped, but it was too late. He smiled slyly as she fell silent.

'Please, Miss Bennett, don't stop now. You've called Prince Khalil a tyrant, a chauvinist—I can hardly wait to hear what else you think of him.'

What was she doing? She'd come here to further her cause, to succeed in a tricky endeavour and convince Sam that she was capable of carrying her weight at Bennettco, and instead she was alienating the Hawk of the North's right-hand man with terrifying rapidity. She took a deep breath, let it out, and pasted a smile to her lips.

'Perhaps—perhaps I got carried away.'

The Prince's emissary smiled tightly. 'You may not be given to subtlety but you surely are given to understatement. Referring to m—to the Prince as a dictator is hardly—'

'I never called him that!'

His brows lifted. 'But you think it.'

'Certainly not,' she said, lying through her teeth. Of course she thought it. If this—this overbearing, arrogant, insolent pig of a man was the Prince's minister, she could only imagine what the Prince himself must be like. 'Besides, my opinion of your Prince is no more important than your opinion of me. You and I have lost sight of the facts, Mr Hassan. We are representatives, I of my father, you of Khalil. I doubt if either of them would be pleased if we reported back that we'd cancelled this meeting because we'd gotten off to a bad start.'

Her smile did nothing to erase the scowl from his face. 'Perhaps we'll simply tell them the truth, that we cancelled it because I resent having been made a fool of.'

He had a point. Much as she hated to admit it, she had twisted the facts to suit her own needs. She'd lied to him, lied to her father. And if Sam found out...

'Well?' She blinked. He was staring at her, his expression as unyielding as stone, his eyes cold. 'What do you say to that, Miss Bennett?'

'I say... I say...' Joanna swallowed hard. Go for broke, she thought, took a deep breath, and did. 'I say,' she said, her eyes meeting his, 'that you have every right to be annoyed.'

His scowl deepened. 'The start of another bit of trickery?'

Colour flared in Joanna's face but she pressed on. 'I

admit I may have stretched the facts, but I haven't lied. I do represent my father. I have his every confidence and I'm fully authorised to act on his behalf. I know you have a problem dealing with me, but—'

But, he thought impatiently, his eyes on her face, but! She was good at suggesting alternatives, this Joanna Bennett. She had insulted him, apologised to him, and now she was doing her best to convince him her father had Jandara's best interests at heart—but for what reason? Why had Sam Bennett sent her? She kept insisting she was Bennettco's representative, but what man would be fool enough to believe that?

His gaze moved over her slowly, with an insolence born of command. She kept talking, although her skin took on a rosy flush, and that amused him. Why would a woman like this colour under his gaze? Surely she was not innocent? She was a beauty, though, perhaps more beautiful than any woman he'd ever seen. What she couldn't know was that her beauty meant nothing to him. Despite what Joanna Bennett thought she knew of him— or of the man she believed him to be—he had long ago wearied of beautiful faces and bodies that hid empty souls. He preferred his women with strength and character, individuals in their own right, not the pampered lapdogs Western women so often were.

The logical thing to do was to tell her that she and her father had wasted their time, that he was not Hassan but Prince Khalil, that he was not interested in whatever game it was they were playing.

But if he did that, he would not learn what game it was. And that, surely, was vital.

'I still fail to see why your father sent you to this meeting, Miss Bennett,' he said sharply, 'unless he thought you could succeed where others had failed simply through the element of surprise.'

'If it makes you feel any better,' Joanna blurted, 'I'm as surprised as you are. I thought you'd be—I thought…'

'Yes?' His eyes narrowed. 'What did you think?'

Joanna stared at him. That you'd be a million years old, she thought, that you'd be a wizened old man… His voice. His voice had sounded old on the telephone. Hadn't it? Maybe not. She could remember little of their conversation except how desperate she'd been to make him commit to this meeting—this meeting that she was on the verge of ruining, unless she used her head.

'I thought,' she said carefully, 'we'd be able to sit down and discuss our differences face to face.'

He smiled tightly. 'But not man to man.'

'The bottom line,' Joanna said, ignoring the taunt, 'is that we—that is, Prince Khalil and Bennettco—*do* have differences.'

'Yes. We do, indeed.' His voice hardened. 'Bennettco thinks it can ignore Khalil and deal only with Abu—'

'Abu Al Zouad is the King of Jandara,' Joanna said with an icy smile, 'or has your Prince forgotten that little item?'

'He is not the King, he is the Sultan,' Khalil said sharply, 'and surely not Khalil's.'

'Abu is the recognised leader of your country, and he has guaranteed Bennettco the right to mine in the northern mountains.'

Khalil's smile was wily. 'If that is the case, why has your father sent you to meet with me?'

'To talk about what is best for Khalil's people.'

He laughed, this time with such disdain that it made Joanna's spine stiffen.

'You spout nonsense, Miss Bennett. That is hardly the issue we're here to discuss.'

At least the man was blunt, Joanna thought grimly. 'Very well, then,' she said. 'My father's sent me to talk about what will most benefit Bennettco—and what will most benefit your Prince, which is why your unwillingness to listen to what I have to say surprises me, Mr Hassan. This meeting is in Khalil's best interests, but—'

'Sir?' They both spun towards the curtained doorway. The head waiter was standing just inside it, smiling nervously. 'The bill, sir.'

Khalil looked at the silver tray in the man's hand, then at Joanna. She was right. It would be foolish of him not to find out what tricks her father had up his sleeve, even if it meant enduring her company.

'Very well,' he said. 'I will give you an hour, and not a moment more.'

Joanna nodded. She was afraid to breathe or even to answer for fear this impossible man would change his mind again and walk out.

Khalil nodded, too, as if they had made a pact, then looked towards the waiter.

'Bring us the meal I ordered,' he said with a dismissive wave of his hand.

'Certainly, sir.'

'Be seated, Miss Bennett.'

Be seated, Joanna thought as she slid into the padded banquette, just like that. No 'please', no attempt at courtesy at all. It was ludicrous. He'd already ordered dinner, even though she'd reserved the table. The man was impossible, arrogant and imperious and—

'So.' She looked up. He had slid into the booth opposite her and he was watching her intently, his eyes unreadable as they met hers. He sat back, his broad shoulders straining just a bit at the jacket of his suit, and a faint smile touched his mouth. 'Why don't you start our meeting by telling me about the Bennettco project?'

She did, even though she was certain he knew all the details. It would only help her make her case at the end, when it became time to ask him for assurance that he'd not try and hinder the project. She talked through the lemon soup, through the couscous, through the chicken baked with saffron, and finally he held up his hand.

'Very interesting—but you still haven't told me why I should permit—why my Prince should permit Bennettco to mine in the mountains?'

'Well, first of all, the operation will bring money into Jandara. It will—it will…' Joanna frowned. 'Permit, Mr Hassan? I don't think that's quite the correct word, do you?'

'English is not my first language, Miss Bennett, but I learned it at quite an early age. "Permit" was the word I intended.'

'But the decision's not Khalil's. It's Abu's.'

'Is it?' He smiled lazily. 'If that were completely true, you wouldn't be here.' He smiled lazily. 'You're concerned that Khalil will interfere with the project, isn't that right?'

What was the sense in denying it? Joanna shrugged her shoulders.

'We think he might try, yes.'

'And have you stopped to consider why he might do that?'

'Perhaps he hasn't given enough thought to how much this project will benefit his people.'

The arrogance of the woman! Khalil forced his smile not to waver.

'He is selfish, you mean?'

Joanna looked up, caught by the man's tone. He was still smiling, but there was something in that smile that made her wary.

'Well, perhaps he doesn't see it that way,' she said cautiously, 'but—'

'But you do, and that's what matters.'

'You're twisting my words, Mr Hassan.'

'On the contrary. I'm doing my best to get to the heart of your concerns. What else am I to tell him, apart from a warning about his selfishness?'

Joanna stared at him. Was he asking her to be more direct about the bribe money? It galled her to make such an offer but reason seemed to be failing. Sam had warned her that this was the way things were done in this part of the world, but—

'Don't lose courage now,' he said coldly. 'Be blunt, Miss Bennett. It's why you came here, remember?'

'Tell him—tell him we won't tolerate any harassment of our workers.'

'I see. You worry he might have them beaten. Or shot.'

There was a lack of emotion in his words, as if having men hurt were an everyday occurrence.

'We are not ''worried'' about anything, Mr Hassan,' she lied, her tone as flat as his. 'This project will go ahead, no matter what your Prince does. We simply want to encourage Khalil's co-operation.'

His nostrils dilated. He yearned to take the woman's slender shoulders in his hands and shake some sense into her.

'Really?' he said, and if Joanna had not been so caught up in her own determination to succeed, if she had not already decided that the only thing that would close the deal was the enormous bribe Sam had suggested, she'd have heard the note of warning in that single word. 'And how are you going to do that, Miss Bennett?'

Joanna gave him a look laced with contempt, then unclasped her evening bag and took out the envelope her father had given her.

'With this,' she said bluntly, and slid the envelope across the table towards him.

He bent his head and looked at it. His anger made the words on the paper a meaningless blur but then, what this female Judas was offering didn't matter. She had accused him of being obstinate, selfish and despotic, and now she had sought to buy him off as if he were a common thief.

'Well?' Her voice was impatient. 'Is it enough?'

Khalil silently counted to ten, first in Arabic, then in English, and then he took the envelope and stuffed it into his pocket.

'Oh, yes,' he said, the words almost a purr, 'it is enough. It is more than enough.'

She'd done it! She'd won the co-operation of the in-famous Prince Khalil—well, Bennettco's bribe had won it, which stole away most of the pleasure. Concentrate on the victory, she told herself, on what this will mean to your future...

He rose to his feet. 'Come, Miss Bennett,' he said softly.

Joanna looked up. He was holding out his hand and smiling. Or was he? His lips were drawn upwards, but would you really call what she saw on his handsome face a smile?

'Come?' she said, smiling back hesitantly. 'Come where?'

'We must celebrate our agreement with champagne. But not here. This place is for tourists. I will take you somewhere much more authentic, Joanna.'

Joanna? Joanna's heart thudded. Don't go with him, she thought suddenly, don't go.

'Joanna?'

That was ridiculous. She had done it, she had closed

the deal her father thought couldn't be closed. What on earth could there possibly be to fear?

Smiling, she got to her feet and gave him her hand.

He led her through the restaurant, pausing only long enough to say something to their waiter, who bowed respectfully all the way to the front door. Outside, the night seemed to have grown darker. He was holding her elbow now, his grip firm, as he led her towards a low-slung sports car at the kerb.

Suddenly, Joanna thought of something.

'Did you say we were going to have champagne?'

He nodded as he handed her into the car, came around to the driver's side, then slipped in beside her.

'Of course. It's a celebration. Why do you sound surprised?'

Joanna frowned slightly. 'Well, I'm just—I guess I *am* surprised. I didn't think your people drank wine.'

He smiled. 'Believe me, Joanna,' he said, 'you are in for a number of surprises before the evening ends.'

He stepped hard on the accelerator and the car shot into the night.

CHAPTER THREE

EVERYONE Joanna knew had had the same reaction to the news that she was going to Casablanca.

'Oh,' they'd sighed, 'how incredibly romantic!'

Joanna, remembering the wonderful old Humphrey Bogart-Ingrid Bergman movie, had thought so too. But after a week she'd decided that things must have changed a lot since the days of Rick and Ilse. Casablanca was ancient and filled with history, it was beautiful and mysterious, but it was also the economic heart of Morocco which meant that in some ways it was not only prosaic, it was downright dull.

The man beside her, though, was quite another story. She gave him a surreptitious glance from beneath her lashes. There was nothing dull about him. She'd never met a man like him before, which was saying a great deal. The circles in which she travelled had more than their fair share of handsome, interesting men but even in those circles, this man would stand out.

Joanna's gaze flew over him, taking in the stern profile, the broad sweep of his shoulders, the well-groomed hands resting lightly on the steering wheel. He seemed so urbane, this Mr Hassan, so at home in his well-tailored suit, his pricey car, and yet she could easily imagine him in a very different setting.

Her lashes drooped a little. Yes, she thought, she could see him in her mind's eye, dressed in long, flowing robes, mounted on a prancing black stallion, racing the wind across the desert under a full moon.

'You're so quiet, Miss Bennett.'

Joanna's eyes flew open. They had stopped at a light and he was looking at her, a little smile on his lips. For some reason, the thought that he'd been watching her without her knowing made her uncomfortable. She sat up straighter, smoothed her hair back from her face, and gave him a polite smile in return.

'I was just enjoying our drive,' she said.

She glanced out of the window as the car started forward. They were passing the Place des Nations Unies, deserted at this hour except for a solitary pair of strollers, a man and woman dressed in traditional garb, she walking barely noticeable inches behind. Like a respectful servant, Joanna thought with a grimace, or a well-trained dog…

'She is not being obedient, Miss Bennett,' the man beside her said, 'she's simply gawking at the sights.'

Joanna swung towards him. He was looking straight ahead, intent on the road.

'I beg your pardon?'

'That couple.' He glanced at her, an insolent smile curled across his mouth. 'You were thinking the wife was following her husband out of custom, but I assure you, she wasn't.'

He was right, but what did that matter? Joanna gave him a frigid look.

'Do you make a habit of reading people's thoughts, Mr Hassan?'

'It isn't difficult to read yours. You seem convinced we classify our women as property in this part of the world.'

She smiled tightly. 'Your definition, not mine.'

He laughed. 'A diplomatic response, Joanna—but then, your father would not have sent you on such a delicate mission if he hadn't been certain of your ability to handle yourself well.'

Some of the tension flowed from Joanna's posture. He was right. This *had* been a delicate mission, and she'd carried it off successfully. Let the Hassans and Khalils of this world have their *baksheesh* and bribes. What did it matter to her? She'd set out to snatch success from the jaws of defeat and she'd done it, despite the arrogant high-handedness of the man next to her.

'You're quite right,' she said pleasantly, folding her hands neatly in her lap and watching as the dimly lit streets spun by, 'he wouldn't have.'

'He has no sons?'

'No.' Her smile grew saccharine sweet. 'I know you must think that makes him quite unfortunate, but—'

'I suspect it simply makes him all the fonder of you.' He glanced at her, then looked back to the road. 'You must be very important to Sam Bennett, not only as vice-president of Bennettco but as the jewel of his heart.'

Joanna looked at him. She was neither, she thought with a little pang, not the vice-president of Bennettco nor even the jewel of her father's heart. It was Bennettco itself that was his love, it always had been, but now that she'd pulled this off...

'Am I right, Joanna?'

She swallowed. 'Yes,' she said quickly, 'I'm as important to him as you are to Prince Khalil.'

His head swung towards her. 'As I...?'

'I mean, you must be very important to Khalil, for him to entrust you with negotiating such important matters.'

'Ah.' He smiled. 'Of course. You are wondering if my word is Khalil's bond.'

'No. I wasn't. It never occurred to me to doubt—'

'I promise you, he will abide by my judgement.' He looked towards her, and suddenly his smile fled. 'I will not repudiate anything I do this night.'

Joanna's brows rose a bit. 'I'm sure you won't,' she said politely.

The man wasn't just arrogant, he was contemptuous as well. '*I will not repudiate anything I do this night*'! It was almost laughable. How could he say that when he was only the Prince's minister?

Khalil would be even worse, Joanna thought with a sigh, rigid and imperious and completely egotistical. It was probably a good thing he hadn't agreed to meet with her. As it was, she'd had difficulty holding her temper with Hassan. Heaven only knew how she'd have been able to deal with someone even ruder.

But she didn't have to worry about that any more, she thought, permitting herself a little smile. She'd done the impossible, pulled the coup that would set her firmly on a path she'd always wanted, and if she'd have been happier managing it without pushing a bribe under Hassan's nose, well, so what? If that was how things were done here, who was she to ask questions? She had succeeded, and now she and Hassan were going to drink a toast to their agreement.

Joanna settled back in her seat. Where was he taking her, anyway? Somewhere far from the streets she knew, that was obvious. In fact, they'd left the streets behind completely. The car was racing along a straight, narrow road that disappeared into the night.

Perhaps he was taking her to some place less Western than the restaurant where they'd dined. Perhaps, for all his seeming urbanity, he'd been uncomfortable in its sophisticated setting.

'You've become quiet again, Joanna.' Hassan stepped down harder on the accelerator and the car seemed to leap forward. 'Have you nothing to say, now that you've got what you wanted from me?'

His tone was nonchalant but Joanna sensed the un-

derlying derision in his words. She shifted into the corner of her seat and smiled politely.

'I think we've each gotten something from the other,'
she said.

'Of course. You have my promise of co-operation and
I—' He looked at her, his teeth showing in a swift smile.
'I have the bribe you offered me for it.'

It was what she had just been thinking but hearing it
from the man on the receiving end made it different.
Surely people who demanded you buy them off didn't
go around admitting it, did they? And, just as surely,
they didn't make it sound as if *you* were the one who'd
done something vile—yet that was what his tone had
clearly suggested.

Joanna caught her bottom lip between her teeth. Was
he still smarting over the clumsy way she'd handled the
bribe offer? She knew she hadn't done it with any subtlety, that she'd come within a breath of insulting him,
something that was not done anywhere but especially not
in this part of the world.

'Everyone benefits,' he said softly. 'Khalil is bought
off, Bennettco turns a handsome profit—and Abu Al
Zouad grows fatter.' He looked at her, his eyes unreadable in the darkness. 'All in all, a fine arrangement, yes?'

Joanna shifted uneasily. 'Look,' she said, 'I don't
know what it is between your Prince and the Sultan,
but—'

'Everyone benefits,' he said again, his tone hardening.
'Everyone—except my people.'

As if he or his mighty Prince really gave a damn, she
thought angrily. But she bit back the words and offered
ones that were only slightly more diplomatic instead.

'It's too late to have second thoughts, Mr Hassan. You
gave me your word—'

'If you intend to speak to me of honour,' he said coldly, 'you are wasting your time.'

Their eyes met and held. All at once, Joanna wished she were anywhere but here, in this fast car tearing through the darkness to some unknown destination.

'I was only going to point out that we agreed on—'

'What would you have done if I'd turned down your bribe money?'

'Listen, Mr Hassan, if you've a problem with Prince Khalil's accepting money...' Joanna clamped her lips together. What was needed here was a touch of diplomacy, not anger. 'I wasn't suggesting that you were— that you should...' She shook her head. 'It's not my place to make judgements, but—'

'Of course it is. You and your estimable father both make judgements. You judged Abu Al Zouad worthy of Bennettco's largesse, you judged Prince Khalil a man to be easily bought off—'

'Easily?' His supercilious tone made Joanna bristle and she spoke sharply, before she could stop herself. 'Who are you kidding? I know how much is waiting for him in that Swiss bank account, remember?' Her eyes narrowed. 'Wait a minute. Is that what this is all about? Are you going to try and hold us up for more?'

'And what if I did? You'd pay it. You'd pay whatever you must to get what you want.' He shot her a look so deadly she pressed back in her seat. 'That's how people like you do things. Don't waste your breath denying it!'

Joanna stared at him. What was happening here? A little while ago, he'd been all silken cordiality, and now he was treating her with an abrasive scorn that bordered on insult. He was scaring her, too, although she'd be damned if she'd ever let him know it. Well, not scaring her, exactly, that was too strong a word, but it was hard not to wish they were still seated in the civilised environs of the Oasis Restaurant.

Was that why he'd dragged her to the middle of nowhere—so he could insult her? That was certainly how it seemed. Even if he hadn't, even if he'd been deadly serious about taking her somewhere for a glass of champagne, she had absolutely no interest in it now. All she wanted was for him to turn the car around and take her back to the city, to lights and traffic and people.

'I've changed my mind about having champagne,' she said, swinging towards him. She waited for him to answer but he didn't. After a moment, she cleared her throat. 'Mr Hassan?'

'I heard you. You've changed your mind about drinking with me.'

'No, I mean, it's not that. I just—I—um—I misjudged the time earlier.' Damn! Why was she offering an explanation? 'Please turn the car around.'

'I can't do that.'

Can't? *Can't*? Joanna stared at him. 'Why not?'

'We are expected,' he said.

'You mean, you made a reservation? Well, I can't help—'

He swung to face her suddenly, and even in the shadowy interior of the car, she could see the sharp anger etched into his face.

'The sound of your voice annoys me,' he said coldly. 'Sit back, and be silent!'

Her mouth dropped open. 'What?' she said. '*What*?' She stared at him, waiting for him to say something, to apologise or offer some sort of explanation, but he didn't. 'That's it,' she snapped. 'Dammit, Mr Hassan, that's the final straw!'

'I don't like women to use vulgarities.'

'And I don't like men to behave like bullies! I'm telling you for the last time, turn this car around and take me back to Casablanca!'

He laughed in a way that made her heart leap into her throat.

'Is that a threat, Miss Bennett?'

'My father will be expecting me. If I'm not at the hotel soon—'

'How charming. Does he always wait up for your return at night?'

Her eyes flew to his face. What was that she heard in his voice? Disdain? Or was it something more?

'He'll be waiting to hear how our evening went,' she said quickly. 'And unless you want me to tell him that you—'

'Why would he do that?' He gave her a quick, terrible smile. 'Was there ever any doubt of your success?'

'Of course. There's always a chance of a slip-up when—'

'How could there have been a slip-up, once he put you in charge of dealing with the bandit Khalil?' The awful smile came again, clicking on, then off, like a light bulb. 'Surely he expected you'd get the agreement for him, one way or another.'

Joanna clasped her hands together in her lap. Something was happening here, something that was beyond her understanding. All she knew was that she didn't like it.

'If you're suggesting my father doesn't have every confidence in me,' she began, but the man beside her cut her short.

'Confidence?' The sound of his laughter was sharp. 'In what? You're no more a vice-president at Bennettco than that woman we passed in the street a while ago.'

'Of course I am!'

'What you are,' he snapped, 'is an empty-headed creature who knows nothing more important than the latest gossip!'

Colour rushed into Joanna's cheeks. 'How dare you?'

'What is the name of your secretary at Bennettco?'

'I don't have to answer your questions!'

'Do you even *have* an office there?' he demanded.

She swallowed. 'Not yet,' she said finally, 'but—'

'You are nothing,' he snarled, 'nothing! Your father insults me by sending you to me.'

'You've got this all wrong,' Joanna said quickly. 'I *am* his confidante. And his vice-president—well, I will be, when—'

'What you are,' he said grimly, 'is a Jezebel.'

She stared at him, her mouth hanging open. 'What?'

'I knew Bennett was desperate to hold on to his contract with that pig, Abu Al Zouad.' His eyes shot to her face. 'But even I never dreamed he'd offer up his daughter to get it!'

'Are you crazy? I told you, my father is ill. That's why he sent me to meet with you!'

'He sent you to do whatever had to be done to ensure success.' He threw her a look of such fury that Joanna felt herself blanch. 'If Khalil wouldn't accept one sort of bribe, surely he'd accept another.'

She felt the blood drain from her face. 'Are you saying my father…are you saying you think that I…?' She sprang towards him across the console and slammed her fist into his shoulder. 'You—you contemptible son of a bitch! I'd sooner sleep with a—a camel than—'

She cried out as the car swerved. The tyres squealed as they clawed at the verge; the brakes protested as he jammed them on, and then he swung towards her, his eyes filled with loathing.

'But it *would* be like sleeping with a camel, wouldn't

it, Miss Bennett? Sleeping with a man like Khalil, I mean.'

'If you touch me,' Joanna said, trying to keep her voice from shaking, 'if you so much as put a finger on me, so help me, I'll—'

'You'll what?' His lips drew back from his teeth. 'Scream? Go right ahead, then. Scream. Scream until you can't scream any more. Who do you think will hear you?'

God. Oh, God! He was right. She looked around her wildly. There was darkness everywhere—everywhere except for his face, looming over hers, his eyes glinting with anger, his mouth hard and narrowed with scorn.

'My father,' she said hoarsely. 'My father will—'

'The scorpion of the desert is a greater worry to me than is your father.'

'Surely we can behave like civilised human beings and—?'

He laughed in her face. 'How can we, when I am the emissary of a savage?'

'I never said that!'

'No. You never did. But you surely thought it. What else would a greedy, tyrannical bandit be if not a savage?' His mouth thinned. 'But I ask you, who is the savage, Miss Bennett, the Hawk of the North—or a father who would offer his daughter to get what he wants?'

He caught her wrist as her hand flew towards his face. 'I've had enough, you—you self-centred son of a bitch! My father would no more—'

His face twisted. 'Perhaps I should have let it happen.' He leaned towards her, forcing her back in her seat. 'Maybe it wasn't your father who suggested you make this great sacrifice. Maybe it was *you* who wanted to share Khalil's bed—or did you think it would be sufficient to share mine?'

'I'd sooner die,' Joanna said, her voice rising unsteadily while she struggled uselessly to shove him off her. 'I swear, I'd sooner—'

His lips drew back from his teeth in a humourless smile. 'Just think what erotic delights a savage like me might have taught you. Enough, perhaps, to keep your useless New York friends tittering for an entire season!'

'You're disgusting! You—you make me sick to my stomach!'

His mouth dropped to hers like a stone, crushing the words on her lips. She struggled wildly, beating her free hand against his shoulder, trying to twist her face from his, but it was useless. He was all hard sinew and taut muscle that nothing would deter.

After a moment, he drew back.

'What's the matter?' he said coldly. 'Have you changed your mind about adding a little sweetening to Bennettco's bribe offer?'

Hatred darkened Joanna's eyes. 'What a fool I was to think I could deal with you in a civilised manner! You're just like your Prince, aren't you? When you can't get what you want, you just—you reach out and grab it!'

'What if I said you were wrong, Miss Bennett? What if I told you that I am not a man who takes?'

Anger made her reckless. 'I'd call you a liar,' she snapped.

To her surprise, he laughed. 'Which of us is the liar, Joanna? Or are you suggesting I not take what you are prepared to give?'

The look she gave him was pure defiance. 'I offered you nothing.'

For a long moment, their eyes held. Then he smiled, and the smile sent her heart into her throat.

'I never take that which has not been offered,' he said, very softly.

She cried out as he reached for her again but there was no way to escape him. He caught her face between his hands, holding it immobile, and bent his head to hers. She stiffened, holding her breath, preparing instinctively for the fury of his kiss, for whatever ugly show of strength and power lay ahead.

But there was no way to prepare for the reality of what happened. His lips were soft, moving against hers with slow persuasion, seeking response.

Not that it mattered. It was a useless effort. She would never, could never, respond to a man like him, a man who believed he could first terrorise a woman, then seduce her. His hands spread over her cheeks, his thumbs gliding slowly across the high arc of her cheekbones. His fingers threaded into her hair, slowly angling her head back so that his lips could descend upon hers again—and all at once, to Joanna's horror, something dark and primitive stirred deep within her soul, an excitement that made her pulse leap.

No. No, she didn't want this! But her body was quickening, her mouth was softening beneath his. Was it the way he was holding her, so that she was arched towards him, as if in supplication? Was it the heat of his body against hers?

The tip of his tongue skimmed across her mouth. She made a sound, a little moan that was barely perceptible, but he heard it. He whispered something incomprehensible against her mouth and his arms went around her and drew her close, so that her breasts were pressed against his chest.

Joanna felt the sudden erratic gallop of her heart as his mouth opened over hers. His tongue slipped between her lips, stroking against the tender flesh. Heat rose like a flame under her skin as he cupped her breast in his hand. She shuddered in his arms as his thumb moved against the hardening nipple.

'Yes,' he whispered, 'yes…'

How could this be happening? She hated him, for what he was and for the man he served—and yet, her hands were sliding up his chest, her palms were measuring the swift, sure beat of his heart as it leapt beneath her fingertips. Her head fell back; he kissed her throat and she made another soft sound that might have been surrender or despair…

He let her go with such abruptness that she fell back against the seat. Her eyes flew open; her gaze met his and they stared at each other. For an instant they seemed suspended in time, and then two circles of crimson rose in Joanna's cheeks.

Khalil smiled tightly. 'You see?' he said, almost lazily. He reached for the key and the engine roared to life. 'I never take what is not offered.'

Humiliation rose in her throat like bile. 'I get the message,' she said, fighting to keep her voice from shaking. 'I'm female, you're male, and I shouldn't have said anything to insult you or the mighty Khalil.'

'I'm happy to see you're not stupid.'

'Slow, maybe, but never stupid. Now, take me back to—'

'We are not returning to Casablanca, Joanna.'

She stared at him in disbelief. 'You can't possible think I'd still go anywhere with you after…'

Her heart rose into her throat. He *was* turning the car, but not back the way they'd come. Instead, they were jouncing across hard-packed dirt towards a long, looming shadow ahead.

'What is that?' she demanded, but the question was redundant, for in the headlights of the car she could now see what stood ahead of them.

It was a plane. A small, twin-engine plane, the same kind, she thought dizzily, as Bennettco owned. But this was not a Bennettco plane, not with that spread-winged, rapier-beaked bird painted on its fuselage.

Instinct made her cry out and swing towards him. She grabbed for the steering wheel but he caught her wrists easily with one hand and wrenched them down.

'Stop it,' he said, his voice taut with command.

The car slid to a stop. He yanked out the keys and threw the door open. Several robed figures approached, then dropped to their knees in the sand as Khalil stepped from the automobile.

'Is the plane ready for departure?' he demanded in English.

'It has been ready since we received your message, my lord,' one of the men answered without lifting his head.

Khalil hauled Joanna out after him. 'Come,' he said.

She didn't. She screamed instead, and he lifted her into his arms and strode towards the plane while her cries rose into the night with nothing but the wind to answer them. Khalil paused at the door and shoved her through. Then he climbed inside and pushed her unceremoniously into a seat.

'Let's go,' he snapped at the men scrambling up after him. 'Quickly!'

The little coterie bowed again, touching their hands to their foreheads. It was a gesture of homage that would, even moments before, have made Joanna laugh with scorn. Now, it made her dizzy with fear.

Suddenly, she understood.

'You're not the Prince's emissary,' she said, swinging towards him, 'you're—you're Khalil!'

He laughed. 'As I said, Joanna, you aren't a stupid woman.'

She leaped to her feet and spun towards his men. 'Do you understand what he's doing? He's kidnapping me! He'll lose his head for this. You'll all lose—' The plane's engines coughed to life and began to whine. Joanna turned back to Khalil. 'What do you want?' she pleaded. 'More money? You've only to ask my father. He'll give you whatever—' The plane began moving forward into the dark night and her voice rose in panic. 'Listen to me! Just take me back. No. You don't have to take me back. I can drive myself. Just give me the keys to the car and—'

Khalil's look silenced her.

'We've a three-hour flight ahead of us. I suggest you get some rest before we reach the northern hills.'

'You'll never get away with this! You can't just—'

Khalil put his hands on his hips and looked at her. His eyes were cold, empty of feeling. With a sinking heart, she thought what a fool she'd been not to have guessed his identity from the start.

'It is done,' he said. 'What will be, will be.'

Joanna stared at him, at that unyielding, harsh face, and then she turned away and looked blindly out of the porthole while the plane raced down the sand and rose into the night sky.

He was right. It was done. Now, she could only pray for deliverance.

CHAPTER FOUR

NOTHING made sense. Joanna sat stiffly in her seat, alone with her thoughts in the darkness of the plane, trying to come up with answers to questions that seemed as complex as the riddle of the Sphinx.

Why had Khalil played out the charade of letting her think he was someone else? He could have announced his identity when he'd discovered she was Joanna, not Joe.

Where was he taking her? This wasn't any quick trip around the block. She glanced at the luminescent face of her watch. They'd been in the air more than an hour now, and she'd yet to feel the tell-tale change in engine pitch and angle of flight that would mean they were readying to land. A little shudder went through her. No, she thought again, this wasn't a short hop by any means. Wherever Khalil was taking her, it was some distance from Casablanca.

And then there was the most devastating question of all, the one her frazzled brain kept avoiding.

Why had he taken her captive?

She had tiptoed around the issue half a dozen times at least, edging up to it as a doe might a clearing in the woods, getting just so close, then skittering off. She knew she had to deal with the question, and soon, for this flight could not last forever and Joanna knew herself well. Whatever lay ahead would only be the more terrifying if she weren't prepared for it mentally.

The plane bounced gently in an air pocket and she

used the moment to try and see beyond the curtain that separated the tiny lounge area in which she was seated from the rest of the cabin. Khalil had gone to the front shortly after take-off, leaving her alone with a robed thug who sat in total silence. Did he speak English? She thought he must, but what was the difference? He was a brigand, the same as his chieftain, left to guard his prisoner. Where Khalil thought she might escape to was anybody's guess.

She closed her eyes. It was too late for that, too late for anything except standing up to whatever fate awaited her and showing this—this cut-throat marauder that Sam Bennett's daughter was no coward.

'Are you cold?'

Her eyes flew open. A man was standing over her, tall and fierce and incredibly masculine in flowing white robes. Joanna's throat constricted. It was Khalil.

'Are you cold, Joanna?'

'Cold?' she said foolishly, while she tried to reconcile the urbane man who'd sat beside her at dinner with this robed renegade.

'You were shivering.' His eyes, as frigid as winter ice, swept over her. 'But then you would be, wearing such a dress.' His tone oozed disdain. 'It hardly covers your body.'

Joanna felt heat flood her face. Her fingers itched with the desire to tug up the bodice of her dress, to try and tug down the emerald silk skirt, but she'd be damned if she'd give him that satisfaction. Instead, she folded her hands in her lap, her fingers laced together to keep them still, and looked straight at him.

'I am certain that Oscar de la Renta would be distressed to learn that you don't approve of his design,

Your Highness, but then, the dress wasn't made for the approval of a back-country bandit.'

The insult struck home. She could see it in the swift narrowing of his eyes, but his only obvious reaction was a small, hard smile.

'I'm sure you're right, Joanna. The dress was meant for a finer purpose: to entice a man, to make him forget what he must remember and concentrate only on the female prize wrapped within it.'

Joanna smiled, too, very coldly.

'I am dressed for dinner at the Oasis. Had you told me we were going on a journey, I'd have worn something more suitable for travel.'

His smile broadened. 'Had I told you that, I somehow doubt you'd have come with me.'

It was impossible to carry off her end of the dialogue this time. He had struck too close to home, and she shuddered at the realisation.

'You *are* cold,' he said sharply. 'It is foolish to sit here and tremble when you have only to ask for a lap robe.'

It was hard to know whether to laugh or cry. A lap robe? Did he really think this was a flight on Royal Air Marroc to New York? Did he think she was wondering what would be served for dinner?

'Ahmed!' Khalil snapped his fingers and the man seated across the aisle sprang to his feet. There was a flurry of swift, incomprehensible words and then the man bowed and scurried off. 'Ahmed will find you a blanket, Joanna. If you wish anything else…'

'The only thing I want is my freedom.'

'If you wish anything else,' he said, as if she hadn't spoken, 'coffee, or perhaps tea—'

'Are you deaf or just a bastard? I said—'

She gasped as he bent and clasped her shoulders so tightly that she could feel the imprint of his fingers, the heat of his body.

'Watch your tongue! I have had enough of your mouth tonight.'

'Let go of me!'

'Perhaps you don't realise the seriousness of your situation, Joanna. Perhaps you think this is a game, that I have instructed my pilot to fly us in circles and then land at Nouasseur Airport before I return you to your hotel.'

It wasn't easy to look back at him without flinching, to force herself to meet that unyielding rock-like stare, but she did.

'What I think,' she said tightly, 'is that you've made one hell of a mistake, Khalil, and that there's still time to get out of it with your head still attached to your neck.'

He looked at her for what seemed a long time, in a silence filled only with the steady drone of the plane's engines, and then he smiled.

'How thoughtful, Joanna. Your concern for my welfare is touching.' He straightened and looked down at her. 'But you may be right. Perhaps I *have* made a mistake.'

A tiny flame of hope burst to life in her heart. 'If you take me back now,' she said quickly, 'I'll forget this ever happened.'

'Perhaps I should have accepted what you so graciously offered before I stole you.'

Joanna flew from her seat. 'How dare you say such things to me?'

'Highness?'

Khalil put his hand on her shoulders and propelled her

back into her seat. He turned to Ahmed, who held a light blanket in his outstretched arms.

'Thank you, Ahmed. You may leave now.' Khalil dropped the blanket into Joanna's lap as Ahmed disappeared behind the curtain. 'Your temper should be enough to keep you warm, but if it isn't, use this.'

'Dammit!' Joanna shoved the blanket to the floor. 'Who in hell do you think you are?'

He bent, picked up the blanket, and dropped it in her lap again.

'I am the man who holds your destiny in his hands,' he said with a quick, chill smile. 'Now, cover yourself, before I do it for you.'

She snatched the blanket from him, draping it over herself so that it swathed her from throat to toe.

'What's the matter?' she said with saccharine sweetness. 'Are you afraid my father won't pay as much ransom if I come down with pneumonia and die?'

His thigh brushed hers as he sat down beside her, the softness of his robe a direct contrast to the muscled warmth of the leg beneath it.

'Such drama, Joanna. You're young and healthy and a long, long way from death.'

'But that is what you're after, isn't it?' The question she'd dreaded asking was out now, and she was glad. Still, it was hard to say the words. 'Ransom money, from my father?'

'Ransom money?' he repeated, his brows knotting together.

'Yes.' She made an impatient gesture. 'I don't know how you say it in your language—it's money paid to a kidnapper to—'

'I speak English as well as you do,' he said sharply. 'I know what the word means.'

'Well, then…'

'Is that what you think this is all about? Do you think me so corrupt that the money you offered me at the restaurant isn't enough to buy my co-operation?'

'What else am I to think?'

Khalil sat back, his arms folded over his chest. 'And just how much do you think you're worth?'

Joanna's jaw tightened. 'Don't play with me, Khalil. I don't like it!'

'Ah.' Amusement glinted in his eyes. 'You don't like it.'

'That's right, I don't. It's bad enough that you've kidnapped me—'

'And I don't like your choice of words.'

She stared at him in disbelief. 'What would you prefer me to call it? Shall I say that you've decided to take me on a sightseeing trip?'

His face turned cold and hard. 'What I do, I do because I must.'

Joanna sat forward, the blanket dropping unnoticed to her waist. 'All you had to do was say you wanted more money. My father would surely have been willing to—'

'Money!' His lip curled with disgust. 'You think there is a price for everything, you and your father. Well, this is what I think of your pathetic attempts to buy me!'

He dug the envelope she'd given him from his robe, folded it in half, and ripped it into pieces that floated into her lap like a paper sandstorm. For the first time, she permitted herself to admit that he might have kidnapped her for some darker, more devious reason.

'Then—then if it's not for the money…' She touched the tip of her tongue to her lips. 'I see. You want to hurt my father.'

Khalil's mouth narrowed. 'Is that what I want? It must

be, if you say it is. After all, you know everything there is to know about me and my motives.'

'But you won't hurt him,' she said, leaning forward towards him. 'You'll just make him angry. And—'

'I don't give a damn what he is!' Khalil reached out quickly and caught her by the shoulders. 'He can be angry, hurt, he can slash his clothing and weep for all I care!'

'Then why—if you don't want money, if you don't care how my father takes the news of my kidn—of my abduction, what's the point? Why have you done this?'

A quick smile angled across his mouth.

'Ah, Joanna,' he said, very softly, 'I'm disappointed. You seem to know so much about the kind of man I am—surely you must have some idea.'

She stared at him, at those fathomless dark blue eyes. A tremor began deep in her muscles and she tensed her body against it, hating herself not only for her fear but for this show of weakness she must not let him see.

Before she'd left New York, the same people who'd teased her about her chances of running into the ghost of Humphrey Bogart had teased her with breathless rumours of a still-flourishing white slave trade, of harems hidden deep within the uncharted heart of the desert and the mountains that enclosed it.

'And what a prize you'd be,' a man at a charity ball had purred, 'with that pale skin, those green eyes, and all that gorgeous red hair!'

Everyone had laughed, even her—but now it didn't seem funny at all. Now, with Khalil's fingers imprinting themselves in her skin, she knew it was time to finally come face to face with the fear that had haunted her from the moment she'd found herself in this plane.

'My father won't let you get away with this,' she said in a low, taut voice.

'Your father will have no choice.'

'You underestimate him. He's a powerful man, Khalil. He'll find where you've taken me and—'

'He will know where I've taken you, Joanna. It will not be a secret.'

'He'll come after me,' she said, her voice rising, becoming just a little unsteady. 'And when he rescues me, he'll kill you!'

Khalil laughed, a soft, husky sound that made the hair rise on the nape of her neck.

'I am not so easy to kill. Abu Al Zouad will surely tell your father that.'

'How about my government? Do you think you can make a fool of it, too?'

'Your government?' His dark brows drew together. 'What part has it in this?'

She smiled piteously. 'I'm a US citizen. Perhaps, in your country, women are—are like cattle, to be bought and sold and—and disposed of at will, but in my country—'

'I know all about your country, enough to know your government won't give a damn about one headstrong woman who runs off—'

'I didn't run off! You—'

'—who runs off with a man on a romantic adventure.'

'Me, run off with you on a romantic adventure?' She laughed. 'No one would accept that! Anyway, my father will tell them the truth.'

'He'll tell them exactly what I authorise him to tell them,' Khalil said coldly.

'Don't be ridiculous! Why would he lie?'

'This thing is between your father, Abu Al Zouad, and me. No one else will be involved.'

'You're unbelievable,' Joanna said, 'absolutely unbelievable! Do you really imagine you can tell my father what to do? Maybe you should have spent more time in the West, Khalil. Maybe you'd have realised you're only a man, not a—a tin god whose every insane wish has to be obeyed!'

'I'm impressed,' he said, with a condescending little smile, as if she were a pet he'd just found capable of some clever and unexpected trick. 'Any other woman would be begging for mercy, but not you.'

Joanna's chin lifted. 'That's right,' she said, determined not to let him see the depths of her fear, 'not me! So if that's why you abducted me—so you could have the pleasure of seeing me grovel and weep for mercy— you're out of luck.'

'I'm sorry to disappoint you, Joanna, but my reasons were hardly so petty.' He gave her a slow, lazy smile. 'I took you because I can use you.'

Her eyes flashed to his. 'Use me?' she repeated. 'I don't—I don't understand…'

His smile changed, took on a darkness that made her breath catch, and his gaze moved over her lingeringly, from her wide eyes to her parted lips, and finally to the swift rise and fall of her breasts.

'Don't you?' he said softly.

'Khalil.' She swallowed, although the effort was almost painful. 'Khalil, listen to me. You can't—you can't just—'

'Shall I have you sold at the slave-market?' He took her face in his hands and tilted it to his. 'You would bring a king's ransom in the north, where eyes the colour of jade and hair like the embers of a winter fire are very, very rare.'

Oh, God, Joanna thought, oh, God…

'You wouldn't do that,' she said quickly. 'Selling me would be—'

'It would be foolish.' He smiled again, a quick angling of his lips that was somehow frighteningly intimate. 'For only a fool would sell you, once he had you.'

'Abducting me is foolish, too!' She spoke quickly, desperately, determined to force him to listen to reason. 'You must know that you can't get away with—'

'What would you be like, I wonder, if I took you to my bed?'

Patches of scarlet flared in her cheeks, fury driving out the fear that had seconds before chilled her blood.

'I'd sooner die than go to your bed!'

He laughed softly. 'I don't think so, Joanna. I think you would come to it smiling.'

'Not in a million years!'

His fingers threaded into her hair; his thumbs stroked over her skin.

'How would your skin feel, against mine?' he said softly. 'Would it be hot, like fire? Or would it be cool, like moonlight against the desert sand?'

There it was again, that sense of something dark and primal stirring within her, like an unwanted whisper rising in the silence of the night.

'You'll never know,' she said quickly. 'I promise you that.'

Khalil's eyes darkened. He smiled, bent his head, brushed his lips against Joanna's. A tiny flicker of heat seemed to radiate from his mouth to hers.

'Your words are cool, but your lips are warm,' he murmured. Her breath caught as his hands slid to her midriff. She felt the light brush of his fingers just below her breasts. 'Fire and ice, Joanna. That is what you are. But I would melt that ice forever.' He pressed his mouth to her throat. 'I would turn you to hot flame that burns only for me,' he said, the words a heated whisper against her skin.

She wanted to tell him that it was he who'd burn, in the eternal fires of hell—but his arms were tightening around her, he was gathering her close, and before she could say anything he crushed her mouth under his.

He had spoken of turning her to flame but *he* was the flame, shimmering against her as he held her, his kiss branding her with heat. His tongue traced the seam of her lips, then slid against hers as her mouth opened to his, silk against silk.

Dear God, what was the matter with her? This man was everything she hated, he was her enemy, her abductor...

He felt the sudden tightening of her muscles and he reached between their bodies, caught her hands and held them fast.

'Don't fight me,' he whispered.

But she did, twisting her head away from his, panting beneath his weight. Still, he persisted, kissing her over and over until suddenly she went still and moaned his name.

'Yes,' he growled, the one word an affirmation of his triumph.

Joanna wrenched her hands from his and buried her fingers in his dark hair, drawing him down to her, giving herself up to the drowning sweetness of his kisses.

Khalil whispered something swift and fierce against her mouth. He drew her from her seat and into his lap, holding her tightly against him, his body hard beneath hers. His hand moved over her, following the curve of her hip, the thrust of her breast. Her head fell back and the dampness of wanting him bloomed like a velvet-petalled flower between her thighs. He bent and pressed his open mouth to the silk that covered her breast, and she cried out.

The sound rose between them, piercing the silence of the little cabin. Khalil drew back and Joanna did too. They stared at each other and then, abruptly, he thrust her from him, shoving her back into her seat and rising to his feet in one swift motion.

'You see?' His eyes were like sapphire coals in his taut face; his voice was cold, tinged with barely controlled cruelty. 'I could have you now, if I wanted you. But I do not. I have never wanted any woman who offered her body in trade.'

Joanna sprang towards him, sputtering with fury, her hand upraised, but Khalil caught her wrist and twisted her arm behind her.

'I warn you,' he said through his teeth, 'you are done insulting me, you and your father both!'

'Whatever it is you're planning, Khalil, I promise you, you won't get away with it.'

He looked at her for a long moment, still holding her close to him, and then he laughed softly.

'It's dangerous to threaten me, Joanna. Surely you've learned that much by now.'

His gaze fell to her mouth. She tensed, waiting for him to gather her to him and kiss her again. This time, she was prepared to claw his face if she had to rather than let him draw her down into that silken darkness— but suddenly a voice called out from beyond the curtain.

Khalil's smile faded. 'We have arrived.'

She fell back as he let go of her. 'Where?' she asked,

but he was already hurrying up the aisle towards the front of the plane.

She knelt in her seat and leaned towards the window. Some time during their confrontation, the plane had not only descended, it had landed. She pressed her nose to the glass. It was still night, yet she could see very clearly, thanks to a full moon and what at first seemed the light from at least a hundred lamps.

Her breath caught. Torches! Those were flaming torches, held aloft by a crowd of cheering men mounted on horseback.

With a little moan, she put her hands to her mouth and collapsed back into her seat.

They had arrived, all right—they'd arrived smack in the middle of the thirteenth century!

CHAPTER FIVE

IT WAS the sight of the horsemen that changed everything. Until now, Joanna had let herself half believe that if what was happening was not a dream, it was some sort of terrible prank, one that would end with the plane turning and heading back to Morocco.

But the line of horses standing just outside the plane, the robed men on their backs, the torches casting a glow as bright as daylight over the flat plateau on which they'd landed, finally forced her to acknowledge the truth.

Khalil had stolen her away from the world she knew. What happened to her next was not in the hands of fate but in the hands of this man, this bandit—and he didn't give a damn for the laws of his country or of civilisation.

'Joanna.'

She looked up. He was standing at the open door of the plane, his face like granite.

'Come,' he said.

Come. As if she were a slave, or a dog. Joanna's jaw clenched. That was what he wanted, to reduce her to some sub-human status, to stress his domination over her and make her cower beneath it. In some ways, he'd already succeeded. She had let him see her fear when he'd first abducted her, let him see it again when she'd pleaded with him to release her.

She drew a deep, deep breath. And her fear had been painfully obvious when he'd kissed her and she'd yielded herself so shamelessly in his arms. It was nothing but fear that had caused her to react to him that way. She knew it, and he did, too.

But his ugly scheme could only work if she let it—and she would not. She would never, ever let him see her fear again.

'Joanna!' Her head came up. He was waiting for her, his hands on his hips, his legs apart, looking as fierce as the predatory bird whose name he bore. 'Are you waiting for me to come and get you?'

She rose, head high, spine straight. He didn't move as she made her way slowly towards him, but she saw his gaze sweep over her, his eyes narrowing, his jaw tightening, and she knew he must be once again telling himself that only a woman who wanted to seduce a man would dress in such a way.

It was laughable, really. Her dress was fashionable and expensive, but it was basically modest and would not have raised an eyebrow anywhere but here or the Vatican. For a second, she wished she'd gone with her first instinct and worn a business suit, but then she thought no, let him have to look at her for the next hours—which was surely only as long as he would keep her here—let him look at her and be reminded constantly that she was of the West, that he could not treat her as he would one of his women, that she was Sam Bennett's daughter and he'd damned well better not forget it.

'You are not dressed properly.'

Joanna smiled coolly. He was as transparent as glass.

'I am dressed quite properly.' She gave him an assessing look, taking in the long, white robe he wore, and then she smiled again. 'It is you who are not dressed properly. Men stopped wearing skirts a long time ago.'

To her surprise, he laughed. 'Try telling that to some of my kinsmen.' With a swift movement, he shrugged off his white robe. Beneath it, he wore a white tunic and pale grey, clinging trousers tucked into high leather boots. 'You are not dressed for these mountains.' Briskly, as if she were a package that needed wrapping, Khalil dropped the robe over her shoulders and enfolded her in it. 'We have a climate like that of the desert. By day, it is warm—but when the sun drops from the sky the air turns cold.'

She wanted to protest, to tell him she didn't need anything from him, but it was too late. He had already drawn the robe snugly around her and anyway, he was right. There was a bone-numbing chill drifting in through the open door. Joanna drew the robe more closely around her. It was still warm from Khalil's body and held a faint, clean scent that she knew must be his. A tremor went through her again, although there was no reason for it.

'Thank you,' she said politely. 'Your concern for my welfare is touching. I'll be sure and mention it to my father so he'll know that my abductor was a gentle— hey! What are you doing? Put me down, dammit! I'm perfectly capable of walking.'

'In those shoes?' He laughed as he lifted her into his arms. 'It was the ancient Chinese who kept their women in servitude by making it impossible for them to walk very far, Joanna. My people expect their women to stride as well as a man.' He grinned down at her. 'If you were to sprain your ankle, how would you tend the goats and chickens tomorrow?'

Goats? Chickens? Was he serious?

'I won't be here tomorrow,' she said curtly.

'You will be here as long as I want you here,' he said, and stepped from the plane.

A full-throated cheer went up from Khalil's assembled warriors when they saw him. They edged their horses forward, their flaming torches held high. He stood still for a moment, smiling and accepting their welcome, and then one of the men looked at her and said something that made the others laugh. Khalil laughed, too, and then he began to speak.

Joanna knew he must be talking about her. His arms tightened around her and he held her out just a little, as if she were a display. The faces of his men snapped towards her and a few of them chuckled.

'Damn you,' she hissed, 'what are you saying about me?'

Khalil looked down at her. 'Hammad asked why I'd brought home such a lumpy package.' His teeth flashed in a quick grin. 'I suggested he remember the old saying about never judging a horse by the saddle blanket that covers it.'

Her face pinkened. 'It's a book one isn't supposed to judge in my country,' she said frigidly. 'And I would remind you that I am neither.'

His smile fled, and his face took on that stony determination she'd already come to know too well.

'No,' he said grimly, 'you are not. What you are is a guarantee that I will get what I want from Sam Bennett.'

So. It was ransom he wanted, after all. Despite all his cryptic word-games, it was money he would trade her for.

One of his men moved forward, leading a huge black stallion that tossed its head and whickered softly. Khalil lifted Joanna on to its back, then mounted behind her. She stiffened as his arms went around her.

'Yet another indignity you must suffer,' he said, his voice low, his breath warm against her ear as he gathered the reins into his hands. 'But only for a little while, Joanna. Soon, we will be at my home, and neither of us will have to tolerate the sight and touch of the other until morning.'

He murmured something to the horse. It pricked its ears and it began moving forward, its steps high and almost delicate. Khalil spoke again, and the animal began moving faster, until it seemed to be racing across the plateau with the wind. Khalil's arms tightened around her; there was no choice but to lean back and let his hard body support hers as they galloped into the night.

How long would it take to get his ransom demand to her father? And how long after that for the money to reach here?

Khalil's arm brushed lightly, impersonally, across her breast as he urged the horse on.

Not too long, she thought. Please, let it not take too long.

It couldn't possibly.

Her father would want her back, and quickly, no matter how outrageous the Prince's demands.

She had assumed the torchlight greeting had been ceremonial. It had been handsome, she'd thought grudgingly, even impressive, but a man who owned a private plane would not also be a man who travelled his country on the back of a horse.

But an hour or more of riding had changed Joanna's mind. There was nothing ceremonial about riding a horse in terrain such as this, she thought, wincing a little as she shifted her bottom and tried to find a spot that hadn't already become sensitised to the jouncing and bouncing of the saddle. The plane had landed on a plateau, but from what she'd seen so far that had probably been the only flat space in a hundred miles.

Ever since, they'd been climbing into the mountains, although calling these massive, rocky outcroppings 'mountains' was like calling the horse beneath her a pony. The resemblance was purely accidental. The moon had risen, casting a pale ivory light over the landscape, tipping the tall pines that clung to the steep slopes with silver.

How far up would they ride? It was probable that a bandit would want to have a hidden stronghold, but this was ridiculous! Only a mountain goat could possibly clamber up this high.

Suppose her father and the Sultan mounted a rescue mission? Could they make it? No. It was best not to think that way. She had to think positively, had to concentrate on how easily they'd find her. And they would. Of course they would. Khalil wasn't invincible and his hideout, no matter how it resembled the eyrie of a hawk, would not be impregnable.

Her father would come for her. He would find her. He would take her back to civilisation, and all this would just be a dream.

A dream. Joanna yawned. She was tired. Exhausted, really, and the slow, steady gait of the horse, the creak of leather, the jingle of the tiny bells that adorned the bridle, were all having a hypnotic effect. She yawned again, then blinked hard, trying to keep her eyes open. It would be so nice to rest for a few minutes.

Her head fell back, her cheek brushed lightly against a hard, warm surface. Quickly, she jerked upright.

'Joanna?'

'Yes?'

'Are you tired?'

'No. I'm not.'

'You must be.' Khalil lifted his hand to her cheek. 'Put your head against my shoulder, and sleep for a while.'

'Don't be ridiculous! I'd sooner—'

'Sleep with a camel. Yes, I know.' He laughed. 'Just

pretend that's what I am, then, and put your head back and close your eyes.'

'Please,' she said coldly, 'spare me this attempt at solicitude. It doesn't become you.'

Khalil sighed. 'As you wish, Joanna.'

The horse plodded on, its movements slow and steady. Up, down, up, down...

Concentrate. Concentrate. Listen to the sounds, to the clatter of the horse's hooves, to the sigh of the wind through the trees.

Stay awake! Take deep breaths. Smell the fragrance of pine carried on the night wind, the scent of leather and horse...

'Dammit, woman, you're as stubborn as the wild horses of Chamoulya! Stop being such a little fool and get some rest.'

'I don't need rest. I don't need anything. And I especially don't need your help.'

'Fine. I'll remember that.' He jerked her head back against his shoulder. 'Now, shut up and stop fidgeting. You're making Najib nervous, and—'

'Najib?'

'My horse. And the last thing I want is for Najib to be nervous on the climb ahead.'

Najib, she thought giddily. She was making Najib nervous. By heaven, this man was crazy! He had kidnapped her, carried her off to God only knew where without so much as giving a damn if she turned to stone with fright, but he was worried that she was making his horse nervous.

Joanna's eyes flickered shut. Still, he was right. It would be stupid to upset the animal on a narrow mountain path. Closing her eyes didn't mean she'd sleep. She'd let her other senses take over. Yes. That was what she'd do, she'd—she'd think about the coolness of the night air—and the contrasting warmth of Khalil's arms, think about the softness of his robe on her skin and the contrasting hardness of his thighs, cradling her hips.

That was the word that best described him. He was hard. Powerful. That was how he felt, holding her—and yet she knew his hands were holding the reins lightly. Still, the black stallion responded readily to his slightest touch, to the press of his heel.

A woman would respond to him that way, too, Joanna thought drowsily; she would move eagerly to obey him, to pleasure him and to let him pleasure her...

A heat so intense it was frightening spread through her body. Her eyes flew open and she jerked upright in the saddle, steadying herself by clasping the pommel. Najib snorted and tossed his head, and Khalil caught her and pulled her back against him.

'Dammit!' he said tightly. 'What did I tell you about making the horse nervous?'

'I know what you said,' Joanna snapped, 'and frankly, I don't much care if I make your horse nervous or...'

A whimper slipped from her throat as she looked down. They were on a ledge that looked only slightly wider than a man's hand. Below, the earth dropped away, spinning into darkness.

'Exactly,' Khalil said gruffly.

Joanna didn't have to ask him what he meant. She turned her face away from the precipice.

'The stallion is sure-footed, Joanna. But I would prefer he have no distractions.'

She laughed uneasily. 'That's—that's fine with me. Tell him—tell him to pay no attention to me, please. No attention at all.'

Khalil laughed softly. 'I'll tell him. Now, why don't you shut your eyes again and sleep?'

'I wasn't sleeping,' she said. 'How could anyone sleep, on the back of this—this creature?'

'I'm sure it's a sacrifice when you're accustomed to riding in the back of a chauffeured limousine.'

She smiled smugly. 'No greater than the sacrifice one makes giving up the comfort of a private plane for the back of a horse.'

'The plane is necessary,' he said, so quickly that she knew she'd stung him. 'My responsibilities take me in many different directions.'

'Oh, I'm sure they do.' Her voice was like honey. 'They take you up mountains and down mountains—clearly, one needs a plane for that!'

He said nothing, but she had the satisfaction of seeing his jaw tighten. They rode on in silence while the moon dropped lower in the sky, and then, finally, Khalil lifted his hand and pointed into the distance.

'There it is,' he said quietly. 'Bab al Sama—Gate to the Sky. My home.'

Joanna sat up straighter and stared into the darkness. There were smudges against the horizon. What were they?

'Tents,' Khalil said, as if she'd asked the question aloud. 'Some of my people still cling to the old ways.'

Tents. Of course. His people lived outside the law. They'd want to be able to strike camp quickly.

But the tents were larger than she'd expected. They were, in fact, enormous. And what was that beyond them? Joanna caught her breath. It was a walled city, ancient and serene in the moonlight. A gateway loomed ahead and the horsemen filed through it, then stopped inside the courtyard of a stone building. The cluster of men dismounted, as did Khalil, and then he looked up at Joanna and lifted his arms to her.

'Come.'

Come. Joanna's chin lifted. There it was again, that single, imperious command. She tossed her head, deliberately turned away from him, and threw her leg over the saddle.

'Joanna!' Khalil's angry voice stopped her for an instant. He moved quickly, so that despite her efforts to avoid him she slid into his arms. 'You little fool! Didn't anyone ever teach you there's a right way and a wrong way to mount a horse?'

'I wasn't mounting him, I was getting off!' She put her hands on his shoulders. 'Put me down!'

'Horses are skittish creatures, Joanna. Surely, even you know that.' His eyes glared into hers. 'They're trained to accept a rider from the left side—but anyone coming at them from the right is asking for trouble.'

'I'll be sure and remember the next time,' she said with heavy sarcasm. 'Now, put me down!'

'With pleasure.' She gasped as he dropped her to her feet. 'Goodnight, Joanna. I suggest you get some rest. You've a long day ahead of you.'

She watched in disbelief as he turned on his heel and marched away from her.

'Goodnight?' she said. Her voice rose. 'What do you mean, goodnight? Where am I supposed to sleep, Khalil? Out here, with the horses?'

He spun towards her, and she saw the quick, humourless flash of his teeth.

'I think too much of them to subject them to an entire night in your company.'

'Damn you, Khalil! You can't just…'

'*Mademoiselle*?'

Joanna turned quickly. A girl had come up silently behind her. She was slender, with long, dark hair and wide-set eyes.

'I am Rachelle, *mademoiselle*. I am to see to your comfort.'

Joanna's mouth narrowed as she looked at the girl. 'I suppose you usually see to the Prince's comfort.'

Rachelle's smooth brow furrowed. '*Mademoiselle*?'

Joanna sighed. It wasn't this child's fault that she had to play slave to a rogue. She forced a faint, weary smile to her lips.

'I could use some comfort. A basin of warm water, a cup of hot tea, and a soft, comfortable bed would be lovely.'

The girl smiled. 'It will be my pleasure, *mademoiselle*. If you will please follow me...?'

Warm water, tea, a comfortable bed—in the mountain hideaway of Khalil the bandit Prince? It was all out of the question and Joanna knew it, but she was too tired to care. A wash in a mountain stream, a cup of cold water, and a blanket spread on the floor were the best she could hope for, but after the last few hours even they would be welcome.

And tomorrow—tomorrow, her father would come for her. He wouldn't wait for Khalil's ransom demand. She was certain of it. Why would he waste time, and risk her life? By now, he would know that she was missing, and it wouldn't take any great effort to know what had happened to her. As for locating her—her father's resources were endless, his contacts enormous. He'd find her, and come after her, before the next setting of the sun.

Joanna's shoulders went back as she marched into the stone building on Rachelle's heels.

'You're the one who's going to need a good night's sleep, Your Highness,' she muttered. 'Because as of tomorrow, you're going to find yourself neck-deep in trouble!'

'*Mademoiselle*? Did you say something?'

Joanna cleared her throat. 'I said, I think I'd like a sandwich to go with that tea, Rachelle. Can you manage that, do you think?'

The girl stopped and turned to face her. 'Certainly. My lord has made it clear that I am to do whatever pleases you, *mademoiselle*. You have only to tell me, and I will obey.'

Joanna gave her a bright, beaming smile. 'How about giving me a map and a ticket out of here?'

Rachelle smiled uncertainly. 'I do not understand…'

'You know, point me towards the nearest highway and send me on my way.'

'*Mademoiselle* jokes,' the girl said, with another little smile.

Joanna sighed. '*Mademoiselle* is dead serious. The only thing I really want is to get away from your lord and master.'

Rachelle ducked her head, as if Joanna's words had unsettled her. 'Here is your room,' she said, and opened the nearest door.

Joanna stepped inside the room. It was dimly lit, and what little light there was fell across a huge bed. An image flashed into her mind. She saw herself on that bed, locked in Khalil's arms, her mouth open to his, her breasts tightening under the slow, sweet stroke of his fingers…

'Stop it,' she hissed.

The girl looked at her. '*Mademoiselle*?'

Joanna puffed out her breath. She *did* need a night's rest. Hallucinations weren't her style, but she'd surely just had one. Any second now, a chorus line of pink elephants would probably come tap-dancing into view!

'I—uh—I think I'll pass on the tea and all the rest, Rachelle.' Joanna sank down wearily on the edge of the bed. 'Just turn out the lights and hang out the "do not disturb" sign.'

'I am afraid I do not understand…'

Joanna sighed. 'I just want to get to bed. It's very late, and I'm exhausted.'

'As you wish, *mademoiselle*.'

Sleep, Joanna thought as the girl moved silently around the room, sleep was precisely what she needed. It would clear her head, drive away the cobwebs. And, when she awoke, her father would probably be here, ready to take her home and make the almighty Khalil eat his every threatening, insolent word.

And that, she thought with grim satisfaction, would almost be enough to make this horrible night worthwhile.

CHAPTER SIX

JOANNA lay asleep in her bed, dreaming... Her father and a rotund little man sat in a pool of light, their heads bent over what looked like a game board while she sat in the darkened perimeter of the room, watching, when the silence was broken by the sound of hoofbeats. She looked up just in time to see a man on the back of a great ebony stallion bearing down on her.

Father, she cried. She wanted to run, but her legs wouldn't move. *Father*, she said again as the horseman leaned down, snatched her up, and tossed her across his saddle.

But her father didn't hear. He was intent on his opponent and on moving his playing piece around the board, and even though she called and called him he didn't—

'Good morning, *mademoiselle*.'

Joanna awoke instantly, her heart racing. The room was unfamiliar, grey and shadowed, and she stared blindly at the figure silhouetted against the drawn window curtains.

'Khalil?' she said shakily.

'It is Rachelle, *mademoiselle*.' The curtains whisked open and Joanna blinked in the golden sunlight that splashed across the bed.

'Rachelle.' Joanna expelled her breath. 'I—I was dreaming...' She sat up, her knees tenting the blanket, and pushed her hair back from her face. 'What time is it? It feels late.'

The serving girl smiled as she placed a small inlaid tray on the low table beside the bed.

'It is mid-morning, *mademoiselle*. I have brought you coffee and fruit.'

'Mid-morning? But I never sleep so…'

'My lord said to let you sleep.'

'Did he,' Joanna said, her voice flat.

The girl nodded. 'He said there was no reason to awaken you until he was ready to see you.'

Joanna snorted. 'That arrogant ass!'

Rachelle threw her a shocked look. 'We do not speak of our Prince that way, *mademoiselle*.'

'No? Well, maybe you should. Maybe you should start seeing him for the miserable donkey's *derrière* he really is!'

Rachelle's eyes widened. 'Please, *mademoiselle*. You must not say such things!'

Joanna sighed. What was the sense in taking out her frustration on a servant? The girl had no choice but to serve her master; hearing unkind things said about him clearly made her nervous. Perhaps she was afraid she'd be punished for permitting Joanna to make such remarks—the Jandaran version of guilt by association. It was the sort of thing that went on in dictatorships, wasn't it?

'Sorry,' Joanna said, with a little smile. 'I'm just feeling out of sorts this morning.'

Rachelle nodded. 'A bath will make you feel better. I have already run it. I added bath oil. I hope the scent is to your liking, *mademoiselle*. Is there something else I can get you?'

Yes, Joanna thought, you can get me my freedom. But she knew it was pointless to ask. The girl was obviously scared to death of Khalil, and desperate to avoid confrontation.

'No,' she said, after a moment, 'no, thanks. I can't think of anything more.'

'I will bring you some yogurt, *mademoiselle*, when you are finished bathing. Or would you prefer eggs?'

'I would prefer you call me Joanna. It makes me uncomfortable to have you address me so formally.'

Rachelle blushed. 'I am honoured.'

'For goodness' sake, you needn't be "honoured"! This is the millennium. Bowing and scraping went out with the Dark Ages.'

'Yes, Joanna.' Rachelle smiled sweetly. 'If you need me, you have only to ring the bell.'

She started towards the door, and suddenly Joanna's good intentions deserted her. She couldn't let the girl leave without at least trying to get through to her.

'Rachelle!' Joanna swung her legs to the floor. 'Rachelle, wait a minute.' The girl turned towards her. 'Prince Khalil brought me here against my will,' she said in a rush. 'He kidnapped me…'

Rachelle's eyes grew shuttered. 'I shall return,' she said, and the door swung shut after her.

Joanna sat staring at it for a long moment and then she muttered several short, impolite words she'd learned during the years she'd spent with Sam in his field operations and had never found suitable to use—until now. She sat up, threw back the blankets, and looked around the room.

It was handsome, she thought grudgingly. The tiled floor, the inlaid furniture, and the white walls on which hung old and beautiful Persian rugs were all pleasing to the eye.

But it was still a prison.

She rose from the bed, kicked aside her shoes, stubbing her toe in the process, and strode briskly to the adjoining bathroom. By now, she knew better than to expect to find a hole in the ground and a basin of cold water, but the tiled room and glass-enclosed shower still were enough to surprise her. Steam rose from a deep tub, and the scent of roses filled the air.

'His Almighty Highness likes to live well,' Joanna muttered as she yanked her slip over her head and tossed it on to the closed bathroom commode.

She glared at the tub, then turned her back on it, pulled open the door to the shower stall, and stepped inside. Khalil had given orders she was not to be disturbed this morning. Had he also given orders she was to be wooed with a scented bath? A shower, quick and modern, was more to her liking.

What insanity this was. First there'd been those silly men last night, riding up to greet Khalil with torches blazing in their hands, looking like nothing so much as a crowd of extras who'd wandered off a movie set, and now there was this silly girl, Rachelle, acting as if she either lived in mortal terror of offending her lord and master—or had been brainwashed to think of him as a tin god. Either way, it was ridiculous.

'Ridiculous,' Joanna said sharply, and she shut off the spray and stepped out on to the bath mat.

She dried off briskly, reached for her slip—and stopped. She'd slept in it last night rather than have to ring for Rachelle and ask for a nightgown or pyjamas. Now, the thought of putting on the wrinkled garment was not appealing. The thought of getting into the bit of emerald silk that lay on a chair in the bedroom wasn't appealing, either, but what choice did she have? Joanna's nostrils flared. Khalil hadn't exactly given her time to pack an overnight bag!

Well, she thought, wrapping the towel around herself, she could avoid wearing the slip, at least. The dress didn't really require more than panties and a bra, both of which...

She cried out as she stepped into the bedroom. A man was standing looking out of the window, his back to the room, but she knew instantly it was Khalil. No one else would have those broad shoulders, that tapered waist, those long, muscular legs. Yes, it was certainly Khalil, making himself at home.

'What do you think you're doing?' she demanded.

Khalil turned slowly and looked at her. Rachelle had said she'd drawn a bath for the woman. Why hadn't it occurred to him that he might well catch her as she emerged from that bath, looking scrubbed and innocent and beautiful when she was none of those things? No. He was wrong. She *was* beautiful, more beautiful now, without her make-up and jewellery, than she'd been last night.

He felt a tightening in his groin and it infuriated him. That he should be stirred by a woman like this was impossible. Despite her beauty, she was hardly a prize, not when she was nothing but the *baksheesh* meant to corrupt him.

'I asked you a question! What are you doing in my room?'

His dark brows rose a little. 'Rachelle told me you were awake, and so—'

'And so you thought you'd barge right in, without permission?'

'I knocked, several times, but you didn't answer.'

'I was in the shower!'

'Yes.' He leaned back against the wall and let his gaze drift over her. 'So I see.'

Joanna flushed. She felt as if he'd stripped away the towel and she was certain that was just the way he wanted her to feel. She ached to race back to the safety of the bathroom or to drag the blanket from the bed and enclose herself in it, but she'd be damned if she'd give him the satisfaction.

'Perhaps you can also see that I wasn't exactly expecting to receive visitors,' she said coldly.

'Rachelle said you were unhappy with her.'

'So?'

'So, she is very young, and very sensitive. And—'

'Let me get this straight. You came barging into my room because I hurt Rachelle's feelings?' Joanna laughed. 'You'll forgive me, Your Lordship—'

'That is not my title.'

'If you're waiting for me to apologise for upsetting your little slave, you're in for a long wait.'

'She is not my slave.' Khalil's eyes turned cool. 'We have no slaves, here in the northern hills.'

'Of course,' Joanna purred. 'I should have realised. The people here are all happy and content. The only slaves in Jandara are in the south, where the evil Abu Al Zouad rules.'

His eyes narrowed. The woman was impossible! How dared she speak to him with so little respect? How dared she stand before him as she did, flaunting her almost naked body?

'Don't you have a robe to put on?' he demanded.

She smiled sweetly. 'I'm afraid the hotel didn't supply one.'

'Rachelle was told to bring you anything you requested. If you had thought to ask—'

'The only thing I thought to ask for was my freedom,' Joanna said, lifting her chin in defiance. 'It was a request your little harem girl denied.'

'I shall see to it that you are given some proper clothing,' Khalil said stiffly.

'Meaning what? If you think I'm going to put on a

robe that drapes me from chin to toe, if you think I'm going to wrap a scarf around my head and look out at the world through a veil—'

'Is that what you have seen Rachelle wearing?'

It wasn't, of course. The girl wore a soft, scoop-necked cotton blouse and a pretty skirt that fell to mid-calf; her hair hung loose and uncovered to her shoulders.

'Or is that description of your own invention, meant to shore up your belief that we are a backward people?' The flush that rose in her cheeks gave him a certain grim satisfaction. He shrugged his white robe from his shoulders and held it out to her. 'Here. Wear this until—'

'I don't want anything from you, Khalil!'

His mouth thinned. 'Put it on!'

Her eyes flashed as he stepped forward and draped the robe over her shoulders. His fingers brushed her bare skin; a tingle raced along her nerve endings, one that sent a tremor through her. Khalil frowned and stepped back quickly.

'I will see to the clothing.'

'Yes. So you said.' Joanna drew the robe around herself. 'But I'm more interested in what my father's had to say.'

His frown deepened. 'What do you mean?'

'Come on, Khalil, don't treat me like a fool! Surely you've contacted him with your ransom demands.'

He looked at her for a long moment, then turned and strolled to the window.

'I have, yes,' he said, his back to her.

'And?' Joanna took a step forward. 'What did he say? How soon will he meet them?'

'I cannot tell you that.'

'What do you mean, you can't tell me?' Joanna moved closer to him. 'I've every right to know how long I'm going to be your prisoner!'

He swung towards her, his face stony. 'You will be here until your father decides to be reasonable.'

'You mean, I'll be here until he can raise the money you've asked for my return!'

'I have not asked for money.'

'No.' Joanna's smile was chill. 'Of course you haven't. I keep forgetting—you're the Hawk of the North. It's Abu Al Zouad who's the villain in this piece.'

'Joke all you wish, Joanna. It will not change the truth.'

Her chin lifted. 'It certainly won't. Abu Al Zouad's supposed to be this—this monster, this evil emperor, but—'

'He is a man who has enslaved his people.'

'Don't be ridiculous! If there were slaves in Jandara, Bennettco wouldn't have—'

'There are all kinds of slavery,' Khalil said sharply. 'People who live in fear of displeasing their ruler may not be slaves in the classic sense, but they are slaves just the same.'

Joanna smiled coolly. 'I suppose *your* people do that ridiculous bowing to you out of love, not fear.'

It pleased her to see a wash of crimson rise across his high cheekbones.

'It is custom,' he said sternly, 'and foolish. I have tried to change it—'

'Yeah.' She laughed. 'I'll bet.'

'My people obey me out of respect. If they thought I was wrong, the elders would say so.'

'Remarkable! You've got yourself believing your own lies!'

'And what, precisely, is that supposed to mean?' he said, glaring at her.

'You know damned well what it means! You make

yourself out to be this benevolent ruler, this wonderful good guy, but you're not! You're—you're—'

'A thief. A despot. A greedy pig who wants whatever he can get from Bennettco, or else I'll—' His brow furrowed. 'I never did ask, Joanna, what is it, exactly, that I'll do to the operation if I'm not properly bought off?'

'How should I know?' she cried angrily. 'Raid the camp. Harass the workers. Disrupt things any way you can. Does it matter?'

'And if I told you that you're wrong…?'

'Listen, Khalil, I'm not going to play this silly game! You want to pretend you're Lawrence of Arabia? Fine. Wear that foolish outfit. Ride that ridiculous horse. Stand around and look fierce while your people prostrate themselves before you. As for me, all I want—'

She cried out as he caught hold of her shoulders.

'All you want,' he said through his teeth, 'is to categorise me. And if I don't fit, you'll poke, prod, shove and squeeze until I do!'

'All I want,' Joanna said, her eyes snapping defiance, 'is to go back to Casablanca.'

'Nothing would suit me better! A scorpion would make a better guest than you!'

'I am not your guest!'

'Indeed you are not.' His lip curled with distaste. 'You are an unwelcome visitor.'

'Fine! Then put me on your plane and send me back!'

'I shall, the instant your father agrees to my conditions.'

'Well, then,' she said, tossing her head, 'tell your pilot to rev up those engines. Your money should be on its way.'

A furrow appeared between his dark eyebrows. 'Your father has yet to answer me, Joanna.'

She stared at him. 'I don't understand.'

'It is quite simple. He knows what I want for your return, but he has not offered a reply.'

Joanna's eyes searched his face. 'You mean, your messenger didn't wait for one.'

Khalil shook his head. 'I mean what I said.' His words were clipped and cold. 'Your father has not responded.'

'Well, how could he? If you asked some unholy sum of money, a million billion dollars or whatever, he'd have to find a way to—'

He gave her a thin smile. 'Is that what you think you're worth?'

'The question isn't what *I* think I'm worth,' she said coldly. 'It's what *you* think you can get for me.'

'I have asked a great deal,' he said, his eyes on her face.

Why did his answer make her heartbeat quicken? The words were simple, yet they seemed to hold a complexity of meaning. Joanna gave him what she hoped was an easygoing smile.

'Really.'

'A great, great deal,' he said softly.

'All right, tell me. How many dollars am I worth?'

'I didn't ask for dollars.'

'Swiss francs, then. Or Deutschmarks. Or—'

'I told you before, I want no money for you.'

Joanna's attempted nonchalance vanished. 'For God's sake,' she snapped, 'what did you ask from my father, then? Diamonds? Gold?'

Khalil's eyes met hers. 'I have demanded that your father withdraw from the contract with Abu Al Zouad.'

'What?'

'I said—'

'I heard you—but I don't believe you. All this talk about how you love your people and how they love you, and now you're trying to blackmail Bennettco into pulling out of a million-dollar deal that would pump money and jobs into your country?'

Khalil's eyes darkened. 'He is to withdraw from it and restructure it, so that the people benefit, not Abu.'

'Oh. Oh, of course. You want him to rewrite the contract—'

'Exactly.'

'—to rewrite it according to your dictates.'

'Yes.'

Joanna laughed. 'You're good at this, you know that? I mean, if I didn't know better, I'd almost believe you! Come on, Khalil. The only benefit you have in mind is for yourself.'

His expression hardened. 'Think what you will, Joanna. I have sent your father the terms of your release. Now, it is up to him to reply.'

'He will. He definitely will. And when he does—'

But Sam should have replied already, she thought with a start. He should have said, OK, I'll do whatever you want, just set my daughter free.

No. No, he couldn't do that. She wasn't looking at things clearly. Sam wasn't about to cave in, not without being certain Khalil would live up to his end of the deal. Kidnappers were not known for honouring their agreements; her father would want to do everything in his power to satisfy himself that he could trust Khalil to let her go before he said yes, otherwise he might put her in even greater jeopardy.

She looked up. Khalil was watching her closely. His expression was unreadable, but the little smile of triumph that had been on his lips moments ago was gone. In its place was a look that might almost have been sympathy.

'I cannot imagine your father will have trouble deciding which he prefers,' he said softly, 'his daughter or his contract with the sultan.'

Joanna flushed. The bastard wasn't feeling sympathy, he was just worried that her father might not give him what he'd asked for!

'My father's an astute businessman,' she said. 'Why should he trust you? He'll want some guarantee that you won't hurt me after he agrees to your demands.'

'My message made no mention of hurting you,' he said stiffly.

'Ah. I see. You simply told him you'd keep me as your guest forever if he didn't do what you wanted.'

Khalil began to grin. 'Something like that.'

Joanna's jaunty smile faded. 'What do you mean?'

He shrugged lazily. 'I suggested that if he did not want you back, we would accommodate you here.'

'Accommodate me?'

'You would learn to live among my people.' Still smiling, he strolled across the room to where her green silk dress lay across the chair. 'It will not be the life you know,' he said, picking up the dress. It slipped through his fingers, incongruously delicate and insubstantial, and fell back to the chair. 'But at least it would stop your complaining.'

'What are you talking about?'

'Our women lead busy lives. Only idle women have time to complain. You would start simply, tending the chickens and the goats, but if you showed you were interested in learning they would teach you to cook, to spin—'

'Never!' The word exploded from her lips. 'Never, do you hear me? I'd sooner—I'd sooner—'

'What would you sooner do?' He looked across the room at her, his eyes dark. 'Surely, you would have to do something. We are all productive here, everyone but the sick, the elderly, and the children.'

He started slowly towards her. Joanna's heart skipped a beat. She wanted to step back, to put as much distance as the confines of the room permitted between herself and the man pacing towards her, but she was determined to stand her ground.

'You fit none of those categories,' he said, stopping inches from her. He gave her a long, slow look, one that left a trail of heat across her skin and she thought suddenly that it was a good thing she hadn't fought him about giving her his robe, for if she had—if she had, he would surely see the quickening of her breath, the flush that she felt rising over her entire body, the terrible, hateful way her breasts were lifting and hardening as he looked at her.

'You are not elderly, or ill, or a child, Joanna,' he said softly. He reached his hand out to her and caught a strand of auburn hair between his fingers. 'I would have to find some other use for you, I'm afraid.'

'My father will come for me,' she said fiercely. 'And—and when he does—' Her breath caught as he put his arms around her.

'I think,' he said, his voice husky, 'I think I would not waste you on the goats, even if you wished it.'

'I would rather—' He put his lips to her hair and she swallowed hard. 'I would rather tend the goats than— than—'

'One of the laws we live by is that every person should do what he or she is best suited for.' He lowered his head and nuzzled the robe from the juncture of shoulder and throat. His mouth moved lightly against her skin. 'And you,' he said, his voice dropping to a whisper, 'you are surely best suited to be with a man, to sigh his name, and drive him to the point where his bones begin to melt.'

His teeth closed lightly on her flesh. Joanna gasped, and he touched his tongue to the pinpoint of pain, soothing it away.

'You smell of flowers,' he whispered, 'of flowers heated by the sun of the desert.'

Trembling, Joanna fought for control. 'I—I smell of soap,' she said as he pressed kisses across her shoulder. 'I—I didn't use Rachelle's precious bath oils to—'

'Then the scent in my nostrils is of you.' He threaded his hand into her hair, knotting it around his fist like a bright, gleaming band, so that she had no choice but to meet his eyes, eyes that had gone as dark as the sea at night. 'By Allah,' he whispered, 'it is a scent more sweet than any I have ever known.'

He bent and kissed her throat again. Joanna's eyes closed and she swayed in his arms, hating herself for whatever weakness it was that possessed her when he touched her, hating him even more for finding that weakness and exploiting it.

'The only name I'd ever call you is bastard,' she said unsteadily. 'And—and that would be only the beginning.'

Khalil laughed softly. 'Has no one ever taught you manners?'

'No one's ever tried to tell me how to live my life, if that's what you mean!'

She had meant to insult him, but her words only made him grin. 'Ah. We're back to that, are we? Khalil the dictator.'

'We never left it! You think—you think you can—'

'The first thing you must learn,' he said, 'is not to talk so much.'

His mouth dropped to hers. She had been expecting

the kiss, steeling herself against it, and she went rigid at the first touch of his lips. But his kiss was like a whisper—gentle, almost soft—and it sent a swift *frisson* of pleasure shimmering through her blood.

Don't, she began to say. But the thought never became a word. Instead, it emerged a sigh against his mouth. Khalil's arms went around her and he gathered her so closely to him that Joanna couldn't tell whose heart it was she felt racing, whose skin it was she felt blazing with heat.

His teeth caught her bottom lip and he drew the soft flesh into the warmth of his mouth.

'Joanna,' he whispered.

He swept the robe from her shoulders and the lightly knotted towel fell to her waist. He drew back, just far enough so he could see her. Her skin was flushed, her breasts full and hardened with desire.

'How beautiful you are,' he said, his voice thick.

Joanna felt as if the room was spinning around her. 'Please,' she whispered, 'please…'

'What? What do you want me to do, Joanna?' He reached out blindly, his fingers trailing across her collarbone, and she caught her breath. 'This?' he said softly, his eyes on her face. He touched the rise of her breast, circling the aureole lightly. Joanna whimpered and now it was he who caught his breath. 'Or this?' he said, bending his head and putting his mouth to her flesh.

She moaned, would have fallen, but he caught her and gathered her fiercely to him, his hands cupping her bottom, lifting her into the hardness of his arousal.

'Joanna,' he whispered, his voice unsteady, and she moved blindly against him, exulting in the hard feel of him, her flesh on fire…

'No!' The strangled cry burst as much from her heart as from her throat. What was he doing to her? She wasn't the sort of woman who fell into bed with a stranger or with a man she loathed! Joanna slammed her hands against Khalil's chest and pushed him away.

'All right,' she said, her breathing swift, 'you've convinced me. You're bigger than I am, and stronger, and—and—' She closed her eyes, then opened them, determined to face her humiliation without flinching. 'And there's something you do that—that makes me—makes me receptive. But—'

'Receptive?' He laughed, and whatever unsteadiness she'd thought she'd heard in his voice was gone, replaced by smug satisfaction at her embarrassment. 'What you are, my charming Miss Bennett, is ready and willing.' Her hand flashed up but he caught it before she could slap him. 'But, of course, you'd have to be, wouldn't you, to have had any hope of carrying out your little scheme?'

'I hate you,' Joanna said through her teeth. 'Do you understand? I hate you, and I'd sooner die than—'

'Yes. So you said, several times.' His smile was chill. 'It must be difficult, trying to play the part of the seductress and the wounded innocent at the same time.'

'You'll pay for what you've done, when my father comes for me, I promise you that.'

'The sooner, the better,' Khalil said grimly, thrusting her from him. 'Rachelle will bring you clothing. Then she will show you the areas in which you will be free to walk.'

'Free? You don't know the meaning of the word!'

'Behave yourself and things will not be as difficult as you imagine,' he said, striding to the door.

'And if I don't?' She flung her defiance after him, some inner need more desperate than fear spurring her on. 'What then? Will you put me in chains?'

He turned and looked at her. 'Only a stupid man

would resort to such measures, Joanna.' A quick smile flashed across his lips. 'Especially when there are ones that would please me far better.'

The door opened, then shut, and Joanna was alone.

CHAPTER SEVEN

'I HAVE brought you some lunch, Joanna.'

Joanna looked up as Rachelle entered the bedroom and set a tray on the table beside the window.

'You will like it, I think. There is *kofta* and *ommu-'ali*—little meatballs—and then some rice pudding, and—'

'Thank you, but I'm not hungry.'

The bright smile dimmed. 'But you haven't even looked at it!'

'I'm sure it's delicious. But I don't want it.'

'Joanna, please. You must eat.'

'Why?' Joanna's attempted good humour vanished in a haze of frustration and disappointment. 'Is that what the Prince said?'

Rachelle flushed. 'The Prince will be concerned about the welfare of his guest.'

'Ah. That's touching. Unfortunately for me, I am not exactly his guest.'

'He will be displeased with me.'

'Send him to me, then. I'll tell him you have nothing to do with my not eating. Perhaps he needs to be reminded that prisoners often lose their appetites—but then, what would a kidnapper and bandit know about such things?'

'Hush!' Rachelle's eyes were wide with shock. 'You must not say that of my lord!'

'Why? Will he have me beaten if I speak the truth? Will he have you beaten for listening to it?' Joanna got to her feet and stalked across the room. 'Why don't you stop defending him? There's no one here but me—you can be honest for once. Your mighty Prince is nothing but a—'

Rachelle gasped, turned, and all but flew to the door.

'Rachelle!' Joanna's voice rose in dismay. 'Rachelle, wait, please! Don't go. I just wanted to—'

It was too late. The door swung shut, and she was alone again. She stared at it for a few seconds, and then she flung out her arms in frustration.

'How could you be so stupid, Joanna?' she demanded of the silent room.

She flung herself into a chair and stared blankly at the wall. She'd lost her temper with a slip of a girl who was too terrified of Khalil and the life-or-death power he held over her and the rest of his people ever to question what he did.

More importantly, she'd lost the chance to ask the only question that mattered. When would she be set free? Surely Khalil had heard from her father by now? Sam must be working as quickly as he could to meet the demands for her release, but—

A knock sounded at the door, as if in answer to Joanna's thoughts. She sprang to her feet, her heart pounding—but it was only Rachelle again, this time bearing an armful of what looked like bright lengths of fabric.

'I have brought you some things to wear,' she said, hurrying to the bed, her eyes downcast. Garments fell across the blankets, along with a pair of embroidered leather slippers. 'I hope they are to your liking, Joanna. If they are not—'

'Rachelle—I'm sorry if I insulted you before.'

The girl looked up. 'It was my lord you insulted, not me.'

'Yes.' Joanna sighed. 'And I suppose it's a capital offence to do that here, isn't it?'

Rachelle's brow furrowed. 'Capital offence? I do not understand.'

Joanna smiled tightly. 'No, I'm sure you don't.'

'The clothing,' the girl said, gesturing to the bed. 'I had to guess at the size, but—'

'I won't need it.'

Rachelle shrugged her shoulders. 'I thought you would be more comfortable in these things than in the jellaba, but if you prefer to wear it—'

'I won't be here long enough to bother changing what I'm wearing.'

The girl's eyes met Joanna's, then skittered away. 'It will not hurt to have these things,' she said.

'There's no point,' Joanna said firmly. 'Surely, by now, Khalil has heard from my father, and…' She stared at the other girl. 'He has, hasn't he?'

Rachelle seemed to hesitate. 'I do not know.'

'Khalil said he'd contacted him. Did he tell me the truth?' Rachelle's face grew shuttered and Joanna's voice sharpened with impatience. 'Come on, Rachelle, surely you can answer a simple question. Does my father know what's happened to me?'

The girl nodded. 'Yes.'

Yes. Yes. Sam knew she was being held prisoner, but he hadn't yet arranged for her release…

'I will take away the things I have brought, since you do not wish to—'

'No!' Joanna shook her head and put her hand on Rachelle's arm. 'No, leave them. On second thought, I don't want to go on wearing this—this bathrobe of Khalil's another minute.' She reached towards the bed, then stopped abruptly. 'What,' she said disdainfully, 'is this?'

'A skirt.' The girl smiled hesitantly. 'And a blouse to go with it. If they please you, I will bring you other—'

'I have no intention of wearing anything like that!'

Rachelle looked bewildered. 'Are the sizes wrong? You are so slender, Joanna, that I was not certain—'

'I'm sure the size is fine.'

'The colours, then. I thought the shade of blue was very pretty, but perhaps you would prefer—'

'A skirt that length is a mark of subservience,' Joanna said, blithely ignoring the fact that New York women were probably that minute strolling Fifth Avenue in skirts even longer than the one that lay across the bed. Her eyes flashed to Rachelle's face. 'I mean no insult,' she said quickly. 'It's only that in my country, women don't dress that way.'

'Then you will go on wearing the jellaba?'

Suddenly, the weight of the jellaba seemed unbearable against her naked skin.

'No,' Joanna said quickly.

Rachelle looked bewildered. 'Then what will you wear?'

What, indeed? Joanna gave the first answer that came into her head.

'Trousers,' she said, taking an almost perverse delight in the shock she saw in Rachelle's eyes.

'Trousers? But—'

'I know. Women don't wear them in Jandara.' Her chin lifted. 'But I am not Jandaran, Rachelle. Be sure and give that message to your high and mighty Prince.'

It was a pointless gesture, Joanna knew. Even if, by some miracle, women's trousers could be found in Jandara, surely Khalil would never agree to permitting his hostage to wear something so Western.

An hour later, Rachelle appeared at the door carrying another armload of clothing.

'I hope these things suit you better,' she said, dumping everything on the bed.

Joanna waited until the girl left, and then she walked to the bed and poked at the garments lying across it. A smile curved across her lips. There were two pairs of trousers—soft, cotton ones—and a stack of shirts, as well.

She picked one up. This was men's clothing, not women's. Everything would be too large, but what did that matter? She wasn't trying to be a fashion plate and besides, getting such things past Khalil seemed like a victory. Perhaps Rachelle had taken pity on her; perhaps she'd got the items on her own, without seeking his permission.

Quickly, Joanna stripped off the jellaba. She pulled on a pair of trousers, then slipped a navy cotton T-shirt over her head.

It was Khalil's, she thought instantly, as the soft fabric brushed past her nose. The T-shirt, the trousers—they were all his. The garments were all clean and fresh, but they bore a scent compounded of the mountains and the wind and the stallion he rode... His scent.

A tremor went through her and she closed her eyes, remembering the endless ride to this mountain stronghold, remembering the feel of Khalil's arms as he'd held her before him on the saddle.

Joanna gave herself a little shake. Impatiently, she yanked the shirt down hard over her breasts. His scent, indeed! The T-shirt smelled of the soap it had been washed with and the sunshine that had dried it, nothing more. Honestly, if she didn't get out of this prison soon...

There was a light rap at the door. She spun towards it.

'Rachelle? Thanks for bringing me this stuff. It's just too bad it belongs to your almighty Prince, but—'

'I assure you, Joanna,' Khalil said with a cool smile, 'none of it is contaminated.'

Joanna's cheeks flamed. 'I thought you were Rachelle.'

He nodded as he shut the door after him. 'Obviously,' he said drily. His gaze flickered over her slowly, and then a smile curved across his lips. 'I am sorry I had nothing more to your liking.'

'This is fine,' she said stiffly.

His eyes darkened. 'I agree,' he said softly. 'That shirt has never looked quite as good on my body as it looks on yours.'

The colour in her face deepened. She was wearing no bra—she had none to wear—and she knew that he must be able to see the rounded outline of her breasts clearly beneath the soft cotton of the T-shirt, see the prominence of her nipples, which were hardening as he looked at her.

'Clothing is clothing,' she said, her voice chill. 'Nothing more.'

His smile tilted. 'Even when it belongs to the enemy?'

Joanna's chin lifted. 'If you've come here to taunt me—'

Khalil sighed. 'I came because Rachelle says you are distressed.'

She stared at him. 'Distressed? *Distressed*?' Joanna laughed. 'Don't be absurd! Why should I be distressed? After all, here I am, the guest of the great Hawk of the North, having an absolutely wonderful time—'

'I take it you are not pleased with out efforts at hospitality.'

'I just told you, I love it here! Especially the security.

Armed guards at the door—how much safer could a guest feel?'

Khalil put his hands on his hips. 'Will you promise not to try and escape if I call off the guards?' He laughed at the look on her face. 'No. I didn't think so.'

'Would you really expect me to make such a promise?'

'I have not come here to debate, Joanna. Rachelle says—'

'Rachelle says! For God's sake, if you want to know what I think, why don't you ask me? I don't need Rachelle as my interpreter!'

A smile twisted at his lips. 'I agree. You have no difficulty speaking your mind.'

'So, what do you want to know?' She gave him a beaming smile. 'Is Room Service treating me OK? Do I like the accommodation? The view?' Her mouth narrowed. 'The shackles on the walls?'

He laughed. 'The only thing I see on the walls are paintings.'

'You know what I mean, Khalil! When are you going to let me out of this prison?'

Khalil's face darkened. 'Your freedom is in your father's hands, not mine.'

Joanna looked at him and tried to keep the sudden desperation she felt from showing in her eyes.

'Well?'

'Well, what?'

'Well, when is he coming for me?'

He hesitated. 'I do not know.'

'You do not know?' Joanna said, her voice mimicking his. 'How could that be? You said you'd contacted him.'

'Yes, of course.'

'And?'

'And he has not replied to my message.'

She shot him a cold look. 'That's very hard to believe!'

Khalil's mouth narrowed. 'I am not a liar, Joanna.'

Wasn't he? He had lied well enough to lure her into the desert and carry her here...

No. She'd lied the night they'd met, not he. He'd simply made the most of things. Besides, what would he gain by lying to her now? He had sent Sam a message and Sam—and Sam had not responded...

Sudden despair overwhelmed her. She felt the unwanted sting of tears in her eyes and she started to turn away, but before she could, Khalil stepped quickly forward and clasped her shoulders.

'Joanna?'

She looked up. There was an unreadable expression on his face, something that might almost approach concern. It startled her—until she realised he would have to have some interest in her emotional condition. The last thing he'd want on his hands was an hysterical captive.

'Don't worry, Khalil,' she said with a brittle smile. 'I've no intention of making a scene. I was only thinking that if you really did ask my father to withdraw from the mining deal, you have asked for a great deal.'

A muscle knotted in his cheek. 'Perhaps. But I promise you, I have not asked him for more than you are worth, Joanna.'

She felt a flush rise over her body. How did he manage to do this to her? When he looked at her like this, everything seemed to fade into the background—everything but him, and the awareness of him that he made her feel. It was perverse. It was impossible. And yet—

He bent his head and touched his mouth to hers. The kiss was soft, almost tender, and yet she felt the heat of it race through her blood and confuse her senses.

'Joanna,' he whispered, and his lips took hers again.

She swayed unsteadily and his hands clasped her more tightly, lifting her on tiptoe, moulding her body to his while their mouths clung together. It was Khalil who finally ended the kiss. When he did, Joanna stared at him, her lips parted, her breathing swift. She wanted to say something clever and sharp, something that would put what had just happened into chill perspective—but it was Khalil who did it instead.

'Your father is not a fool,' he said, with a little smile. 'He will do what any man in his right mind would do for you.'

Of course. Any man would meet the ransom demands of his daughter's kidnappers, and Sam was no exception.

Joanna forced a thin smile to her lips. 'You don't have to tell me that, Khalil. I know it. My father will pay what you ask—but you'll never have time to enjoy it. Not when you're going to be rotting in one of Abu's prisons.'

His hands fell away from her. 'Ah, Joanna, Joanna. Whenever I begin to wonder if your spirits are sagging, you say something sweet and loving and reassure me that you're the same soft-hearted creature you've always been!'

'That's the difference between us,' she said. 'You need reminding—but I never for a moment forget what an impossible bastard you are!'

His eyes went dark. 'You play with fire, Joanna.'

'What's the matter? Can't you handle the truth? Or do you expect me to bow and scrape and worship you adoringly, the way Rachelle does?'

To her surprise, he burst out laughing. 'You? Bowing and scraping? It is an interesting thought, Joanna, but I think the only things you will ever scrape will be the chicken coops.'

'What?' She moved after him as he turned and started

for the door. 'Never,' she said, 'not in this lifetime...'
the door opened '...or any other,' she finished, but it
was too late. Khalil was gone.

After a moment, she sighed and walked to the window. Why had she wasted time letting him bait her?
There were things she'd meant to ask him, things that
would make whatever time she had to spend here more
bearable.

There was an enclosed garden just outside, a handsome one, from what she could see of it. Would he permit her to walk in it? Surely, he didn't intend to keep
her locked up in—?

A flash of colour caught her eye. Joanna leaned forward. A little girl dressed in jeans, sneakers, and a pale
blue polo shirt was playing with a puppy. Despite her
own worries, Joanna began to smile. There was something about children and small animals that never failed
to move her.

The child laughed as she held out a bright yellow ball,
then tossed it across the grass. The puppy wagged its
tail furiously, charged after the ball, and brought it back.
Joanna's smile broadened. The two were having a wonderful time, judging by the way the girl was laughing.
The puppy looked as if it were laughing, too, with its
pink tongue hanging out of its mouth.

Joanna tucked her hip on to the window sill and
watched, chuckling softly as the game continued, until
the ball bounced crazily on the cobblestoned pathway,
tumbled into the dark green hedge that bordered it, and
vanished.

The puppy searched, as did the little girl, but neither
had seen where the ball had gone.

Joanna tapped the window pane. 'There,' she said, 'in
the hedge.'

Neither the child nor the dog could hear her.

She tapped the window again. If the girl would just look up...

The child's face puckered. She plopped down in the grass, snatched the puppy to her breast, and began to sob. The puppy licked her face but the child only cried harder as she rocked the animal in her arms.

Joanna turned from the window, hurried to the door, and flung it open. The guard standing outside looked up, startled.

'Excuse me,' she said, brushing past him.

He called out after her, his equivalent, she was certain, of 'Hey, where do you think you're going?' but she was already halfway down the hall, heading towards an arched doorway that she knew must open on to the garden. She went straight through it, pausing only long enough to be sure the child was still sitting in the same place, holding her dog and weeping.

'Don't cry,' Joanna said when she reached her. The little girl looked up, her eyes widening with surprise. Joanna smiled and squatted down beside her. 'Do you understand me? You mustn't cry so hard. You'll make yourself sick.'

The child raised a tear-stained face. 'Who are you?' she said, in perfect English.

'My name is Joanna. And who are you?'

'I am Lilia.' The tears began rolling down her plump cheeks again. 'And I've lost my ball!'

Joanna took the girl's hands in hers. 'It's not the end of the world,' she said softly.

'It was a special ball. My father gave it to me, and—' The tears came faster and faster. 'And he's never coming back!'

Joanna rose to her feet. 'In that case,' she said, 'we'll just have to get that ball, won't we?'

She spotted not one guard but several hurrying

towards her. Too bad, she thought defiantly, as she hurried towards the hedge that had swallowed the child's toy. When she reached it, she saw that the foliage was denser than it had seemed from her window. She hesitated, then shook her head over her foolishness. It was only a hedge, and the guards were almost upon her. Quickly, she plunged her hand deep into the bush's green heart.

'Joanna!'

The ball was here somewhere, dammit. If she could just—

'Joanna! Stop it! Do you hear me?'

There! She had it now. She winced as she felt something needle-sharp hit her hand, but what did it matter? Face flushed with triumph, she pulled the yellow ball from the tangle of branches and looked up into the dark, angry face of Khalil.

'Relax, Your Highness,' she said coolly. 'I'd love to escape, but I doubt if burrowing through some shrubbery will get me very far.'

'You fool.' He barked something at Lilia, who had followed after Joanna. The little girl wiped her eyes, dropped a curtsy, and ran off with the puppy at her heels.

Joanna's eyes flashed. 'You see? Everyone bows and scrapes to you, even a slip of a child who—'

Khalil grabbed the ball from her and tossed it aside. 'Would you risk everything for something as stupid as a child's toy?'

'I know a little girl's tears mean nothing to you, oh great one, but then, you're not exactly known for having a heart, are you?' Her chin tilted. 'What now? Do I get flogged? Put on bread and water?'

Khalil snatched her wrist. 'Look,' he growled, lifting her hand.

She looked. There was a single puncture mark in the flesh between her thumb and forefinger.

'So?' Joanna's mouth narrowed. 'Don't tell me all this rage is over my getting scratched by a thorn.'

'No thorn did that, you little idiot! Do you see any thorns on that bush?'

'So what? It's nothing but a little cut. What's the matter, Khalil? Are you afraid I'll sue you?'

'Damn you, Joanna.' He caught hold of her shoulders and shook her. 'Someone should teach you that a smart answer isn't always a wise answer!'

'It won't kill me,' she said coldly. 'I assure you, I've survived worse.'

'You fool,' he said sharply. 'When will you learn to shut up long enough to listen?'

'If you're finished, I'd like to return to my room.' Her teeth flashed in a tight smile. 'Even being locked inside those miserable four walls is preferable to standing here and dealing with you!'

A muscle knotted in Khalil's jaw. 'I couldn't agree more.'

'Well, then,' she said, and turned away from him. But she hadn't taken a step before he caught hold of her and swept her up in his arms.

'Put me down!' Joanna pounded her fist against his shoulder as he strode through the garden and into the coolness of the house. 'Are you deaf, Khalil? I said, put me down!'

'With pleasure,' he growled through his teeth. 'The instant I am done with you, I will do just that.'

'What do you mean?' She pounded on his shoulder again as he swept down the corridor past her room. 'Dammit, where are you taking me?'

He glanced down at her, his eyes shimmering like the heat waves on the desert.

'To my rooms,' he said, with a smile as cold as any she had ever imagined.

Before she could answer, he shouldered open a huge wooden door, then kicked it closed behind him.

Joanna glimpsed a high ceiling, a tapestried wall, and a massive, canopied bed—and then Khalil dumped her on to the mattress, put his hands on his hips, and glared down at her.

'Now, Joanna,' he said, 'let's get down to business.'

CHAPTER EIGHT

KHALIL was angry, angrier than he should have been, considering the circumstances, but what man wouldn't be angry when an educated, intelligent woman insisted on making a damned fool of herself?

'The woman is trying to escape, Highness,' one of his people had cried out, bursting into the library just as he'd begun a strategy session with his ministers.

His men had let her run when they'd realised she had made for the enclosed garden from which there was no escape.

'I'll get her,' Khalil had said, tight-lipped, but instead of chasing down a fleeing Joanna Bennett, he'd stumbled upon a foolish one, up to her silken elbows in a shrub she should have known better than to touch in the first place.

No. That was ridiculous. Even he had to admit that. How could she have known that the seemingly innocent shrub could conceal a venomous insect? It was obvious she hadn't been trying to run away, even though he knew she could hardly wait to see the last of him.

His teeth ground together. Then why was his temper so close to boiling point? He glared down at her. He knew she prided herself on maintaining self-control but in this moment she was as transparent as glass. Looking into her green eyes, he could see her indignation and anger giving way to something else. To fear—and to the bone-deep determination not to let him see that fear.

Instantly, he realised how his sharply spoken words must have sounded. His glare deepened. Did the woman really think him such a savage that he would take her in violence, in some barbaric, retaliatory rage? His nostrils flared with distaste. He would tell her that she was a fool, that he had never in his life forced a woman into his bed and that she was not a woman he would choose to have in his bed, even if she came willingly…

…But then he looked at the glossy auburn hair that lay tumbled over her shoulders, at the rapid rise and fall of her breasts beneath the ridiculously oversized T-shirt she'd insisted on wearing, and it was as if a fist knotted suddenly in his gut. His gaze fell to her mouth, soft as a flower and slightly parted, as if a breeze had disturbed its petals. Desire raged through him, as hot as the fire that sometimes followed a strike of summer lightning in the mountain forests, hardening his groin with a swiftness that stunned him.

What nonsense was this? He was not a boy, given to uncontrollable bursts of adolescent desire. And she was not a woman he would ever want. She was clever and beautiful, yes, but she was soft and spoiled, selfish and stubborn and altogether unyielding.

And yet, she had yielded to him, when he'd kissed her. Each time he had taken her in his arms to humble her, she had instead kindled a fire in his blood, then matched it with a scorching heat of her own.

His breathing quickened. What would happen if he came down on the bed beside her? It was what she expected, he knew, that he would take her now. What would she do if he did? Would she fight him? Or would she ignite with a quicksilver flame under his touch?

'Joanna,' he said, his voice a little thick, and instantly she rose up on her knees and bared her small, white teeth.

'Go on,' she taunted, 'do whatever you're going to do. It's all the excuse I need to claw out your eyes!'

So much for her igniting under his touch! Khalil burst out laughing.

'If you claw out my eyes,' he said reasonably, 'how will I attend to you properly?'

'You couldn't,' she said. 'I mean, you can't. There's nothing you could do that would make me...'

'Relax, Joanna.' The look he gave her was cool, almost disinterested. 'I assure you, I've no designs on your body.'

Her face coloured. 'Then why—?' Her voice rose as he strode into the adjoining bathroom. She could hear water running, cabinet doors opening and closing, and then he reappeared, bearing a small tray arrayed with a small basin, a bottle, cotton pads, and adhesive tape. Joanna's eyes lit with suspicion. 'What's all that for?' she demanded.

He sighed dramatically as he put the tray on the bedside table and rolled back his sleeves.

'I hate to disappoint you,' he said. 'I know you're convinced I'm about to subject you to some ancient and terrible ritual.' He dipped a cotton pad into the basin. 'But I'm not planning anything more exotic than cleaning your hand.'

She jerked her hand back as he reached for it but his fingers curled around her wrist like a vice.

'Come on, Khalil, give me a break! Surely, we're too old to play Doctor.' Her breath hissed through her teeth as he dabbed the pad against her skin. 'Hey! That hurts.'

'Not as much as it will if the bite isn't tended. Hold your arm to the light, please.'

'It's nothing,' she said impatiently. 'No one dies from—'

'You may be an expert on many things, Joanna, but you are hardly one on the flora and fauna of my country. The spider that bit you might well be poisonous.'

'Poisonous?' she said stupidly. 'Hey! Hey, what are you doing?'

'Drawing out the venom.' The breath caught in her throat as he lifted her hand to his mouth. A shudder went through her as she felt the tug of his lips, the light press of his teeth, and then he dropped her hand into her lap and strode into the bathroom. She heard water running in the sink and she closed her eyes, fighting for control, but she could still feel the imprint of his mouth, the heat of it...

'Joanna? Are you feeling faint?'

Her eyes flew open. 'I told you, it's just a bite. I'm not...' She frowned as he uncapped a bottle and dampened a cotton pad with its contents. Her breath hissed as he applied it to her skin. 'Ouch. That stings! What is it?'

'An ancient medication known only to shamans and holy men.' He looked up, and she could see laughter in his eyes. 'It is peroxide, Joanna. What did you think it was?'

'How should I know?' she said stiffly.

Khalil worked in silence for a moment, and then he looked at her again.

'My men think you were trying to escape.'

'I told you, I'd be delighted to escape,' she said with a quick, cool smile. 'But I'm not stupid enough to escape into your garden.'

He laughed softly. 'No. I did not think so.'

She watched as he bent his head and began dabbing at the tiny bite mark again.

'What were you doing, then?'

Joanna shrugged her shoulders. 'The little girl lost her ball. I saw where the ball landed but she didn't, and when she started to cry—'

'Her crying annoyed you?'

'Annoyed me? Of course not. I felt sorry for her. One

minute she'd been laughing and the next—' She caught her breath as he ran a finger lightly over her skin.

'The bite will itch, for a day or two,' he said, 'but it will be fine after that.'

'Fine.' Her voice shook a little and he looked up, frowning.

'What is it, Joanna? Does it hurt when I touch you there?'

'No,' she said quickly. 'It doesn't hurt at all.'

What it did, she thought wildly, was send a wave of sensation along her nerve-endings. The feeling was—it was...

'That's great,' she said, snatching her hand away. 'Thank you. I'm sure I won't—'

Khalil clasped her hand in his again. 'I am not done,' he said. 'I want to put some ointment on your hand and then bandage it.'

'It's—it's not necessary. Really.'

'Just hold still, please. I'll try and be more gentle.' His hands moved on her lightly, without pressure. 'It will only take another minute.'

Joanna sat beside him, her spine rigid, as he smoothed a healing cream over her slightly reddened flesh. He would try and be more gentle, he'd said—but he was already being more gentle than she could ever have imagined. She had no doubt that those large, competent hands could tame the wildest desert horse; that they could also stroke her as if his fingers were satin and her skin silk came as a surprise. He was touching her with such care, as if she were too delicate for anything but the most careful caress.

Her breathing quickened. Khalil's head was bowed over her hand. She could see the way his dark hair curled lightly over the nape of his neck, as if it were kissing his tanned skin. The fingers of her free hand tightened against her palm. What would his hair feel like, if she were to touch it? And what would he do, if she reached out and lightly stroked that ebony silk?

Some time between the last time she'd seen him and now, he'd changed his clothes. Gone was the white jellaba; in its place was a very American blue denim shirt and jeans. It was amazing, she thought, how little he looked like a fierce mountain bandit and how much he looked like a man who could walk down a New York street without drawing attention to himself—except that he would always draw attention, wherever he went. He was too self-assured, too ruggedly handsome not to be noticed.

Joanna bit down lightly on her lip. Moments ago, he'd dumped her on this bed and stood over her, fury gleaming in his eyes, and she'd thought he was going to force her to submit to him. The thought had terrified her—and yet, if she were brutally honest, she'd had some other far, darker reaction deep within herself as she'd looked up at him.

What if she'd opened her arms to him? Would the fire of anger have left his eyes and been replaced, instead, by the shine of desire? Her lashes fell to her cheeks and she imagined the feel of his body against hers, the excitement of his possession…

Dear God! Joanna's eyes flew open. She really was going over the edge! She wasn't a woman who wanted to be taken against her will any more than he was a man who would take a woman in that fashion. Why would he, when surely any woman he wanted would come to him willingly, when any woman in her right mind would turn to flame in his arms…?

'There,' he said briskly. He capped the bottle, put it on the tray, and rose to his feet. 'That should do it. The next time you want to do something heroic—'

Joanna blew out her breath. 'I wasn't being heroic. I told you, Lilia was crying, and I—'

There was a light knock on the door. 'My lord?' a little voice whispered, and Lilia stepped carefully into the room. She looked from Joanna to Khalil, who folded his arms over his chest in that arrogant posture Joanna had come to recognise. 'I am sorry, my lord,' the child said.

He nodded, his face stern. 'As well you should be.'

Joanna stood up. 'Khalil!'

'Will the lady be all right, my lord?'

'I'm fine,' Joanna said quickly.

Lilia nodded, but her attention was centred on Khalil. 'I really am sorry.' She sniffed, then wiped her hand under her nose. 'I didn't mean—'

'What you mean is, you didn't think.'

'Khalil,' Joanna said, 'for goodness' sake, tell the child that—'

'You have a place to play, Lilia. A safe place, with swings and toys—and with a nursemaid to watch over you.' Khalil's brows drew together. 'You ran away from Amara again, didn't you?'

The child hesitated. 'Well—'

'Tell me the truth, Lilia!'

'Amara fell asleep,' she said, hanging her head. 'She ate her lunch and then she ate most of a box of sweets and then she said she would just sit in the sun and rest...'

The child's mouth twitched. Joanna's eyes flashed to Khalil's face. Astonished, she watched his mouth begin to twitch, too, and then he squatted, held out his arms, and grinned.

'Come and give me a hug, you little devil,' he said. 'I haven't had one in days.'

Lilia laughed as he swung her into his arms. 'I love you, Uncle,' she said.

Uncle? *Uncle*?

He kissed the child on both cheeks, then set her on the floor and gave her a light pat on her bottom.

'Go on,' he said gently. 'Find your puppy and play some other game. I shall speak to Amara.'

'You won't be angry at her?'

He sighed. 'No.'

Lilia smiled. 'Thank you,' she said, and then she turned to Joanna. 'And thank you, for finding my ball.'

Joanna smiled, too. 'You're very welcome.' The child skipped out the door and Joanna cleared her throat. 'I didn't expect—' Khalil looked at her. 'I, um, I never imagined… I didn't know Lilia was your niece.'

'It's an honorary title,' he said.

'She's very fond of you.'

'Yes.' His expression was impassive. 'It is many years since any of us ate children for breakfast, Joanna.'

She flushed. 'I never meant to imply that you—that your people…'

'No.' His expression grew cold and forbidding. 'That's true enough. You never "imply". Why should you, when you are a veritable expert on our behaviour and customs?'

'Look, I suppose I deserved that. But you can't blame me for—for…' She sighed. 'She's a sweet little girl,' she said, after a minute.

Khalil nodded. 'I agree. She's the daughter of Amahl. He was one of my closest advisors.'

'I've never seen—'

'And you won't.' He snatched up the tray of first-aid equipment and stalked to the bathroom, Joanna trailing after him. 'Amahl was killed during a skirmish.' He yanked open the cabinet door and began slamming the first-aid equipment into it. 'Lilia was alone to start with—her mother died in childbirth—but after Amahl's death she had no one.'

Joanna could see the muscles knotting in his shoulders. Her throat tightened. She wanted to reach out, to touch him, to stroke away the tension that held him prisoner and tell him it was all right…

Prisoner? She was the prisoner, not he! She was—

Khalil swung around and faced her. 'Abu is evil, Joanna.' His voice was harsh. 'If your father signs this contract with him, it will ensure that he has enough money to buy the arms he needs to defeat us!'

She stared at him, her eyes wide. The bathroom was mirrored, and she could see their faces in its silvery walls. Khalil's and hers, their reflections seeming to slip into infinity.

What was reality and what was not?

'Abu is the Sultan of Jandara,' she whispered.

'He is a tyrant, and your father knows it.' Khalil reached out and clasped her shoulders. 'He knows it, and yet he would fatten Abu's coffers.'

'You're lying!'

'I told you, Joanna, I do not lie.'

Joanna drew a deep breath. 'I don't understand. How can he be the rightful leader of Jandara if—?'

'*I* am the rightful leader of Jandara! Abu snatched the throne from me when I was a boy.' His face darkened, and she gasped as his fingers bit into her flesh. 'My parents died in a plane crash when I was only a child. Abu and a council of elders were to rule until I came of age. Instead, he killed the elders he couldn't corrupt and seized absolute power.'

Joanna shook her head. 'If he did that, why did he let you live?'

Khalil smiled grimly. 'Perhaps because I would be

more dangerous dead, as a martyr, than I am alive.'

'Then—then why haven't you done something? Why haven't you taken back the throne?'

'There is a war raging here, Joanna! You haven't seen it because it isn't the kind that's fought on great battle-fields, or with planes and tanks. We meet the enemy when we can find him, we inflict damage—and wait for the day we can destroy him without destroying our-selves.' His mouth twisted. 'I cannot let my men offer their lives for me unless I am certain we can win.'

Joanna stared into Khalil's burning eyes. She wanted to believe him—but if she did, then her father would be the liar. He would be a man who had knowingly struck a deal with a tyrant...

Joanna drew a shaky breath. 'You talk about moral-ity—and yet you deny me my freedom.' She ran the tip of her tongue over her lips. 'If you want me to believe you—if you're telling me the truth, let me go.'

Khalil's face darkened. 'It is out of the question.'

'You see? You make speeches about what is right, but...' She wrenched free of him. 'It's impossible. You stole me, Khalil. You've locked me away, kept me pris-oner...'

He said a word under his breath, clasped her shoul-ders, and spun her towards him.

'I took you for a reason, Joanna. I had no choice.'

'Everyone has choices! Make the right one now. Let me go.'

Their eyes met and held. 'No,' he said. 'I cannot.'

'I'll tell my father what you said about Abu, I prom-ise.'

Khalil shook his head. 'I have spoken, Joanna. I will not free you!'

Angry colour flashed across her cheeks. 'You—you

pig-headed, insolent idiot! Why should I believe anything you say?'

'Stop it, Joanna!'

'I won't stop it! You're an arrogant, imperious bastard, and I can hardly wait to see you in chains!'

She cried out as his arms swept around her. 'If you won't keep quiet, I'll silence you myself,' he said, and kissed her.

Joanna twisted wildly in his arms. 'Damn you,' she hissed against his mouth. She bit down, hard enough to draw a bead of blood, but he only laughed and gathered her closer.

'Fight me,' he said, his arms holding her like bands of steel. 'What does it matter, Joanna? Soon you will be crying out my name, moving against me and pleading with me to end this war between us in the one way we both understand.'

'No,' she said, 'that's not true!'

But it was. He wanted her, and she wanted him, and whatever remained of reason fled in Khalil's impassioned kisses, kisses that demanded her submission yet promised his in return. Joanna gave a moaning sob. She wound her arms tightly around his neck and lifted herself to him, pressing her body to his, opening her mouth to the thrust of his tongue. He growled his triumph, lifted her into his arms, and carried her to his bed.

'Joanna,' he whispered.

She looked up as he lowered her to the mattress. He smiled a little, the triumphant smile of a man who knew what he wanted and was about to have it—and, with that smile, passion drained from her bones, leaving behind cold, harsh reason.

How could she let him do this to her? How could she *help* him to do this to her? He had stolen her! She was his prisoner, denied even the right to walk free in the sunshine, and he was telling her ugly lies about her own father and now here she was, in his bed, letting him use the weakness he'd found within her, use this terrible passion she had not even known existed, to make her not just his captive but his ally. She would become not only his hostage but her own, a hostage to her own sexuality.

'Let go of me!'

She slammed her hands against his shoulders and he drew back instantly.

'You're clever,' she said bitterly, 'oh, yes, you're very clever! I have to hand you that, Khalil.' She edged upwards against the pillows, her eyes locked with his. 'If you get me to sleep with you, you can't lose! You'll have me as a playmate so long as I'm here and as an insurance policy after I'm gone.'

He rose to his full height and stared at her. 'What the devil are you talking about?'

'I suppose you're right.' Joanna swung her legs to the floor and stood up. 'It would take a stronger woman than me to watch them hang the man she'd willingly gone to bed with!'

'That's nonsense!'

'Everything my father said about you is true, especially the part about you being a—a barbarian who wants to keep his stranglehold on his pathetic little fiefdom!'

She thought, for an instant, he would strike her. The bones of face showed white through his tan, and his eyes grew dark as stones. She could see him collecting himself, marshalling control of his emotions, and finally he spun on his heels, stalked to the door, and yanked it open. A man standing guard outside snapped to attention. Khalil spat a command at him, and the man nodded.

He looked at Joanna. 'Come,' he said, his voice hard as ice.

'You needn't throw me out.' She fought the desire to

run and instead strolled casually to where he stood. 'I'm more than eager to leave.'

'I'm sure you are.' He put his hand in the small of her back and shoved her none too gently into the hall. 'My man will keep you company while you wait.'

'Charming. But what am I to wait for?'

Khalil smiled coldly. 'Smile, Joanna,' he said. 'Your days as a cloistered prisoner are about to come to an end.'

CHAPTER NINE

JOANNA stood in the corridor outside Khalil's bedroom and tried to look as if she found nothing unusual in being guarded by a man wearing a head-dress, a long robe, and a ferocious scowl.

Was she really going to be set free? It was dangerous to let herself believe she was—but what else could he have meant when he'd said she'd been a prisoner too long? Or something like that; she'd been so stunned by the suddenness of his declaration that she wasn't quite sure exactly what it was he'd said except to know that, for the first time since he'd carried her off, she felt a stir of hope.

It would be wonderful to be free, to be away from this awful place and this terrible man. He'd stolen her and now he was feeding her lies, keeping her locked up and under guard—she'd never forgive him for that or for the other indignities he'd heaped on her. Taking her in his arms, kissing her when the last thing she'd ever want were his kisses, sparking a wild passion in her blood that she'd never before known...

'Are you ready, Joanna?'

She spun around. Khalil stood in the open doorway, seeming to fill it. He wore an open-throated white shirt and black, snug-fitting trousers tucked into riding boots. A white cloak was thrown over his shoulders.

'Oh, yes,' she said with a dazzling smile. 'All I have to do is pack my suitcases and—'

'I have no time for games,' he growled.

'No. I'm sure you don't. I'm the only one around here with time on my hands.'

He smiled tightly. 'Perhaps we should discuss the goats and chickens again.'

'Perhaps we should discuss the fact that I'm not accustomed to sitting on my hands all day.'

'Had you shown me you could behave yourself, I intended to give you greater freedom.'

'Had I shown you I could...' Joanna tossed back her head. 'I'm not Lilia, Khalil. You can't make me do your bidding by promising me a reward.'

His eyes narrowed. 'Would you prefer that I threaten you?'

'I would prefer,' she said coldly, 'that you treat me with dignity.'

'You mean, you would prefer that I treat you as if we were in your world, that I dance attendance upon you and meet your every whim with a smile?'

'Is that how you think I live my life? Like some pampered princess in a fairy-tale?'

'Don't be silly. I know better.' Khalil folded his arms over his chest. 'You go to your office at Bennettco every day and put in long, gruelling hours, working side by side with your father.' He smiled grimly. 'That's what you wanted me to believe, isn't it?'

Joanna flushed. What was the sense in pretending? 'I would have gladly put in twenty-four-hour days at the office,' she said. 'But my father is as much of a male chauvinist as you are!'

'Another crime to add to my list.' Khalil turned as one of his men came hurrying down the hall. 'Ah,' he said, taking a silver-trimmed white cloak from his hands, 'you've brought it. Thank you, Ahmed.' He held it out to Joanna. 'Put this on.'

She eyed the garment with scorn. 'I'm not one of your

women. You can't wrap me up like a Christmas package!'

Khalil sighed wearily. 'I would not dream of making a Christmas package of you. You are far too prickly a gift to give anyone.'

'Good. Then you can forget about me wearing that thing.'

He stepped forward and draped the cloak about her rigid figure, drawing the hood up and over her bright auburn hair.

'You will wear it,' he said.

Joanna glared at him. 'Why?'

Khalil put his hand in the small of her back and pushed her gently ahead of him along the corridor.

'For no more devious reason than your comfort. It's cool in the mountains this time of year.' He looked at her and shook his head. 'Why must you always search for hidden meanings?'

'Dammit!' She shrugged free of his hand and swung towards him, her mouth trembling with anger. 'Anyone listening to you would think you've treated me with honesty and respect from the moment we met!'

His eyes darkened. 'I've dealt with you as you deserved.'

'Would you respect me more if I'd spent my life herding goats?'

To her surprise, a grin spread across his face. 'Are we back to that? It might be a good idea for me to have you spend the day with the goat-herders!'

'I'd rather spend it with Lilia,' she snapped. 'That poor little girl seems almost as miserable as I am.'

Khalil's smile vanished. 'I try my best to make her happy,' he said stiffly.

'She's very lonely.'

'Do you think I don't know this?' His mouth tightened. 'I realise that she could use companionship—but it never occurred to me that you would enjoy spending time with her.'

'No. Why would it, considering that you're so certain you know all there is to know about me? You accused *me* of trying to categorise *you*, but you've done the same thing to me from the instant we met!'

'I know what I see.'

'Really. Then I suppose you know that I like children very much, that for a while, when I was at school, I thought of studying to be a teacher.'

'You?' He smiled again. 'A teacher?'

'That's right. Me, a teacher. And I'd have been a good one, too.'

'What stopped you, then?'

Joanna hesitated. 'My father didn't approve.'

'And you changed your course of study, because of that?' Khalil's smile was open this time, and genuine. 'That's hard to believe.'

'I changed it because…' She hesitated again, uncertain of why she was telling him something she'd never told anyone. 'I thought he disapproved of teaching because he wanted me to come into Bennettco.'

'But he didn't,' Khalil said softly.

Joanna shook her head. 'No. He—he just wanted me to—to—'

'He wanted you to be what I have accused you of being: a handsome accessory for a man to wear proudly on his arm.'

'Yes!'

Her head came up sharply; she was more than ready to tell him what she thought of such an attitude. But he wasn't looking at her with derision; what she saw in his eyes was nothing she understood.

'Perhaps we see only what we wish to see,' he said after a moment.

It was a strange thing for him to have said, Joanna thought. She wanted to ask him what he'd meant, but he put his arm lightly around her shoulders and they stepped out into bright sunshine. Ahead, two horses stood waiting in the cobblestoned courtyard. She recognised Najib instantly. The big stallion was pawing impatiently at the ground. But there was another horse standing beside him, a smaller, more delicate one, as white as Najib was black. Her bridle was hung with tiny silver bells, and her saddle was a masterwork of finely tooled leather.

'This is Sidana,' Khalil said, gently stroking the mare's long nose. He smiled. 'She is gentle, although even she may object if you mount from the wrong side. I promise you that she will take us safely to our destination and then back.'

Joanna looked at him. 'You're not setting me free, are you?' she said, with a sinking heart.

He shook his head. 'I am not.'

She nodded. 'I see.'

'No,' Khalil said fiercely, 'you do not see! But you will. After today, you will not believe the lies you have been told by your father.'

'What lies will I believe, then? Yours?'

The muscle in his jaw knotted with anger. 'Go on,' he said tightly, 'get on the horse.'

'This is pointless! If you really think I'm dumb enough to fall for some charade you've set up in my honour—'

'Get into the saddle, Joanna—or I'll lift you on to Najib's back and you will ride with me!'

Ride with him? Feel his arms around her, his heart beating against her back? Feel his breath warm at her temple, his thighs hard as they enclosed hers? Colour flamed in her cheeks.

'I'd sooner ride with the devil,' she muttered, and she grabbed for the pommel, stabbed her foot into the stirrup, and climbed into the saddle.

'All right?' She nodded and Khalil sprang on to Najib's back in one fluid motion. 'Hold the reins loosely but firmly, so the mare knows you're in command. You'll have no problem with her. She is sweet-tempered and obedient, and very well trained.'

'The perfect female,' Joanna said sweetly as they started from the courtyard. Behind them, two of Khalil's men and their horses fell into place at a slight distance.

Khalil laughed. 'I never thought of it that way, but now that you point it out, I suppose she is.'

'You still haven't told me where we're going.'

'You'll know the place when you see it.'

'I've no idea what that's supposed to mean.'

Khalil smiled. 'Why don't you relax, Joanna? You've complained about being cooped up—well, here's your chance to enjoy some fresh air and new sights. Look around you, and enjoy this beautiful day.'

He was right, she thought grudgingly. It was, indeed, a beautiful day. The dark green mountains pierced a sky so blue and so bright it almost hurt the eyes. It was spring, and wild flowers were beginning to carpet the gentler slopes, filling the air with their sweetness.

It was lovely here. Joanna thought of New York and Dallas, of crowded city streets thronged with people and automobiles. All of it seemed far, far away. How easy it would be to be happy in a place like this, she thought suddenly. Unbidden, her gaze flew to the man riding at her side.

What was wrong with her? Here she was, being taken out on a tether and thinking nonsensical thoughts, while somewhere her father must be agonising over her welfare.

'Listen,' she said, glaring at him, 'if you think taking me to some—some staged bit of theatre will turn my head around…'

'There is the stage, Joanna, and the players.' Khalil reached out and caught the reins of her horse. 'An hour from now, you can tell me what you think of the production.'

Before she could speak, he tapped his heels into Najib's flanks and both horses shot forward. Joanna clung to the mare's reins, too intent on what she saw to be afraid of the sudden swift motion.

They were entering a town, a real one, with houses and narrow streets. Not even Khalil could have had this place created overnight, she thought wildly as he brought their horses to a stop.

'Would you like to get down and walk around, Joanna?'

She started. Khalil had dismounted. He was standing beside the mare, looking up at her, his face as expressionless as a mask.

She nodded, too bemused to offer any objection when he held up his arms. She went into them readily, her hands light on his shoulders to steady herself, and he eased her gently to the ground.

'What is this place?' she asked.

'It is Adaba. Our central marketplace.' He took her arm and they set off along the narrow street, his two men trailing behind them. 'I thought you might like to see some of my downtrodden subjects with your own eyes.'

She wanted to make a clever retort but already her gaze was moving towards the market ahead. People were selling things and buying things, and she could hear bursts of chatter and laughter. It looked very much like the outdoor markets that flourished in lower Manhattan. People were busy. And happy. But—but…

'Observe the way my people cringe at the sight of me,' Khalil murmured.

In fact, most of the people didn't seem to notice him or, if they did, they paused in their transactions only long enough to smile and touch their foreheads.

'What did you do,' Joanna asked with a chill smile, 'tell them you'd chop off their heads if they threw themselves at your feet this one time?'

His hand tightened on her arm. 'Why be so uncreative, Joanna? Perhaps I threatened to skin them alive if they didn't behave.'

'No doubt!'

A woman came hurrying up to them. She touched her hand to her forehead but Khalil stopped her, put his arm around her shoulders, and kissed her cheek. The woman glanced shyly at Joanna and said something that made him laugh before she melted away into the crowd.

Joanna tried unsuccessfully to wrench her arm from his grasp. 'What's so funny?' she demanded. 'Or does the sight of a captive always rate a chuckle in this crowd?'

Khalil grinned. 'She wanted to assure me that even though your eyes are an interesting colour, she still prefers the blue of mine.'

'A fan,' Joanna said drily. 'How wonderful. Did she want your autograph, too?'

'Her name is Cheva. She was my nurse, when I was a boy. She loved my English mother very much, and it always pleased her that I inherited her—'

Joanna stared at him. 'Your mother was English?'

He laughed. 'Close your mouth, Joanna. It is a warm day, and there are flies about. She was, yes.' His arm slipped to her waist as he led her deeper into the crowded marketplace. 'She was an archaeologist, come to Jandara on a dig. I know you would like me to think my barbarian father abducted her, but the truth is they met at an official function, fell in love, and were married ten days later.'

'And were they happy?'

'The barbarian and the Englishwoman?'

'No,' Joanna said quickly, 'I didn't mean—'

'They were very happy. Is that so difficult to believe?'

Joanna looked at him. 'I—I'm confused,' she whispered. 'I don't—I don't really know what to believe.'

His arm tightened around her. 'Perhaps you will know, by the afternoon's end.'

When the sun began dropping in the sky, they made their way back to the horses. By then, Joanna's head was spinning. Nothing was as she'd expected—and yet, in her heart, she knew that everything was as she'd begun to suspect it might be.

She didn't speak the language of Khalil's people, but it didn't matter. Many of them spoke English, especially the younger ones.

'It is an important language, the language of nations, Prince Khalil says, so we learn it,' a horse trader told her earnestly. 'We start young, when we first enter school.'

'Ah,' said Joanna. 'Only boys learn a language, then?'

'Is that how it is in your country?' the young man said, frowning. 'That only boys may learn?'

She stared at him. 'No. Of course not. Boys and girls both learn what they wish.'

'Here, too.' He smiled. 'I am glad to hear that America believes in educating its women.'

Khalil laughed. 'I assure you,' he said, clapping the young man on the shoulder, 'it does!'

At a stall where fresh fruits lay heaped in abundance, a group of young women stood chatting.

'It must be difficult,' Joanna said to one of them, 'to raise a family here, so far from modern conveniences.'

The young woman nodded. 'It is not simple.'

Joanna's brows arched as she glanced at Khalil, who stood several feet away, lounging against a stall.

'Why don't you leave, then?' she said. Her voice fell in pitch. 'Is it because Prince Khalil will not permit it?'

The young woman repeated Joanna's words to her friends, who covered their mouths and laughed.

'We are free to leave, if we choose,' she said, turning back to Joanna. 'But only a fool would wish to live in the south, under the rule of Abu. Surely, you know this.'

Joanna stared at the woman. *I don't know* what *I know*, she wanted to say... But she only smiled.

'Thank you for talking with me,' she said.

She was silent when Khalil took her hand and drew her forward along the dusty street.

'Well, Joanna?' he asked softly. 'Have you seen reality?'

'It's been a long day, Khalil. I'm tired. Can we go back now, please?'

He looked at her, then nodded. 'As you wish.'

They made their way to where the horses waited. Joanna walked to the mare's side and put her hand on the animal's neck. She closed her eyes and pressed her forehead lightly against the coarse hair.

'Joanna.' Khalil's voice was gentle and so was the hand he placed on her shoulder. He said her name again but she didn't answer. After a moment, he spoke to his men. One of them reached for the mare's reins, and they led her away.

Khalil clasped Joanna's waist and lifted her on to the back of the stallion, then swung into the saddle behind her. His arms went around her as he gathered the reins into his hands, but she didn't protest. A terrible languor had crept over her.

The town fell behind them as they rode slowly towards the mountains. Finally, in a field of wild flowers, Khalil reined in the horse and slid to the ground. He looked at Joanna and held up his arms. She hesitated, then put her hands on his shoulders and dropped lightly to the ground.

'What is wrong, Joanna?'

She bowed her head, not wanting him to see the sudden dampness she knew must be glinting on her lashes, but he framed her face in his hands and lifted it to him.

'Is the truth so awful to see?' he said softly.

She shook her head again. Had she seen the truth, or had she seen illusion? It was becoming harder and harder to tell.

'Then why are you crying, Joanna?'

'I'm not,' she said, while one small tear coursed down her cheek.

He smiled a little and caught it on his fingertip. 'What is this, if not a tear?'

She sighed as she stepped away from him. Slowly, she bent and plucked a daisy from the chorus nodding at her ankles. She lowered her face to it, inhaling its sweetness, and then she stared blindly into the distance, where the mountains rose towards the sky. At last, she turned to Khalil and said what she had not even wanted to think.

'You told me the truth when you said the price of my freedom would be my father's willingness to give up his deal with Abu, didn't you?'

He nodded. 'Yes.'

Joanna swallowed hard. 'And he's refused to do it, hasn't he?'

Khalil nodded again. 'I'm sorry,' he said in a low voice. 'The only reality I wished you to see was that of my people.'

'There are many different realities, Khalil. Perhaps— perhaps it's time I finally faced my own.'

'Joanna.' She lifted her head and the hood of her cloak fell back, revealing her pale oval face and the long, fiery spill of her hair. 'I am certain he thinks I will change my mind and send you back to him.'

'And will you?' Her eyes caught his. 'Will you send me back, even though you haven't gotten what you wanted from Bennettco?'

Khalil came closer to her and cupped her face in his hands. 'How can I send you back?' he said fiercely. 'How can I do that, Joanna?'

He couldn't. She was his pawn, his bargaining chip— and, knowing that, believing she was in the hands of a man he thought a bandit and a barbarian, her father was still reluctant to do the one thing that would free her, to give up a fortune in the earth for his daughter's release.

No. No! It couldn't be! Khalil was lying. He was lying about everything.

'If there's a shred of decency in you, you'll free me,' she said.

His eyes darkened. 'I told you, I cannot.'

'You've lied to me! You haven't really contacted my father—'

'Joanna!' He took her by the shoulders. 'Listen to me.'

'My father loves me,' she said, her mouth trembling.

'In his way, I'm sure he does. But—'

'There is no "but", Khalil. Whatever you showed me today was—it was interesting, but—'

'Interesting? What do you mean, "interesting"?'

'I mean, it's interesting to—to see a little backwater town where—where people aren't living in poverty and misery, and I suppose—I suppose it must be quite a salve to your ego, hearing them talk about how wonderful you are, but that's not the whole story. There's more to it.'

'Joanna, dammit! If you won't listen to me, listen to yourself! What you're saying makes no sense.'

'No!' She flung her hands over her ears. 'I won't listen! I won't!'

'You will listen,' he said fiercely, catching her wrists and forcing her hands to her sides. 'You will, because—because...' He looked into her eyes, and then he pulled her into his arms and his mouth fell on hers.

'Don't!' Joanna pushed against his chest. 'I hate you, Khalil!'

'Liar,' he whispered, catching her mouth with his again.

'You think you can solve everything this way,' she said, twisting her face away from him. 'You think you can silence me and—and make me believe things that aren't true!'

Khalil's arms tightened around her. 'The only truth that matters is this one, this hunger that has been between us since the night we met.'

'Don't try and make it sound romantic! We met because you were determined to make it impossible for Bennettco to conduct legitimate business, and—and then you—you kidnapped me! You carried me off on your plane and—'

'And desired you, even then.' He laughed huskily. 'A hundred years ago, I would have carried you off on the back of my horse.'

'Exactly!' Joanna thrust her hands against his shoulders. 'Your ancestors were barbarians, and you—'

'My ancestors knew what they wanted and took it.' He caught her hands in his and held them against his heart. 'As I want you now—as you want me.'

'No! That's not true! I despise you, Khalil, I—'

He kissed her again, his mouth moving softly against hers.

'Despise me all you will,' he whispered, 'but do not deny me—or yourself.'

He was wrong. She was not denying anything. She didn't want this, didn't want his mouth on hers or his hand moving against her skin...

No. No, she didn't. She didn't...

Oh, God! With a desperate cry, Joanna threw her arms around Khalil's neck. He whispered her name and then his open mouth met hers in a wild kiss. His fingers speared into her hair as they sank to the ground and she fell back among the flowers, taking him with her. Khalil groaned and kissed her again and again, his mouth hot against hers.

It was as if Joanna were being swept along in a fever of desire. Her fingers flew to the neck of his jellaba, burrowed beneath his open-throated shirt. She had to touch his skin, had to feel its heat against hers or surely she would die.

Khalil lifted her to him, curving her soft body into the hardness of his. He kissed her deeply, crushing her mouth under his until she knew the taste of him would be a part of her forever.

He knelt and drew her up with him. 'Joanna,' he whispered as he slipped the white cloak and then her cotton shirt from her body. The air was cool against her skin, but his mouth and hands were hot. She caught her breath as he cupped her breasts and when he bent and kissed the nipples, she cried out in pleasure.

Khalil lowered her gently to the grass, then drew back.

'No,' she cried, reaching out to him—but he had only left her so he could strip off his jellaba and then his shirt. How beautiful he was! His skin was the colour of honey, his muscles hard and clearly defined. He was male perfection, and he was hers.

'Touch me,' he whispered, taking her hands in his and bringing them to his chest.

She gasped at the feel of his skin, hot from the sun and from desire.

'Joanna, my beautiful Joanna.' He came down beside her and stroked his fingers along her skin, over the curve of her breasts, down over the slight arch of her belly. 'How I want you,' he whispered, 'how I have wanted you from the moment I saw you.'

She reached up and clasped his head, brought his mouth to hers and kissed him, and then she smiled.

'How much do you want me?' she whispered.

A dark flush rose along his cheeks. He clasped her hand, brought it to his mouth and bit lightly at the soft skin below her thumb, then drew it slowly down his body, to where his aroused flesh pressed against his trousers. Her lashes fluttered to her cheeks as he cupped her hand over him. His erection seemed to pulse through the cloth, the heat of it burning her palm like flame.

'That much,' he said thickly. He bent to her and kissed her, his tongue moving within her mouth as she knew his body would soon move within hers.

A primitive rush of joy and desire swept through her. This was what she wanted, what she'd wanted from the start. Khalil, in her arms. Khalil, kissing her and touching her and bearing her down, down into the soft, sweet grass...

…Khalil, her captor. Her keeper. He had spoken of reality, and of truth, and yet wasn't that the one truth that mattered? She wasn't here of her own free will, she was here because one man refused to bargain for her freedom and another refused to grant it—and now she was in the arms of the man who'd caused the conflict, behaving as he'd predicted she would from the first night he'd met her.

With a cry, Joanna shoved free of Khalil's arms and scrambled to her feet, snatching up her cloak and whipping it around her, trembling with rage at him, at her father, but most of all, at herself. Khalil rose too, his eyes blurred with desire, and held out his hand.

'Joanna,' he whispered, 'what is it?'

'Who in hell do you think you are?' she said shakily. 'Treating me like—like one of your slave girls!'

His brows knotted together. 'What?'

'I've read a lot of stuff about women and—and this kind of sex,' she said, her words rushing together, 'about—about rape fantasies, but—but I never believed any of it, not for a minute, until—'

'Stop it!' Khalil's mouth twisted as he took a step towards her. 'You're talking nonsense.'

'I'm talking reality. Aren't you the one who's big on that?' Her breath was coming fast, in hard little gasps; she felt as if she'd been running for her life and it occurred to her that, in some strange way, she had been. 'I don't know how you set up today's performance in Adaba, my lord Khalil, but it doesn't matter. The point is, I've seen through it. Sam was right. You *are* a savage, and you always will be!'

He stepped forward swiftly and she flinched back, determined to show him no fear but unable to stop herself from reacting to the terrible darkness in his eyes.

'Get on the horse,' he said softly, in a voice that sent

a shudder along her spine. 'Sit still and say nothing until we reach the palace.'

Joanna tossed her head. 'Certainly, my lord. Of course, my lord. Your every wish is my—'

She gasped as his hands closed on her shoulders.

'Push me, Joanna,' he growled. 'Push me, and you'll find out exactly how savage I can be.'

Her lips parted, preparatory to another quick rejoinder, but then she looked into his eyes and saw the coldness in them. The Hawk of the North, she thought, and a shudder went through her.

'That's right,' he said, very softly. 'I could do anything to you now, and no one—no one!—would ever call me to task for it. Now, turn around, get on the horse, and obey my every order. If you can do that, perhaps you'll get back to the palace safely.'

Joanna clamped her lips together defiantly, swung away from him, and did as he'd commanded. But as he swung into the saddle behind her and jabbed his heels hard into Najib's flanks, a little part of her wondered if she'd ever really be safe again.

CHAPTER TEN

JOANNA paced the confines of her room. Twenty paces
to one wall, fifteen to the other, then back again. After
a week, she knew the dimensions as well as she knew
those of the garden, of the palace grounds, of Khalil's
library. And she knew, too, that she would never again
look at a caged beast without feeling a swift pang of
compassion.

Not that she was being mistreated. Never that. If anything, the circumstances of her captivity had improved
since that day in the meadow. Rachelle had brought her
the news the following morning.

'You may walk with me where you wish, Joanna,'
she'd said with a smile, 'and you may use my lord's
library at will.'

Joanna's lips tightened. Perhaps Khalil had thought he
could convince her he wasn't the savage she'd called
him by allowing her to read his books and stroll the
grounds. But he was wrong. She knew him for what he
was, and nothing would ever change that now. The reality he'd wanted her to see wasn't in Adaba, it was here,
in the way he kept her captive, in the way Rachelle
turned pale each time Joanna dared to speak of her lord
and master as the scoundrel he was.

Adaba! Joanna laughed bitterly. The dog and pony
show that had been staged there only proved just how
much power Khalil really wielded. Adaba had been a
stage set! Oh, the thriving marketplace had probably
been real enough—but the idiotically happy villagers
had been straight out of Disneyworld!

Had Khalil bought their compliance with threats? Had he bribed them with promises? Or were the people who'd been so artfully displayed for her benefit simply among the worshipful followers that inexplicably collected around every tyrant the world had ever known, from Attila the Hun straight through to Josef Stalin?

Joanna kicked her discarded shoes out of the way and stalked the length of the room again, remembering how she'd awakened here that first morning, coming hazily out of a dream in which her father had been so busy moving a piece around a game-board that he hadn't noticed the horseman riding down on her.

'Stupid,' she muttered, flinging back her head. 'You were so stupid, Joanna!'

Her father wasn't blind to what was happening to her. He just didn't care!

No. No, that was putting things too harshly. Her father cared. It was just that he wasn't worried about her being held here. Why should he? He'd figured what she should have realised all along, that although Khalil had not hesitated to abduct her he wouldn't harm her, no matter what he threatened. He needed her to get what he wanted.

Sam had understood from day one. He had lots of time to wheel and deal and see if he couldn't come up with a way to secure her release without giving up the lucrative contract he'd worked so hard to get. So what if she'd been sitting here, docile as a clam, waiting to be rescued while Khalil spun a web of confusion around her!

Joanna spun towards the mirror on the far wall and stared at her reflection. The woman in the mirror looked well. Her cheeks had taken on a pink glow from the hours she spent in the garden. The sun had burnished her hair, and her eyes gleamed brightly.

'It is our mountain air that brings such a glow,' Rachelle had said just this morning.

Joanna smiled coldly. The girl was almost pitiably naïve. What her eyes glowed with was rage—and yet, for
all her anger, she'd been able to do nothing to alter
things.

But that was about to change. After days of scheming,
she had finally come up with an idea that might work.

'With an idea that *will* work,' she whispered to her
reflection.

God, it had to!

She took a deep breath. There was no reason to wait
another minute. It was time.

Determinedly, she stabbed her feet into her shoes, then
stalked to the mirror again. She peered into the glass and
took half a dozen slow, deep breaths. Good. Now to
relax her features. Yes. That was the way. She looked
wistful, almost forlorn. Now a little tilt of the head. Not
too much. Just enough to… OK. That was fine.

'It's now or never,' she said softly, and then she
turned and walked to the door.

The guard in the corridor snapped to attention the instant the door swung open.

'*Ya?*'

Joanna gave him what she hoped was a tremulous
smile. 'I should like to see the Prince.'

His brow furrowed and he shook his head.

'The Prince,' she said. 'Khalil.'

'Dee Prinz?'

'Khalil. Yes. I must speak with him.'

'Rachelle, *ya?*'

'No. I don't want to see Rachelle. I want to see your
Prince.'

'Prinz. *Ya.* Rachelle.'

'Oh, for heaven's sake,' Joanna snapped, her modest
smile gone in a flash, 'if everyone here speaks English,
what stroke of bad luck put *you* at my door?'

She elbowed past the man before he had time to react and began marching down the corridor. His voice called after her, rising in intensity, and then she heard the thud of his footfalls following her. His hand closed none too gently on her shoulder.

'Let go of me, you ape,' she snarled. 'Let go, or I'll kick you in the—'

'What is going on here?'

Joanna and the guard both swung towards the sound of that steely voice. Khalil stood in the doorway of a room just beyond them, his hands on his hips, his expression grim.

The guard began babbling an explanation, but Joanna cut it short.

'Tell your Dobermann to let go of me,' she said.

Khalil's brows rose a little, but he barked out a command and the man released her.

'Now, Joanna, suppose you tell me what you are doing here.'

'I have to talk to you,' she said stiffly. 'I told this—this creature that, but he didn't understand me.'

'Mustafa is neither an ape, a dog, nor a creature. It is hardly his fault he doesn't speak your tongue. He was told to send for Rachelle if you needed something.'

'Rachelle can't help me. Only you can do that.'

'I am busy.'

'I'm sure you are. But—'

'Speak with Rachelle,' he said as he stepped back inside the room. 'She will convey your message to—'

'Wait!' Joanna sprang forward and thrust her hand against the door. The guard sprang forward too, clasping her arm and growling a warning, and almost too late she remembered that she'd come here with every intention of playing the reserved, unhappy maiden. 'Please,' she murmured softly, and turned her face up to Khalil's with a desperation that made her stomach threaten to give up her breakfast.

But it worked. She could see the faintest softening along the hard, set line of his mouth. He stared at her for a few seconds and then he waved his hand at Mustafa, who let her go instantly.

'I will give you five minutes, Joanna.'

She nodded as he opened the door and motioned her past him. She glanced around curiously. This was his den, she thought, or—

'This is my office.'

She swung around. Khalil was standing at the closed door, looking at her.

'I didn't realise I'd spoken aloud.'

'You didn't.' Frowning, he walked quickly to a handsome old desk that stood before the window. 'But I knew you must be wondering what possible use a savage could have for a room such as this, so I decided to save you the trouble of asking.'

'I didn't come here to quarrel, Khalil.'

'Why did you come here, then?' He pushed aside a stack of papers and leaned back against the desk, his eyes cool and steady on hers. 'If it is to ask if I have had any word from your father, I have not.'

'No.' She touched the tip of her tongue to her lips. 'No, I—I didn't come for that, either.'

'What is it, then?' He frowned, pushed back the sleeve of his shirt, and looked at his watch. 'I have much to do, and little time to spare.'

You arrogant s.o.b., Joanna thought. You impossible, imperious bastard...

'Well? What was so important that you saw it necessary to push past my man and disgrace him?'

She ached to tell him that it was she who had been disgraced, from the minute she'd walked into the Oasis

Restaurant almost a week ago. But she had a plan, and she was going to make it work.

'I've been thinking about something we touched on the day you took me to Adaba—'

'Nothing that happened that day is worth discussion,' he said, his face hardening. He leaned away from the desk. 'Now, if that's all—'

'I told you that I was bored, sitting around and doing nothing,' Joanna said quickly. He looked at her, and she forced herself to smile politely. 'Surely, you can understand that.'

'I have granted you the freedom of the grounds,' he said. 'And the use of my library.'

'Oh, yes. You've been very generous.'

His eyes narrowed, and Joanna groaned inwardly. Don't overdo it, she told herself. The man may be arrogant, but he's not a fool.

'Then what more do you want of me?' His look hardened. 'If you have come to ask to spend time with Lilia, I must tell you that I have changed my mind about permitting it. I do not think you would be a good influence on her.'

Joanna's chin lifted. 'No,' she said evenly, 'of course not. She's much better off in your company.'

His eyes flashed to hers and she smiled pleasantly. After a moment, he nodded stiffly towards the shelves that lined the walls.

'There are more books here, but I doubt if they would be to your liking. However, if you wish, I will tell Rachelle to bring you—'

'Thank you. But I've enough to read. I need to do something active.'

'Rachelle takes you walking each afternoon.'

Like a pet dog on a leash, she thought. 'Yes,' she said evenly, 'she does. But I need more activity than that.'

His lips drew back from his teeth. 'I wish I could help you, but, unfortunately, we haven't much to offer in the way of parties or discos.'

'Exercise,' she said, hoping he couldn't hear the sharp edge of anger in her voice. She gave him another stiff smile. 'That's what I'm talking about. I'm not used to sitting around, Khalil. When my father and I are in New York, I work out at a gym.'

'I know this will astound you,' he said, his eyes cold, 'but somehow I've not got around to having a Nautilus machine installed.'

Oh, how pompous he was, how arrogant...

'I didn't think you would have,' she said pleasantly.

'Well, then—'

'When my father and I are on our ranch outside Dallas, I ride.'

'Ride?' he said, his brows angling up in his otherwise expressionless face.

'Yes. We have horses, and—'

'You?' He laughed. 'On a horse?'

'What's so funny?' she said, the carefully drawn smile slipping from her face.

Khalil shook his head. 'Nothing much. I was just remembering how you couldn't tell the front of my horse from the rear.'

'I was upset.'

'Not as upset as Najib,' he said, chuckling. 'He must have thought he was—'

'I don't give a damn what that miserable black beast thought!' Joanna slammed her hands on her hips. 'He's not a horse, he's—he's a creature come straight out of a nightmare.'

'Like his owner,' Khalil said, very pleasantly.

'Yes! Exactly like...' She stared at him, horrified. 'No,' she said quickly. 'No, I didn't mean—'

'Stop this farce, Joanna!' His smile vanished; the stony look settled on his face again and he rose to his full height and glared at her. 'I am not for a moment going to believe that you have suddenly turned into a sweet-tempered lamb when we both know that what you are is a sharp-toothed vixen. Tell me what it is you want, and be quick about it.'

Joanna nodded. 'All right. I was quite serious when I said I was going crazy with boredom and just as serious when I said I like to ride. Don't look at me that way, Khalil! I was too upset the night you brought me here to think straight, about getting on and off your horse or anything else.'

He nodded curtly. 'Perhaps.'

'It's the truth! I didn't have any trouble the other day, did I? I didn't need you to tell me how to handle the mare.'

He scowled. 'She is docile.'

'I can ride, I tell you. And I came here to ask you to let me ride an hour a day, to—'

'It is out of the question.'

'Why?' Joanna folded her hands in front of her so he wouldn't see them tremble. If he denied her this... 'Why?' she repeated. 'I do know how! If you don't be-lieve me, you can take me out yourself the first time, you can watch me—'

'No.' He swung away from her so she couldn't see his face and walked around the desk. 'I'm much too busy to waste time in your company, Joanna.'

The sharp words knifed into her breast, although surely what she felt was anger at his insolence, not pain at his dismissal.

'I wouldn't expect you to.'

He looked at her and smiled. 'Do you really think me so stupid, that I would let you ride by yourself?'

'What I thought was that you could let me ride with an escort.'

'It's impossible.' He sat down behind the desk, bent over some papers, and began rifling through them. 'Now, if you're done—'

'Why is it impossible?'

Khalil looked up. 'Because I said it was.'

'You could let me ride the mare—heaven knows the only thing she'd do is plod along obediently beside my guard's horse.'

'Joanna—'

Desperation made her do what she'd promised herself she would never give him the satisfaction of doing. Her eyes grew shiny with unshed tears, her mouth trembled, and when she spoke, her voice did, too.

'Please,' she whispered, 'Khalil, please! I'll—I'll die if I have to sit around like a caged bird.'

Her words drifted away and she fell silent, hating herself for having thrown herself on his mercy, hating herself even more for the real wave of despair that suddenly threatened to overwhelm her. Why was looking at him, seeing that coldness in his eyes, so agonising?

She swung away. 'I'm sorry I've wasted your time.'

His chair scraped against the floor. She heard the sound of his footsteps coming towards her, felt the weight of his hands on her shoulders.

'Joanna.' He turned her towards him. 'Look at me.' When she did, he frowned down at her. 'Is it so terrible here for you?'

'Of course it is. How do you think it feels to be a captive?'

'Yes.' His voice was low. 'That is what you are, Joanna. My captive.'

Their eyes met. A soft sound rose in Joanna's throat

as she looked into the dark blue depths of his eyes. He was right. She was his captive. She belonged to him.

There was a sudden tension in the room. Her heart began to race. She remembered how he'd kissed her in the meadow, how he'd drawn her down into the soft, sweet grass, how the heat of his mouth and the heat of the sun had seemed the same...

She stepped back before he could reach for her. 'I know what I am.' Her voice was cool and steady, although her heart was still pounding. 'And if you are half the great humanitarian you claim to be, I think it's time you considered my feelings and not just your own.'

Khalil's mouth thinned. 'Is that what you think this is about?'

'I've no wish to argue the issue, Khalil. I came to ask a favour of you. Will you let me ride, or won't you?'

Long seconds passed. Then he moved past her, marched to the door, and wrenched it open. The guard stepped forward, and Khalil barked a series of orders. When he finished, he looked at Joanna.

'It is done.'

She could hardly draw breath. 'You mean—you mean, you've given permission for me to ride?'

'Once daily, and only in the company of two of my men.' His face turned stern. 'I will be away the next few days, Joanna. My men will guard you well and keep you safe.'

'They'll make sure I don't run away, you mean.'

His expression didn't change. 'I must have your word that you will never try to slip away from them.' When she hesitated, he closed the slight distance between them and clasped her shoulders. 'Your word, Joanna! Or I will not permit you to ride.'

Joanna bit down lightly on her bottom lip. What did

it matter if she lied? She wasn't his guest, she was here against her will!

'You have it,' she said.

She smiled faintly, then made her way past him and out of the door.

'Do you speak English?' Khalil heard her say to the guard, and when the man answered that he did, Joanna nodded. 'We will go to the stables,' she said, as if she had spent her entire life giving orders to men with fierce faces and flowing robes.

Despite himself, Khalil smiled as he walked slowly to the window. They were out in the sunshine now, Joanna and the guard. Another of his men joined them so that they flanked her. They were big men, better than six feet tall, and she was a woman of average height made smaller looking by fragile bone structure. Yet, in some strange way, she looked every bit their equal, if not physically then surely in determination.

And in courage. Sighing, he turned and sat down slowly at his desk. She was not quite what he'd thought she was, this Joanna Bennett. Khalil frowned and picked up his pen. It would be good when her fool of a father came to his senses and agreed to do that which had to be done. His people would be safe, Abu would take a step back, and Joanna—she would go back to the pretty world in which she belonged. He would forget her in an instant…

Certainly he would.

The pen dropped from his fingers. It seemed a long time until he picked it up again and bent over the papers strewn across his desk.

Joanna's guard seemed confused early the next morning when she opened her bedroom door and stepped out into the hall.

'I'm going horseback riding,' she said as she pushed past him and strode briskly down the corridor. She knew he couldn't understand her; knew too that she wasn't supposed to simply make her announcement and walk out, but it was all part of the painfully simple plan she'd hatched.

Pathetically simple was more like it, although now that she knew Khalil would be absent from the palace for a few days the odds of the plan working had improved. Still, everything would have to fall into place at once, if she were to make good her escape. It was why this initial attempt had to be done just this way.

Would the guard stop her?

He wouldn't, she thought with fierce exultation. He'd obviously been told she'd been granted a new privilege and now he was torn between that knowledge and whatever it was he was supposed to do next, perhaps notify the stable boy to saddle the mare, perhaps notify the men who were to accompany her that she was ready to ride.

At the door, she glanced over her shoulder. He'd finally started after her, but that was unimportant.

All that mattered was that he had let her get past him.

The next morning, she opened her door at the same hour. The guard was waiting, along with the men who'd ridden with her the prior day.

Joanna smiled. 'Good morning,' she said pleasantly. 'I was hoping Rachelle was here, with my breakfast.' She made a show of peering up and down the corridor. 'Not yet? Well, that's all right.' Still smiling, she stepped back into her room and shut the door.

At two in the afternoon, she repeated the performance of yesterday, pulling open the door, stepping past the surprised—and solitary—guard, and marching to the door. After a bewildered pause, he went trotting off in the other direction, looking, she was sure, for the men who were to ride with her.

She reached the stables first and caught the stable boy short. He was lying in an empty stall, dozing, and she had to clear her throat half a dozen times before he heard her.

Shamefaced, he sprang to his feet and said something in an apologetic tone.

Joanna smiled at him and pointed towards the mare. By the time the men who were to ride with her came scuttling into the stable, Sidana was saddled and ready.

The third day, she made her move in late morning. No one seemed too surprised this time; her erratic pattern had become the norm. That was what she'd counted on, and Khalil's absence only made things easier. Even if her guards had thought to report her, who would they have reported her to?

Besides, she was careful not to arouse suspicion. Each time, she waited politely for the men to catch up to her at the stables and once they were on their way, she made a point of not seeming to be anything but a clumsy rider.

At lunchtime that third day, she took the fresh grapes and nuts from her plate, along with the slices of bread that always accompanied her meal, and stashed them inside the deep pocket of the hooded robe Khalil had given her the day he'd taken her to Adaba.

'You ate well today, Joanna,' Rachelle said with a pleased smile, when she came to collect the lunch tray.

Joanna nodded. 'Everything was delicious. The grapes and nuts, especially, were wonderful!'

The girl's smile grew. 'I am glad you liked them. I shall make it a point to bring you more, for a snack.'

Joanna felt a twinge of guilt, but then she reminded herself that Rachelle, too, was her gaoler, the same as Khalil.

She smiled brightly. 'I'd like that.'

The snack went into the robe's pocket, too, along with the bread, cake, and raisins from dinner. It wasn't much, but it would have to do. She had no idea how long it would take her to reach the south, and freedom, but tomorrow she was going to make her break.

The next morning, well before breakfast, Joanna dressed, put on her hooded robe, then flung open her door. A guard she'd never before set eyes on stepped in front of her.

'Good morning,' she sang out and started past him.

The guard moved quickly into her path. He didn't have to speak. His body language said it all.

Joanna's heart pounded harder. 'Out of my way, please,' she said, dodging to the right. But he dodged, too, blocking the corridor. She faced him squarely, her back rigid with displeasure. 'I am going riding,' she said. When he didn't move, she repeated the words, more loudly and more slowly. 'I—am—going—riding. Do you hear me? Step aside, man!'

She thrust out her hand. It landed on his chest, a steel wall under the press of her palm, but he didn't move an inch. Joanna drew herself up.

'Get out of my way, you fool! I have the Prince's permission to ride. I'm going to the stables. Dammit, are you deaf?'

'What's the matter, Joanna?'

Joanna spun around. The child, Lilia, was standing behind her, her pretty face wearing a frown.

'Lilia.' Smiling, Joanna dropped to her knees and took the girl in her arms. 'How good to see you! I've missed you.'

Lilia smiled shyly. 'It is good to see you, too. I meant to ask Uncle Khalil if I might come to visit you, but he went away before I had the chance.' The little girl looked at the guard. 'Is Ali giving you trouble?'

It was hard not to laugh at the regal tone in the young voice. Joanna stood up, her hand on Lilia's shoulder, and nodded.

'Yes, he is. Your uncle gave permission for me to ride whenever I wished, but Ali doesn't seem aware of it.'

'Oh, you're just like me, Joanna,' Lilia said happily. 'I, too, like to ride just past dawn, when the earth smells sweet!' The girl stepped forward, a little figure accustomed to command. 'I will take care of Ali.'

Joanna held her breath while Lilia spoke. Ali's eyes darted to her. He didn't look happy, but, after a moment, he touched his hand to his forehead and stepped aside.

'Thank you,' Joanna said. Her knees felt weak with relief.

'May I ride with you?'

Joanna stared at the child. In her pleasure at seeing her, she'd all but forgotten her reason for this early morning ride. Now, guilt shot into her breast like a poisoned arrow.

'Oh, Lilia,' she said softly. 'I don't think—'

'Please?'

She glanced at the guard. The man was obviously uncertain of what to do next and suddenly she realised he'd yet to notify anyone that she was about to go riding.

Forgive me, Lilia, she thought.

'Yes, all right,' she said with a forced smile. She took the child's hand and they began walking, Lilia babbling happily and the guard trailing uncertainly in the rear. When they reached the stables, Lilia hesitated.

'I almost forgot,' she said. 'I may not ride without an escort. I will tell Ali to send for—'

'No,' Joanna said quickly. She bit her lip, then squatted down and framed the child's face in her hands. 'No,' she said softly, 'not yet. Why don't we have our horses saddled first? That way, we'll be ready to ride when the escort arrives.'

Lilia shrugged. 'As you wish, Joanna.'

The girl gave an order to the sleepy-eyed stable boy, who led out the white mare and a roan pony. The pony was saddled first, and then the boy turned to the mare. But he'd only got the bridle on when the guard, who'd grown increasingly restless, said something sharp-toned, spun on his heel, and trotted out of the door.

There was no time to spare. Joanna bent quickly, kissed Lilia's puzzled face.

'Forgive me, Lilia,' she whispered.

She straightened up, pushed the boy aside, and leaped on Sidana's back. Quickly, she gathered up the reins and kicked her heels hard into the mare's flanks. Before anyone had time to move, the horse was out of the door with Joanna bent low over its neck, riding hell-bent for freedom.

CHAPTER ELEVEN

By DUSK, Joanna was ready to admit what she'd known but refused to admit for hours. She was in trouble. She was hungry, thirsty, bone-weary from riding the mare without a saddle—and she was hopelessly, helplessly lost.

At first, she'd been so intent on making good her escape that she'd paid no attention to direction. All that had mattered was following the narrow dirt trail that led down the mountain to freedom.

She'd counted on the element of surprise to give her a decent head start and it had, at least five or six minutes. Eventually, though, she'd heard the pounding of hooves behind her. Glancing over her shoulder, she'd barely been able to make out the puffs of dust that marked the progress of the men riding after her. Even though she had the advantage, Joanna had known she could not outrun them for long.

Wildly, she'd glanced about, measuring her surroundings. There was a small copse of trees just off the trail. Desperate, she'd taken refuge in it only seconds before the riders had come thundering past. She'd been about to move out after them, seeing no choice but to play the risky game of following her followers, when she'd spied what had seemed to be a parallel path on the far side of the trees. Joanna had gritted her teeth and decided to go with the unknown.

For a while, her choice had seemed a good one. The path was narrower than the first and it twisted and turned like a snake, but it did lead down—only to suddenly peter out on the edge of a dizzying cliff.

A stone, dislodged by the mare's delicate hooves, had gone tumbling down into oblivion. Heart racing, Joanna had edged the animal away from the precipice but she hadn't gone all the way back up the trail for fear of losing too much time. Instead, she'd cut through the trees, pausing only long enough to dismount and rip the telltale bells from the mare's bridle. Then she'd ridden on until, at last, she'd come out in a narrow gorge.

Now, as the sun dropped a crimson mantle over the surrounding mountain peaks, Joanna was trying to decide what to do next. She stared up at the sky. If the setting sun were there, ahead of her, then east was directly behind her, and north and south were—they were...

A little sob of despair burst from her throat. What did it matter? The points of the compass didn't mean a damn if you were trapped in a cage and didn't know the way out.

An owl hooted mournfully in the trees. Joanna shuddered and burrowed more deeply into her jellaba. The night was cool, and steadily growing cooler. The mare was exhausted, head drooping, legs wobbly. She'd been wonderful and courageous, running like the wind after the first shock of being asked to do so, but for the past hour she'd moved at little more than a walk.

Except for the crescent moon hanging like a scimitar over the trees, the darkness was complete. The owl's cry came again and just after it came another cry, that of some small creature which had evidently met the owl and lost the encounter.

Joanna shuddered again. She had to do something, but what? Should she ride on, without any idea of where she was going? In the dark, the horse could easily mis-step;

they'd both end up at the bottom of some abyss, breakfast for the vultures she'd seen circling on the warm
thermals of morning.

She could stop, give herself and her horse a rest. But
if she did, she would lose whatever time she'd gained,
perhaps give Khalil's men just the edge they needed to
pick up her trail.

The mare lifted her head and snorted.

Joanna sat up straight, eyes wide as she peered into
the darkness. Had the animal heard something?

Sidana snorted again and pawed the ground with a
hoof. Joanna bent over her neck, patted it soothingly.

'What is it?' she whispered. 'Is there something out
there?'

The horse took a tentative step forward. Joanna hesitated, and then she loosened her hold on the reins and
gave the animal its head. Wherever the mare was leading
had to be better than this.

Sidana's pace quickened. She was almost trotting
now, and all at once Joanna understood. Ahead, just visible in the pale wash of moonlight, a spring bubbled
from a rocky cairn and trickled into the trough-shaped
depression it had worn into the rock over the centuries.

Joanna smiled. 'Good girl!'

She slid carefully to the ground, groaning. Muscles
she hadn't known existed ached. She had not ridden
bareback since a childhood summer spent on a Montana
mining property.

The mare buried her nose in the shallow water and
Joanna squatted beside her, sipping from her cupped
hands, not caring that she and the horse were sharing
their drink. Thirst had become a growing discomfort;
she'd known it might be, but how could she have stolen
a Thermos of fruit juice from her meal tray without
drawing Rachelle's attention?

The horse, replete, lifted her head and whinnied softly.

'It does taste good, doesn't it?' Joanna murmured. 'I'm glad I gave you your head, girl, otherwise—'

What was that? Joanna stiffened. She could hear something. Voices. Male voices, low-pitched but carrying clearly on the still air, and now the sound of hooves and the creak of leather.

Khalil's men! They'd picked up her trail! Joanna snatched up the mare's trailing reins and led her back into the trees.

'Shh,' she whispered frantically, holding the animal's bridle with one hand and stroking its nose with the other, 'shh!'

She couldn't let them find her now, not after she'd come so far. Even if it took her until dawn to find the path that would lead her down the mountain, she wasn't going back, she couldn't go back, she—

There! She could see them now. They were heading for the spring. A dozen men, not any more than that— but—but—

But who were they? Surely, not Khalil's followers. She had never seen their faces before, and their clothing was all wrong.

The men dismounted, all but one obscenely fat man who she knew instinctively must be their leader and who barked out commands. One man scurried to the spring, dipped a cup into the water, hurried back and offered it with downcast eyes. The fat man drank thirstily, tossed the cup into the dirt, and slid clumsily from the saddle to the ground.

Joanna's gaze flew over the other men. They were heavily armed and had a grim, ugly look to them. And you didn't have to understand their words to shudder at their tone of voice.

The fat man snarled another command and one of the

men bowed and answered. His answer meant nothing to Joanna, except for the last words and the fearful respect that laced them.

'…Abu Al Zouad.'

Joanna's breath caught. Of course! The fat man was Abu Al Zouad! Her father had described him to her. Abu was a big man, he'd said, grossly overweight and clumsy, given to expensive Italian suits and too much gold jewellery.

What would he say now, if he saw him dressed in a greasy jellaba, his chest bristling with bandoliers of ammunition?

The men were clustered in little knots, smoking cigarettes and murmuring quietly to each other. Abu clapped his hands and they looked up as he began to speak. It was a long speech, and again incomprehensible to Joanna, except for two simple words that were repeated over and over.

Joanna Bennett.

Abu was talking about her! Had he come to free her? This looked more like a raiding party than a rescue mission, but Joanna wasn't a child. It wasn't only the good guys who wore white hats.

But why would her father authorise a risky attempt at rescue instead of negotiating for her freedom? Joanna blew out her breath. Perhaps—perhaps Khalil had not told her the truth? For all she knew, Sam might have made every possible effort to gain her release, only to be rebuffed by Khalil. In desperation, he might surely send men to find and free her.

It was reasonable, even logical—but if it were, what was keeping her from stepping out into the clearing and yelling, hey, here I am, Abu? Why was she still hiding, still praying that her horse would not suddenly whinny and give away her position?

Abu finished speaking. One of his men said something; she heard her name fall from his lips, and the others chuckled. Abu shook his head and pointed to himself, and their laughter grew.

There was something in the sound of the laughter, in the way her name had been used and in the way Abu had stabbed that pudgy finger at himself, that sent a chill along Joanna's spine.

She swallowed hard. The men were mounting up. In another moment, they'd ride out of here and she'd be alone again, and just as lost as she'd been before they arrived.

Now was the time to step forward, to call out Abu's name and identify herself. Determinedly, before she could lose courage, Joanna began rising slowly from her crouched position—

A hand clamped over her mouth and an arm, powerful and hard as steel, closed around her. Joanna cried out soundlessly and began to struggle, but she was helpless against the strength of the man holding her.

'Joanna!' Khalil's voice whispered into her ear. 'Stop it, Joanna! It's me.'

She almost sobbed with relief. She went still, and Khalil lowered her slowly to the ground, his arm remaining around her waist.

'You mustn't make a sound,' he said softly. 'Do you understand?'

She nodded and he took his hand from her lips. Beyond the trees, the little group of riders was just vanishing into the night.

She swung around and looked at Khalil. In the moonlight, she could see that he was unshaven, that there was a grim set to his mouth and that lines of weariness fanned out from his eyes, and yet she had never seen a man so beautiful. She had escaped his silken prison, she thought with a sudden catch in her breath, but how would she ever escape the memory of him?

The realisation was as stunning as it was bewildering. She whispered his name, but he shook his head, the stony expression on his face unchanging.

'There will be time for talk later.'

Najib stood just behind his master, ears pricked forward. Khalil took the animal's reins and set off through the trees, in the opposite direction from the spring with Joanna and her mare following after him.

A ten-minute walk brought them to what looked like a labyrinth of giant boulders and, at its end, the yawning, dark mouth of a cave.

Khalil tethered the horses in a blind passageway among the boulders, where no casual observer would see them, and then he took Joanna's hand and led her through the maze up into the cave.

'I played here often, as a boy,' he said, his voice echoing off the stone walls. 'It's deep enough for safety, and there's even a narrow cleft in the rocks at the cave's end that we can use to get out, if we should have to.'

Within minutes, he'd swept together a small pile of kindling and brush and lit a fire deep in the cave's interior. Joanna held her breath as he turned towards her. They had been alone before, but this time was different. She had been running away from him, it was true, but now, seeing him again, being so close to him, she felt— she felt—

'What the hell did you think you were doing?'

She blinked. Khalil's face was taut with barely contained fury.

'I don't—I don't know what you mean.'

'I don't know what you mean,' he mimicked. His mouth tightened. 'For a woman who always has a clever answer at her fingertips, that one is pathetic!'

Her spine stiffened. 'It is not!'

'If you behave like a fool, I'll treat you like one.'

She stared at him for a moment, and then she whirled around and started towards the mouth of the cave. His hand fell on her shoulder.

'Where do you think you're going?' he growled.

'Where I should have gone in the first place. With Abu. If you hadn't come along and ruined things—'

Khalil spun her towards him. 'You gave me your word, Joanna! But I should have known that such a simple pledge was beyond you.'

'What are you talking about?'

'You promised you would not ride alone!'

Joanna tossed her head. 'But I didn't promise I'd willingly remain your prisoner.'

'You little idiot! I'm not talking about escape. I'm talking about danger.'

'The danger of disobeying the rules of a petty dictator, you mean!'

'It is dangerous for anyone, but especially for a woman, to ride these mountains alone.'

'You never said that.'

'I didn't think I had to,' he said, glowering at her. 'Anyone with half a brain—'

'Stop it! I'm tired of your insults!'

'Then don't set yourself up for them. If you'd used your head, you'd have realised I gave you those instructions to keep you safe.'

'Oh, yes.' Joanna's voice shook, and she could feel the sting of tears in her eyes, although there was no reason to want to cry. 'Yes, you'd want me kept safe, wouldn't you? If I were hurt or damaged, what sort of bargaining chip would I be?'

His eyes narrowed. 'Bargaining chip?'

'What's the matter? Isn't your English good enough

to understand a simple phrase? A bargaining chip is what a hostage is. It's—'

She cried out as he swept her into his arms and kissed her, his mouth taking hers with a passion so urgent it stole her breath away, and then he clasped her face in his hands and drew back just enough so he could look into her eyes.

'You cannot be so blind,' he whispered. 'Surely you see that you have become much more than my hostage.'

'No,' she said shakily, 'no, I don't see.'

He smiled, and suddenly his eyes were tender. 'Let me show you, then,' he said softly, and slowly, his head descended to hers.

He kissed her gently, his mouth moving softly against hers, his hands spreading under the hood and into her hair. A tremor went through her, but she didn't respond.

'Joanna,' he said, his lips still clinging to hers, 'Joanna, Joanna…'

And suddenly a wave of emotion, as unexpected and as fierce as a tidal wave, swept through her. She began to tremble.

'Khalil?' she whispered, and the question inherent in the single word was enough. He caught her in his arms and kissed her insistently. Her lips parted beneath his, her arms stole around his neck, and she clung to him and knew she would never, not in a thousand lifetimes, want to let him go.

'How did you find me?' she sighed, while he pressed little kisses to her temples and eyelids. 'And where did you come from? You were gone—'

'I was drawn away deliberately by Abu. It was a clever scheme, but there are few secrets that can be kept in this part of the world. I turned back when the information reached me, contacted my men, told them to put you under armed guard.'

'Abu was coming to free me, then?'

Khalil hesitated. 'It might be better to say that you were all the excuse he needed to ride against me.'

'But—what will happen when he reaches your village? Will your people be safe?'

He smiled grimly. 'He's riding into a trap. My men are waiting for him.'

'But how…?'

'Joanna.' He stroked the hair back from her face. 'I don't want to talk about Abu now,' he whispered.

His mouth took hers again, this time in a deeper, more passionate kiss. Joanna moaned softly, and he lowered his head and put his mouth to her throat, as if to measure the racing pulse beating in its hollow.

She whispered his name as he eased the jellaba from her shoulders. His eyes burned into hers as he undid the buttons of her shirt. When it fell away, he drew back and looked at her with such hunger that she felt her breasts lift and harden under his gaze.

'You are so beautiful.' He reached out slowly and stroked his fingers across her nipples. 'You are more beautiful than any woman I have ever seen.'

'You're beautiful, too,' she whispered. The skin tightened across his cheekbones as she slid his jellaba from his shoulders. Her fingers trembled as she undid the buttons on his shirt. She slid her hands under the soft cotton, exulting in the feel of his silken skin, his taut muscles, and in the hiss of his breath when she touched him.

He caught her hand in his, carried it to his lips and pressed a kiss into her palm.

'I want to see all of you, Joanna.'

She stood still as he stripped away her shoes, her trousers, and, finally, her panties. Colour raced up under her skin as she watched him look at her, not from embarrassment but from the sweet pain of wanting him. Her body was already damp, ready for his, and although he had barely touched her so far, her blood was at a fever pitch.

'Now you,' she whispered.

She lifted her eyes to his as she reached out to his belt buckle. He made a sound in the back of his throat as she opened it. She swept her hand lightly down the length of his fly, her breath catching when she felt his arousal. His fingers curled around her wrist and he smiled tightly.

'Be careful,' he said. 'If you go on playing this game, the night may end before it begins.'

A smile curved across Joanna's mouth. 'Am I to obey you, my lord?'

He laughed as he caught her up in his arms, snatched up Najib's saddle blanket, and walked deeper into the cave, to where the fire's glow was only a soft reflection.

'We will obey each other on this night, my beloved.'

Slowly, he eased her down on the blanket, laid her back, and bent over her, his face shadowed and mysterious in the firelight.

'I wanted you from the moment I saw you,' he whispered.

Joanna laughed throatily. 'I thought you wanted to throttle me from the moment you saw me.'

Khalil chuckled. 'You are right. There have been times I didn't know which I wanted to do more.' His smile faded as he looked at her. 'But tonight—tonight,' he whispered, 'there is only one thing I wish to do tonight.'

He touched her with his fingertips, slowly following the curve of breast and belly, then moving lightly against her thighs. She whispered his name, held out her arms to him, but he ignored her, bending over her body so that he could trace the same path again, this time with his mouth. She moaned softly as his lips closed first on one breast, then on the other. When he drew back and bent again to kiss her thighs, her voice rose quavering into the silence of the cave. And when, finally, his mouth closed on the sweet centre of her, Joanna cried out his name in ecstasy.

The stars were still tumbling from the sky when he rose over her.

'Look at me,' he said. Joanna opened her eyes and he smiled down at her, a sweet, fierce smile of possession and dominance that made her heart seem to stop—but when he entered her, slowly, so slowly, with his eyes never leaving hers, she knew that her possession of him, her dominance of him, was as complete as his was of her.

She loved him, she adored him, and it stunned her that it had taken her so long to recognise the truth.

She wanted to tell him that, to whisper that he was the captor not of her body but of her heart and of her soul, but he was deep within her now and she was, oh, she was—

'Beloved,' he said fiercely, and kissed her deeply. Joanna cried out as she spun into the night sky, where she became a burst of quicksilver among the stars.

Joanna awoke once, during the night, drawn from sleep by the sweet touch of Khalil's mouth. Her awakening was slow and dreamlike, and after they'd made love she settled into his arms and fell back into deep sleep.

But when she awoke again, she was alert, uncertain as to what it was that had roused her. She lay very still, tension building in her muscles, and then she heard the faint whicker of a horse and she sighed with relief.

That was what had awakened her, the mare or Najib,

offering gentle protests at having spent the night tethered.

Joanna smiled. She, too, had spent the night tethered,
held closely in Khalil's arms—and it had been the most
wonderful night of her life. She turned her face against
his shoulder, inhaling the clean, masculine smell of his
body, touching her lips lightly to his satiny skin, and
gazed at his face.

How different he looked in sleep. The little lines that
fanned out from his eyes were almost invisible, his
mouth was soft, as if, in sleep, he could put aside, at
least for a while, the burden of leadership he carried.
She sighed and put her head against his chest, listening
to the steady beat of his heart. And that burden had to
be even heavier, knowing that part of his country had
been stolen from him, that it was in the grip of an evil
despot, for Joanna no longer had any doubts at all about
Abu Al Zouad.

Her father had been wrong, whether through accident
or design. Khalil was not the bandit. Abu was, and the
sooner she was able to tell Sam that she knew the truth
now, the better.

There it was, that sound again. Joanna sat up, tossing
her hair back from her face. She was sure it was one of
the horses, but what if the animal was whinnying a warning instead of protesting against inactivity?

She dropped a gentle kiss on Khalil's forehead, then
rose to her feet, found her clothing, and dressed. It had
been hard to see much last night, but she remembered
that the cave entrance was on a slight elevation. Quietly,
she made her way forward. Perhaps she could see what
it was that—

A hand whipped across her mouth. Joanna gasped,
kicked out sharply, and other hands caught hold of her

and dragged her into the sunlight, where Abu and the rest of his men waited.

'Good morning, Miss Bennett.' Joanna glared at the fat man as he slid from his horse. He strolled towards her, smiling unpleasantly. 'I am His Excellency, Abu Al Zouad.' His smile became a grin, revealing a shiny, gold tooth. 'You don't look very happy to see me.'

Joanna's mind was spinning. Abu wasn't bothering to drop his voice. And now that she'd appeared, no one was paying any attention to the cave.

They had no idea Khalil was with her! He could escape through the rear of the cave. All she had to do was be certain he heard this fuss and awakened.

She bit down hard on the hand that covered her mouth. The man cursed, let her go, and lifted his hand to strike her.

'I wouldn't do that,' she said in her best Bennett voice. Whether he understood her English or not, her tone stopped him. He glanced at Abu, who motioned him away.

'Well, Miss Bennett. It is good to see that captivity has not dulled your spirit.'

Joanna's chin lifted. 'How did you find me?'

Abu smiled. 'My spies alerted me to your rather abrupt departure from the fortress of the bandit Khalil, and then it was simply a matter of following your trail— although I must admit, my scout stumbled upon your little hideaway quite by accident.' He moved closer to her. 'And now I have my prize.' Without warning, he reached out and ran his hand down her body. 'And what a prize it is, too!'

Joanna's blood went cold. She thought of Khalil's hesitation last night, when she'd asked him if Abu were coming to rescue her.

'It might be better to say that you were all the excuse he needed to ride against me,' he'd said.

Abu had no intention of taking her back to her father! He would kill her—after first taking his pleasure—and blame her death on Khalil.

Joanna slapped his hand away. 'I am not your prize!' The man nearest Abu snarled something and put his hand on the scabbard hanging from his belt. 'You have forgotten who I am,' she said, her voice so sharp and chill that only she knew she was really trembling with fear.

'I forget nothing.' Abu growled. 'You are a woman, stolen by a bandit. Whatever happens to you will be his doing, not mine.'

'And losing the reward for my return will be your doing—or are you so rich you can't use a million dollars in gold?'

'A million dollars? Your father did not say—'

Joanna drew herself fully erect. 'A million dollars, and the contract you want so badly with Bennettco. You will get neither, if I am not returned safely.'

'You are only a woman! You make no rules for Sam Bennett.'

'I am his daughter.'

'That is a guarantee of nothing.'

Joanna smiled tightly. 'Perhaps—and perhaps not.' With a last bit of bravado, she looked him straight in the eye. 'Are you willing to take that chance?'

She could almost see the wheels spinning in his ugly head, but her most desperate thoughts were deep within the cave. Had Khalil got away? Had he heard the noise, made good his escape? Had he—?

Her answer came in a sudden burst of sound, a blood-chilling yell that froze her with terror. It must have had the same effect on Abu's men, too, for when Khalil came bursting from the cave entrance there was time for him to lunge at Abu and almost curl his hands around the man's throat before anyone moved.

'Go on,' he yelled at Joanna as two men pulled him back and pinned him against the rocks, 'make a run for it! Dammit, woman, why are you standing there?'

Abu rubbed his dirty fingers over his throat. 'Well, well,' he said, very softly, 'this is indeed a morning of prizes—and of surprises.' He grinned, then pointed at one of his men. 'Kill the bandit!'

'No!' The word ripped from Joanna's throat. She stepped forward. 'No,' she said again, 'don't kill him.'

'We will spare you,' Abu said, as if it were an act of humanity that impelled him and not the threat Joanna had made. 'But I have waited too long for a reason the people will accept to kill the bandit.' He smiled. 'And now I have one. Kill him!'

'Very well.' Joanna's voice was cool. 'Kill him, if you like—but if you do, you are a fool.'

'Watch your tongue, woman!'

'He is not only your enemy, Abu, he is also my father's. He has dishonoured him—and me.' She took a breath. 'My father will surely want the pleasure of killing Khalil himself.'

Abu laughed. 'Westerners do not believe in taking blood for dishonour.'

'Do you think my father got where he is today by being soft-hearted?'

She looked over at Khalil, expecting to see a dark glint of admiration for her off-the-cuff cleverness in his eyes, needing to see it to give her the courage to go on. Her heart dropped like a stone. Khalil was watching her as if she were something that had just scurried out from under a rock. She turned away quickly, forcing herself to concentrate on Abu.

'My father will pay for having Khalil delivered into his hands,' she said coldly, 'and he will be grateful to you forever.'

'I think you say this to save the neck of the man who has become your lover.'

Joanna stared at him. 'No. No, I—'

'I think I am right, Miss Bennett.' He looked at one of the men holding Khalil. 'Go on,' he said, 'kill him!'

'He took me,' Joanna blurted. 'He forced me! That's why I made such a desperate escape.' She knotted her hands into fists, marched up to Khalil and looked into his eyes, which were almost black with rage. My love, she thought, oh, my love!

Swiftly, before she lost courage, she drew saliva into her mouth and spat full into Khalil's face.

'He's a barbarian,' she said, swinging away so she didn't have to look at him, 'and I'll have no peace until my father takes my revenge.'

A heavy silence descended on the group, broken only by the laboured sound of Khalil's breathing, and then Abu nodded.

'Very well. We take him with us and—'

Cries filled the air. Joanna shrank back as Khalil's men came riding up the slope. Within minutes, it was over. Abu and his men were defeated.

With a little sob of joy, Joanna ran to Khalil and threw her arms around him, but he shoved her away.

'Don't touch me,' he said in a soft, dangerous whisper.

'Khalil. My love! I was bargaining for your life! Surely you didn't believe—'

'And now you are bargaining for your own!' He stepped forward, grasping her arms and yanking her close. 'Be grateful I am not the savage you think I am,' he growled. 'If I were, I would gladly slit your throat and leave you here for the vultures.' He flung her from him and strode to Najib, who stood waiting beside the white mare. 'Take her to the airstrip,' he snapped to one of his men, 'and have her flown to Casablanca. We have Abu—Sam Bennett can have his daughter.' He leaped on to Najib's back, grasped the reins, and gave Joanna one last, terrible look. 'They deserve each other.'

He dug his heels hard into Najib's flanks. The horse rose on its hind legs, pawed the air, then spun away with its rider sitting proudly in the saddle.

It was the last Joanna saw of Khalil.

CHAPTER TWELVE

THE doorman pushed open the door and smiled as Joanna stepped from her taxi and made her way towards him.

'Evening, Miss Bennett,' he said. 'Hot enough to fry eggs on the pavement, isn't it?'

Joanna smiled back at him. 'Hello, Rogers. Yes, but New York in August is always pretty awful.'

The lift operator smiled, too, and offered a similar comment on the weather as the car rose to the twelfth floor, and Joanna said something clever in return, as she was expected to do.

It was a relief to stop all the smiling and stab her key into the lock of her apartment door. Smiling was the last thing she felt like doing lately. With a weary sigh, she stepped out of her high heels and dropped her handbag on a table in the foyer.

Sam kept saying she'd developed all the charm of a woman sucking on a lemon, and she supposed it was true—but in the three months she'd been back from Casablanca she hadn't found all that much to smile about.

Joanna popped off her earrings as she made her way towards her bedroom. She was vice-president of Bennettco now, she had an office of her own, a staff, and even her father's grudging respect.

So why wasn't it enough? she thought as she peeled off her dress and underthings.

She stepped into the blue tiled bathroom and turned on the shower. The water felt delicious but she couldn't luxuriate beneath it for long. In less than an hour, Sam was picking her up. They were going to another of the endless charity affairs he insisted they attend, this time at the Palace Hotel.

A mirthless smile angled across her lips as she stepped from the shower and towelled herself dry. The Palace. She had been to it before, knew that it dripped crystal chandeliers and carpeting deep enough to cushion the most delicate foot. But she remembered a real palace, one that boasted no such touches of elegance, yet had been more a palace than the hotel would ever be.

Damn, but she wished she hadn't seen that little squib in the paper at breakfast! 'Jandaran Prince Consolidates Hold on Kingdom, Seeks Financing for Mining Project', it had said, and she'd shoved the paper away without reading further, but it had been enough. A rush of memories had spoiled the day, although she couldn't imagine why. She didn't care what happened to Khalil. She had never loved him. How could she have, when they came from such different worlds? It was just that she'd been frightened, and despairing, and there was no point pretending he wasn't a handsome, virile male.

An image flashed into her mind as she reached for her mascara. She saw Khalil leaning over her, his eyes dark with desire. Joanna, he was whispering, Joanna, my beloved...

Her hand slipped and a dark smudge bloomed on her cheek. She wiped it off, then bent towards the mirror again and painted a smile on her lips. What had happened in Jandara was a closed chapter. No one even knew about her part in it, thanks to Sam.

'I didn't tell a soul,' he'd said, after she'd finally reached Casablanca.

'Not even the State Department?' she'd asked, remembering shadowy fragments of something Khalil had said the night he'd abducted her.

'Not even them. I was afraid I might compromise your safety. How could I know what an animal like Khalil might do if I called out the troops? That's why I couldn't give in to his demands. I figured once I did, the bastard might kill you. You understand, don't you?'

Joanna had assured him that she did. Sam hadn't been saying anything she hadn't thought of herself. Sending Abu after her had been the only way he'd thought he could rescue her. As for Abu—Sam had been duped, he'd said with feeling.

'The guy had me fooled. How could I have known what he really was like?'

Joanna slid open the wardrobe in her bedroom and took a sequinned blue gown from its hanger. The only fly in the ointment was that the proposed mining deal had gone down the tubes. Khalil had wasted no time making sure of that. Within twelve hours, Abu had been sentenced to life imprisonment, Khalil had been restored to the throne of Jandara, and the Bennett contract had been returned by messenger, accompanied by a terse note, signed by Khalil.

'We will develop the property ourselves.'

Sam had turned red with anger and cursed and then said hell, win some, lose some, what did it matter? He had his Jo back. That was all that counted.

Joanna whisked a brush through her hair. He was right. That was what counted, that she was back, and if sometimes, at night, she awoke from dreams she could not remember with tears on her cheeks, so what? She was getting ahead rapidly at Bennettco and that was what she wanted. It was all she wanted.

She glanced at the clock. It was time. Quickly she stuffed a comb, tissues and her lipstick into an evening bag, slipped on a pair of glittery high-heeled sandals, and made her way out of the door.

Sam was waiting at the kerb in his chauffeured Lincoln. 'Hello, babe,' he said when she stepped inside. 'Mmm, you look delicious.'

Joanna's eyebrows rose. 'What gives?'

He chuckled as the car eased into traffic. 'What do you mean, what gives? Can't I give my girl a compliment?'

'You're as transparent as glass, Father,' she said with a wry smile. 'Whenever you want something from me and you expect a refusal, you begin laying on compliments.'

He sat back and sighed. 'I was just thinking, on the way over here, what a terrible time that bastard put us through.'

Joanna's smile faded. 'Khalil?'

He smiled coldly. 'What other bastard do we know? To think he locked you up, treated you like dirt—'

'I really don't want to talk about him tonight, Father.'

'Did you know he's in town?'

She shrugged, trying for a casual tone. 'Is he?'

Sam grunted. 'Abu may have been a brute,' he said, 'but Khalil's no better.'

Joanna looked at him. 'You know that's not true!'

'You're not defending him, are you, Jo?'

Was she? Joanna shook her head. 'No,' she said quickly, 'of course not.'

'It burns my butt that the man treated you the way he did and gets rewarded for it,' Sam said testily. 'There he is, sitting in Abu's palace, snug as a quail in tall grass, counting up the coins in the national treasury.'

Joanna closed her eyes wearily. 'I doubt that.'

Sam chuckled. 'But we'll have the last laugh, kid. I've seen to that.'

Joanna turned towards her father. There was something in his tone that was unsettling.

'What do you mean?'

'We may have lost the mining deal—but so has Khalil!'

'He's not. He's going to put together a consortium himself.'

'He's going to try and milk a fat profit straight into his own pockets, you mean.'

'No,' Joanna said quickly. 'He'd never—'

'How do you think he'll like having the world hear he wanted the fortune tucked away in those mountains so badly he killed for it?' Sam said, his eyes glittering.

Joanna stared at her father. 'Killed who?'

'Abu. Who else?'

'But Khalil didn't kill him. He's in prison. And it isn't because of the fortune in those mountains, it's—'

'For God's sake, Jo!' Sam's voice lost its cheerful edge and took on a rapier sharpness. 'Who cares what the facts are? I'm telling you I've come up with a way to put a knife in that s.o.b.'s back for what he did to us!'

'Us? *Us*? He didn't do anything to us. I was the one he took, the one whose—'

'What? What were you going to say?'

She stared at him in bewilderment. She knew what she'd been going to say, that she was the one whose heart was broken. But it wasn't true. She was defending Khalil, yes, but not because she loved him. It was only because it would be wrong to lie about him, to raise doubts in the minds of his people.

'You can't do something so evil,' she said flatly.

Sam's face hardened. 'Listen to me, Joanna. Khalil's trying to put together this mining deal, sure. But when the banks and the power brokers know the truth about him, how he abducted you and how he treated you—'

'But they won't.' Joanna's eyes flashed with defiance. 'The story's mine, and I'm not going to tell it.'

Sam's mouth thinned with distaste. 'It's useless, treating you as if you understood business! You're not the son I wanted, and you never will be.'

Tears glinted on Joanna's lashes. 'Well,' she said, 'at least it's finally out in the open. I'm not, no, and—' The car jounced to a stop at the kerb. Joanna grabbed her evening bag from the seat. 'We can discuss this later, Father.'

'Jo. Wait!'

She snatched her hand from his and reached for the door, too angry and upset to wait for the chauffeur to open it. Sam cared about protocol, but it had never meant a damn to her.

'Joanna,' Sam said sharply, but she ignored him, swung open the door—and stepped straight into a bewildering sea of cameras and microphones.

'Miss Bennett!' Someone shoved a mike into her face. 'Is it true,' an eager voice asked, 'that you were abducted and held for ransom by the new ruler of Jandara?'

Joanna stiffened. 'Where did you—?'

'Is it true he abducted you because he'd demanded bribe money from your father's company and your father refused to pay it?'

She spun towards Sam, who had stepped out of the car after her. 'Did you do this?' she said in a low voice.

His eyes narrowed. 'We'll discuss this later, you said. I think we should stay with that idea.'

'Answer me! Did you set this up?'

'Do unto others as they do unto you, Jo,' Sam said out of the side of his mouth. 'Khalil's in New York, his hat in his hand. It's my turn now.'

Joanna's mouth trembled. 'You would lie about Khalil, let the media swarm over me, all to get even?'

Sam glared at her. 'Business is business, Joanna. How come you can't get that straight?' He pushed past her, making it look as if he were defending her against the press, and held up his hands. 'My daughter finds this too emotional a topic to talk about,' he said. 'I'll speak on her behalf.'

He launched into a tirade against Khalil, about his greed and his barbarism, about how he'd been angered by Bennettco's refusal to pay enough *baksheesh* and how he'd stolen Joanna in retaliation, then demanded a king's ransom for her return—

'No,' Joanna said.

The microphones and cameras swung towards her and Sam did too, his eyes stabbing her with a warning look.

'The only reason we've decided to come forward now,' he said, 'is because my daughter refuses to let Prince Khalil trick our bankers into investing in—'

'No!' Joanna's voice rose. 'It's not true!'

'Do you see what the bastard did?' Sam roared. 'She's still afraid to talk about how he imprisoned her, starved her, beat her—'

'It's a lie!' Joanna stepped past her father. 'Prince Khalil asked for no ransom, no bribes. He's a good, decent man, and my father's trying to blacken his name!'

There was a moment's silence, and then a voice rang out.

'Decent men don't abduct women.'

There was a titter of laughter. Joanna lifted her chin and stared directly into the glittering eyes of the video cameras.

'He didn't abduct me,' she said in a clear voice.

'Your father says he did. What's the story, Miss Bennett?'

What had Khalil said, the night he'd taken her? That he could tell the world she'd run off with him and be believed, that no one would doubt such a story. Joanna took a deep breath.

'I was with Khalil because I wanted to be with him,' she said. She heard her father growl a short, ugly word and her voice gathered strength. 'The Prince asked me to go away with him—and I did.'

A dozen questions filled the air, and finally one reporter's voice cut through the rest.

'So, you don't hate the Hawk of the North?'

Joanna's lips trembled. 'No,' she said, 'I don't hate him.'

'What, then?' someone called.

Joanna hesitated. 'I—I—'

'Well, Miss Bennett?' another voice insisted, 'how do you feel about him?'

Joanna stared at the assembled cameras. How did she feel about Khalil? What did she feel?

A woman reporter jostled aggressively past the others and stuck a microphone under her nose.

'Do you love him?' she said, her crimson lips parting in a smirk.

Joanna looked at the woman. The time for lies and deceit was past.

'Yes,' she whispered, 'I do.'

She heard Sam's groan, heard the babble of voices all trying to question her at once, and then she turned and fled into a taxi that had mercifully just disgorged its passengers.

Joanna stalked the length of the terrace that opened off her living-room. The night had proven even warmer than the afternoon; the long, white silk robe she wore was light against her skin but even so, she felt as if she were smothering.

But she knew it had little to do with the temperature.

She was smothering of humiliation, and there was nothing she could do about it.

She groaned out loud and sank down on the edge of a *chaise longue*. How could she have made such an ass of herself?

I love him, she'd said—but she didn't. She *didn't* love Khalil, she never had.

So why had she said such a preposterous thing? Anger at Sam, yes, and pain at how he'd been prepared to use her, but still, why would she have made such an announcement?

She rose and walked slowly into the living-room, just as the clock on the mantel chimed the hour. Four a.m. If only it were dawn, she'd put on her running shoes, a T-shirt and shorts, and go for a long run through Central Park. Maybe that would help. Maybe—

The phone shrilled, as it had periodically through the night. Would it be the Press, which had found her despite her ex-directory listing, or Sam, who'd called three times to tell her she had ruined him? She snatched it up and barked a hello.

It was Sam, but the tone of his voice told her that his rage had given way to weariness.

'Will you at least apologise for making fools of me and of Bennettco, Jo?'

Joanna put a hand to her forehead. 'Of course. I never intended to embarrass you, Father.'

'How could you do it, then? My reputation and the company's are in shambles.'

She smiled. 'You've survived worse.'

Sam sighed gustily into the phone. 'I'm not saying you were right,' he said, 'but maybe my idea wasn't so hot.'

Joanna's smile broadened. 'Are *you* apologising to *me*, Father?'

'I've always walked a thin line between what's right and what's wrong and sometimes—sometimes, I lose my way.'

It was an admission she would never have expected, and it touched her.

'You're one tough lady, Joanna,' Sam said quietly.

'I love you, Father,' Joanna whispered.

'And I love you.' She heard him take a deep breath. 'Jo? I really did believe I'd endanger you by negotiating with Khalil. That's the only reason I didn't tear up that blasted contract. I want to be sure you know that. You mean the world to me.'

Tears stung her eyes. 'I know.'

'Well,' Sam said brusquely, 'it's late. You should get some sleep.' There was a silence. 'Goodnight, daughter.'

Daughter. He had never called her that before. Joanna's hand tightened on the phone.

'Goodnight, Daddy,' she said.

She hung up the phone and smiled. So, she thought, stretching her legs out in front of her, some good had come of this mess after all. She and her father might yet be friends—

She started as the doorbell rang. Who could it be, at this late hour? Who could the doorman have possibly admitted without calling her on the intercom first?

Joanna stood and walked slowly to the door. A reporter, she thought grimly, a reporter who'd sneaked in the back way.

The bell rang again, the sound persistent and jarring in the middle of the night silence.

'Go away,' she called.

Someone rapped sharply at the door.

'Do you hear me? If you don't get away from here this minute, I'll call the police!'

'You call them,' a man's voice growled, 'or your neighbours will, when I break this door down!'

Joanna fell back against the wall. 'Khalil?' she whispered.

'Do you hear me, Joanna? Open this door at once!'

'No,' she said, staring at the door as if it might fly off its hinges. 'Go away!'

'Very well, Joanna. We'll wait for someone to phone the police. They'll probably show up with a dozen reporters in tow, but that's fine with me. Jandara can use all the publicity it can get.'

She flew at the door, her fingers trembling as they raced across the locks, and then she threw the door open.

'How dare you do this?'

'This is America,' Khalil said with a cold smile. 'People can do anything they want in America. Didn't you tell me that once?'

'No! I certainly did not. I—'

Joanna fell silent. Khalil was dressed much as he had been the night they'd met, in a dark suit and white shirt, but somewhere along the way, he'd taken off his tie, undone the top buttons of his shirt, and slung his jacket over his shoulder. He looked handsome and wonderful, and the sight of him made her feel giddy.

She clutched her silk robe to her throat. 'You can't come in!'

He smiled, showing even, white teeth. 'Can't I?'

'No. This is my apartment, and—' The door slammed shut behind him as he pushed past her into the foyer. 'Damn you,' Joanna cried. 'Didn't you hear what I said? I don't want you here. Get out!'

Khalil shook his head. 'No.'

No. Just that one word, delivered in that insolent, imperious voice...

Joanna tossed her head. 'All right, then, wait here and get thrown out! The doorman's probably on the phone this very minute, calling the—'

'The doorman,' he said with a smug little smile, 'is chatting with my minister.' He folded his arms over his chest in that impossibly arrogant manner she detested. 'Did you know the man was born a stone's throw from Hassan's birthplace?'

Joanna's eyes narrowed. 'Hassan was born in Brooklyn?'

Khalil grinned. 'Well, perhaps he stretched things a bit. But it is true that Hassan has a cousin who was born in Brooklyn.'

Joanna lifted her chin in defiance. 'As far as I'm concerned, you and Hassan could have a string of cousins who—'

'We were at a dinner party all this evening, Joanna.'

'Isn't that wonderful,' she said sweetly. 'I'm delighted for you both.'

'I only just got back to my hotel, and I turned on— what do you call it?—the twenty-four-hour-a-day news channel—'

'I am certain there are lots of people who'd be interested in a minute-by-minute accounting of how you spent your evening, Khalil, but personally—'

'I saw your news conference.'

Joanna felt her face go white. 'What news conference?' she said with false bravado. 'I don't know what you're talking about.'

'That informative little gathering you arranged outside the Palace Hotel.' A cool smile curved over his lips. '*That* news conference.'

'It wasn't a news conference, it was a circus. Now, if you're quite finished—'

'What a clever pair you and your father are, Joanna.'

She gaped at him. 'What?'

'Telling two such disparate but fascinating stories to the Press.' Khalil's eyes narrowed. 'What better way for Bennettco to garner publicity, hmm?'

'What better way for...' Joanna burst out laughing. 'Is that what you think? That Sam and I set that up?'

'Didn't you?'

'No, of course not. What would be the point?'

'How do I know? Perhaps the price of Bennettco's stock has fallen and you two decided front-page headlines would shore it up.'

Joanna shook her head in disbelief. 'My father would be proud of you, thinking of something like that.'

'You didn't arrange it, then?'

'Me? I had nothing to do with it. It was my father who...' She stopped in mid-sentence and colour spotted her cheeks. 'Look, if that's all you came here for—'

'Why?' He moved forward quickly, before she could back away, and took her by the shoulders. 'Why did he want you to pretend I had hurt you?' His eyes darkened. 'Heaven knows I would never do that.'

'I—I told Sam that. But—but he had some crazy idea that—that he could influence things in Jandara—'

'By destroying my reputation,' Khalil said, his voice flat.

'He knows it was wrong,' she said quickly. 'I swear to you—'

'But you wouldn't let him lie.'

Joanna's throat worked. 'I—I didn't think it was right.'

Khalil's hands spread across her shoulders. 'And so

you told two hundred million people that you went away with me willingly.'

She felt the rush of crimson that flooded her cheeks. 'Please go now, Khalil.'

'Not yet, not until I have the answers I came for.'

'You have them. You wanted to know if my father and I—'

'I wanted to know why you told the entire population of the United States that you love me,' he said softly.

'It was—I mean, I thought it was—' She looked up at him helplessly. 'I couldn't think of anything else to say.'

He grinned. 'Really.'

'Yes. Really.' Joanna swallowed hard. 'I didn't mean it, if that's what you think.'

What he thought was that she was still the most beautiful woman in the world, and that he would surely have died if he had never looked at her wonderful face again. He smiled and traced the fullness of her bottom lip with his thumb. The last time he'd gazed into Joanna's eyes, his heart had been so filled with pain that he had been blind to everything but his own anguish.

But the passage of time had made him begin to wonder if he'd reacted too quickly that terrible morning three months before. He had dreamed of her for weeks, thought of her endlessly, and now he had come to the States on a mission for his country—but in the back of his mind, he knew he had come to find her, to find the truth…

…and there it was, shining along with the tears that had risen in her beautiful green eyes. He was certain of it, certain enough to do something he had never done before, put aside his pride—and offer up his heart.

'Didn't you?' he said softly.

Joanna swallowed again. 'Didn't I what?' she whispered.

'Didn't you mean it when you said you loved me?'

She closed her eyes. 'Khalil—please, don't do this—'

'I think the only time you lied about how you felt was that morning outside the cave.'

Her lashes flew up and she looked at him. 'You're wrong. I don't love you. I never—'

He lowered his head and gently brushed his lips over hers.

'How could I have been such a pig-headed fool? You told Abu you loathed me to save my life—didn't you, Joanna?'

Joanna stared into Khalil's wonderfully blue eyes. She could walk away from this with her pride intact. Well, sure, she could say, smiling, I did—but that doesn't mean I love you. I just did what I could to save your neck because it was the right thing to do...

'Joanna.' He cupped her face, tilted it to his, and when she looked into his eyes again, her heart soared. 'Beloved,' he whispered, 'will it be easier to tell me the truth if I tell it to you first?' Khalil kissed her again, his mouth soft and sweet against hers. 'I love you, Joanna. I love you with all my heart.'

Her breath caught. 'What?'

'Why do you think I kept you captive, even after I knew your father would never negotiate for your release?'

'Well, because—because—'

He smiled and put his arms around her. 'It was wrong, I know, but how could I let you go when I'd fallen in love with you? I kept hoping you would stop hating me, that you'd come to feel for me what I felt for you.'

Joanna felt as if her heart were going to burst with joy. 'Oh, my darling,' she whispered, 'my love—'

He drew her close and silenced her with a kiss. Then he sighed and brought her head to his chest.

'That night in the cave, I let myself believe you loved me, but the next morning—'

Joanna leaned back in his embrace and flung her arms around his neck. 'I do love you,' she said, laughing and weeping at the same time, 'I do!'

He kissed her again. After a long time, he lifted his head and smiled into her eyes.

'Lilia speaks of you. She is very happy. Her father was found alive, in one of Abu's dungeons.'

'That's wonderful!'

He grinned. 'Rachelle still speaks of you, too. She says she hopes some day you will see the error of your ways and admit what a wonderful person I really am.'

Joanna laughed. 'I'll do my best.' Her smile faded, and she touched the tip of her tongue to her lip. 'Khalil—about Lilia. I felt awful, involving her in my escape, but—'

'Do you still have it in your heart to be a teacher, beloved?'

She looked at him with a puzzled smile on her lips. 'What do you mean?'

'There is much to do in my country. Lilia, and all the children, are eager to learn.' Khalil kissed her tenderly. 'Do you think you could give up your job at Bennettco and come back to Jandara with me to teach them?'

Joanna's eyes shone. 'Is that all you want me to do?'

'What I want,' he said, holding her close, 'is for you to be my wife and my love, and to live with me in happiness forever.'

As the sun rose over the Manhattan rooftops, Joanna gave Khalil her promise in a way she knew he would surely understand.

MILLS & BOON®

Makes any time special™

By Request™

*Bestselling themed romances brought
back to you by popular demand*

Each month By Request brings you three
full–length novels in one beautiful volume
featuring the best of the best.

So if you missed a favourite Romance
the first time around, here is your chance
to relive the magic from some of our
most popular authors.

**Look out for
Passion in August 1999
featuring Michelle Reid,
Miranda Lee and Susan Napier**

*Available at most branches of WH Smith, Tesco,
Asda, Martins, Borders, Easons,
Volume One/James Thin
and most good paperback bookshops*

THE Regency COLLECTION

Where rogues find romance

**Look out for the fourth volume in this limited
collection of Regency Romances from
Mills & Boon® in August.**

Featuring:

The Outrageous Dowager
by Sarah Westleigh

and

Devil-May-Dare
by Mary Nichols

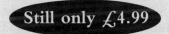

Still only £4.99

Our hottest

TEMPTATION

authors bring you…

Blaze

Three sizzling love stories available in one volume in September 1999.

Midnight Heat
JoAnn Ross

A Lark in the Dark
Heather MacAllister

Night Fire
Elda Minger

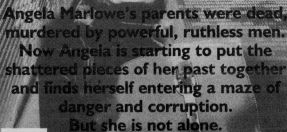

THE DISAPPEARANCE

from

JASMINE CRESSWELL

One chilly morning Summer Shepherd
disappeared…

Ordinarily the FBI refuses to negotiate with
kidnappers, but they will make an exception for
the daughter of the U.S. Secretary of State.

But when they begin to suspect that Summer staged
her kidnapping, she must expose the shocking truth
that lies behind her disappearance…

MIRA®   **Published 23rd July 1999**

EMILIE RICHARDS

Beautiful Lies

Since the day it was discovered in
Australian waters, the pearl has cursed the
Robeson and Llewellyn families. Now it is
in the possession of Linda Robeson, and
tragedy has struck again—her son has
gone missing and so has the pearl. Linda
and her ex-husband embark on a terrifying journey to find their son, stumbling
into a deadly game with a rival who will
go to any lengths to possess the pearl.

Published 23rd July 1999